REVIEWS

D1662166

PRAISE FOR *FAIRHAVEN*

'We can't navigate our way to a better future fed on a diet of nothing but doom and gloom. We need stories to challenge, provoke and inspire to help us dare to imagine and act with hope - Fairhaven does just that!'
Nigel Topping, UN High Level Climate Action Champion, COP26

'May the climate crisis be a spur to a million imaginations--we're going to need some new ideas to get out of this century!'
Bill McKibben, author, The End of Nature

'No turning back now. We have crossed the threshold where fact will be stranger than fiction. Ironically good climate fiction like Fairhaven, may help us envision a path forward and give us inspiration for the challenging journey ahead.'
John Englander, Author, Moving to Higher Ground, Rising Sea Level and the Path Forward (2021)

It's wonderful to see more solutions-focused climate fiction being published by people with the expertise to see a future that's really possible. Fairhaven fills me with hope.'

Lauren James, founder of Climate Fiction Writers League

'Climate change is the most pressing environmental topic of today, as it has already affected this generation and is expected to be a more severe issue for future generations to cope with. Reading this climate fiction novel will educate and entertain you, and more importantly, it will tell you that individual actions can alleviate the climate crisis.'

Edwin Lau, Executive Director, The Green Earth

'Fairhaven takes the reader on a compelling journey through climate change challenges and solutions, crafting memorable characters that feel real and prescient. With gripping storylines that immerse the audience in the urgent struggle to protect vulnerable lands and communities through ambitious geoengineering projects, Fairhaven deftly spotlights the importance of climate adaptation work while entertaining and informing readers of all backgrounds.'

Dr William Yu, Founder & Chief Executive Officer, World Green Organisation

'This engrossing novel offers a rare combination of in-depth technical knowledge with a flair for telling compelling stories. It brings the story of a diverse cast of characters to life as they try to solve real climate change problems - before it's too late.'

Catherine Cole, Sustainability Advisor, MOTIF

'Gripping drama bursting with inspiring ideas of what is possible: a

map to the future'

D.A. Baden, founder of Green Stories and author of 'Habitat Man.'

'In a time when the narrative matters more than we can possibly imagine, the need for story telling that lets us reflect on who we are, who we're becoming, and the world we wish to create is incredibly important. This book is that story. It will open up a door to your imagination while serving as a bridge to the place of yourself that remembers our strengths and why we're here. It's beautiful and engaging and a true testament to our times. Here's to even more optimistic and inspiring climate fiction!'

Anne Therese Gennari, Climate Optimist, Author & Speaker

Fairhaven

A NOVEL OF CLIMATE OPTIMISM

STEVE WILLIS AND JAN LEE

Habitat Press

HABITAT PRESS

To all those striving for a future that doesn't suck

CONTENTS

MAPS

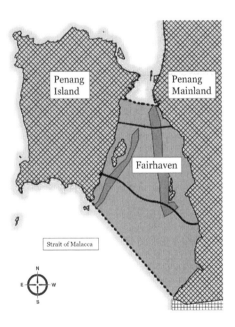

Penang Island

Penang Mainland

Fairhaven

Strait of Malacca

Penang is a Malaysian state and Fairhaven is a fictional construction that connects Penang Island with the Mainland.

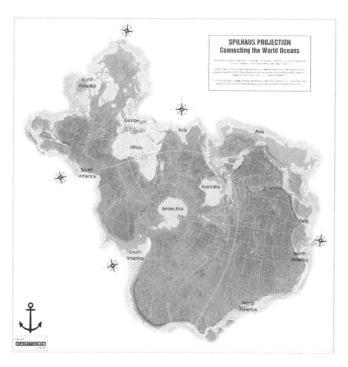

Spilhaus projection map used with permission from Terry Steinkey.
This illustrates the view of the world seen from the perspective of the
oceans, presenting them as one body of water.

BAZALGETTE

2.00 am, Tuesday, December 30, 2036

Penang Fairhaven – 8 Gurney Drive

Global temperature: 2.3°C above pre-industrial average

It would be the second time Grace Chan fought for her life in the waters of the Fairhaven Project.

Her note, left under a mug on the kitchen counter, read, 'Out for some air. I need to let off steam and think about my speech. Back by breakfast.'

Wearing jeans and carrying an ancient phone, she tiptoed to the lift, trying not to wake up her flatmates. It was funny to think of them as flatmates after all these years; there was still no better way to describe the communities of peers that were replacing many of Malaysia's older, multi-generational households in the latter half of the 2030s.

She'd heard a rumour that someone had spotted a manatee. It was unlikely, but just in case, she checked the old phone to see whether its camera was still working. It was still in selfie mode from the last time it had been used, decades earlier. Before making a hasty switch to the front camera, Grace saw her own face, skin fair like her father's, weathered but still smooth, her 'famous' hazel eyes, and her short hair, wavy like her mother's, still black.

Having descended 38 floors to the car park, she climbed into the old Rivian R1T, registered her annoyance with its oversized cabin (so impractical for a 154cm tall driver), and fastened her seatbelt. She pressed 'record' on the phone and shoved it into her front pocket.

The electric pickup passed through the ornate, green-painted gates.

She disengaged the pickup's autopilot, useless now, as she took the North Dyke service road towards the Bazalgette pump house, speeding up as she recited her speech. She frowned; her message was still too banal considering the unprecedented situation in the world over the past fortnight, and the momentousness of her own accession.

The streets were deserted in a way not seen since the pandemic days of her youth. Other than her pickup, the lights of a few fishing boats and the glow from a small soup kitchen were all that broke the darkness.

Without warning, a large monitor lizard appeared in the headlights.

2.15 am, Tuesday, December 30, 2036
Penang Fairhaven – North Dyke

Grace cursed herself for her instinctive decision to swerve. A collision would have been bad news for the lizard, of course. But she was well aware that the most important decisions in life create collateral damage.

Pinned in by the crumpled side door of the truck, she strained against the seat belt, designed for someone twice her weight. She struggled to push the deflated airbag out of the way. The truck had burrowed nose-first in the soft, deep mud of the dyke. The vast dyke behind her was discernible through the shadow it cast on the rippling water, blocking the reflections of the stars.

She spoke aloud, hoping that the old phone, unreachable in her front pocket, had survived the impact and was still recording. She needed a listener, even if it was insensate.

'After all these years of tight scrapes, this is the one that gets me. And I'm still at least half a kilometre away from the lock.'

Bazalgette Lock, where she first worked at Fairhaven all those years ago, was her destination when she needed to think. It was an unprepossessing block of concrete, a droning pumping station. Now, it was also a place to ground herself amid the chaos that surrounded her. Long after others were asleep, she would stand on the lock for hours and look north to the Malacca Strait. To the south lay the enormous Fairhaven land reclamation project, which had joined Penang Island to the Malaysian mainland after a million years of separation. On clear days, she could just see the South Dyke, 17 kilometres away.

'It all happened so fast, but I think when I swerved away from the lizard, the truck clipped the edge at the top of the dyke, and slipped down the outside towards the sea. I can't believe I was so stupid.

'To be honest, I was distracted – nothing could have prepared me for the past two weeks.'

11.00 am, Monday, December 29, 2036
Consulate General, Ocean Independent State

'That's all the time we have this morning,' said her press secretary, earlier that day. 'We look forward to seeing you at the inauguration.'

Grace thanked the journalists assembled in the stifling room and retreated towards her office.

Grace's relationship with the media, ever since the early days when her series first launched on Streamberry, had always been prickly. This press conference had been a bad one, without the usual barrier of a screen between her and the reporters' questions. Although most routine news – weather, sports, and so forth – was now reported by automated feeds (or had been, before the Cloud Bust), nothing could replace a live journalist when it came to badgering a politician until she cracked. The journalists were all local, of course; no international correspondent would fly to Malaysia when both air traffic control and international satellite navigation were unavailable.

The absence of the air conditioners, most of which could not function without an internet connection, increased the pressure.

One reporter caught up with her just before she entered her office. He must have sensed a fracture in her defences.

'President-elect Chan. One more question. Considering the current situation, how are you planning to address wage gaps for the historically disenfranchised populations that make up much of the new Ocean Independent State?'

Grace raised an eyebrow. If the current situation could not be fixed, there would be no populations of any kind to talk about, let alone disenfranchised ones.

Aloud, she delivered a more measured response. She concluded, 'That will be all for now,' and slammed her office door as her press secretary hustled the reporter away.

She flinched at the next knock, but it was an aide, bringing her an early lunch of *assam laksa*. She took it eagerly, and realised she had not yet been in touch with Auntie Janis and the rest of the clan. She wondered how Auntie Annie was managing in the crisis. She could at least visit; it was one of the few addresses she remembered without consulting an electronic device.

She knew she would not be able to get to sleep that night.

3.00 am, Tuesday, December 30, 2036
Penang Fairhaven – North Dyke

Grace continued to address the unseen phone, as her eyes grew more accustomed to the darkness.

'I have to accept at this point that the seat belt clip is jammed solid. I've spent half an hour trying to open it. My fingernails are gone.

'At least the tide is still far out. I'd guess I have about four hours before it reaches me.

'I can just about reach the side pocket in the door, but there's not much in there. The problem is that this truck hasn't collected any junk. Nobody has left a screwdriver, or a bottle cap, or a handy Swiss army knife. All I've found is an empty crisp packet and a mint without its wrapper.

'I've eaten the mint.

'Be careful what you wish for. All I wanted was a quiet moment. The press will have a field day with this. Or will they? Given the current situation, most of them won't hear about it.'

'Even if I survive the night,' she told the patient, soulless phone, 'I don't know if I can survive the next few weeks.'

4.00 am, Tuesday, December 30, 2036
Penang Fairhaven – North Dyke

The hands of Grace's diving watch had lost their phosphorescent glow hours ago. But by listening to the gentle plashing of water against the dyke, she could tell that it was no later than four o'clock.

She hummed to herself before she recognised the tune: it was the soppy, old Beverley Craven song she used to listen to with Hans, 'It's Four O'Clock in the Morning'. The song was a staple of her Spotify playlist, before that service was superseded by the largest of the newer mega-platforms, Orac.

'Does Orac still exist?

'I need to talk about that in my speech.'

She had been searching for a new analogy to describe the climate situation. Years ago, her hit series on Streamberry established the sinking of the *Titanic* as the standard metaphor, but it had become a cliché. The story that had won her fame, fortune, and political success was already losing its power.

'Come to think of it, being trapped here in this seat has all the makings of a good analogy. If I ever get out. Trapped in a situation of my own making, because of ill-considered moves I did without thinking, let down by the elaborate trappings we have built for our complex society.'

Another analogy: she could do nothing to address the bigger problem of the climate crisis if she didn't tackle the immediate problem first.

'Okay, enough philosophy. As usual, I'm procrastinating on the real problem: how am I going to get out of here? The clip? The seat back? Is there anything at all?'

5.00 am, Tuesday, December 30, 2036
Penang Fairhaven – North Dyke

On a normal night, lights from the North Dyke offered respite from the total blackout of night. Not this time.

It was silent, too, apart from the faint swish of crabs and mudskippers, and the unwelcome sound of approaching wavelets.

Grace was wondering if she should have panicked earlier.

She took another inventory of the truck. Could she make a sharp edge out of something? The clunky old phone was too heavy, and wouldn't break into clean shards.

'There must be something. What am I overlooking?'

There was nothing.

She concentrated on the phone. Would a text message still work? But to whom? All the networks were down.

'I'm on my own. Again.'

6.00 am, Tuesday, December 30, 2036
Penang Fairhaven – North Dyke

The phone.

'Oh my God. That's it. The screen protector! Gorilla Glass. I remember.'

Almost dislocating her shoulder, she wiggled the phone out of her pocket with the tips of her fingers. She picked the glass off the phone casing with her last remaining piece of fingernail and used the limited space she had to bend the glass across the steering wheel.

To no avail. 'It's tougher than I thought. How am I going to break it into shards without slashing my arm in the process?'

She dug out the crisp packet from the door pocket, slid the glass inside, and tried again. And again. On the fifth attempt she succeeded: the glass broke in two, scratching her hand.

'Okay, so I've gone from having nothing at my disposal to having two Stone Age tools. That's a big step. I hope this is sharp enough to cut through the seat belt. Who on earth thought that carbon fibre-reinforced seat belts were a good idea?'

She sawed away at the seatbelt with quick, persistent cuts, making headway with excruciating slowness. She saw the first signs of water leaking into the truck.

A glimmer of distant lightning illuminated the horizon. The mosque would call soon. It began to rain.

'This isn't working. My hands are so sore. Damn. Do I leave a final message for the world? Tell them how this all started?'

9.00 am, Saturday, November 4, 2017
George Town – Penang
Global average temperature: 1.2°C above pre-industrial levels

In the week since young Grace Chan arrived back in Penang for her college's term break, the floods were getting worse.

Her Auntie Janis cautioned her as she left the sprawling family compound. 'Don't bother going to the refugee camps today. Let one of the other idealists do it. Just because you're going to college doesn't mean you have to solve every single one of the world's problems.'

'I'll be careful. For now, Jack needs to be walked. He hasn't been out yet this morning.'

'Your Auntie Annie and I told your parents we'd look after you while they're working abroad. Don't do anything dangerous.'

'I'm 19 already. I don't need any additional looking after. If my parents cared about my welfare that much, they wouldn't be working in Iraq. Why couldn't we have stayed in Dubai? Or Cape Town. Or better, Vienna.'

Auntie Janis shouted, 'Take your umbrella!' as Grace let the door slam behind her.

It was true, Grace thought as she ambled toward the refugee area, that her local attempts to help people wouldn't solve the big issues that got them there. Many of those who fled to Penang were from areas that suffered from perpetual water problems: drought half the year, and floods the other half. But she needed to do something.

Jack tugged at the leash as he strained to inspect a fascinating piece of rubbish. Grace pulled him back. 'You can't go running after every interesting little bug and stick you see! You have to prioritise; not everything is important. That's why you're the only dog in the neighbourhood that has to be leashed up like this, you disappointing, adorable, little mutt.' She wondered if he had a hunting or tracking dog in his ancestry, but it was impossible to know; Jack, like Grace herself, was beautiful, intelligent, and irrepressible, but was also a mongrel. She yearned for him while she was away at school. It was only in Jack's eyes that she ever saw the unconditional love that others took for granted. Her amiable parents saw her as a distraction; her aunts were happy to have her as an extra hand around the house. But to Jack, she was everything.

The excited dog didn't mind the rain, and continued to explore the corners of drains and edges of garbage bins. Grace's umbrella made no difference, since the block-long puddles were already shin-deep, and the cars and motorbikes created waves that soaked her as they passed. There was irony in people's attempts to overcome the forces of nature: bicycling through a waist-high puddle was unpleasant, but possible; driving through one with a motorbike, however, risked a drowned carburettor and an expensive trip to the repair shop.

Two streets away from the refugee housing compound, she heard the shouts of an agitated crowd.

'Come on, Jack. Let's go. We need to get out of this rain.'

As they turned a corner, a government utility truck passed, leaving a giant wake behind. The wall of water knocked Grace off her feet. As she struggled to stand upright, losing her grip on Jack's lead, a smaller car ploughed through the flood. She recognised the growing sounds of the crowd as shouts of fear. A swell of water, higher than anything she had crossed so far, flowed toward her. She tried to run, but the moving water was more powerful than her shaky legs.

'Jack! Where are you? Come here!'

The water was faster than she could have imagined. A woman screamed from a window above, and men cried out conflicting instructions to each other. A large piece of floating debris – a vegetable bin? – almost knocked her over again, but she grabbed a street sign and managed to stay upright. The water, churning and filthy, roared past her as she cried out Jack's name again and again. A man in full rain gear, attempting to push his stalled motorbike through the inundation, slipped under the moving water and did not re-emerge. A Nissan hatchback floated down the street at a crazy angle and crashed into a Toyota.

Grace searched for Jack as she continued to clutch the street sign. Perhaps his attempts at a furious paddle against the relentless water had brought him to an open window. Perhaps a well-meaning passer-by had caught him.

For many years afterwards, she saw him in her dreams.

FAIRHAVEN

9.30 am, Friday, April 1, 2026
George Town, Penang – Fairhaven Site Office
Global temperature: 1.4°C above pre-industrial average

'I know you're only a few years out of college. But the "Client Representative" role is a new one and we need new ideas,' Zygmunt explained, still perusing Grace's resume through a pair of reading glasses. 'Our client is the city of Penang, and Fairhaven Development Corporation has been contracted to implement the entire project. But, like yourself, we're all engineers, and we can get hyper-focused on the day-to-day operations. So we need someone to help keep our client informed of what's going on, and understand what their priorities are. You'd have to get involved in everything to do with the project – you'll be a contractor-customer liaison.'

Grace examined the older man. His thin hair was still dark, but his creased complexion gave him the appearance of someone older than his 60-something years. Perhaps he had spent more time on construction sites than was obvious at first glance.

'Working at Fairhaven is a step up from the contract I just finished at Shipham, but I'm confident I can handle the role. To be honest, it's my dream job,' Grace replied.

He looked up from the document. 'I like to see that kind of enthusiasm in the team. And I'm guessing that working with a pump and valve supplier has given you the practical experience you need. Long story short – let's do it. How soon can you start?'

Grace grinned. 'How about Monday?'

Zygmunt nodded with satisfaction, but was distracted by a tall, fair-haired man in his early 30s, passing the site office hut. 'Hold on. Hey, Hans!' Zygmunt's cry caused the man to pause, and, at a gesture, to enter. 'Come on in. We've hired a partner for you.' Turning back to Grace, he continued, 'You're in luck. I thought he was out on the site today. Hans is my chief of staff; you'll be working with him. Hans de Jong, this is Grace Chan.'

'Nice to meet you, Ms Chan,' Hans replied affably. 'Is today your first day?'

His genuine smile helped quell a tiny doubt nagging at the back of Grace's mind. 'Nice to meet you, too. I'm here for my interview, but it seems to have gone very well! My first day is going to be Monday.'

'Congratulations! Do you have a bit of time now? I can show you around. Why not get a head start?'

'Why not?'

Zygmunt indicated his approval with another short nod, and Grace grabbed her mini backpack. Moments later, Hans was leading Grace toward the docks.

'How familiar are you with the whole operation? You know, they call it a dyke project, or land reclamation, but it's so much more than that. Fairhaven is the biggest climate adaptation project in the world. FDC, which runs it, is a quasi-autonomous NGO – so we have a certain amount of leeway in how we manage things.'

Stretching across the water in front of the docks, half a dozen dredge-and-crane stations and piling barges punctuated the shimmering waves. They could see the opposite side of the strait, about a kilometre away; marshy areas were already emerging from the mud flats as the tide dropped. Small boats darted between the barges and around the heaps of construction rubble that would form the bulk of the North Dyke, while crows wheeled above. The blazing, mid-day sun beat down, as a smell of mud, rotting fish and diesel fuel mingled with the aromas of simmering curry *mee* from the shore.

A group of fishermen, squatting on plastic chairs, scowled at Grace and Hans as they drew closer to the water's edge. 'It's been attracting bad press, though, hasn't it?' she queried.

'Yeah, the fishermen are complaining. I mean, I understand. The place where they fish is literally going to become a piece of land once the two dykes are completed and the land reclaimed.

'But what they don't realise,' continued Hans, 'is that the choice is not between keeping the satisfactory status quo, versus a future unknown risk. Doing nothing won't keep things the same. Without this project, sooner or later this whole area is going to be like 2017 every day.'

Grace was surprised. 'You mean the floods. Were you here then?'

Hans nodded. 'I was about 26. I'd been working in Japan for a few years and my family came here on holiday from the Netherlands, so I flew down to join them. My mother wanted to cut our trip short, once it became obvious what was going to happen with the floods, but my grandmother said we should stay, so my sister and I would see what things would be like at home if we didn't have all of our own dykes.'

'Your country is at risk, too.'

'We are. Our entire history is about managing flood risk. My grandfather was a farmer, but I'm like my father, a civil engineer working on water and land management. I came back here to join the Fairhaven project because I thought it was about time we put our expertise to work outside of Holland.' Grace glanced up at his serious expression, and liked what she saw.

A slim, blue boat perched at the shoreline, and a tanned boatman held on to a sharp, red-painted bar that jutted from its prow. 'Let's take a look at one of the barges,' Hans offered, shouting instructions to the boatman, who nodded and gave him a thumbs-up sign. As they clambered over the side, he donned a life jacket from the rail and handed one to Grace. 'You know, all our boatmen are former fishermen, too.'

The boatman brought the old Mercury outboard motor to life. A few minutes later, they coasted to a halt alongside a larger vessel. Grace peered at its stern, dominated by a two-tonne A-frame and hydraulic drive lift; despite the appearance of its broad deck, it was, in its structure, a catamaran. Stable, compact, and with a shallow draft, it was the type of craft that could carry a huge load and stay flat when the tide went out. A radar arch topped the upper observation platform above the helm station. 'They use scanning gear to explore the mud below the surface,' explained Hans. 'Sometimes we help explore archaeological sites.'

'That kind of work must be fascinating.'

'Yes. You see there? There's a 40 metre or longer wooden, ribbed structure. It's deep in the mud; over 20 metres. It could date back to the end of the last ice age.'

'Wow! Of course, I'd heard the rumours about World War II submarines in these waters.'

'The ones with gold still on board? Treasure-hunters have discovered flasks of mercury and jet engine parts, but no gold. A few boats are still unaccounted for, but they might have been lost anywhere in the region.'

'Oh, well! Do you think the gold really exists?'

'Sure. But will it ever be found? We've got more sophisticated scanning technology now than ever before, but it's a big ask. By the way, we're getting a new civil engineer on the team this week, Ivan. He's an avid wreck diver in his spare time; that's the original reason he came to Penang. He'll be able to tell you all about it.'

8.30 pm, Friday, April 1, 2026
George Town, Penang – Mutiara Heights

That evening, she scrolled through the news on her phone.

Fishermen in uproar at Malaysia dyke

Massive geoengineering project threatens UNESCO World Heritage Site

Malaysian prime minister defends dyke plan against fishing lobby

'What they don't say is that if nothing is done, their precious UNESCO site will be flooded in a few years,' Grace commented to Nant, showing her the headlines as they ate their bowls of Maggi instant noodles. 'They're also getting it confused with the existing land reclamation projects, the old "three islands" project. If the sea level rises even a metre within the next few decades, not only the islands but all the other recovered land will be lost. Not to mention all the low-lying land on Penang island and coast.'

'Really?'

'Yes. The airport has tidal gullies around it. It wouldn't survive. All of those new apartment blocks on the seafront, the historic town, rice-growing areas hundreds of kilometres north and south. The choice is to lose everything, or protect what it is viable to protect.'

'Listen to you!' her flatmate crowed. 'You haven't started the job yet, and you're already an apologist.' Nant's long hair, coloured with a fashionable, dark blue wash, fell over her shoulder, threatening to dip into the noodles. Grace compared the attractive, casual style to her own frumpy haircut, just reaching below her chin; should she bother going to the hairdresser again? No; it never seemed to fix anything.

The two women sat cross-legged on a tattered sofa in a tiny living room; a laptop played a Streamberry series on mute. 'It's tragic, honestly. But it's true,' Grace continued.

'Just be careful. Don't put yourself in danger.'

'I have no choice. This is a climate engineer's dream job. It's the biggest thing I can do.'

'Climate engineer? Since when? Sounds sinister. Aren't you a chemical engineer?'

'Sinister! No more so than people who manufacture SUVs and single-use plastic containers and ... fast fashion.' She gave a reflexive glance at Nant's sequined yoga pants.

Nant laughed again and took a contented slurp of her noodles. 'How did you get to be such an activist? Childhood trauma?'

'Where were you in 2017?'

'In 2017?' Nant regarded Grace with surprise. 'I was still at university, in Scotland, darling, with all the best people. Why?'

'I think how you see the world depends on where you were at key moments.'

10.30 am, Friday, September 2, 2008
Cape Town, South Africa – Encotsheni Public Primary School
Global temperature: 1.0°C above pre-industrial average

Grace was, once again, curled up with a book. This time, it was a copy of an old Enid Blyton story; newer books, like Rick Riordan novels, never made it to the poorer South Africa primary schools until decades after they were published. As she turned the pages, she didn't notice that all the other children had already left the classroom for play time. It didn't matter; in another half a year, she knew, it would be time for a new country, a new school, and a new group of kids who would accept her or taunt her or ignore her according to their own rules. As usual, her mother would dismiss it all as unimportant. If she noticed at all.

She had come up with several shortcuts to help her fit in. One was a quick-and-dirty explanation of her unusual features: I'm from Malaysia; my father is Chinese and my mother is Indian. Of course, the full story was more complicated – her mother was Indian/Malaccan, while her father was from a sprawling Chinese/Peranakan family who had inhabited Penang for generations.

She'd also devised a simple way to explain why their family moved so often: my father is an engineer, and he goes around the world working on power plants. Again, the truth was more interesting, had any of them cared to listen to an explanation. Her father worked on installation projects for power stations, slum electrification, and post-war rebuilding – the tougher the better from his point of view. Her mother, a teacher, took on classes at posh international schools, at rough-and-tumble local schools, and everywhere in between. The problem was that her parents' work was more interesting than anything their daughter could offer.

At last, a cleaner noticed her sitting in the deserted classroom, and shooed her out onto the dusty playground.

'Go get fresh air! You can't be inside all day.'

Grace obeyed, tucking the book into her backpack, and wandered out-of-doors. Standing in the narrow band of shade provided by the eaves of the concrete building, she listened to the chatter of the other kids, absorbing new words in Xhosa and Zulu. After watching for a long time, she drifted into the margins of a game – something with a ball and two sticks – cataloguing the rules in her mind.

A girl of her own age accosted her, speaking in the type of joyful patois that can be found in playgrounds around the world. 'Hey! You play with us now now?'

Grace joined the circle with a grin and gestured toward the ball. 'I take this one?'

The girl grinned back. '*Haikona*! Hands off. You think we have so many balls we can give you one? I show you how first.'

Some things are precious, Grace thought to herself, while others take them for granted.

6.00 pm, Friday, March 9, 2012
Penang, Malaysia – Chan family compound
Global temperature: 1.0°C above pre-industrial average

The noise at Auntie Annie's house was never deafening, but always present, and never consistent enough to be ignored. A younger cousin was crying, Jack was barking, and Auntie Janis was scolding an older cousin. The television showed a middle-aged woman in a sparkling dress, wailing out her misery in front of an orchestra.

'Janis!' shouted an uncle. 'Change the channel. Don't you know the football is on?'

'Change it yourself! Can't you see I'm busy? Grace! Why is that damn dog barking again?!'

All the chaos distracted Grace from the Agatha Christie novel she'd found at the public library. She placed a bookmark at the beginning of Chapter 6 (Poirot had not shown up yet), held the book under her arm, and wandered outside to the courtyard to find out what was bothering Jack.

'And to think my parents consider it dangerous over there!' Grace muttered to herself. 'At least in Iraq there might be a proper reason for getting a headache.' She found Jack under the mango tree, launching intermittent, joyful barks at a small child and worrying a plastic toy, while the child howled with indignation. As usual, someone had drawn a ridiculous (and hilarious) set of eyebrows on poor Jack's forehead.

'Stop it, Jack! You are incorrigible. If you don't calm down and give back that toy, I'm going to have to ...' she stopped. The long-legged dog was already seated at her feet, his tail wagging and tongue lolling. Her cousin retrieved the toy and toddled back to the kitchen. 'What do I do now? Hug you or scold you?' The tail continued to wag as Grace squatted next to him. 'Fine. You can read with me.' She sat with her back against the mango tree and returned to Chapter Six. She read aloud, 'The photograph of Jane Finn, which would have been of the utmost value to the police in tracing her, was lost beyond recovery ...' and Jack curled up, his head on her lap.

9.30 am, Thursday, April 23, 2026
George Town, Penang – Bazalgette Lock

'So I'm not an orphan,' Grace explained, 'but I wouldn't see my parents more than once a year when they came back on leave. I wasn't a real child of any particular house, just one of a crowd of cousins at one of several houses.'

Hans replied, 'I would guess that sort of upbringing gave you unusual empathy.'

Grace had learned more about empathy over the past several

months, as she completed her site orientation. She was studying excavation permits, how to place a crane without collapsing the ground, and the details of concrete slump tests. She learned about scaffold design, diesel bowser organisation, and operational safety at heights. Working alongside various team members, one by one, helped her understand how they did their jobs. They taught her the risks involved and other tricks of the trade, along with a wide variety of personal back stories. Every so often, to her delight, Hans made surprise visits to her work site at Bazalgette Lock.

'Yes and no. It made me self-reliant. And a loner, too. But after the age of 14, I spent weekends helping out at the refugee centres in Penang. Teaching English to the younger kids. You know, a lot of those refugees were fleeing their homes because of climate change.' Grace handed Hans a digital clipboard with the update of the work around the Bazalgette lock site.

'But you didn't want to go into development work? Join an NGO?'

'I suppose the closest I got to that was joining the Girl Guides when we were in Liverpool! Whenever they weren't ignoring me, my family were always trying to tell me what I should be doing. My Auntie Annie told me I was "too old for all this refugee nonsense" and that I should focus on my studies, and find a good job with the government. Or else find a young man with a good job.'

Hans laughed as he signed off on the update and handed the clipboard back. 'What about your other aunt, the one you like?'

'Auntie Janis? She always tells me I'm perfect just as I am, which is maddening in its own way. I've learned not to rely on anyone but myself. But I can't ignore what's happening around me. This is the first time I've been working on a project that makes a difference. Anyway, tell me more about the other locks. Is there anything we should learn?.'

'You'll see them soon enough.' Hans changed the subject. 'By the way … what do you think of Zygmunt?'

'He's the first boss I've ever had where I thought he believed in what he's doing. Where is he from?'

'He's Polish,' Hans replied. 'But he's been working in Asia all of his life.'

Grace grimaced. 'Is he one of those "yellow fever" men who came here for the women?'

'I don't think so. But he's single at the moment; and he doesn't seem to have much luck as a husband. He has at least three ex-wives in three different countries, and he's paying child support for at least four kids.'

'How awful.'

'It's not something I bring up at the department head meetings.'

LEMMINGS

8.30 pm, Thursday, October 22, 2026
Penang, Malaysia – Chan family compound
Global temperature: 1.4°C above pre-industrial average

Occasional babysitting duty was the price she paid for free rent. But as Grace attempted to clean up crumbs from an unsanctioned bag of Mr Potato crisps off the bed, she wasn't sure it was worth it. She was already exhausted from a long day at Bazalgette Lock.

'Auntie Grace, why did you move back here with us?' asked Sasha. 'I thought you weren't coming back, because you're a grown-up now.'

At six, she had not yet learned about tact, although she had stopped objecting every time Grace asked her to put on her pyjamas.

'Well, it's too expensive for me to rent an apartment by myself. And my roommate Nant had to go away to Singapore, because she got a new job.'

'Nant is our auntie, too. You can tell because her name sounds like aunt,' declared Sasha's brother. He was two years older and knew almost everything.

'No, she's not related to you at all. She was my friend. Is my friend. In fact, I am not your aunt, either; I'm your first cousin once removed, because —' he had already stopped paying attention. 'Where did your cousins get to?'

'They're in the living room! They're playing Orcraft again!' Sasha reported, bouncing up and down on the bed. 'And Auntie Katherine said they couldn't!'

The moment their parents leave, Grace thought to herself, they revert to savagery. 'Kids! Get in here!' she bellowed. 'It's bedtime!'

'We're not done yet! Ten minutes!' returned a shout from the other room.

'Five minutes! Or no story!'

Three dramatic groans came from the other room, followed by their shout of assent. For now, the threat still worked, since they still enjoyed her stories. But she didn't know how long she could keep it up. The eldest, Clara, turned 12 a month ago.

When five minutes elapsed, they put down their controllers and headed into the big bedroom. Grace sat in the middle of the group. 'Okay, you little lemmings. What's it going to be this time? You want the one about the *Titanic* again?'

'No, tell us, tell us one about a volcano. And it should have animals. And helicopters. And snow.'

'Okay, let me think. Once upon a time ... there was an enormous volcano. It was the biggest volcano in the whole world. Its name was Mount Erebus. And do you know where it was? It was far away in Antarctica! One day, a little lemming climbed all the way up the side of the volcano, because he wanted to see what was going on.'

'And although the sky was blue, and the sun was shining, he was very, very, very, very, very, very cold. And he was so cold, and there was so much snow, that he couldn't walk there. He had to go everywhere on little lemming skis or little lemming ice boots. So he was looking at the lava. And before he knew it, there was an enormous BOOM!'

The two youngest shrieked. 'Did he fall in the volcano?'

'Yes. And that's the end of the story!'

'Wait! No fair!'

'Okay, that's not the end of the story. But the little lemming did see something very strange. The volcano was erupting! So he went down the side of the mountain, as fast as his skis could carry him. And what do you know, when he got there, his lemming friend had already started up the helicopter! So he got in, and they flew away as fast as they could.'

'Where did they go?'

'They went to McMurdo Station. But as they were flying away, they looked down, and saw a river of burning lava running down the side of the mountain! The lava was going straight into the ice sheet. And it made huge explosions, because you know what happens when something very hot hits cold water? Steam. So the lemming had to figure out whether they should stay there, since it looked extremely dangerous. In fact, pretty soon, they realised that it was going to be a big disaster!'

The 9-year-old, who had kept quiet until this moment, objected. 'Auntie Grace, your stories are always about disasters!'

'Oh? I guess we'll just have to find out whether they get out of this one. Anyway, all over the world, the lemmings were very worried. In particular, they were very worried if they lived in Shanghai, or Singapore, or New York. Why do you think those lemmings were more worried than the others?'

'I know! They're all near the ocean.'

'Yes. They were worried because the ice in Antarctica was going to melt, and make all the oceans rise 10 metres. And it was going to happen all at once, not in ten years, but in just one year! So, do you know what they did? They decided to move every lemming in the world to new homes. And every single one of them had to be 20 metres above sea level.

'But there were problems. First of all, it was very expensive. Second, there would be places that couldn't be saved. And third, once the seas rose, there would be fewer airports, because most of them would be drowned!'

'Why couldn't they just live in Fairhaven? I thought you said it's supposed to be okay if the sea rises.'

'Well, even huge projects like Fairhaven can only protect against a few metres of sea level rise. But you see, there was one more problem and it was the biggest of all. Do you know what it was?'

'What?'

'They were all fighting with each other about what to do! Something I believe you five are familiar with. But they realised that if they wanted to solve their problems, they could only depend on themselves.

'And they took down as many buildings as possible, and moved everything to the new locations: windows, bricks, wood, steel. And in their new houses, each lemming had to learn how to live without using up so much stuff. How do you think they did that?'

'How?'

'In their new cities, they decided that since all the lemmings had four feet, they didn't need cars, and they could go around on roller skates, or else take the MRT or the tram. And since they were so tiny, they didn't need such big houses. And since they were lemmings, which are herbivorous, they decided to eat more vegetables.

'And they all escaped from the sea level rises and lived happily ever after. At least until the point where the demographic calculus no longer made sense in terms of the planetary carrying capacity, and they needed to embark on a multilateral program of gender equity and female empowerment in order to manage out-of-control birth rates and the resulting increase in global emissions.'

'What? What do you mean?' Sasha was bouncing on the bed again.

'Sorry, I got carried away. What I meant to say was that they all lived happily after, until the end of their days! The end.'

The four youngest children got into bed, but Clara lurked outside the door. 'Auntie Grace, I think your story wasn't about lemmings and volcanoes. It was about climate change.'

'You're cleverer than I had you down for. Must have been all those vegetables. It's true that an eruption of Mount Erebus could cause a ten metre sea rise, although the chance of that happening is super low.'

'The sea level rise is happening already, though, isn't it.'

'Yeah. Does this stuff bother you?'

'Sort of. We hear about it in school all the time. But it's not so bad, at least not for us.'

'How so?'

'We know you're working on it. You'll fix it.' Clara hugged her, got into bed, and switched off the light.

Sitting in the living room, Grace texted Hans, tears in her eyes.

> I can't live here any more.

She saw the word 'typing ...' and waited.

> Why not?

> There's too much pressure.

6.30 pm, Friday, November 27, 2026
George Town, Penang – Zur Bratpfanne

'So this is it,' Zygmunt concluded, surprising them with a vulnerable expression as he swiped through the images on his phone.

The older man was wearing a polo shirt and shorts, his white legs conspicuous.

Grace was sitting at the plastic table with Hans. Ivan, the new civil engineer and wreck diver, joined them. They sipped their cold tea to temper the heat, looking at the views in the photos. 'That apartment is gorgeous,' Grace sighed. 'Nant got a new job in Singapore a few months ago, so I had to move back into the family compound with my aunties. I'm grateful, but it's stifling.'

Ivan, distracted by the television, whooped at something on the screen – a sudden save by the team in blue and green livery. Too slight ever to be an athlete himself, he was an enthusiastic fan. As he and Hans analysed the play, Zygmunt put away the phone and turned back to Grace. 'Have you tried their German sausages? Not quite like the Polish ones back home, but acceptable.'

'I've never tried them. Are you buying?'

In response, Zygmunt went to the counter to order and returned with the receipts.

'How did you get that contract sorted out with the concrete supplier?' Hans asked Zygmunt as he sat down again.

'It's pretty straightforward. The cement will be delivered in bulk by ship to the harbour, and then trucked to the readymix units around the construction sites.'

'They might struggle to supply the amount needed,' Hans pointed out. 'Did they really agree?'

'You can trust me on this one. I've been doing contracts my whole career.'

'But back to the apartment,' Grace pressed on. 'How would this be possible? You know what our salaries are. And that place looks well out of our range.'

'The market's tight, but there are still empty apartments. And by living as a group, we can enjoy a very good lifestyle.' Zygmunt was fiddling with the paper wrapper on his cutlery, folding it this way and that, and soon constructed a clever little holder to perch them on. It was the kind of thing he did when he was nervous.

'I didn't know you were such a real estate tycoon.'

'There are many investment properties that are bought but not lived in. I've made enquiries and there are at least nine empty units in Gurney, the block next to our site office. And they are big apartments, six bedrooms in each.'

'I'd have thought it was a load of small apartments,' said Ivan.

'Each floor is two massive apartments. So I tracked down one of the owners. He has no desire to rent, and less to sell. But I'm a contract negotiator, right?'

'And you talked him into it?' asked Grace.

'I subscribe to the theory of standing side by side with your negotiating partner. I've stayed in communal apartments in other cities, and wanted to do the same here. So, I'm asking, would you like a room?'

'I'd love to! I need to ask my aunties, though,' she frowned. 'They won't approve of me staying with a group of unmarried men.'

'But you're half my age! And there will be others there. Hans, Ivan – well, I suppose they're also unmarried – but it's 2026, and these old-fashioned attitudes must give way.'

Hans piped up, 'In the Netherlands, such arrangements are quite common.'

'When would you want us to move in?' asked Grace.

'Beginning of next month, if we can manage it. You three were at the top of my list.'

Ivan clapped his hands, his infectious smile lightening the mood. 'I'm willing to take a look. We've had sausages together. I think that counts as knowing each other well enough!'

NONKIYA

10.00 pm, Friday, November 13, 2026
Shinjuku, Tokyo – Nonkiya Bar
Global temperature: 1.4°C above pre-industrial average

After the seminar, four men descended to the little underground bar, a dark, old-fashioned place with a single employee standing behind a polished, wooden countertop. Bundles of chopsticks stood upright in shiny, black cups. Outside, the November air was already creating tiny clouds of vapour around the mouths of the pedestrians.

Strangers at the start of the evening, they each watched a well-advertised presentation about the melting of the arctic from the Cambridge Centre for Climate Repair. By the end of the talk, they were connected by their common response: a strong need for a strong drink, to shake off the inevitable sense of doom.

The speaker had droned, 'As melting ice caps have darkened, replaced by open water, sunlight is no longer being reflected into space. What we have feared for decades is happening. We've tipped over into a positive feedback loop, meaning our ice caps will now melt faster and faster. Scarier still is the methane time bomb. Rising temperatures will cause this greenhouse gas, more than 80 times more potent than carbon dioxide, to be released from the permafrost and the shallow Siberian Seas, spiking global heating, and ending civilization as we know it.'

They bid him farewell with bows, handshakes, and goodwill. But their mood darkened the moment he was out of sight.

At the bar, they exchanged cards, ordered beers and chatted about the visiting professor's gloomy warnings and possible solutions. After half an hour, a man with rimless glasses turned to a tall, younger man, who had stayed quiet in the background.

'Fujimoto-san. What would you do about this, if you could?'

Kenji Fujimoto stood up, alert. He ventured, 'I do have some ideas, Ito-san. Would you like to hear about them?' He pushed a lock of unruly hair from his eyes.

'At this point, we are ready for any options,' Ito replied.

Kenji pulled a map from his briefcase and unfolded it before speaking. At first, only Ito listened. But as Kenji went on, the casual conversation between the other two died down, and they paid closer attention. One of them signalled to the bartender to serve another round of beer.

By the time he answered all their questions, it was almost midnight, and the last train would be leaving soon. Kenji mentioned the lateness of the hour. Ito-san considered each of the other three men.

After a long moment, he said, 'I will pay.'

Kenji and the others thanked him for his hospitality. He interrupted – the prerogative of the most senior member of the group. 'No, no, no. Fujimoto-san. I will pay for your plan.'

'What?'

'It is November. Can we have everything in place for February?'

Kenji bowed deeply. 'Ito-san, I will put together a team and prepare a complete project plan for you. We will make it our united goal to put everything in place by the time the ice arrives.'

'Good. I have already given you my card, I believe? Please contact my secretary to make an appointment for Monday morning.'

12.10 am, Saturday, November 14, 2026
Penang, Malaysia – 8 Gurney Drive

Hans had just stood up from his gaming console and was stretching after an all-out raid with Ivan, when his laptop pinged with an unfamiliar chime. A moment later, he realised that he did recognise it, after all: it was from the Line app, which he hadn't used since the days when he worked in Japan.

He was delighted to see that the message was from Kenji Fujimoto, a man he worked with for several months soon after arriving in Osaka. Kenji had been a grad student at the time and was now an assistant professor of oceanography. Hans was still learning Japanese, but Kenji spoke and wrote English well, having grown up next door to an American military base. They had earned each other's mutual trust. Hans typed out an immediate reply.

> Kenji! Long time no see. How are you?

> I am very well, thank you, Hans!

> Good to hear from you. What's up?

> I am very sorry to bother you, but I have just been asked to develop a new project and would like your advice.

Hans smiled and replied, falling into the pattern of conversation he had learned during his time there. He continued typing:

> Would be honoured to help! My advice probably useless tho. You're the expert.

> I have good news. Last night, I met Mr Ito, an industrialist, and I told him all about our plan.

Hans smiled again as he replied.

> *Our* plan? The Arctic plan? It's *your* plan LOL. I just listened while you developed it.

> Your contribution was valuable. But I was surprised that Mr Ito has agreed to pay for a large-scale trial. I asked him for $2 million, and he said yes.

> Really? OMG. That's incredible. Congratulations!!1!

> However, Hans, I need your help. I do not know what to do next.

> Would love to work on it with you right now if I weren't committed here in Fairhaven. Will do what I can. Tell me about Mr Ito.

> He owns and runs a big machinery company, Rakki. It is well known in Japan.

> Good. Ask for help w/ equipment procurement.

> What else?

> Dedicated procurement specialist. Defined budget. SAP code. a Gantt chart. Project administrator. Technical specialists. Specific equipment to do the project.

> What about the experiments?

> That's the easy part LOL. U need to try all methods to make the ice thicker. Don't buy the equipment – try to rent. Ask for funding for specialists to operate it.

> Did I ask for enough money? I made a rough estimate.

> $2 mn? Should be enough for 1 season trial. Tugboat runs ~$10-15K per day, including crew, not including fuel. You need to prepare a decent budget tho.

> Thank you very much, Hans. It is late here, and I must go to bed. I must give a lecture tomorrow morning at 8.00am.

> Np. Great news. Keep me posted.

COP31

4.00 pm, Friday, November 6, 2026

Malaysia Airlines – en route to Sydney

Global temperature: 1.4°C above pre-industrial average

Tengku Marina Zainal, with flashing, dark eyes, dressed in the exact clothes that would be expected of someone from her background, turned away from the first-class view out the window of the Boeing 777x, and toward the woman in the next seat. Her expensive outfit chafed; she would be happier in overalls and rubber boots.

'We shouldn't be flying to COP31. We should be walking, or sailing, or something. We should think about the optics, if nothing else.'

Her companion's attire revealed a more frugal budget. She replied, 'It would take months to sail from Malaysia to Sydney. Not to mention the fact that your sister and your brother-in-law have the yacht this week.'

'Stop being so practical, Elizabeth,' Marina pouted, and took a moody sip of her coconut drink. Here on an international flight, far away from anyone who would judge her, she still could not bring herself to taste alcohol. 'I'm 39 years old; I'm too old to be reasoned with. Plus, I get enough rational arguments in my scientific work. What I want is irrational action.'

Elizabeth remained calm. 'Unlike you, Marina, I can't afford not to be practical. We are there to represent the interests of our community of businesses, and I'm there to ensure you get everything done that you need to get done.'

'And remind me what these interests are, again?'

Elizabeth tapped the large, in-seat entertainment screen, turning off the latest blockbuster, from the new Orac Studios, and gave Marina her full attention. 'Growth and shareholder value. Which, I should remind you, are what keep the Zainal family office solvent. Don't forget, I'm 39, too, and it is my job to be reasonable.'

Marina smiled. 'It's your job to further the aims of the Zainal family, and at the moment, those aims are to take a hard look at the real situation we're in, and help us find a way forward so that we're still successful in the next generation. I've learned something from being the black sheep of this family; while you were in business school with Amir, I was working on my dissertation in the Cocos Islands. I learned that it takes more than business to keep the planet solvent. We should be treating Earth as a service provider, one that gives us water, land, food, and air; but at the moment, we're a terrible customer. We've never settled a single invoice.'

'What do you mean?'

'The entire premise of what we are doing is flawed. Every time we talk about growth, all I can see is the Cocos people. They speak a Malay language, and from a legal point of view they are part of Australia. But the difference between their lives and how the rest of Australia lives – between our lives in Kuala Lumpur and theirs in their village – it's intolerable. Growth to them means someone coming to take away their livelihood and devastate their fishing grounds, while they get nothing.'

'There are different ways of achieving growth.'

'We should find a different way, then.'

'Hm.' Elizabeth tapped the elaborate entertainment screen again, resuming the movie.

'You know at this meeting, they are going to propose that governments cut all subsidies to oil and gas companies. And everyone in the family has been telling me it's impossible. Among other things, we have massive assets tied up in offshore oil platforms. You told me yourself that they're going to demand cuts of 10% emissions every year, from this year, every year, until we get to net zero. And then they want us to go net negative.'

As she answered, Elizabeth regarded the screen in front of her with a steadfast gaze, where a blue-and-white logo was twirling as the opening credits appeared. 'That's why we're going there, to explain the economic consequences of such a move. There's no way it will work. You know that as well as I do.'

'I have another idea. Will you help me?'

'You know what I'm going to say.'

'Yes, yes, "As long as it furthers the aims of the Zainal family!" I assure you, it will. My granddaughter is going to be telling people about how this all started.'

'All right,' Elizabeth smiled. 'Then let's hear it.'

7.00 pm, Sunday, November 8, 2026
Sydney, Australia – COP31

Three aides, briefcases in hand, scurried to keep up with the sour-faced Prime Minister of Canada as he strode through the crowd.

'He found the sandwiches too expensive, maybe?' Marina observed. There had not yet been a COP conference where the catering was anything close to acceptable, and this one was no exception. Elizabeth laughed.

A photographer was attempting to wrangle two heads of state and the executive director of a multilateral agency into a photo against the playful, rainbow-coloured backdrop. Every time she had them in position, a new person came out of the crowd to distract them, by shaking hands, starting up a new conversation, or requesting their own selfie.

A group of protestors outside the glass double doors were chanting incomprehensible slogans. The two women glanced at each other and shrugged their shoulders. Elizabeth put a hand on Marina's shoulder. 'We've got to get over to the symposium. Do you want to grab a coffee first?'

'No. This event has the worst coffee I've ever tasted. Maybe it was better last year in Brazil. Anyway, it's too late. It will make our jet lag worse.'

They walked for several minutes to the conference room, their paces matched. 'When do you think we should announce?' Marina asked after a long silence.

Elizabeth waited before answering. 'I don't think we should make commitments we can't keep.'

'We have before.'

'It's different this time.'

Marina remained silent until they arrived. 'All right.'

'All right, what?'

'Your advice is good, as always.'

She nodded, and held open the door for Marina, who sailed through. Elizabeth persisted, 'We'll announce it when we have projects to show.'

'It is my intention to have that happen sooner than you expect.'

9:00am, Monday, January 4, 2027
Oil Platform – Natuna Sea, 18 kilometres from Vietnamese border

The once proud, bright yellow structure was streaked with corrosion and long lines of rust stains, like dried blood from old wounds. Marina was grim as she regarded the scene.

The landing area on the lowest deck was broken, with walkways and handrails missing. The smell of oil lingered, perhaps from subsurface leaks. The only sound was the waves as they passed the legs of the platform.

The platform was small, big enough for no more than 30 workers. Somewhere above her were the accommodation block, control room, and workshop. She was not optimistic about there being anything left that hadn't been stolen.

Below her feet, shafts of bright sunlight pierced deep into the clear blue water. Shoals of fish flitted between the platform legs.

It doesn't look like much, she thought to herself, but the Sea Orchards will be our future.

10.00 pm, Wednesday, March 10, 2027
Kuala Lumpur, Malaysia – Grand Hyatt Kuala Lumpur

Marina was the only one at the dinner table not queasy from overindulgence. Every year, her mother's *Ramadan Buka Puasa* celebration became less of a religious observance, and more of a way to overwhelm guests with her generosity. Still, it was hard to resent the satisfaction surrounding her, heightened by the weeks of fasting that preceded the meal. She turned around to appreciate the magnificent city view, glittering many stories below and extending to the horizon.

'And what are you up to these days?' her cousin Amir asked, as he picked his teeth behind a napkin. 'We haven't seen you in town for ages.' Marina noticed that his jowls were more obvious than ever. Not that she was one to criticise. With all the time she spent out of doors, her skin was as rough as sandpaper.

'I've been down south, working on my offshore project. The Sea Orchards.'

'Oh, yes, with the fish!' Amir's mother trilled, her face flushed from the exertion of doing justice to the extravagant dinner. 'What extraordinary ideas you have.' She took another chocolate. 'Your mother must have picked up these delicious little sweets when she was in Switzerland last week. They're marvellous. So, is everything going well with your little project?'

'Yes, although we are still in the start-up phase.'

Amir's father intervened. 'It's past time you got involved in our philanthropic activities, Marina, so we're all happy to see you putting aside your hobbies and working on a charitable venture. But I wish you would choose something in our family's core giving areas. You know, your aunt is still looking for help with her scholarship program.'

Marina thought of what she wanted to say, cast it aside, and allowed herself a brief smile. 'I've been working for the Department of Fisheries as a marine biologist for the past fifteen years. It's not a hobby. And this new project isn't a charity, although we do expect to help the fishermen displaced by the Fairhaven project.'

Amir sat back in his chair with a philosophical frown, and commented, 'The fishermen do have a valid point. Their traditional space will be lost when the Fairhaven project is complete.'

'Yes, but they need to change – they're not only the injured party but also the perpetrators. They've been trawling, dredging, overfishing, and polluting from their fish farms.'

'What a dreadful business,' Amir's mother clucked, reaching for another chocolate.

Marina pressed on. 'Most of the catch from the flats is already small. It's about developing a way to fish that ensures the long-term abundance of the wider fishery area.'

Amir's father clasped his hands over his substantial midriff. 'If you need any help, let me know – remember, the Penang vice-governor is my mother's brother-in-law.'

For a moment, Marina thought of asking then and there for a permit to conduct a trial she'd been thinking of; however, she already had a reputation in the family, and they would look at her askance if she went into all the details of her oddball project at a *Ramadan Buka Puasa* dinner. Instead, she thanked her aunt's husband and changed the subject.

The 'little' project was, indeed, little more than an idea, at least for now. She had secured the use of one of the family's inactive oil platforms. She had also set up the initial group of rope pillars. But it would take time for fish to discover the new location, and still more time for them to become established in their new habitat – and she could not afford to scale the project without the benefit of additional primary research.

Her own dissertation, conducted on the Cocos reefs, already formed the principal basis of the initiative: she was wagering that if an artificial habitat could be set up in one of the 'deserted' areas of the ocean, a new ecosystem would form around it. It happened often enough on the sea floor, when shipwrecks, fallen pieces of equipment, and bits of doomed aircraft acted as the nucleus of new reefs. Marina wanted to duplicate the effect, vertically, at the 10m to 20m depth, using oil platform legs and buoyed ropes.

It could take ages for the ecosystem to develop. Yet giving it a boost with extra nutrients would be too risky, since it might cause a dangerous algal bloom. She had seen the damage runaway blooms could do along shorelines.

If she was successful, however, all the areas chewed up by trawlers could be rehabilitated on the same scale at which they were destroyed, and then tended and farmed by the coastal fishermen who had lost so much to the big commercial operations. Redundant and retiring oil platforms would all become part of her new system, deterring trawling and providing habitat. Platforms would be cut into pieces and planted in designed and managed areas.

She wished she could talk to Elizabeth about it, but it would have been impossible at a dinner like this one. From her mother's point of view, Elizabeth was no more than an employee. She would have to find another time.

ANXIETY

11.00 pm, Thursday, January 14, 2027
George Town, Penang – 8 Gurney Drive
Global temperature: 1.6°C above pre-industrial average

Once again, Grace Chan sat alone on her balcony, looking at the extraordinary view.

On paper, her life was perfect. She was doing meaningful work, well-paid. She lived in a beautiful penthouse apartment, with people whose company she enjoyed. But none of it could stop the dread.

'You'll fix it,' her young cousin Clara had told her. But in reality, nothing could be done. Fairhaven itself, the largest climate adaptation project in the world, could not stop the world from boiling as she watched. There on the 38th floor, she could enjoy a breeze at night, but thousands, millions, billions of people were once again facing violent floods and typhoons. Winter in the northern hemisphere brought wildfires to the south.

And nobody was coming to save them.

It was spiritual vertigo: invisible from the outside, until the moment the victim reeled from its effects. Among others, she could hold it off, but there, alone on her balcony, she too often felt the 'call of the void' – a wild impulse to scream at the top of her lungs, smash her fist right through the sliding glass doors, or hurl herself headlong over the edge.

It's all pointless, she thought.

Auntie Janis recommended she keep a diary, that she quit her job, or that she at least make herself a soft boiled egg.

Later. She had already been keeping a diary for ages, where she wrote stories and vignettes to make herself feel better. In another hour she would wipe away the tears. But in the moment, all she could do was to sit on the plastic outdoor furniture, staring at the skyline.

She had given up the idea of asking her parents for sympathy or advice long ago. Her resources must come from within.

7.00 pm, Friday, March 19, 2027
George Town, Penang – India House

Sixteen chairs were arranged in a circle, with fourteen occupied. As Grace entered the room in the shadow of her Auntie Janis, the meeting was just getting started. Preoccupied with the thought that they might be interrupting, it took Grace several minutes to realise that the large figure in the far seat was Hans de Jong.

'Sorry we're late,' trilled Janis, oblivious, wrapping herself in a voluminous shawl against the air conditioning. 'Grace, sit, sit, sit!' In that instant, Grace once again felt 12 years old, but managed to give a surreptitious nod to Hans, evoking a sheepish half-wave in return. She scampered over to the empty seat nearest the door. To her surprise, she recognised two other people from work. Auntie Janis, satisfied, plopped herself down next to the meeting's leader and offered a broad smile to the room. 'Don't mind us!'

The leader pressed his lips together, but seemed more amused than disturbed. 'Okay, now that we're all here, as I was saying, I'm Wen Xin. Who'd like to go first?'

He waited a beat before nodding at a thin woman in her forties. Only then did Grace notice that the woman's hand was half-raised.

'Go ahead. The floor is yours.'

She stood. 'My name is Yong. And I'm terrified that we are the last generation of people to live on this planet.'

Everyone in the room gave a polite smile, and clapped.

An hour and a half later, Auntie Janis left, Yong and Wen Xin drifted away somewhere, and Grace and Hans were the last to remain in the room.

'Wanna go get curry *mee*?'

'After that ordeal? Absolutely.'

Two bowls of noodles plonked down on the melamine surface of the table, followed by two bottles of Tiger beer, condensation pearling on the surface. Chilli oil floated on the surface of the noodles.

'Careful,' warned Grace. 'The curry *mee* here is spicy.'

'I can take it.'

'We'll see,' she said. 'So did you cry?'

Hans slurped a large spoonful of the broth. Before he could answer, tears began to stream down his face.

Grace laughed. 'I didn't mean that kind of crying!'

'Very funny. Strong men don't cry. Except when their team concedes a goal – that's different.'

'Zygmunt said that it's wrong to say football is a matter of life and death – because it's much more important.'

'I know people in Holland who think like that. But I'm not one of them. I don't even like football.'

'You make a pretty good show to the contrary! I hear you and Ivan going on about it all the time. It's the one thing he's more interested in than wrecks.'

'There's nothing else men are allowed to bond over, so I make it a point to learn enough to have an intelligent discussion. But it's not my passion.'

'That's a relief. I was bracing myself.'

Hans laughed. He took his bottle, looked in vain for an opener, shrugged, and popped off the cap with the end of a spoon.

Grace admired the trick. 'How did you do that?'

'Oh, I learned it from Zygmunt.' He showed her again.

'That explains it. He's always doing stuff like that; I didn't realise when I started working at Fairhaven that our boss would be the world's biggest life hack man.'

Hans laughed and offered his bottle, and they clinked. Grace found, once again, that something about his smile released a fragment of the constant tension that had tied ever-tighter inside her over the past years.

'So if football isn't your passion, what is?'

'Flower pressing! Penang is great for flowers. And I bake a good sourdough loaf. During the pandemic I was teaching everyone else, because I'd already been doing it for years.'

'Flower pressing? Bread? You're not winding me up?'

'My mother and grandmother did those things, so I took them up, too.'

Grace shook her head in disbelief. 'You need to bake your bread for the rest of us. I buy the square, white stuff from the supermarket, but it's pretty bad.'

'I've already established a starter culture for the sourdough. It's on the kitchen counter behind the knife block.'

'Is that what that is! I was wondering. Did you have one of those big bread ovens when you were growing up?'

'Yes, when I was small. We lived on a farm on Vlieland, an island outside the main dykes. The 2017 flood here wasn't the first one I'd seen. Cyclone Anatol hit when I was eight. We all got out, but we had to go live in Rotterdam after that. You could say we were climate refugees, of sorts. They reinforced the dykes, but we never went back.'

'I had no idea.'

'We kept an axe in the attic on the farm. Maybe you've heard about that practice among the Dutch; my grandmother was strict about it. Her parents chopped their way out through the roof during the great flood of 1953. And she was prepared for it to happen again.'

'Wow. How old is she?' Grace asked.

'She's 88. I'd love to introduce you to her some day. You know, she used to read to me all the time. She's the reason I was able to get an education. I didn't like school much, but she made it interesting for me.'

'I'd love to meet her.'

Hans took a smaller slurp of his noodles, his eyes crinkling. 'My family's very close. I miss them.'

'But you did a good job of ignoring my question,' Grace pressed.

'You noticed.'

'And?'

'The answer is no, I didn't cry. At least, I didn't let anyone see it.'

'Have you been going to these meetings for a long time?' she asked.

'This was my second one. Are you going to come back?'

Grace, her mouth too full of curry *mee* to speak, her eyes watering from the chillies, nodded her head in confirmation. When she swallowed, she continued, 'So what did your grandmother read with you?'

'All sorts of stuff. Lots of it was ancient. Jack London, HG Wells,

Asimov, Tolkien, Wyndham. Thea Beckman.'

'I loved all of those, too. I was a real bookworm. But I had to read it to myself. My parents were never around.'

'It's what I do instead of crying,' Hans explained. 'I disappear into a good book, or into a film. That's not to say I don't sometimes cry as well. Sometimes there's nothing else you can do.'

Grace continued, 'You know, I've always known it was coming. In primary school, we learned about it in science class. But it was this distant thing, like that massive cliff in Yosemite Valley. In my mind's eye, that's what it was like: big, but far away. Now, thinking about it at work every day has brought me to the foot of the cliff. It fills my whole view. There's nothing else.

'And now we're on the cliff, a hundred metres up. My nose is pressed against the rock and my knees are trembling. Meanwhile, you and the rest of the team always look so confident; I always thought I was alone.'

'Obviously not, given the company tonight.'

'But I'm still terrified. For all of us. We'll fail in a valiant effort and all get picked off one by one. We can't fix it.'

'By the way, you're pretty good with extended metaphors. Have you ever tried writing it down?'

'I do. My auntie gave me a journal.'

'I'm not much of a writer,' Hans mused. 'Typical engineer. Good with a calculator, bad with a pen.'

'I don't just stick to diary-writing,' she confessed, after a long pull from the bottle, 'I've been writing short stories. Alternative histories of the past and future. Something that can give me hope, where problems are solved, and we can look forward to what's ahead. What I really want is to get these stories in front of people, so they can see how disasters can be averted, or at least made less devastating.'

'It's possible. If you do it right.'

'In the stories I can say what I want. But in real life I can be impatient, and blunt.'

'Too blunt – are you sure you're not Dutch?'

Grace laughed. 'Given my family background, it's possible! We're just about everything you can think of – Chinese, Malay, Indian, Portuguese, and who knows what else. Maybe Dutch. One of my other aunties tried to assemble the family tree a couple of years ago and had to give up.'

'Are you coming back to the next Climate Anxiety session?' Hans asked.

'I have to. Auntie Janis made me go because she found me crying after family dinner last week.' Grace didn't add that part of the reason for her tears was the harangue from her Auntie Annie, who told her that at 28, she was risking being 'left on the shelf', that she herself was already married with three children by that age, and that Grace was getting old and ugly. She was grateful she could go home to the casual, anonymous commune of 8 Gurney Drive.

'Maybe you should bring along something you've written.'

'I'll think about it.'

'Do. I want to read it.'

'It's personal. But I might make an exception for you.'

Hans had finished his noodles but remained still in his seat. 'Grace, speaking of personal things ... do you want to ... come over to my place tonight?'

She laughed and took his hand. 'I live there, after all. But yes. I'd like that. I've been waiting for an invitation. Later, I can show you some of the stuff I've been writing. I've been working on a piece about the *Titanic*.'

DEFYING FUTILITY: A STORY BY GRACE CHAN

The sinking of the Titanic *is one of the most horrifying calamities of modern history. More than 1,500 people lost their lives on that January night in 1912. For more than a century, we have been asking: could they have been saved?*

In April 1912, the global temperature was 0.1°C above the pre-industrial average. As we approach a modern calamity on a planetary scale, we must ask ourselves the same question. Can we act now to avert a climate disaster, or at least mitigate its impact?

This is us: it is too late for us to change the past. But we still have a chance to change the future.

***

The *Titanic*, still moored at the Southampton dockside on that chilly April morning, was like nothing anyone had ever seen. Two ladylike

Patrols of Girl Guides, 14 girls in all, were murmuring to each other, but they fell into awed silence as they piled out of the hansom cabs and retrieved their haversacks. Several of them stopped in their tracks, congesting the growing crowd for a moment.

'Come along, Guides! We've got to get going,' said Lady Agnes Baden Powell, in a measured contralto.

One of the older girls gathered the rest of the Company. 'The 1st Pinkeys Green Girls should be prompt and considerate of others!' she admonished. The sound of their own Company's name was enough to set them moving again, breaking the spell of the enormous vessel before them. Even the prospect of their arrival in the United States of America, one week hence, was not as daunting as the idea of climbing on board – but as Girl Guides, they were ready for any opportunities to build their character. Their motto was the same as the one the Boy Scouts used: be prepared.

In that spirit, they spent the first day of the voyage, a Wednesday, exploring the ship. Lady Agnes had written to White Star Line, who arranged that the sixth officer, Sub Lieutenant James Moody, would be their liaison.

James greeted Lady Agnes with unexpected politeness for a rough-and-ready sailor. 'Good morning, Miss Baden-Powell, and a warm welcome to all of you. I am to be your liaison officer while you are aboard, and I am at your service.'

'How do you do, Lieutenant Moody? Girls, Mr Moody will answer your questions in due course, but you must not disturb him from the proper operation of the vessel.' The Guides murmured their assent. 'The girls are so interested in how the ship has prepared itself for any eventuality.'

As the day and their explorations progressed, some Guides tittered behind their hands when any of their number admitted to feeling the motion of the vessel. But another would rush to the aid of their stricken comrade, bearing a knob of ginger, or a box of black horehound lozenges. Those who could manage it cast aside all thought of seasickness, and marched to the bridge, where they found Captain Smith, a commanding gentleman with a trim naval beard, bewildered by the sight of a gaggle of schoolgirls. They saw the engine room, the kitchens, and the Marconi room. They visited the crow's nest, the bow, and the coal store.

'Lieutenant Moody is so much fun,' wrote Constance that evening, who had sworn to send a postcard to her parents every single day they were away. 'He let us address him by his Christian name, which is James! He let us clamber around the lifeboat, as long as everything was put back in place neat and tidy. My friend Dorothy knows everything about ships and asked a thousand questions.'

At breakfast on the following morning, Dorothy approached Lady Agnes.

'Miss,' she asked, with a curtsey, 'Why is there space for 1,178 when there are 2,208 passengers and crew?'

'What on earth do you mean, Dorothy? There is accommodation for every one of the passengers and crew, each in staterooms that meet their accustomed style of lodgings.'

'I mean the lifeboats, Miss. I asked James – I mean Lieutenant Moody – and he said there were lifeboats enough for 1,178 people.'

'That leaves 1,030!' piped up Ivy, who had a good head for figures.

Lady Agnes sipped her coffee. 'Surely not everyone in the ship would need a lifeboat at the same time.'

'Excuse me, Miss, but on the contrary, there is one singular case in which the lifeboats would be needed, and in that case, surely everyone would need them.'

'You raise an interesting point, Dorothy. It is not anything we need to concern ourselves with, since the ship is said to be unsinkable. But you may use this occasion to exercise your mind. If you believe there is a shortage of lifeboats, then I encourage you to think about it and come up with a solution. Do not forget our motto: be prepared!'

'Yes, Miss. We'll do so, just as you say!' Dorothy curtseyed again and, hand in hand with Ivy, ran back to a group of chattering girls.

Within two days, the navy blue uniforms of the 1st Pinkeys Green Girls were known throughout the ship. To some passengers and crew, they were a perpetual annoyance; others found their enthusiasm refreshing. Young Mary Chater possessed an endless repertoire of tunes, and could get them all singing along at a moment's notice. 'Listen to this one!' she would cry; and in short order, both men and women would be whooping out the words to the chorus.

On the fifth evening of the voyage, Captain Smith was smiling to himself as he stood at the bridge of the ship and peered through a pair of binoculars. The girls were doing a marvellous job of raising the spirits of a group of rich, elderly passengers. Those tended to be the crankiest and most demanding, and the girls distracted them all through the long, cold afternoon. The view over the North Atlantic, with its wine-dark waters and distant icebergs, was mesmerising to someone in love with the sea, but less so to jaded socialites. The young folks helped even the crotchety millionaires John and Marian Thayer appreciate the gorgeous vista.

The Captain lowered the binoculars and passed them to Second Officer Lightoller, who had the watch. 'Have an eye out for those bergs. 22 knots is well enough for the open sea, but we don't want to give our First-Class passengers any bumps to complain about.'

'Aye-aye, Sir!'

Late that evening, well after the Guides turned in – since it was well known that going to bed early, and rising with the sun, was both healthful and built strong moral fibre – a heavy, grinding thud and a tearing screech jolted the lighter sleepers awake. 'What is it?' asked Constance, one of the youngest Guides. 'Why have the engines stopped?'

Having shed their nightclothes and donned their uniforms, the Guides emerged by twos and fours from their berths. Helen, the eldest, sent a pair of scouts down the passageway to assess the situation. It took no more than a few minutes for them to return with the news.

'We've struck an iceberg,' Edna reported, steadfast despite her shivers. 'The purser told us we should not concern ourselves, but I caught a glimpse of James – I mean Mr Moody – and he had quite the grim look in his eye.'

'Did you speak with him? Lieutenant Moody, I mean.'

'No. But my assessment is that the situation is serious.'

Ivy, who had been huddled with Dorothy for the previous day, working on a mysterious project, was the first to state out loud what they all knew – the 'exercise for the mind' they had been discussing for the past two days. 'There are not enough lifeboats.'

Space for 1,178, when there were 2,208 passengers and crew.

'We've been working on this, you know,' Dorothy addressed Helen, and then the entire company. 'Do you remember last year at Windermere?'

'Where we built the canoe tent?' Helen asked. 'Modelled on the Polynesian double-hulled canoes? Those ocean-going canoes?

'Yes,' replied Ivy. 'Each of them could carry hundreds of people.'

The girls nodded. Yes. They remembered.

'I've got my notebook ready,' Ivy offered. 'With our sketches. Shall we show Lady Agnes?'

'I'll wake her,' Helen nodded. It was not a task to be taken on lightly, but as the eldest, she was ready to don the mantle, and the risks, of command.

To their surprise, Lady Agnes was already awake and dressed. They found her on the deck, wrapped in a heavy rug, agitated, speaking with James.

'Miss Baden-Powell?' Helen asked. 'Please excuse us. This is important.'

'What is it, Helen?'

'Dorothy has a plan.'

Lady Agnes examined the beautiful pencil drawing, doubtful at first, but with increasing interest as the girls explained the details.

'We can make one,' said Dorothy. 'I'm sure of it. A single lifeboat can only hold 65. But with two lifeboats of this size, each pontoon can hold several hundred people. It will be more than enough for everyone.'

'Your plan has merit. And given that we are already feeling a slight list to the vessel, I am inclined to put it into practice.'

Lady Agnes called James over and explained the plan, showing him the sketch.

'Thank you, but there's not much time, Miss Baden-Powell. I've been ordered to launch these boats and get the women and children on board. You'll all be safe, as I'll make sure you're on the first boat.'

'No, Mr Moody. I believe we can do better than that. Allow us to launch the two boats together, and build the pontoon to show it can be done. And in the meantime, I shall convince the Captain to do the same for the others.'

For the past five days, the Lieutenant had been plagued during every waking hour by the questions and proposals of fourteen clever girls. He wanted to cut them off several times. But with persistence as maddening as the girls themselves, their questions stayed in his head. He was realising that they had converted him to their side.

'It goes against the Captain's direct orders. But he's a reasonable man, and this is not a situation we anticipated. You there! Petty Officer Green! Stop what you're doing and follow the instructions of Miss Hollingsworth. Here is a sketch for you to refer to.'

Dorothy smiled and curtseyed, despite her shivers.

James continued, 'I shall return before long, Green, and I expect to see the design carried out.' Only the Petty Officer's long years of training kept him from challenging the orders of someone with a superior rating, and could not prevent him from casting a sceptical glare at the younger man. 'Meanwhile, Lady Agnes, we shall go together to Captain Smith.'

After a brief, intense discussion with Dorothy and Ivy, Petty Officer Green supervised the descent of the first boat, with four of the Guides aboard. Surrounded by 20 passengers and two crew, the girls were struck with a sudden fit of shyness. Violet, one of the newer guides, bounded across the boat and sat next to Ivy and Dorothy. Helen was still on board, rounding up the rest of the Guides.

Dorothy whispered, 'Violent – I'm sorry, I shouldn't call you by your nickname in such a situation – do you think our plan will work? How will we get these seamen and passengers to do what is needed?'

'Never mind the name. I know I've got a reputation for playing hard at hockey. In fact, I rather like being known as Violent. I've been watching you and Ivy these past few days, and I think you've got the right idea. You're just getting the jitters, like I do before a big match. You've got to learn to love the anticipation. But if you're not feeling up to it, you tell me what you want everyone to do, and I will get it done.'

Dorothy agreed, grateful. Soon, she and Ivy were providing quiet descriptions to Violet, who bellowed orders to Green, who then relayed them to the passengers. An older woman in furs attempted to shush the brash young woman. 'I say! Sit down, young lady, and be quiet! We need to get to safety!'

Green, without missing a beat, replied, 'I've got my orders, Ma'am, and I'm starting to see what they're about. These girls have a plan and you'll do well to stay out of the way.'

'I say! I shall have you reported!' the woman replied, as she har-rumphed back onto the uncomfortable bench.

Violet was bawling at the passengers, 'Everyone! Yes, you! Form up into pairs! Who's got a knife? Cut that rope into 12-foot lengths. We'll need you to lash the oars together. Like this.'

The seamen manoeuvred their boat alongside Lifeboat 5, despite the interference of the passengers. They were soon bridging the gap between the two boats with a frame made from the masts, gaffs, and oars that came with each lifeboat, and covering the frame with the sail. By this time, Green and the two sailors on the other lifeboat understood the plan, and were pitching in with gusto. Violet stood at the centre of the scrum. 'Lay the mast across the central rollocks!' she cried. 'And the same on the other boat! What next, Dorothy?' The sailors' laughter at the young ladies' use of nautical jargon created plumes of vapour in the icy night.

It took 10 minutes to get all the cross-pieces in place. To the surprise of both the sailors and the Guides, the woman in furs was tying quick, elegant knots. 'I've spent enough of my life around horses to know a clove hitch from a bowline,' she said with a sniff.

Installing the first sail, however, presented more of a struggle: too many hands were trying to help, becoming frantic, and fumbling in the semi-darkness. Just when Violet's shouting capability was threatening to devolve into hoarse whispers, she heard the calm, clear voice of young Mary Chater coming from Lifeboat 5 like a beacon, singing one of the sea shanties that she had already taught many of the First

Class passengers. Grinning with recognition and joining in on the chorus, the passengers relaxed into the work. The second sail was much smoother, as most of the eager hands were still tightening and securing the knots of the first sail. Two of the other guides on Lifeboat 6 moved with cool confidence among the frightened women and children, teaching or reteaching them how to tie reef knots and do lashings, retying granny knots, and providing general organisation.

Lady Agnes, followed by James, ran down the starboard side of the ship, each minute growing more unsteady as the deck dipped towards the sea, searching for the Captain. She had, of course, understood that the *Titanic* was among the largest ships ever to sail, but its enormity never struck her with such dreadful awe as when it prevented her from finding the man who could save more than a thousand lives.

It was a full 20 minutes before they found him, on the port side of the bridge wing, in heated discussion with a man she recognised as Thomas Andrews, the *Titanic's* builder.

'Captain!' she shouted, before James could speak a word. 'I need your help.

He turned his attention away from the builder with a look of frustration. 'You should be at a boat, Miss Baden-Powell. Indeed, if you go now, you might still get on one – it's women and children first.'

'Captain – we can still save everyone – but we need your orders.'

'I wish it were the case, Miss Baden-Powell. But it can't be done. There's not enough space. Mr Moody, please conduct Miss Baden-Powell to one of the remaining boats.'

James spoke up. 'Captain Smith – Sir – please listen to Miss Baden-Powell. She has a scheme which may save all of us.'

'Captain, I must insist,' Lady Agnes shrilled. 'Come with me to the starboard side. I'll show you it can be done!'

'Madam —'

'Do you want to go down with your ship,' she thundered, 'or do you want to go down in history?'

Helpless against her tirade, the Captain relented, and pulled out his binoculars. 'Where? Be quick about it.'

He paused when the deck creaked in a way that none of the three had heard before. Its starboard list was, ominously, correcting itself. Andrews spoke up. 'Captain, it is my estimate that we have less than two hours before she goes down.'

The Captain remained silent, squinting into the binoculars, searching the moonless night. 'Here,' Lady Agnes replied with impatience, reaching into a voluminous carpet bag. 'Our astronomical spyglass is more powerful, I believe. We were planning to do planet spotting on the top deck, you know. There – there! Look at that pair of boats.'

Captain took the telescope and peered into the darkness, focusing. 'What the blazes are they doing?'

'They are making a pontoon, Captain. A catamaran. Like the Polynesian canoes that Captain Cook recorded with the *Endeavour*. And that is what will save us.'

As they watched, the girls on the pontoon waved at the ship, while the crew loaded more passengers on board. An empty boat was already heading back.

'Well, I never!'

'If we can get all the other lifeboats set up like this, we can still save everyone.'

At that moment, the Captain made his decision. From a subdued, fateful determination, he roared to life. 'Mr Moody! Get me First Officer Murdoch! We've got a way out, by God, and we're going to take it!'

He turned to another officer, standing by. 'Boxhall. Work your way down the starboard side. I'll take the port side. Tell every boat crew that my new orders are to make every boat already on the water part of a pontoon, like that one, and to shuttle everyone out to these rafts with the remaining boats.

'Miss Baden-Powell, go with him, and take this whistle – it will help attract their attention around the boat davits.'

'Yes, Captain.' She rushed with Boxhall towards the milling crowds, desperation replaced, at last, by determination and hope.

The flurry of action did little to calm the desperate passengers, however. Within an hour, the tentative list to starboard was first replaced by a slight list to port, and then by a subtle but unmistakable descent of the bow, with the inexorable flood of water from one compartment to the next. The Guides returned again and again to the ship, to help with the lashings on the next pontoons. The first pontoon, now as laden as it would ever be, rode dangerously low in the water, but on a calm sea, it held steady.

The smallest boat, with the Second Officer on board, along with eight strong oarsmen, volunteers from third class, raced between the pontoons. He shouted through a megaphone, passing orders from the Captain and organising the shuttling of passengers.

Three burly cooks gathered dogs from the kennels. Ivy took a moment to calculate the total fares collected from the canine passengers, who were each brought aboard for the price of a First-Class child, and shook her head with wonder at the frivolities of wealthy Americans. Within 90 minutes, seven pontoons were carrying over 2,000 people. One of the smaller collapsible boats was used for the dogs, which had to be muzzled and bound or put in sacks. 'I do believe the same treatment should be accorded to certain First-Class children,' Ivy commented, as they worked away at the knots.

As the ship's bow grew ever lower, the Captain, Agnes and James found themselves on the last boat, a collapsible. Murdoch, with his eight oarsmen, drew alongside. 'The men are doing the final count, sir, but we believe we have all of them. We've determined that each of the pontoons can bear more than 300 people, as long as they don't shuffle around much.'

'Very good. I've had word from the Marconi operators that the Carpathia is not far away, and has been apprised of our situation. For now, we've got to keep these people warm! Let's think how: it's no use telling them to do callisthenics if the pontoons won't bear it, so we'll have to gather them in groups – men with men, women with women – and use the heat of their own mortal forms to keep up their temperature.'

'Sir,' piped up James, we've checked that all the pontoons are now a safe distance away from the ship. Two had to be rowed further out, but everything should be in order now.'

'Very good, Mr Moody. Mr Murdoch, take note.'

From across the flat, shining water came the explosions of the dying ship. But they were no more than an arrhythmic percussion behind a clear, treble voice from one of the pontoons, issuing forth a soaring hymn. A tentative violin from the ship's band joined in, and then played with confidence. Soon, knots of passengers, huddled together, covered with a motley collection of furs, rugs, and coats, were singing along.

'We're lucky, Captain,' commented James. 'The night is mirror calm. The pontoons would have been harder to build on a rough sea.'

'We're lucky in more ways than one,' he replied. 'Miss Baden-Powell, we're not out of this yet, but by the Lord God and the Devil himself, I beg your pardon, Miss, we'll have a story to tell when we get to New York.'

HOKKAIDO

8.00 am, Tuesday, February 2, 2027
Hokkaido, Japan – Harbour dockside, Abashiri
Global temperature: 1.6°C above pre-industrial average

Kenji Fujimoto thought he understood what cold weather was, from snowy winters in Tokyo and an occasional New Year's visit to relatives in Morioka. That was before Hokkaido. The plan he described to Ito-san with such enthusiasm in that underground Nonkiya bar never included the gnawing throb of sub-zero temperatures.

At the Abashiri dockside, he found with bone-aching clarity that a changing climate could freeze as well as boil. By the second half of November, the temperature had stayed below zero for three weeks. And on the morning of February 2, it plunged to negative 20, as a vast mass of freezing air edged ever closer from the North.

It was a portent. The Okhotsk sea ice was arriving.

Kenji donned his snow pants, a long overcoat, and a fur hat before pulling on his boots – a pair of mukluks given to him by a Russian who had spent time in Siberia – and shoved his hands into giant mittens.

Anticipating the frozen cheeks, he wished again that he could grow the great beards that the Russian workers did. In any case, he had stopped shaving weeks ago, giving him a disreputable appearance.

Despite everything, he could not contain his excitement. He'd spent the past months preparing at breakneck speed. They were well into winter, weeks behind schedule before they started. But at last, today was the day.

Ito-san had arrived by helicopter the night before. Although his company, Rakki Holdings, was the principal funder, many other parties were present: observers, scientists, and curious locals. It all added to the overall sense of a performance, surrounded by the audience in a large, circular theatre.

One group of visitors was a camera crew, with their director, a Rakki Holdings corporate communications manager. Kenji noticed a wisp of grey hair sneaking out of her fur-lined hood and mused that Ito-san was bringing more than one kind of innovation into his company; it would have been unheard of a few years ago to have employed an older woman for a role like this. But Ito-san was willing to pull talent into the organisation wherever it could be found.

She bowed, her smile as warm as the conditions would allow, and introduced herself. 'I am Hiroko Mizutani from the corporate communications department. Please, Fujimoto-san, explain the idea behind this project so that our valued investors can understand what you are trying to achieve.'

Kenji faced the camera, bowed, and began. 'Welcome to our Abashiri project. The idea behind our project is simple. As we all know, the Arctic ice is melting. In order to help manage climate change, we need to manage the melting of the ice. We will do that by making more ice. And we will make ice by spraying large volumes of sea water into the freezing air.'

He paused, and Hiroko regarded him expectantly. 'Please continue. I apologise, but not everyone understands how making more ice would be helpful, considering that temperatures are still rising.'

Kenji bowed again. 'We are in Hokkaido because, for two months every year, there is a vast area of sea ice that comes down from the Sea of Okhotsk in Russia. It is arriving today. This ice melts away each year as the weather warms, which makes it ideal for our trial – no lasting harm can be done. We will make a few areas of thickened ice, marked with a harmless food dye, and compare them with the natural formed ice. This will allow us to calculate the longevity of the thickened ice, and to determine whether this method can be used in the Arctic. This is Phase One of the plan.' Kenji did not mention all the problems they had with the food dye.

'And what is Phase Two?'

'During Phase Two, we will move our operations to Arctic waters. Throughout the winter, we will thicken as much ice as possible. We will monitor the new ice with satellites and drones.'

Kenji looked beyond the camera, at the new ice-breaking tug, the crew of experienced sailors, and the eclectic collection of equipment: water cannons, snow machines, and high-powered pumps. He could not believe that his staggering scheme was coming to fruition. Deep inside, in his personal self that nobody would ever see, he was convinced that the entire thing was a delightful, expensive game. Yet this was just the beginning.

He continued. 'In Phase Three, we will increase the number of boats and deploy a series of new technologies to create thousands of cubic kilometres of thickened ice. We hope, or, I should say, we expect, that a larger and thicker build-up of ice will increase the albedo – the proportion of light and heat that is reflected back into the atmosphere – which will create a positive feedback loop.'

'This is an ambitious plan. Will there be a return for our investors?'

'As of now, the project is being funded by the Japanese government in the form of tax breaks amounting to more than 150 million yen. Later, however, we aim to include albedo credits as part of a carbon credit portfolio. At the early stage, it would make up no more than 10% of a carbon credit portfolio. After the project is established, albedo credits could be sold like other credits, but for a better price. Our colleague in the Rakki finance team is dedicated to this task. But, excuse me for my impoliteness, I would like to bring your attention to Phase Four.

'This is the boldest part of our plan. We aim to create, in the high Arctic, as much ice as there was at the end of the last ice age. This will be an enormous, man-made cooling block that can balance the centuries of man-made heating. Others have proposed schemes with a similar goal of planetary cooling. One of these is the atmospheric injection of particulates to mimic the temporary, global cooling effect that took place in 1991 when the Pinatubo volcano erupted. However, our huge reflective shield of ice will be less damaging than these other proposals. Yes, it will be vulnerable to melting as long as temperatures continue to rise. But it will buy time to get our global emissions under control. If we can make it through the next two decades, then there is still hope for a future beyond that time.'

Kenji gave a final bow and headed toward the operations team lead. Although he designed the entire project, he had little control over the actual events of launch day. Once all the vessels reached the sea ice, the chief meteorologist would give the go-ahead based on its position; the pump operations team would bring in the seawater and add the food dye, in multiple colours; the spraying team would direct the placement of the new ice; and the monitoring team would keep track of the process.

He felt a growing sense of unease when he contemplated the next phases of the project. Here in Japan, with a small crew, and with the paternal support and encouragement of Ito-san, he managed to get things started. But he lacked the management experience for a project of this scale. When they moved to the next phase, to the Arctic itself, he would need to use English every day to communicate with international crews, he would need to know how to negotiate mega contracts, he would need ... that was the problem: he didn't know what he would need.

The boats launched, and within a short time they reached the sea ice.

At a word from the meteorologist, the pumps began their steady churn, and the spraying commenced. Hiroko was now directing her camera operator to take footage of the colourful spectacle. A gangling youth with bare wrists held a large boom microphone to catch the cheers of the crowd of watchers from their ice tour boats. The amount of the dye was minuscule in order to maintain the reflective properties of the ice. But it was as brilliant as a rainbow against the frozen background of dark waters, a pale grey sky, and shining white sea ice. The incredible cold meant that most of the water froze the moment it touched the existing sea ice. Layer upon layer built up. A short cry from the pump crew leader halted the process for several minutes while the team checked the electrical hose heaters. After a long discussion between the pump crew and the dyers, the spraying recommenced. The little crowd on the tour boats cheered once again.

What am I attempting? Kenji thought. This is insane.

After many rounds of spraying, the operations lead called time – they could deploy workers in such extreme conditions for no longer than two hours between heat breaks, lest the labour union baulk – and the little group of tour boats dispersed. Kenji, standing at the monitoring station, watching and listening to the real-time information feed, declared the launch day a success, although it would take many more days of work to complete the first phase. Ito-san was striding towards him, rubbing his mittens together, an enthusiastic grin on his face.

A success! He did not know whether to express relief, joy, or terror.

3.00 pm, Wednesday, February 17, 2027
Hokkaido, Japan – Harbour dockside, Abashiri

> Hans, we have solved the dye problem!

It was a text message, but Hans could feel Kenji's relief. It was the latest issue in an endless series of unpredictable challenges.

> How?

> We will use *kyudo*. That is Japanese traditional archery. We will fire arrows with stripes and radio markers into the target areas, and use the drones to take visual measurements before and after.

Hans searched for a laughing emoji.

> Cool! Do you have an archer?

> Ito-san funds an archery program in Tokyo. They will find us archers. We'll need hundreds of arrows, but I think bamboo poles will work.

Over the next six weeks, with the help of their old drift ice tour boat, long strips of fresh ice were built on top of the drift ice, travelling at different speeds. Although the weather paused operations for several days, the excitement carried them through the blizzards. To catch up, they worked through the long nights, and showed that the extra cold at night allowed higher water flows, quicker freezing and better results.

The ice road crew worked as a separate team, in a small bay choked with ice. Ice ridges, blocks, lumps and holes made it almost impossible to get from the shore to the larger pieces they wanted to work on.

Within a short time, the largest ice sheets in the bay increased their thickness by up to two metres – enough for a regular ice road.

The ice season would end faster than they thought possible. The question was how long the new ice would last.

PLATFORM

4.00 pm, Tuesday, May 11, 2027
Oil Platform – Natuna Sea
Global temperature: 1.7°C above pre-industrial average

'Yes, I'm calling you from an oil platform!' Adam Park shouted in Korean. His wife's voice was strong, considering that the signal was coming all the way from their home town in Seoul. It had travelled to a satellite somewhere above before returning to the clunky device he held in his hand. 'The insurance company called us to inspect it, after a pirate attack.'

'Did you say pirates?'

'Yes, pirates.'

He waited a moment for her to react, which she did with shocked silence, before continuing. 'They hijacked a coaster out of China with a mixed cargo of bagged fertiliser. They needed a crane to move the bags to their own vessel, so they tried to use the one on an idle oil platform. But the crane driver was inexperienced and in a hurry, so they dropped ten tons of bags on the edge of their barge.'

'Did you see this? Are you safe?'

'I'm fine. This all happened before we got here. We're dealing with the aftermath.'

'What aftermath?'

'The barge started to sink. And it was attached with a wire *hawser* to a side *bollard* on the coaster,' – he used the English words – 'and it took the ship down with it. So now a barge and a coaster with 2,000 tons of fertiliser are jammed against the legs of the platform. The cargo was worth almost two million dollars.'

'This is terrible. If the pirates can be caught, I think they should go to jail for life.'

'I agree. Darling, do not worry about me. The pirates are already gone. They fled away in their speedboat, once they realised what was happening. No one will see them here for a long time.'

At a sharp glance from the insurance man, he gave a warm goodbye, ended the expensive conversation, and surveyed the situation in front of him.

Oil still spotted the surface of the water.

To the left of the rusty stairs was a designated smoking corner, where three workers were gazing at the moody sea as they puffed. Adam knew that despite the thought of the platform burning with them aboard, nicotine addiction was too powerful for a complete smoking ban.

Cormorants had made the lower deck their home; it stank of fish and guano.

Adam had been on the platform for two days when a government marine biologist arrived by helicopter, wearing her own hard hat and steel-toed boots. She shook her head as she looked down through the gratings at the capsized hulk.

'Tengku Marina Zainal. I'll be looking after this one.'

'Adam Park. Our team runs the Remote Operated Vehicle.'

She nodded. 'The good news is that only one hatch on the coaster was open, so most of the fertiliser is trapped inside. The bad news is that it's still dissolving into the sea.'

The fertiliser, combined with the water in the hold, had formed a solution as wet and mushy as a dish of overcooked *kangkung belacan*. It seeped through the hatch and oozed along the dark seabed.

Tengku Marina brooded as she leaned on the peeling railing. 'We need to stop the leaking, or we'll have an algal bloom worse than anything we've ever seen.'

She stood upright, in the manner of someone who expected those around her to defer, and spoke to the waiting salvage crew. 'Get some rest, men. As of tomorrow morning, you all work for me.'

Adam, who preferred to receive his instructions through official channels, wanted to ask whether the insurance company had agreed. But her demeanour brooked no objection.

Indeed, an email from General Oceanic early the following morning confirmed the new assignment. Tengku Marina was already shouting orders to insert a large hose in the ship's hold, to pump out the seawater and spray it onto the surface of the sea.

'We want to measure how much nutrient has been added to the ocean, and what it was. There are several types of fertiliser in there, and I estimate that about one ton is dissolving every day.'

Several hours later, Adam's ROV was easing a long hose, attached to its grabbing clamp, into the hold of the distressed vessel. A magnetic anchor fixed the hose to the far end of the hold. However, on its return to the platform, the ROV became enmeshed in a wad of loose bags and tarpaulins.

'Ho! Stop that thing!' shouted Tengku Marina.

Shuffling back and forth, the crew attempted to ease the ROV out of the hold. It was stuck.

'Can't we just winch it?' someone asked.

Adam shook his head. The standing instructions would never permit it. 'We will lose the ROV!' he cried. But after a sharp look from Tengku Marina, the crew engaged the winch.

As they pried the mess through the hatch bit by bit, like a plumber unclogging a toilet, a massive, white plume burst out into the sea along with it.

Adam gaped. 'What is that?'

'Entrained fertiliser. 100 tons. Maybe twice that,' commented his flabbergasted crewmate.

Tengku Marina's face wore a curious expression as she watched the disaster unfold with agonising languor, the enormous plume feathering into the sea.

'This is bad. This is very bad. But I'm a scientist. I measure things. As long as it's happening, we should at least record the results.'

Adam approached her with caution. 'We should report it, right? What shall we do?'

'Right now, we need satellite data. We need glide drones. And we need information. I've got to go make a few calls.'

'And my crew?'

'Find out what was in that hold! I need the cargo manifest.'

'The owner is waiting for approval from their senior management. We must follow the correct procedure. It may take time.'

'There is no correct procedure for this situation. Just get it done.'

11.00 am, Tuesday, June 1, 2027
Oil Platform – Natuna Sea

Two more lab technicians and an additional oil field crew member came on board within the week. In the meantime, Tengku Marina called in every favour she could – from former students, colleagues, and ex-husbands of ex-girlfriends – to get access to satellites, drones, submarines, remote submersibles, and any other available observation equipment.

The team took hundreds of samples from around the platform and in nearby waters, using discarded water bottles until they ran out. Two days away from the platform, the transmitted images showed long, straight lines of algae, growing thicker as they left the immediate area, before eventually dissipating. The plume was also visible in the satellite images.

'This and the Great Wall of China,' commented one of the new lab techs to Adam, resigned. 'The only man-made structures you can see from space.'

'First, that's not true,' retorted Tengku Marina from behind them. Adam and the lab tech whirled. 'Chinese astronauts reported back in 2005 that they couldn't see the Great Wall. But there's another reason all this activity is going on. This awful plume of fertiliser we've created is allowing us to do something unprecedented: we can conduct a large-scale, long-term baseline trial on the effectiveness of ocean nutrification, both for ocean restoration and for carbon sequestration. This is what might take our Sea Orchards program to the next level.'

'I thought you said the plume will kill everything?'

'Well, it might. That's why a trial like this would never be approved if we applied for it, and never with this quantity of fertiliser. But it would be wasteful not to learn from the event, now that it has occurred. And as long as we can get that original manifest to check the details, we can do it properly.'

'You said "long term",' Adam observed with a frown. 'How long?'

'I've talked to the insurer, General Oceanic. You'll represent them, since they are now the ship owner. They'll need your ROV services for most of the coming year. You'll get two weeks off every four months, plus a bonus for project completion. I've secured additional funding from a ... family source.'

A full year. Adam nodded as he took in the new information, mentally composing an email to his wife.

Outreach

Two years after she moved in, very little in Grace's room could attest to its being lived in. A neat bed, a small table with a lamp, a desk, and a chest of drawers in the corner made up the complete set of furniture; a monk's cell would have more personality.

The spareness of her room reflected the spareness of her life. She spent her days on the Fairhaven site, or at the client's offices, in meeting rooms giving endless status updates. Her evening meals were either a quick bowl of noodles at a shop, or fast food in a shopping mall. Once a month, she and Hans met the other anxious people whose emotions were brought to a standstill by climate change. She spent her weekends at the old Penang Public Library on Jalan Scotland, writing out stories to distract herself.

Her little collection of 'alternate history' stories was growing. They were a little old-fashioned, in the sense that every story she wrote had a moral and a happy ending. However, she didn't know how to publicise the stories. The idea of exposing her innermost thoughts in public was horrifying. Yet she yearned to share them with the world, to give people the feeling that society might not be doomed, after all, that ingenuity and action could save things. Hans was an enthusiastic reader, but he knew nothing of the publishing world.

Grace rolled over on her empty bed and opened her phone. She had seen on LinkedIn that Nant was now based in London full time, and had something to do with books or magazines. Maybe her old flatmate would have advice.

Nant was using the new social platform, Orac. Grace opened a chat window.

'Are you up for a virtual coffee later next Friday?' she typed. She waited, and then a little icon of a keyboard flashed.

8.00 pm, Friday, February 4, 2028
Penang, Malaysia – 8 Gurney Drive

A week later, Grace wandered to the communal kitchen to pour herself a mixed drink. Living with her aunties, she would never have dared, but her easy-going colleagues had taught her the appeal of a cocktail to end the working week. She brought it onto her balcony, leaned back in the chair, and opened the laptop. As Nant's image appeared on the screen, adjusting her earphones, she laughed to see that the other woman was sitting in a cafe, holding a tall glass filled with an amber liquid, foamy at the top.

'Look at you, Nant! I thought it was lunchtime over there. Has living in the UK made a day drinker of you?'

Nant shrilled with laughter. 'I could say the same about you! I bet you anything that your glass has more than a Fanta in it.'

'Guilty! That's what comes of leaving the family compound for good. So, how have you been? That's an extraordinary hat you're wearing, by the way.'

'Busy, busy, busy. You're letting your hair grow out! It looks brilliant. You're still working at Fairhaven; the vengeful fishermen haven't got you yet?'

'Who? Oh, the fishermen! No, there's a new offshore project that is providing jobs for them.'

'That's good to hear,' replied Nant. 'I was worried about you, but I also always felt a little guilty about those men losing their jobs.'

'Speaking of jobs: remind me what it is you do now. Didn't you study fashion design?'

'I started out at one of the women's magazines here, but, you know, the whole media business is dying, so that magazine closed down, but my boss's boss liked what I'd been doing, so she asked me to stay on at one of the company's other divisions. By the way – are you on a balcony?'

'Oh, you didn't know! I moved into this new penthouse apartment with a bunch of guys from work. It's incredible! Let me show you.' She turned the computer around, giving Nant a full view of the lights scattered over mud flats that would one day become a new city. 'I'll bring you inside for a minute. Here's my room.'

'Did you just move in? There's nothing in there.'

'I spend a lot of time at work,' Grace replied defensively. 'We have six bedrooms, and mine has its own bathroom. We all share the communal space. Zygmunt is the one who uses the kitchen most of the time, though – that's him, right there; say hello! – because he's the only one of us who knows how to cook.'

Zygmunt came out, with two Ziploc bags in hand. 'I'm marinating the tofu first. Did you know you can fasten two of these together by turning one upside down? Then you have a double-sided bag.' Grace smiled at the trick – another of Zygmunt's perpetual life hacks – and continued Nant's tour.

'And this is the living room. Hans and Ivan use the TV to play games. Ivan is the little one. And that's Hans, with the beer. Johnnie is always travelling, so he's never here. And Scott keeps this weird schedule where he gets up before dawn to work out and goes to bed before anyone else is home in the evening. But I guess he's doing something right. The other day when his phone fell underneath the sofa, he lifted the end of the sofa with one arm like he was the Incredible Hulk.'

'You should see the little hole I'm in. It's one step away from coal stoves and cholera in the drains. So you live with a bunch of guys?'

'It took a lot of convincing to explain it to my aunties, but they came around in the end.'

'Is any of them more than a friend? What about that tall one, the blond guy with the beer? He was cute.'

Grace felt herself blushing. 'Hans? On the record, we're colleagues, and I can't date someone I work with. Off the record, we've been ... baking a lot of sourdough bread together.'

Nant shrieked with delight. 'I knew it! And don't let the colleague thing get in the way. You yourself said that you spend all your time at work. So it's not like you're going to date anyone else.'

'Hey, I didn't call you to be interrogated. What about you, anyway? Where's your husband and your 1.5 children?'

'Children? I wouldn't dare! London will be underwater by the time they're out of secondary school.'

'No kidding. Wait, I left my drink on the balcony. Let's go back out there.'

'Suits me. In reality, I'm still sitting here at a cafe in Shoreditch waiting for a screenwriter to come and pitch me.'

Grace frowned. 'That doesn't sound like magazines.'

'Streamberry. I'm a talent agent now. I acquire rights to stories from glamorous and famous people, and get them to sign away their lives. It's terribly dull.'

'That sounds like the perfect job for you,' Grace said. 'I mean, except for the part about asking them to sign away their lives. You've always been such a fashionista; I bet the glamorous people look at you and know they'll be in glamorous company.'

'The main problem is that it's hard to know who your true friends are. So tell me the truth: you didn't get in touch because you have a screenplay to flog? If you didn't, that would be a first! Everyone we ever knew in secondary school has contacted me because they have got the perfect new series for Streamberry.'

Grace reddened again, this time with real embarrassment. 'In a certain way, yes. But not like that.'

Nant sighed. 'That's what they all say, darling. Well, go ahead. What have you got for me?'

'I remembered you had something to do with magazines and thought you might be able to give me advice. I'm not trying to sell a new series to Streamberry. I've just written a series of short stories, and I was wondering ...' she trailed off. What did she want? To be published in an erudite literary magazine? No. She wanted everyone to see her stories. She wanted them to change the world.

Nant spoke gently. 'Darling, that's not how it works now. People don't get rich and famous by writing short stories and selling them. They already are rich, or famous, or both, and that's why their stories sell.'

'So what do the rest of us do? Those who are neither?'

'Keep writing. Get better at it. Send me your stories, just in case. And try to build up your own audience online. Orac offers a lot of tools to make it easier nowadays. And I'm not saying that because they're our new parent company.'

It was good advice, although not what she wanted to hear. 'Thanks, Nant. And I did want to know how you were.'

'Of course you did!'

'Is there any chance of you ever coming back to Penang?'

'What, to that awful construction site you call a city? No thank you! Call me again when you've closed the locks.'

Grace smiled. 'I don't suppose you want to watch a show with me, the way we used to? We could each get snacks, and you and I could stream it at the same time. No,' she realised, snapping out of the fantasy, 'it doesn't make sense. It's the middle of your working day, and I'm sure you spend all of your time overwhelmed with video content as it is.'

'Darling, I would absolutely love to do that, and I'm not kidding at all. I can't today, but maybe another time? In the meantime, here's a tip for you: assuming you have a Streamberry account, you should watch this new show that launched last week. It's one of the ones I scored.' Nant typed the name into the chat window.

'Thanks for the tip! Okay, have a great afternoon. Let's talk soon.' Grace ended the call on more of an abrupt note than she intended, and felt a twinge of sadness in her certainty that it would be years before they spoke again.

Empty glass in hand, she wandered into the living room, where Hans and Ivan were wrapping up a game. 'Okay if I watch TV for a while?'

'Sure!' replied Hans, tossing her the remote and getting up. 'We just finished.'

Grace navigated to 'New Releases', where the Orac algorithm had pre-selected a group of 'Suggestions for You'. To her surprise, the series

Nant recommended was already at the top of the list. 'I swear that thing listens to my conversations!' she chuckled. As the opening scenes played, Hans returned with a beer and sat back down next to her.

Ivan stayed in a half-standing, half-sitting position in the easy chair, ready to move if the show was boring, ready to watch if it had promise.

BARGE

Between the two dykes, one at the northern boundary of the strait between Penang Island and the mainland, and the other at the southern boundary, hundreds of men on barges were hard at work.

Grace stood at the Bazalgette Lock administration hut. The client was asking again for ways to increase productivity, and Grace was determined to make it happen. A few more piles per day from each barge would make a vast difference to how fast they could reclaim land from the strait and protect it from the rising seas.

She planned to inspect the pile drivers. With 38 smaller floating barges out in the bay, installing the main piles was taking up precious time. The process would last until the completion of the main dykes in three years, when they would drain the bay.

A sour-faced woman from the administration pool handed Grace the permit book, the slapping sound as it flopped down on the counter reflecting her pointed look. Grace signed it and stowed the walkie-talkie in her bag. The administration team was staffed by former government bureaucrats who preferred to do things according to the book, and didn't appreciate it when upstarts like Grace wanted to try new methods.

'How are you getting to the barges?' asked the administration woman, her curiosity overwhelming her resistance to change.

'Kayak.' Grace grinned at the surprise her answer produced.

Travelling under her own arm power, she could choose a random barge, spend as long as needed to get to know the team, and then move on. The crews' techniques varied, meaning that there was plenty of potential for efficiency gains. Her plan for the day was to see a selection and get some decent photos, before suggesting changes.

She covered her head with a hat, slathered her skin with sunscreen, and pulled down her long sleeves and long leggings.

It would be an exhausting exercise, and she would have to start soon; it was always easier to paddle when the tide was higher. She was looking forward to her regular lunch with Hans the following day. Given their busy schedules, she seldom saw him either at work or at the flat. His usual reminder, whenever they crossed paths, was a cheerful warning: 'Watch out for the jellyfish!'

11.50 am, Monday, March 13, 2028
Penang, Malaysia – Fairhaven North Bay

Grace unclipped her kayak from Barge #12, and paddled towards a smaller, purplish piling barge, the furthest of four in the vicinity. It was almost noon, and the sun was beating down. She glanced upward; not a single cloud mitigated the burning heat. After paddling for a long time, she re-clipped the kayak to the purple barge, scrambled aboard, and introduced herself to the crew, who had gathered to watch her as she approached.

Something made her stop short as she did so. For a moment, she tried to figure out what was so awkward. Then it hit her: not one of them had returned her smile.

As one of the few women working on the barges, she was conspicuous. She found the men either shy, giggling whenever she was around, or else awkward and formal. But they were always happy to have a visitor. This was different. The men replied to her in monosyllables and spoke to each other in low voices.

The setup of the rig itself struck her as peculiar. She moved towards the opposite edge of the barge, trying to understand. Three of the men followed her, while the others went back to their work. She called out to the youngest one, 'It looks as if you haven't done any piling at all today. Can you tell me what's holding you back? Maybe it's something I can help with.'

He glanced at an older man before responding. 'No.'

Neither moved or made any effort to engage with her. The younger man gave a surreptitious tug at his neckline; Grace thought she glimpsed him tucking away a small pendant. The sparkle of the gold chain made an eccentric contrast to his ragged jeans and stained football top. The older man, also in worn jeans, had thinning hair and a hard expression. He gave a small nod to the younger man.

Grace pushed ahead. 'Is the wire broken? Have you hit a stone?'

'No.'

'Is the barge leaking?' She tapped the lid of an enormous, unlabelled crate. 'What's this? Part of the equipment?' As she peered at the lid, the sky, the deck, the men, the crate, and everything else around her turned black.

12.10 pm, Monday, March 13, 2028
Penang, Malaysia – Fairhaven North Bay

She couldn't tell whether it was minutes later or hours later, when she heard someone crying: a whining, quiet, affectless 'aah – aah – aah'. She could not tell who was making the maddening noise, since her eyes were closed. She wanted to go back to sleep.

Bit by bit, she realised that it was her own voice. Her first coherent thought was not to bother anyone; no one liked a girl who pushed her problems on other people. She had to take care of it by herself; she mustn't let her mother know. She wanted to stop the crying, but couldn't. Something was forcing the desperate bleats from her, try though she would to quell them.

Then the pain began.

It built up like a stuck pressure release valve on the right-hand side of her head, in the back, and washed over her entire body. Her face quivered; her arms and legs straightened with a spasm. She gasped for breath, and felt the 'AAH – AAH – AAH,' deafening in her mind but too quiet in reality, explode through her sinuses.

She could do nothing for several minutes but experience the pain. She tried to form a coherent thought, to test her mouth and throat. An eternity passed.

She managed a tentative croak at last. 'There was a crate?'

No one answered, and the pain did not abate; it was building with screaming intensity. She thought of opening her eyes. With an enormous effort of will, she managed to crack her eyelids apart by a sliver. A harsh band of dusty light shone through a hair-thin chink in the boards above her head.

Yes, there was a crate. It was now her prison.

Overwhelmed, she turned her head to the right – in time to avoid vomiting on herself. Outside, a shout went up, followed by the un-mistakable sound of her kayak scraping along the deck of the barge. Yes. She had a kayak. She was on a barge.

Grace still could not make a sound any louder than her pitiful cries. The putrid stink of her own vomit and sweat and the unrelenting pain in her head conspired to keep her immobile. Grimacing, she was beginning to remember the sequence of events, but still could not put together anything that had happened before she got into the crate. Had someone injured her? She thought of opening the lid of the crate, but couldn't lift her hand above her body, let alone pry open a lid. Would there be a padlock? Nails? Her thoughts were muddied. At last, with another enormous effort, she turned herself to her left side, away from the filth, and put her palm under her cheek: the most primitive cushion against a hard surface. As she did so, her fingers, instinctively reaching around to touch the other side of her head, came away sticky.

Despite the screaming, throbbing agony that emanated from her skull and flowed through her entire body, she fell into a stupor that passed for sleep.

Much later, through the haze of her torpor, she heard shouts again, and the rattle of a lock. When the lid of the crate opened (it was hinged, she realised), she could just make out a sprinkling of stars overhead. Without warning, a bucket of muddy, brackish water inundated the small space, making her gasp, and then cough, setting off howling at the back of her head once again. A voice she did not recognise cried out, and another bucket of brackish water followed the first. Then, two sets of muscled arms grabbed her own, dragging her out onto the deck, where she collapsed.

Before her, three men were arguing in a language she did not know. As she continued to gasp and cough, one of them hoisted her to her feet with long, gorilla-like arms, while another, with thinning hair, pulled a length of duct tape from a roll, tore it off with his teeth, and stuck it over her mouth. The duct tape man hissed a question at the one with the gorilla arms, who answered with a low, angry voice. She got the impression that they were arguing about her. Grace found herself able to stand, but did not know how long her legs would hold up. Fighting the pain and nausea, she peered at the third man, who was standing to the side, and the word 'pendant' came into her mind, although she could not explain why. Duct Tape twisted away for a moment, said something to Gorilla Arms, and returned with a rough sack, which he lifted over her head. She wanted to shake her head in protest, with the increasing rage she was feeling, but the thought of moving her aching skull was too much to endure. The sack went on and a big zip tie was threaded through the cloth and tightened around her neck, while her wrists were secured with more zip ties.

Moments later, she was in the crate again.

1.00 pm, Tuesday, March 14, 2028
Penang, Malaysia – Hing Fat Noodles

Hans felt frustrated. His entire morning had been spent quelling an unnecessary dispute between two department heads. He was looking forward to lunch with Grace, where he could let off steam and maybe hear how she was managing her latest plot twists. She was ten minutes late, which was unusual. He tapped out a brief message to ask when she was expecting to arrive, and smiled to himself. Seeing Grace evolve from tentative diarist to confident writer charmed him. Maybe it would be her second career. She was getting more insistent all the time that if she could only get her stories about averting disasters in front of the public, that might help real people avert real disasters. In any case, talking through her stories would be a pleasant distraction.

The server once again came over to ask whether he was ready to order. Hans glanced at his phone; Grace was now twenty minutes late. He shook his head at the server and decided to call Grace. No answer; the call went through to voicemail. From force of habit, he hung up without leaving a message, but thought better of it. He called again, and this time left a short voice note asking if everything was okay.

Ten minutes and four messages later, he called Zygmunt.

'Zygmunt. It's Hans.'

'I know that. Your name shows up on my phone when it rings. What's happening? It usually takes a big emergency for one of you young people to make a phone call.'

'Do you have any idea where Grace is?'

'Hmph! I feel as if I should be the one asking you that question. And before you say anything, yes, we've all known about you two for ages. But the answer to your specific question is no, I haven't seen her today. She's due for a meeting with me and the client at four.'

'We were supposed to meet for lunch, but she hasn't shown up yet. And I can't get hold of her.'

'That's not like her.'

'I'm going to go down to the administration hut and find out when she checked back in.' Hans put down his phone, brooded for a moment, and then stood, apologising to the server. 'Sorry, my friend can't come.' He scanned the server's code and added a little money as an apology.

At the admin hut, the same woman was still minding the shop. She glanced at Hans, and gave an annoyed, 'What?' as he entered. 'Can't you see we're busy?'

'Did Grace check back in yesterday evening?'

'Who?'

'Grace Chan. You know her. Everyone knows her.'

'Let me check.' The woman took a moment to glare at him, before looking down to shuffle through the pile of permit books. 'There's a record of Grace Chan picking up a waterproof walkie-talkie at 9.15am yesterday morning. Yes, I remember her.'

'But did she come back?'

'No. There's no record of a return. But it's not reliable. Maybe she didn't sign the book when she came back. Or she landed somewhere else, and still has the walkie-talkie and hasn't had a chance to check it in.'

'Do you have another one of those walkie-talkies?'

Grumbling, she dug out a walkie-talkie from a lower shelf. 'Here. Hey, not so fast! Sign first.'

Why couldn't anyone else understand that something was wrong? His pen poked through the flimsy paper as he signed the book. He turned on the walkie-talkie, and made the same request on all four of the live channels. A few minutes later, a response cracked through.

'Barge #12 here. We had Grace Chan onboard yesterday morning for a couple of hours. She left a little before noon.'

'Do you know where she was going?'

'She said she was checking out one of the other barges. There are three in this sector, including our own.'

'Thank you.' He gave back the walkie-talkie, and signed his name in the book with a pointed flourish. He addressed the doyenne of the admin hut. 'Listen, we need to find out what happened. I'd like you to call all the site offices and equipment huts.'

'All of them?' She sniffed.

He scribbled in the margin of the logbook. 'Here's my number. Let me know if you find anything.'

The woman raised an eyebrow. 'Really? Your number ends with 123 123?'

'Yes. You can imagine all the spam calls I get. Now please, call. This may be an emergency.'

The woman at last was starting to feel Hans's anxiety, and picked up her own phone from under the counter. Hans thanked her with a word, and headed towards the main Site Office. On the way, he dialled 999.

1.45 pm, Tuesday, March 14, 2028
Penang, Malaysia – Fairhaven North Bay

Grace could tell by the angle of the sliver of sunshine that noon had passed again. She could now almost control her body, although her head and limbs still felt wooden and the scrapes across her belly were burning where she had been dragged out of the crate. She managed to remove the bag by tearing the cheap cloth, but the long zip tie remained around her neck like a collar. She searched her pockets in vain for her phone and camera. The men gave her nothing more than a little drinking water in a plastic bottle. It was just as well. She would not have been able to eat anything; every tiny motion of her jaw magnified the searing, throbbing pain at the back of her head.

Although the sides and top of the crate blocked out most light, she could hear the same three men arguing with each other. Throughout the afternoon, she heard the constant, high whine of drones, and the chatter of the seaplane, three times. Then nothing.

When darkness had fallen again, the men opened the lid, tugged the bag over her head again, and took her to the edge of the barge; when she finished, they put another water bottle in her hand and lifted her into the crate.

It was odd to feel such gratitude for a simple thing like water.

5.00 pm, Tuesday, March 14, 2028
Penang, Malaysia – Fairhaven Main Site Office

Hans was giving Zygmunt the latest update. 'They found someone who saw her around 10am, meaning that she set off later than she expected. We know she was on Barge #12 around 10:30 or 11am, and left not too long after noon. We still don't know where she went next. Scott is at home, so he checked her room; he says it doesn't look like anyone slept there last night.'

'Where is barge 12?'

'Northern half, mainland side.'

Something made Zygmunt frown as he fiddled with his stapler, inserting a bit of plastic coated wire into the front. 'What did the Coast Guard say?'

'They're called the Maritime Enforcement Agency, remember? They said they'd contacted every ship passing through the strait to keep an eye out, but no one has seen anything yet. There's a steady southward current – if she's afloat, she could be far away by now.'

'What about the aerial search?'

'No kayak. No hat. No life jacket. I asked them to look into the fishermen, because we know they have been against this project from the start. And the press agrees with me; they're not just treating it as a missing person's case. They've been running a new story every hour on her disappearance, tying it all back to the fishermen's protests last year. The local media think it will jeopardise the project. And in the meantime it's also become international news.'

'How on earth did that happen?' Zygmunt wondered.

'Grace's friend Nant in the UK posted about it on her Orac channel, and a member of one of those popular Thai boy bands shared it. That was all it took.'

Zygmunt shook his head in disbelief. 'You really can't tell what's going to go viral. Makes you wonder who's controlling it all. So what do you think? Is it the fishermen?'

'I don't know what to think. The cops said it was my imagination running wild.'

Zygmunt nodded. 'Sometimes imagination is what solves problems, though.' He set down both the stapler and the wire, now neatly stripped, two centimetres from the top.

7.00 am, Wednesday, March 15, 2028
Penang, Malaysia – Fairhaven North Bay

Not long after high tide, when the sun was rising above the dark water, a black speedboat bearing the white, capital letters MARITIM MALAYSIA pulled up alongside the small, purple barge and hailed the workers with an electric megaphone. A short, stocky petty officer, in a clean blue uniform, held up a photo for the bargemen to see.

'We're looking for this woman. Have you seen her?' The speedboat's motor continued running as its sailors waited, tired and bored. One stared with envy at the cigarette in the hand of the youngest bargeman.

The men on the barge conferred among each other before answering. An older man with a balding head nodded toward the speedboat. He spoke in accented Bahasa. 'Yesterday morning.'

'What time?'

'She come here 10 o'clock. Then she go. We don't know where.'

'If you see her, let us know.' The blue-uniformed officer shouted a radio frequency and added a mobile phone number for good measure. At first, no one made a move to write either down. Then, at a sharp glance from the balding man, one of the other bargemen took out a phone and entered the numbers. The speedboat's engine roared, and it was out of sight within a minute.

Inside the crate, Grace heard their conversation, and thumped her foot against the wooden walls. She realised the men must have removed her boots; stockinged feet were ineffective in generating anything louder than a muffled thud, too quiet to be noticed over a running speedboat. She wondered what had happened to her hat.

After the noise of its engine receded, the men lifted the lid of the crate, and brought another batch of zip ties, this time to bind Grace's ankles together.

BIRTH

11.00 pm, Wednesday, March 15, 2028
Penang, Malaysia – Fairhaven North Bay
Global temperature: 1.8°C above pre-industrial average

Grace counted individual voices, giving each one a name, to help her remember. Duct Tape and Gorilla Arms – she knew them well. She also thought she recognised Pendant, although it was rare to hear him speak above a mutter. She counted at least four more, speaking several languages, and ticked them off on her fingers. Deep Voice. Whiny. Raspy. And one she was sure was Russian, although he spoke Bahasa Malay to the others. Sometimes they referred to each other by name – Vladimir, Ismail, Michael – and she memorised them all.

They spoke to each other in tones of quiet, urgent instruction. Sometimes she could catch no more than individual words: *'zoloto'*, *'emas'* and *'kepal selam'*.

Nevertheless, it became obvious what was going on: the barge was not a piling crew at all, but a salvage crew, operating in plain sight among the piling barges. They had discovered one of the rumoured

World War II treasure submarines, and they were determined to get the gold before anyone else.

Voices from the salvage crew grew more urgent. Two unfamiliar voices emerged on the other side of the barge. Both Russians – it was unmistakable this time – with deeper, more commanding tones. She reached deep into her memory to retrieve what Russian she knew, from the year she spent with her parents in Kazakhstan. 'Tell them we need to offload it before 5.00 am,' said the one whose name she determined was Ivan Mikhailovich. 'The big ship is meeting us at Pantai Robina at 9.00 am, so we need to finish before then.'

She tested the board in the crate once more. Over the course of several hours, she pried it loose bit by bit, wedging her shoulders against the opposite side of the crate and concentrating the full force of her legs against one knotty edge. At last, it cracked. No one noticed; the drone of the crane drowned out any other sound.

In the meantime, as she lay in the stinking mix of seawater and human filth, an image of Zygmunt came to mind, showing off one of the little tricks he was so fond of. Ziploc bags. Bottle caps. Staplers and wires. 'Zip ties are funny things,' he'd said. 'They are impossible to undo. Except for one way: you push the tail of one, backwards, into the teeth of another. Then, they open with ease, and you can re-use them multiple times.'

She tried it. Thank God. A life hack that worked. One by one, she removed the infuriating ties.

Through the gap in the crate, she saw only darkness.

She squeezed through, first her aching head, then her shoulders, and then her hips. Born again, she thought to herself. Stifling her own cries of pain, she slipped over the side of the barge into the water and swam out into the darkness.

10.45 am, Thursday, March 16, 2028
Penang, Malaysia – Police Headquarters

A familiar blond head emerged, well above the rest of the crowd. 'Oh, God, Grace, thank God!'

Although relief washed over her, she resisted giving into it. 'Hans! Wait for me; we'll talk at home. There are too many people here. I have to get away first.'

Reporters surrounded her: public, private, local, international, bloggers, YouTubers, Orackers, Instagrammers. They had already grilled her for half an hour at the official press conference. Still, they shouted questions at her. 'When did you realise they were gold smugglers?' and 'How did you remember all of their names and voices?' and 'Would you like to say a word of thanks to BangkokBoyz and all their fans around the world?' She worried that her responses didn't matter; the Orackers would use the latest tools to fabricate something plausible that she should have said.

The reporters continued to shout at her, as Zygmunt's lawyer guided her towards a car. She spotted Hans from afar, towering above the others, caught in the middle of the crowd. When she was inside the vehicle, the lawyer asked, 'Do you want to go home?'

She nodded and then grimaced. 'Yes. I went directly from the hospital to the press conference, so I still have to watch out for the aftereffects of the concussion. Not to mention the fact that the jellyfish stings ended up being just as serious as being bashed over the head.'

When she arrived, her Auntie Janis was waiting in the living room. 'Hans said he and your flatmates will take care of you, but I couldn't let them try to do it by themselves.'

Grace showed her most offended expression. 'I don't need help.' Hans had already tried, and failed, to visit her in the hospital that morning; only family members were allowed. 'Is he here?'

'No, I assume he's still caught up in the traffic jam. You know men!'

Grace rolled her eyes. Her heart begged Auntie Janis to stay and take care of her, but her pride cut off the request.

As Janis brought cushions and pillows to the living room, she described the exaggerated media frenzy that surrounded Grace's disappearance and escape. 'The first day it wasn't such a big story. Then people started to wonder where you were. Then it became crazy because one of the opposition used your disappearance as a reason to stop the Fairhaven project. People had all kinds of ideas – you ran away, you were murdered by the fishermen, you drowned in your kayak, you were a Chinese spy – I have to say, they treated you more like a soap opera character than a real person. And then there was that Orac post.'

'But all I did was get hit over the head, and then pry my way out of a box!'

'People need something to talk about, something to distract them from the election.' Grace pulled a face. 'You frown, but you know it's true. Things are ridiculous this year, and that's why people need to be distracted.'

'It's always ridiculous. I'd never want to be a politician. I'm just glad they caught the crooks.'

'I am, too. Otherwise, there would always be a sword hanging over your head. Those criminals would not want you to stay alive.'

'I'll still have to give evidence at the trial.'

'The trial about your own kidnapping and assault, yes. And your boss, Zygmunt – he said that the project would fund your lawyer. He's a good man. But for the gold smuggling, all the police needed to find was on that barge. Yes, you led them there, with your description, the names, the position. And they were caught red-handed, loading the gold onto a fast skiff.'

Grace grimaced.

Janis continued, 'I talked to your mother, you know. She said she wanted to come, but it was impossible to find a flight.'

'From N'Djamena? I'm not surprised.'

'She said she would fly through Lagos if she had to. But it would be at least four more days before she could get here.'

'Tell her not to come. I'll be fine.' Grace preferred her interactions with her parents to stay cool and professional. After all these years of benign neglect, her mother was a near-stranger. She hated the thought of appearing vulnerable, of needing help.

Auntie Janis took over the kitchen, preparing an herbal soup, while Grace stewed on the living room sofa. Zygmunt arrived but stood aside, a perturbed, almost petulant look on his face. Ivan, she'd heard, was out of town, spending his holiday in Palau diving at sunken Japanese warship sites. For a moment, Grace wished that he'd spent more time investigating the wrecks here in Penang; she could have avoided this whole thing if someone had already stripped the damn sub.

A few minutes later, the apartment doors opened. Hans crossed the living room in an instant. Ignoring Janis and Zygmunt, he knelt on the carpet.

'Oh, Grace. Oh, my God. I'm so glad you're okay.'

She imagined falling into his embrace, his powerful arms encircling her, but winced as he attempted to put a hand on her shoulder. 'Ouch! Sorry, I got a lot of stings there.'

They stared at each other, wordless, each thinking of his usual greeting: watch out for jellyfish.

'Where did they find you?

'Chenaam – south of the Kerian River. There was a local fisherman on the beach when I got to shore just before dawn.'

'Why did you call me first, before the police?

'I was confused. They brought me someone's phone to use, and I thought of your phone number first, because of the 123 123. But I somehow didn't remember how to call 999.'

'I suppose I should be grateful. At least I knew you were alive, although you didn't tell me where you were, and then hung up a second later.'

'Hearing your voice, just for a moment, helped me gain a little coherence. Otherwise, I think they wouldn't have understood what I was talking about.'

Hans attempted to adjust a pillow behind her, making her wince again. He pressed his lips together. 'Okay, I get it. I shouldn't be trying to do what I think you might want. I should ask. Grace, what do you want right now?'

'I want to sleep, but I can't. I'm still too worked up. Maybe – can you bring me my laptop? I could just surf for a while, as long as I can keep my vision clear.'

'Sure. Hold on.'

Grace settled in with her laptop, scrolling through cat videos and photos of surprised babies. She couldn't handle anything more serious, so when an Orac chat notification popped up, she handed the laptop back to Hans. 'Tell me if I have to deal with it.'

'You shouldn't have to deal with anything right now. You're still recovering. Anyway, it's a message from Nant.'

'My old flatmate Nant? What does she have to say? Is she going to apologise for the boy band?'

'She says, "Hello, darling! Quite the grisly affair you've been through. Didn't think you'd take quite such a dramatic step to seek fame." I think she's still typing.'

'Never mind. I don't want to hear from her.'

'I'm not so sure. Listen. She says, "In any case, it worked. They're interested in your *Futility* story, and anything else you have on hand. You've got quite the stage presence! Those hazel eyes look stunning on camera." Does this mean what I think it means?'

'I think it means my life has just changed in more ways than one.'

RECOVERY

8.00 am, Friday, March 31, 2028
Penang, Malaysia – 8 Gurney Drive
Global temperature: 1.8°C above pre-industrial average

After an initial burst of energy upon returning home, Grace fell into a profound lethargy, exhausted by basic tasks. At work, she could understand written documents but a simple diagram on a slide baffled her. Thirsty, she'd pick up her water glass, say the words, 'I need to drink!' but then stand, transfixed, with the glass in her hand, trying to figure out what to do with it. Her hair, which was tickling her shoulders, threatened to become ratty when her hand would not obey her brain's commands to brush it.

Zygmunt told her to take off as much time as she needed. But she knew his patience wouldn't last forever.

The pressure from Nant to keep herself 'relevant' was no help. Following the burst of media attention when Grace escaped, Nant hounded her to make her Orac channel public and to start up a video presence. Grace's follower requests were already in the tens of thousands.

Nant set up an Oracall with her boss in California, the producer from Streamberry.

'Eliot John Mather-Winthrop the Third. I go by Trip. I saw your picture on the news,' he began. 'Your profile is sky high. Brave escape from capture, mysterious barge, gold smuggling, BangkokBoyz stans all rooting for you – it's great content. We want to start with a documentary feature by the end of this month, and after that, you can follow it up with your own stuff. I can feel it; this is going to sell.'

'I'd love to see my stories being shared. I'm not interested in being famous as myself, but I really want people to read or see something that gives them hope for the future. People need to know that we can prevent disasters, or at least survive them.'

'Sure. Your disaster narratives are a little preachy, but fun. Optimistic. Look, I read your story about the *Titanic*. And the one about the earthquake. It's good stuff. But we need you to work with us.'

'What do you mean?'

'I've seen your social media presence, or should I say, lack thereof. We need to fix that.'

Grace shook her head and regretted it instantly as the waves of pain overwhelmed her. 'I want to work on the climate crisis, not generate fluff and have guys comment on my body. And I definitely don't want to go over all of what happened on that barge.' It was an understatement. She never wanted to think about the barge, ever again. She grieved for her camera and her lost kayak gathering silt at the bottom of the strait.

'Grace, the way it works is that when you have the momentum, you need to keep it up. While we're putting the documentary together, you need to get your own content out there. Show 'em your hazel eyes, but talk about yourself. Be vulnerable. Be authentic. If you want the stories you wrote to succeed, you need to get your own story out there.'

'I guess so.'

'Good girl! Hey, I have to get on another call. Let's talk tomorrow. I'll have Nant set it up.' He grinned, his white teeth flashing against his tanned skin.

Desperate as she was to get her stories in front of a larger audience, she couldn't force herself to relive her ordeal so soon. Instead, she began with a short, tentative video, filmed on her phone, introducing herself and the Fairhaven project, but never mentioning a word about the barge. To her surprise, it was shared across every network within days, and she gained followers faster than she could keep up with them. Her reluctance to discuss the incident became the best possible method to win a fan base; those who watched her first video started to get to know her, and were enthralled with the knowledge of what was to come; those who learned about it second-hand were caught up in the anticipation.

Under Trip's relentless pressure, she began a series of ten short videos, one each week. Her follower count leapt from the thousands to the hundreds of thousands by the time the third video went live. The fans came for her grisly story, but stayed for her hazel eyes, her plain talk about climate issues, and her air of unspoken sorrow. They did not know that it was borne of a deep reluctance to make a show of herself in front of the world, and her growing fear that she was going down a path from which she could not backtrack.

When disgusting men or enraged women sent private messages to her, Nant advised her to ignore and block them. She said nothing about what to do when the messages repeated themselves in Grace's head again and again at 3.00 am, as she tried in vain to capture a few minutes of sleep.

It's the apraxia, she told herself, as she attempted to re-learn how to brush her teeth, or to use a mouse. Her typing speed was slower than when she first encountered a keyboard as a child. She returned to work, but abandoned kayaking.

The jellyfish stings continued to itch long after they should have stopped.

Trip's crew arrived in Malaysia to film the short documentary feature, and wrapped the filming within a weekend. It aired two weeks after that, its rapid production schedule supported by a thousand of Trip's clever technical tricks. She frowned when she saw the final version; it made too much of the suspected fishermen's connection, and dramatised her injuries with lurid medical diagrams. The timing was right, but it struck her as a sensationalist effort.

I want to get my stories out, she reminded herself. This is just a means to that end. She continued to post videos about herself and her work, steadily amassing followers. She was surprised at how much she enjoyed the technical aspects: filming, editing, and optimising. She bought herself a new camera, an upgrade from the one lost in the bay.

In April, when the documentary aired on Streamberry, public excitement exploded, and she learned for the first time what it was to belong to her followers, and not to herself. Strange men from Europe and Australia travelled to Penang, to lurk around the gates of 8 Gurney Drive. Her flatmate Scott appointed himself bodyguard: whenever she complained of a new lurker at the gate, Scott would take the elevator down to the ground floor, fix the unwelcome guest with a pointed look, and fold his arms, 'accidentally' showing off his swelling biceps and revealing a glimpse of the skull tattoo on his shoulder. Although it was obvious he enjoyed the posturing – he returned from each intimidation session with a satisfied grin – Grace could not find comfort in the idea that she was dependent on his protection.

All her life, she had been self-sufficient; the indifference of her parents and the distracted chaos of the Chan family forced it upon her.

It was time for her regular meeting with Trip.

'Your numbers are looking good, Grace, but we need more. All that science content makes them think you're smart. It's like MacGuyver meets Rod Serling.'

Grace had never heard of either of the men Trip was referring to. She wondered how old he was; his skin was taut and his hair was blond. 'I've been posting about my work; it's what I do every day. The most important thing is that we're trying to save ourselves from destruction. And if we have the power in our hands to do so, we need to get it done.'

'See, right there! That's what we're looking for. And all the rest, the fish, and all that – it's good stuff.'

'Trip, I can't – this is too difficult. I haven't recovered yet. The apraxia is almost gone, but I'm not ready.'

His face hardened, then, the change as dramatic as a gate slamming shut. 'Listen, Grace. Nant let you have a very favourable contract, much against my advice, I might add, because now we're committed to a level of marketing that your work does not deserve, although you are pulling in the numbers. But now is when you need to grow up. We're racing against the clock, here. By the time we're finished production on your little stories, you may very well have faded into obscurity. So I don't want to hear how ready or not ready you are.'

Grace hardly remembered the contract process. Zygmunt had offered to take it over, and found an agent for her with Nant's help.

'I don't think the contract …'

'As I hope I have made clear, I am no longer interested in what you think. We've got the schedule for the writers' room all booked out now, so you'll need to get your bags packed.'

'The writers' room?'

LEGS

9.00 pm, Friday, December 8, 2028
Oil Platform – Natuna Sea
Global temperature: 1.8°C above pre-industrial average

Adam Park missed his wife. Every evening he stood at the railing of the platform and watched the lab techs emerge, miserable, from their review meeting with Tengku Marina. One of them, a tiny, middle-aged woman from Singapore, confided in Adam.

'We're going to have to get iron sulphate and soluble silicates on board. Then you have to use your ROV to run hoses to different parts of the hold, to give more nutrient-in-water compositions.'

'That sounds more complicated. But not impossible. Why do you look unhappy?'

'Where do you think the materials are going to come from? And how are we going to get them on board?'

'Tengku Marina arranged the guard boats almost as soon as she arrived. The guard boat men will do it.'

The petite lab tech barked with laughter. 'Oh, yes, she's quite an arranger. Do those guys look like they're Maritim Malaysia?'

Adam came to an unpleasant realisation. 'I see. What else is she planning?'

Within days, his question was answered. A group of smaller craft resembling miniature submarines arrived to conduct comprehensive surveys of the coral under the platform and the new installations.

Over the years since the original construction of the platform, life underneath had blossomed into a kingdom of colour, clustering around the legs of the platform and extending in all directions. The fertiliser plume gave a dynamic boost to the growth, transforming the little grove into a sensational marine forest. Flush with experimental zeal, Tengku Marina toyed with yet another idea. She explained to Adam what she wanted to do.

'We have made 50 simulated platform legs,' Adam told his wife in an email. 'We use a piece of scrap as a weight, a thick rope, and a home-made buoy. We are using old trawler hawsers which are supplied by the so-called "local fishermen". I suspect these fishermen are not very legal, but I do not want to make trouble. Marina says that algal blooms are bad for shallow waters, but here, they can become a foundation for the food chain. She says it will become part of her project called the Sea Orchards. We still have not found the original ship manifest, but we will at least learn something.'

The crew placed each of the makeshift legs 45 metres from the platform, in lines and squares, extending the habitat in all directions. 'That's twice the fish we had a few weeks ago,' an excited Indian oil platform worker announced at the daily round-up, as he squinted at the day's photos and scans.

'Yes,' confirmed the Singaporean lab tech. 'From a fish's point of view, these rope legs are like platform legs, but thin, and further out. But they are still cover. And because the buoys stop around five or ten metres below the surface, they aren't a nuisance to the boats. Still, I'd like to see how we can scale it up with more weights and marine debris. There's a lot of potential here if we get it right.'

Like a tendril of cool air on a hot, muggy day, a cirrus of optimism was beginning to take hold on the creaking platform.

WRITERS

7.30 pm, Thursday, November 9, 2028
Penang, Malaysia – 8 Gurney Drive
Global temperature: 1.8°C above pre-industrial average

Grace caught Hans in front of the TV again, blasting digital aliens into bits. Ivan stood up, stretched, and went to the kitchen looking for a beer, while Hans continued to play against the blue-and-white Orac avatar. She watched for a while, until Hans finished a level, and sat back on the sofa with a satisfied grin.

'Hans, can I ask you something?'

'Sure thing! What's up?' He paused the game and turned his attention to her.

'Have you ever been to America?

'I have. You haven't? I always thought you were so well-travelled.'

'No. When I was little, we went to all kinds of bizarre places, but never to the United States. My parents went, but they didn't say much about it. I'm nervous, but I can't tell you how much I'm looking forward to it.'

'I'm not,' Hans replied. 'I'm amazed Zygmunt is letting you take all that time off. The few times you've been away, the client always gets sort of peevish.'

'That's no surprise. They're always like that. The entire Penang Development Board is composed of peevish government workers and political appointees who exist to make our work as inefficient as possible. Anyway, Zygmunt's not that generous; I'm only getting unpaid leave. Plus, Fairhaven was doing fine before I came on board, so I figure you all can spare me for a month.'

'When you were – when the barge thing happened, I had to deal with the PDB myself, and they kept asking me when you would be back, and I got the idea it wasn't just because they cared about your well-being.'

For a moment, he saw the troubled look in Grace's eyes that appeared after the barge incident. It passed before she noticed. She raised her face towards his, and asked, 'So tell me about America! I want to hear about the famous Hollywood stars everywhere, and all the places I've seen on a screen. Mountains, valleys, cowboys. The land of opportunity. It's where I'll get my stories out at last.'

Hans tried to decide how he should answer. 'I worked there for a few months. I could tell you more about Japan! But – America, well, there is no generalisation that holds true, except to say it's a land of contrasts.'

'How do you mean?'

'Fabulous landscapes, rural, urban, rich, and poor. Vast suburban sprawl, cars everywhere, strip malls, fast-food places, and then a thousand kilometres of desert. The most and least progressive people you'll meet, and often on the same day.'

Grace nodded, but her gaze fixed on the image in her imagination. 'It's everything everyone has always dreamed of. But onto more important things. What movie do you want to watch?'

'I'm indifferent. How about you?'

'Anything that doesn't involve smugglers, climate change, or concrete contracts.'

He laughed. 'This may not be easy. Let's take a look.' They settled back onto the couch as he flipped through the options. It was a performative gesture; the algorithm always ended up selecting something they liked.

Later, after the movie was over, Grace's tone grew serious. 'Hans, don't let the PDB get you down while I'm away.'

'I won't. As long as you promise America won't make you into someone else. And don't stay there too long.'

10.30 am, Friday, December 15, 2028
Fremont, California – Santa Vista Science Park

The atmosphere in the room chilled, and not from the cold, damp weather.

Despite Hans' warning, she thought California, at least, would resemble what she had imagined. It did not. There was no beach volleyball in Silicon Valley in December. When she asked about the open-air cafes, a staff writer hooted with laughter. 'Not when it's 45 degrees outside!' Grace attempted to do a quick calculation – in Celsius, was that closer to zero degrees, or to ten degrees? – but gave up and pulled her fleece jacket tighter around herself. She had a dim memory of the six months she spent with her parents in Norway, where she enjoyed playing in the snow, whooping with the other children and sliding down the sides of drifts at the roadside. But that was a long time ago; the children she once played with would no longer recognise her.

Creased paper Red Bay Coffee cups and plates of half-eaten doughnuts littered the table. A story editor was once again indulging in a kind of bluntness that Grace found not far from cruelty.

'I've got to tell it like it is. Where's the love interest? This is the first episode. Does this, Miss something, what's her name, Agnes, does she hook up with James or what? Or is she an old bag?'

'It's a survival story,' Grace explained, 'about quick thinking and ingenuity. It's not a love story.'

The executive story editor leaned back in the room's only Herman Miller chair. 'But it's supposed to be about climate change, right? As far as I can see, it has nothing to do with climate change. Nobody's trying to introduce windmills or solar panels. It's set more than a century ago, for Christ's sake. It's a historical drama.'

'It's a metaphor,' she replied. 'And it's also about adaptation, not mitigation. Yes, a few people are still trying to turn the climate *Titanic* away from the iceberg, but for the rest of us, we have to talk about what we're going to do when they fail. We have to prepare our pontoons.'

'Adaptation? Mitigation?' The writers accused her of relying on jargon, which, she gathered, was a sin against the holy gods of entertainment.

She had arrived two days ago, but Grace already wanted nothing more than to go home.

Emboldened by the executive's prodding, the others climbed on board, criticising, arguing with each other, sidelining Grace from the discussion.

'It's too preachy.'

'Plus, it's riddled with mistakes; they're called Girl Scouts, not Girl Guides.'

'No, that's what they're called in England.'

'That's too arcane. What do they call Boy Scouts? Boy Guides?' A co-producer, sitting at the head of the table, looked up from his phone long enough to guffaw.

'No matter what they were called 100 years ago, we can't call them Girl Guides in our show. It's too foreign. I can picture the comments now. So let's make them Girl Scouts, coming back from their Grand Tour of Europe. Did people do that in 1912? Or make them Boy Scouts. Boys would have known how to tie knots.'

'That's sexist.'

'It's set in Victorian England! Women weren't even allowed to vote.'

'Come to think of it, how are we on diversity? Is this going to be another hashtag Oscars So White moment?'

Grace pointed out, 'On board the *Titanic*, according to the passenger manifest, there was one black man, his two children, one Japanese, and eight Chinamen.'

'Oh my God, Grace, you can't just say "Chinamen"!'

'She can say it; she's Chinese herself. It's like the N-word for them.'

Grace clarified, '"Chinamen" was the word used on the passenger manifest. And, since you mention it, I'm mixed race, from Malaysia.'

'Isn't that part of China?'

'Girl Scouts saving all the people on the *Titanic*; it's too corny.'

Would their arguments never stop? Grace's head ached. They bickered over whether to call it an adventure story on the high seas, or a love story. If the former, then it lacked action scenes; building boats was too dry. If the latter, they decreed that Agnes and James were an unbelievable couple.

They proclaimed that building a catamaran in the way described in the story was impossible. Grace remembered the group of Sea Scouts she saw achieving that very thing, the inspiration for the original story. They completed a pontoon in under 17 minutes. It didn't sound as if this group wanted to hear about it.

'Maybe everyone in those days knew how to tie knots, like the horsey woman in Act III. Just because modern man has lost those skills, doesn't mean they never existed.'

'It's a century ago, Dawn, not the Ice Age. They weren't hunter-gatherers. They were more like people from Downton Abbey.'

'Come to think of it, didn't Downton Abbey have a *Titanic* scene in it?'

'We need a fight scene.'

'Don't forget, 13% of our viewers still don't believe climate change is real.'

Grace thought of the George Town floods; of the tornadoes in Poland; of the 23 mega-typhoons that battered the Philippines in the past year. She wanted to look out the window, but none existed in the bright, artificial conference room. Perhaps that was the real issue: Americans, and the ones who created their entertainment, were forever indoors, cut off from the natural world.

'Where are the jokes?'

'We can add jokes. Mike's a good hand at that. There's good comic potential in that hockey captain character.'

At 11.00, someone called for a bio-break. In the corridor, Grace was surprised to meet Trip in person for the first time. 'I thought you must be out of town!' She was still resenting being left to face the writers' room on her own. His teeth really were an incredible shade of white, she noticed. Was there something in the food they ate in America, or was it the product of an artificial bleach?

'So how was it? Did they manage to make something out of your little bits of fiction?'

She was exhausted from the ordeal, and his casual dismissal of her work was almost too much. She managed to compose herself long enough to reply, 'I think half of them hadn't read beyond the first few paragraphs of the story.'

'Grace, baby, you've got to understand things around here. Writers are either lazy, or else they're insecure egomaniacs who don't like using other people's material and want the story to reflect their own work. Or both. But what that means is that the first session is always a knock-down, drag-out fight to determine who's going to call the shots. Remember, everything here is about eyeballs, because eyeballs are money. It's always been like that, since the first dot-com boom.'

She wanted to ask what the sudden 'Grace, baby' thing was about, but he had piqued her curiosity. 'The dot-com boom? The first one? Do you remember that?'

'Don't tell anyone. I graduated from USF in 1994.' He flashed his toothy grin again, and Grace blinked. Was he in his mid-50s? She would have guessed that he was 20 years younger. He looked into his eyepiece, a new Orac product that was rumoured to cost almost $15,000, said, 'Gotta go! I have a thing,' and strolled away.

The break was over, and Grace stood outside the depressing meeting room, willing herself to enter. The writers passed her, laughing with each other, ignoring her, one going so far as to push her aside with an outstretched elbow. As he shoved past, his coffee spilled on her thin blouse. Instead of apologising, he went on the offensive, asking why she was blocking the door, and demanded that she get a new cup for him. Mute and shocked, she returned several minutes later with a tray. The conversation was continuing in her absence. One writer was musing over the possibility of making the Girl Guides into American Marines, and adding a forbidden romance between their drill sergeant and one of the sailors. Another suggested setting the action on a spacecraft. Grace continued to stand and listen, aghast at the changes being wrought to her simple story.

For the duration of the spacecraft discussion, no one acknowledged or noticed her as she stood. But as they turned to another proposal, a young staff writer who couldn't be more than a year out of school cried, 'Sit down, Grace! You're giving me the heebie jeebies.' The room roared with laughter. Ashamed, Grace found a chair in the corner and tucked herself out of the way.

Home. There was nothing to do but flee. She allowed herself to close her eyes for a moment, and pictured herself at Bazalgette Lock in the sunshine, talking to one of the workers, taking notes, and collecting water quality measurements. She opened her eyes again and remembered that she had asked for this; hoped for it.

It was lunchtime. She had not uttered a word for an hour.

Lunch in the staff cafeteria was every bit as awkward as those she experienced on the first day of every new school. But one thing was different. Four Streamberry staffers approached her with cameras upheld, hopeful looks on their faces. 'Is that really you?' one asked, a young woman with red hair and a complicated arrangement of headbands. The headbands were in imitation of herself; she had taken up wearing headbands as her hair grew out after the barge incident, and joked that they were all that prevented her brain from falling out the back. Grace gave an automatic smile as the recording continued. 'I'm a huge fan. Do you remember when I commented on your livestream, the one you did standing on that dock? Thank you so much for liking my comment!' Now addressing her phone camera, she continued, 'This is the amazing thing about working at Streamberry! You can be in the middle of the cafeteria and you meet, and this is totally true, the real Grace Chan. I didn't know she was in California. Grace, I love your stuff! You are so amazing.' She threw an annoyed glare at one of the other young women who also wanted a chance at reflected fame. 'Look, wait your turn, okay? Some people are so rude.'

Grace fielded seven impromptu interviews by the end of the lunch break, staying as polite as she could, addressing their questions without revealing details of the new series, which was still under a non-disclosure agreement. She realised again that her reticence would drive anticipation to a frenzy, and tried not to resent it. After they finished recording, the would-be streamers drifted away to their own friends and lives.

Grace knew that here in California, she would never be solitary again, but she would be just as alone as ever.

At least her stories would be seen.

THE YELLOW RAT: A STORY BY GRACE CHAN

The 2008 earthquake in Sichuan, China was felt a thousand miles away. By the time the final toll was counted, it was clear that more than 69,000 people had lost their lives.

Most of those affected were in no position to construct monumental fortifications or implement Herculean solutions. But when we listen and think ahead in places where others only speak and react, opportunities can reveal themselves that we would otherwise overlook. Not everyone will grasp these opportunities, but the one who does may come from anywhere.

This is us. In 2008, the global average temperature was 0.9°C above pre-industrial levels. As our climate changes, natural disasters are increasing around the world. Where will your opportunity come from?

***

The village had not changed since the last time Huang Ning was home.

In the industrial city of Dongguan, every week brought a new batch of migrants, a new group of workers, a new factory opening, a new chance. But back in Luobozhai, in Sichuan Province, it was the same as ever. Small, rainy, and boring. The name of the little hamlet itself was banal, laughable: Radish Village.

Ning descended from the rattling bus, annoyance and defeat showing on his face. As the bus pulled away, he kicked a clod of early spring mud, sending a squawking chicken running in the opposite direction.

His final pay cheque, including severance, was enough to buy one of the cheaper mobile phone models. In Luobozhai, however, no mobile phone tower was close enough for him to get a signal. Frustrated, he checked the phone again, but the characters 'no network' were all that showed on the little screen. He'd heard that the government was merging the phone companies into three large groups; maybe one of them would bring a tower to Radish Village. For now, the rest of the world might be living in 2008, but Luobozhai was stuck in the past.

Three other young people were in the same situation, including his younger sister, Huang Luo. All four left the village together on an over-crowded, long-distance bus to Guangdong Province, found work at a new electronics factory in Dongguan, and were all sacked together. Luo and the other two, disheartened, returned home right away. Ning swore that he would find a new job, and stayed for three more weeks, until his money ran out. But at last, he had to admit that he was a rare breed: a healthy 25-year-old man in Dongguan who couldn't find work.

They were lucky to receive a final pay cheque. 'I've been keeping my eye on the American market,' the blunt factory boss told his laid-off workers. 'I think they're going to have a financial downturn, and that's where most of our customers are. This isn't the first time I've managed a business through difficulties: I was here during the 1998 crisis, the dot-com bust in 2001, and the post-SARS slump in 2003. So I'm not going to risk keeping on extra workers, when the buyer might cut my contract at any moment.'

He was a fool! thought Ning, frustrated: according to the TV, both the Chinese economy and the American economy were as strong as ever. Was this not 2008, the year of the auspicious number eight? In less than half a year, the Summer Olympics would take place in Beijing for the first time ever, beginning on August 8. He was proud: at last, China was ready to step onto the global stage.

If only he could get a hukou, a residence registration, he would go to Beijing to find a job. No jobs were to be had in Luobozhai, and wages were pitiful for those jobs that did exist. How was he going to support his mother and four grandparents now? Giving birth to Luo 20 years earlier already strained his mother's finances; she tried to argue that her grandmother's heritage as a member of the Qiang ethnic minority gave her the right to a second child, but the village family planning council disagreed, and levied fines all the same. She never let Luo forget it, reminding her again and again how lucky her daughter was not to have been abandoned at birth, or given away.

Ning himself was not sure whether to feel guilty or resentful about having a second child in the family. Most of all, he wished he could have stayed in school, and not had to go out to earn. For as long as he was allowed to attend, he loved learning about science, dissecting creatures and finding out what was inside, and tinkering with batteries and resistors and electrical wires. If he had been able to stay for a few more years, perhaps he could have performed a more useful function at the Dongguan factory, more than cleaning the equipment. But when his father died, there was not enough money.

The morning after his arrival back in the village, a rooster's crow, followed by the clucking of chickens and the squeals of the neighbour's pigs, conspired to wrench Ning out of bed before it was light. The dormitories in the factory, crowded though they were, had never antagonised him like the cacophony of a working farm.

His mother was already up, squatting before a fussy little coal stove, persuading it to light. 'As long as you're here,' she nodded towards the bag of feed. It was the longest sentence she'd spoken to him since he returned.

He rose, scratched himself, and went out to tend to the chickens.

As he scattered the feed in front of their coop, he saw how agitated they were. Two would not come out of the coop at all. Only one had laid an egg. It was a plucky little hen, smaller than the others, with soft grey feathers. He smiled and scratched her head. 'Good girl! What's wrong with the rest of them?' he asked Luo, who was standing in the yard, brushing her teeth.

'There was a little earthquake last night. Didn't you feel it?'

'No. I was too exhausted from the trip, I guess. Nothing damaged, though, it looks like.'

'It was just a shake.'

Minor quakes were a fact of life in Sichuan, an annoyance that kept people on their toes, but posed no real threat to daily existence. Indeed, the last big one happened ages ago, seven years before Ning was born.

He listened to the clucking of the chickens and the chatter of the wild birds. Birds in villages and cities are different, he thought. Sparrows, crows, pigeons, swifts.

He brought the single egg back into the house and presented it to his mother without a word. Resigned, she nodded, and sat back on her heels. She tucked it away into a little cabinet.

That evening, as they ate a small meal of spicy noodles, with a few mustard greens on the side to provide a little variety, Ning asked his sister if she knew of anyone in town who might want to buy his phone. 'Without a connection, it's a useless piece of metal. But maybe someone who's travelling out of town soon will want it.'

'Don't you want to wait until the village gets a service tower?'

'We don't know when that's going to happen.'

Their mother picked at the greens, eating a tiny amount. Luo put another bunch into her bowl. 'You're too thin. These will be good for your blood.'

'We don't have enough for one person,' she grumbled. 'I don't know how we're going to feed three.'

'Are my grandparents well?'

'They have enough. Your father's father has a little bit of pension from the army, and their sow gave birth to three pigs this spring.'

'What about your own parents?'

She shook her head, dismissive. 'If they had a son, I wouldn't have to worry.' She drew out a single noodle from her bowl and ate it with deliberate slowness. 'You can visit them if you like.'

Ning nodded. 'I thought I'd go around the village tomorrow, and see if anyone might need help with harvesting the winter wheat. It's a bit early, but ...'

'I heard the Zhu tea farm is harvesting tomorrow,' commented Luo. 'You can try there.'

Big Zhu, the tea farmer, paid Ning a pittance, but was good for conversation. They smoked cigarette after cigarette together, as they gathered the tea leaves along with several other day labourers. 'Little quake last night,' Zhu commented.

'I missed it; I was asleep. To be honest, I kind of miss the ground shaking from time to time. But it spooked the chickens, that's for sure.'

'They always know about it first,' Zhu laughed. 'Hey! Focus on the top three leaves. Don't forget, this is the early harvest. We shouldn't pick the leaves lower down until later in the year.'

'Will do. By the way – what do you mean, they always know about it first?'

'Oh, everyone knows that,' Zhu replied with a breezy wave. 'Chickens, all kinds of birds, and the other farm animals know when a quake is coming.'

'I suppose I've heard that. My father's mother used to say the same. But I was never sure if it was just out-of-date thinking. We're a modern people now; we shouldn't be listening to old wives' tales.'

'I assure you, it's true, and the scientists at Peking University have proven it. Birds' ears are more sensitive than ours. Sometimes they'll know about a quake a good five minutes before it arrives.'

As the long day continued, the germ of an idea formed in Ning's head. He'd have to get a few long wires.

That night, he hung his head as he handed his paltry wages over to his mother, but glowered with defiance. She accepted them without comment and served a simple dinner to all three of them.

'Luo, you've been back for a few weeks now. Do you know where I could find copper wire?'

'Have you forgotten so fast? A couple of years in Dongguan, and you don't remember where Peng Ni's hardware shop is! When I came back home, it was easy for me to see that everything was where it had always been.'

'How would I know if it's still there?' he shot back. 'I've been home for a day.'

'Do you think you can sell him your phone?'

'No, I'm keeping my phone. I have another idea.'

The next evening, after a gruelling day cutting winter wheat, he dragged himself to the shack where Peng Ni always kept his shop. To his surprise, the door flew open, as if he was expected.

'Oh. You're not —'

'No. I'm Huang Ning. From down the road. We keep chickens.'

Peng Ni gestured towards the spare racks. 'What do you need?'

'I'm looking for wire.'

Peng Ni showed him spools of wire, drawers of connectors, switches, and toggles. He saw one piece that was decades old; others were new, cheap and cheerful junk from the plant in Chongqing.

Ning looked through all of them, but had to concede. 'It's too difficult for me.'

'Maybe I can help. What do you need to do?'

'I want something that can throw a switch whenever it detects a noise.'

'Why didn't you say so!' He dug through a pile in the back of the shop, and found a small Zave sound sensor. 'Here you go. Ten yuan.'

'But I'll need a switch, too.'

They discussed it for a few minutes, and Ning brought out a piece of soft school notebook paper to draw a little diagram of what he wanted. Half scoffing, and half entertained by the young man's earnestness, Peng Ni offered to teach him the rudiments of circuitry.

'I won't be able to pay,' Ning confessed.

'If you strip this pile of old phones and cart them to the recycler, I'll let you keep a percentage of the gold he extracts. He lives in the next village over. Let me show you how.'

By the time Ning left, he knew he would be late for dinner. 'Don't tell my mother about this.' The older man smiled.

Luo, with sunken eyes, hemming a neighbour's dress, kept her head down when he arrived. 'We already ate,' she said. Their mother lay exhausted in the corner, on a pallet that served as her bed.

'Everyone is broke here.'

'Don't you remember why we left to begin with?'

The chickens had begun to lay again, after their little scare. Every morning, Ning fed them, cleaned their coop, gathered their eggs, and listened. He was convinced that they had at least a dozen distinct types of call. Perhaps more. One day, a new cry burst out, one that he hadn't heard before. A moment later, a swift, grey form snuck from the corner towards the brooding racks. Ning stood still, a large block of wood in his hand, for what felt like an eternity, and then struck. Bullseye!

He held the dead rat aloft by its tail, and crowed about his victory to anyone who could hear. He then recorded his notes about the chickens' cries in his little notebook, his pencil digging into the soft, grey paper.

During the day, he went from shop to shop, from farm to farm, finding whatever work was available. Sometimes Peng Ni would give him a phone to strip, or a tangled collection of wires and parts to sort through. As he sat prying metal loose with a pair of rusted pliers, he understood that this was another kind of education.

A week later, an old lady came to him with a request to deal with three rats in other chicken sheds. There was not much to talk about in a small village, and news of a vigorous, young rat assassin was spreading to every house. If it served to protect the flocks, the villagers could still dig out a few coins and dirty bills from under pillows or inside old tea canisters.

With the earnings from his rat killing, he bought additional bits and pieces of old wires or half-depleted batteries from Peng Ni. By running noise sensors, microphones, trip switches, and connectors throughout the village, within a month he put together a network of 14 chicken coop monitoring stations.

Everyone knew him now. They no longer called him by his name, Huang Ning, which meant 'yellow mud', but by a new nickname, Huang Shu.

Huang the Rat.

He didn't mind. It fit him, since he was born in the Year of the Rat. And he felt like a rat, sometimes, stashing away bits and pieces of electronics in a corner of the house or in the back of Peng Ni's shop. He was learning more every day: his occasional visits to the recycler gave him a new appreciation for the vast variety of electronics that existed in the market. He determined that one of the discarded 'junk' phones from a city many kilometres from their village was a high-spec Japanese model, with more computing power than the old desktop his boss used at the factory.

Although it was good and dead, after an accidental plunge into a puddle, he kept it to one side.

Meanwhile, he monitored the chicken sounds day and night. He set up Zave sound sensors to activate whenever one of the coops became suddenly louder. In a moment, just by listening to the birds, he could determine whether the threat was a fight over chicken feed, excitement from the farmer's arrival, a rainstorm, a motorbike, a stray dog, or a rat.

No one, he mused, had ever listened to so many chickens for so long – and never not across such a wide area.

After drying the Japanese phone next to his mother's coal fire, he wheedled it back to life, although the battery was useless. It was a 'smart' phone, one of the first he'd come across: full of apps he'd never seen before, although most needed a live connection: games, entertainment, a notepad. He was fascinated by an earthquake warning app. He recognised certain Japanese characters borrowed from Chinese so many centuries ago. He smiled: looking out for earthquakes was a point of commonality between their two cultures. The Japanese were better at it, he had to admit.

He coaxed his mother, that evening, to tell him about the quake that happened before he was born. 'Can you tell us what it was like?'

'You don't want to hear about any of that.'

Luo piped up, 'Yes, we do. Do you remember it?'

'Remember it? Of course I remember it!' she snapped. 'It was the worst day of my life.'

They gaped at her.

'I was 18 years old. I was going to be married that year. There was a man from Anshun, who was introduced by my father's old boss. He was the handsomest man I'd ever seen.'

'Did ... something happen to him in the earthquake?'

'No. But this whole village was devastated. Don't you know that since that day, my mother could never again walk as she used to? The house collapsed into ruins. But the worst part of all was that my older brother was inside when it happened.'

'You had a brother? We had an uncle?'

'Not after that day. If they'd had a moment's notice to get out of the building, maybe he could have been saved. But he and my mother were having a meal, and she was going outside to check on something, when it struck. It was like a thunderclap. The door frame was made of wood and stones, and it fell on her. It took them a day and a half to dig her out. The infection in her leg almost crippled her. And they didn't dig out my brother until a week later.'

Luo and Ning sat, frozen.

'The man who was supposed to marry me took back his proposal, of course. My father spent too much money on my mother's medical treatment and on my brother's funeral, so I became too poor for a man like that. And a year later, when your father came here, and offered to pay for our debts, it was my duty to go with him.'

'And the house was rebuilt?'

'No thanks to the village People's Committee! Those rats ate away every bit of spare money they could find. It took my father ten years to gather enough earth and stones to put it together again. He used whatever materials were at hand. If there's ever another quake, it won't be any different from the last one.'

Luo and Ning whispered long into the night. They worried that they would keep their mother awake, but recounting the grim tale had exhausted her, and she fell asleep on her pallet in the corner, still wearing her clothes.

The next morning, after feeding the chickens and taking notes on the other coops, he was back at Peng Ni's shop. 'The Yellow Rat has arrived!' he shouted, by way of introducing himself. They sat together for several hours, going over Ning's plan.

'It's worth showing to the People's Committee,' Peng Ni admitted at last.

'My mother told me never to trust them.'

'Maybe, maybe not. It's their job to look after our village, after all. And they have access to the loudspeaker system.'

Over the past decades, the village leaders had installed a public address system, whose blaring noise penetrated into every residence. In the afternoon, it played patriotic songs, announced important political topics, and gave advice on family planning. Every day at 4.00 pm, an enthusiastic voice cried, 'Villagers who want to get rich: have fewer children but grow more trees!' or 'Carry out family planning, implement the basic national policy!' Ning had never considered the system as a possible tool – the village residents ignored or ridiculed much of the content – but he understood the practicality of Peng Ni's plan.

The People's Committee laughed, but agreed to the idea, as long as they would not be required to pay anything. 'We don't have the funds. But we've always heard the same thing, of course, and your idea has merit. If it really happens, then the worst that could go wrong is that people are a bit vexed, and have something to joke about; the best is that we save lives.'

Ning thanked them, and within days had put a basic system in place that connected to his chicken network.

Yet, after all the weeks spent on planning and rigging wires and sensors, Ning felt a keen sense of anticlimax as they made the final connection and ran a test. Seeing his glum expression, Chang, the People's Committee representative, said, 'Cheer up. Something terrible may yet happen!' and chuckled at his own joke.

'It's not that.'

'What, then?'

'What if our system works? If the big one comes, the village will still be destroyed.'

Comrade Chang became serious. 'Huang Shu, if your system works, you will be a hero of this village, and of all Sichuan Province. Buildings can be rebuilt; but remember, people are the most precious resource we have.'

It was less than a week later when, in an insane moment of cosmic synchronicity, Ning heard the chickens make a new sound.

Throughout the morning, there were rumbles of discontent among the flock. But as Ning relaxed after lunch, they made a more irritating babble. At first, he couldn't understand what he was hearing. Every sound sensor in the network was firing at once.

The birds' cry transformed to a wail.

He dropped his little ceramic cup and shouted to his mother and sister, 'Get out of the house! Now! Right now!' At the same moment, he took up the direct 'hotline' connection to the People's Committee office, and roared into the receiver. 'It's happening! Right now! Sooner than we could have imagined! Put out the alarm!'

Seconds later, an alarm siren sounded on every loudspeaker in the village. 'Earthquake warning! Get out of your houses! Earthquake warning! Get out of your houses!' it shrieked, again and again.

Ning's mother and sister came out into the yard, confused and annoyed, and asked what was going on.

Hearing the loudspeakers, people rushed into the street, shouting for others to follow.

And the world collapsed.

A violent noise like a highway full of container trucks roared through the earth, shaking the very land on which he stood. Waves billowed through the ground, as if it were the ocean itself. At first, Ning attempted to stay upright, but gave in to the relentless undulations, and fell to his knees. A pig shrieked next door, its scream worse than the sound of slaughter, and the chicken coop collapsed in on itself. Luo turned back towards their house, horrified, just in time to see the roof cave in. She and her mother both sat down heavily, and Luo held the older woman to her chest, cradling her as they felt the ground roll beneath them.

The quake went on as seconds ticked by.

Ning attempted to glance at his watch, but lost his balance and put his hand down. It had been at least a minute since the quake began. A utility pole swayed, and then toppled. Across the small lane, he saw several neighbouring families sitting in their front yards, stunned at the chaos surrounding them.

At last, after more than two minutes, the roaring subsided. Huge clouds of dust floated everywhere, forming a haze that filtered out the sun. The stink of chicken manure, charcoal, and motor oil combined with that of burning rubber and plastic. Shouts came from across the street, as his swineherd neighbours tried to put out a small fire with an ancient extinguisher.

Stunned, he got up, and stood, unsteady for a moment, wondering whether it was he or the earth that was still swaying. The dust was settling, the finest particles still hanging in the air, while the heavier motes drifted downwards.

Where was everyone?

Ning heard a pitiful noise coming from one of the loudspeakers. It was emitting an incomprehensible wheeze from its felled utility pole. He turned toward the main road.

And then he saw them.

People.

His neighbours, standing in the dust, confused, angry, or terrified, but alive. Up and down the road, they were struggling to their feet, talking, shouting, crying. Mothers held wailing babies. Children clung to their parents' legs. An elderly man squatted on his heels, unwilling to rise.

Ning moved among them, reeling at the sight of so many collapsed houses, asking, again and again, 'Did everyone get out? Was there anyone left inside?' They shook their heads in a daze. They were all out. One had a scrape along her arm; another had bumped his head as he rushed outside. There were no serious injuries.

At last, he returned to attend to his own mother and sister, who sat, silent and confused, in the middle of the chicken run. Wordless, Luo gestured to the collapsed chicken coop.

A small, grey hen lay on its side, crushed under the weight of the corrugated steel roof. Ning lifted the bird and cradled it to his chest.

'It's a fortunate year for us, after all.'

MARKET

Grace Chan pulled the windbreaker across her chest, her teeth chattering. She reminded herself that she was just walking to an ordinary California grocery store. It was less than half a kilometre away, according to what she'd seen online; she couldn't justify using a ride share service. Did America have Grab? No, they had Or-V nowadays, self-driving cars. She shook her head.

A narrow sidewalk teetered along the edge of a six-lane road. Although she was not walking on the road itself, she was almost blown off her feet as the traffic rushed past, the drivers hidden behind their tinted windows and elevated to a level where no pedestrian would be visible. And indeed, there was no one for them to see: the streets were empty of pedestrians. In this artificial, inhuman sprawl, nothing existed outside except for trucks, highways and parking lots, hectare upon hectare of parking lots, most of them half-empty. The 500 metres from her temporary serviced apartment to a nearby Walmart stretched before her in monotone.

She plodded, squinting her eyes against the wind. On her right: an enormous glass building with a manicured lawn and three puny saplings, their roots covered with thick layers of wood-chip mulch and their scrawny trunks guy-wired to the dry earth. On her left: a boxy self-storage unit with large solar panels perched atop its flat roof. How many solar panels could be saved, she grumbled to herself, if these people could build energy-efficient, dense housing and install a decent system of public transportation?

When it was time to cross the main road, she approached the crosswalk and waited. The trucks continued to whip past; whether they had drivers or auto-pilots made no difference. After an eternity, the light changed to green; she took a tentative step forward and froze. A black Ford SUV with a forbidding grill the size of a bedframe accelerated in front of her, careening out of the shopping mall entrance.

As she entered the Walmart at last, she laughed aloud with relief. Or perhaps she was laughing at the preposterous size of the shopping carts; was there no such thing as an ordinary shopping basket in America? It took her more than half an hour to find basic ingredients like rice, tofu, noodles, and fish sauce. She wandered for another 45 minutes, gaping at items she never expected to see in a grocery store: riding lawn mowers, funeral caskets, and something that was labelled 'airgun' but looked like a rifle. There were also products that bordered on the absurd. A colouring book featuring farting dinosaurs. A bacon-scented fake moustache. Dog nail polish.

Was this the ultimate expression of human desire, an abundance so great that selecting what to consume became a baffling ordeal? If so, then the planet was headed for disaster.

She laughed out loud for the second time. Why on earth was she here, if not to show how disasters could be mitigated, or averted?

As she watched several shoppers navigate the self-checkout machines, a young woman approached her, phone held high. 'Are you, sorry, has anyone ever told you that you look like Grace Chan?'

After her experience at lunch the previous day, Grace had an answer ready. 'No. But most of them don't need to say so, since that's who I am.'

'Oh, my God, I knew it!' the young woman shrieked, and continued to film, speaking into the phone as if it were her closest friend. When she finished, she turned to face Grace. 'You know we have all been rooting for you ever since the beginning. You've got, like, a whole army behind you lmao!' She pronounced the final word 'le mao', just as Grace always did in her videos, just for fun. Grace gave a secret smile of satisfaction, to think that she was affecting how people spoke.

She said goodbye to her fan and walked out into the bitter afternoon. Before the next meeting, on Monday morning, she had to think.

9.30 am, Monday, December 18, 2028
Fremont, California – Santa Vista Science Park

The second writers' room session went on for half an hour, much in the same manner as the previous one: criticism, dismissal, and outright ridicule of her story.

At last, Grace raised her hand. The crowd of writers ignored her at first, but, one by one, fell silent.

The producer cleared his throat. 'You don't have to raise your hand, Grace. This isn't elementary school. Go ahead.'

'I don't think what you're doing here is helpful in understanding how we will make this a success. What you are all not getting is that the entire point of this story is hope. In their hearts, people are optimistic.

Your audiences want to see action, quick thinking, Yankee ingenuity. They like go-getters, who pull themselves up by their bootstraps. They want to see the hero win in the end.

'And that's what happens here. Everyone knows the bad guy already, which is the hubris of mankind itself, thinking that we can overcome the forces of nature. The viewers will have seen the classic movie, or maybe read a book.'

'A book? That's not likely!' snorted Jamie, a staff writer.

'The connection to our current situation might not be obvious at first. That's why Trip suggested the intro format: I appear on camera to introduce each episode and give a teaser about the storyline and the metaphor. I've been watching the old Twilight Zone episodes from the last century, and I can tell you that this format works. In this case, it also makes it more interactive. The viewers will be talking to each other as the episode airs, trying to figure out the puzzle. What's the metaphor? What does this mean? What could we do? How can we escape from an impossible situation, using nothing more than what we've learned along the way, grit, and courage?

'And I know this is what they want, because my 22 million followers have told me so.'

There it was, at last: her leverage. It was something she had never experienced before. For years, she had been in the position of a supplicant. Now, the moment she mentioned her followers, the others shifted in their chairs.

Kaitlin, the other co-producer, spoke in an ironic tone, making it obvious that she was quoting something. 'Yes, sure, "You can make deals in a boardroom, but always do so with your angry mob in the street outside the boardroom window."'

'Who said that?' asked a staff writer.

'Kwame Nkrumah, the African revolutionary.'

'Ha! I think Grace has been taking lessons.'

Francis, the producer, spoke. 'We get it, Grace. We should use this meeting not to second-guess the concept, and try to change it to fit the audience we already have, but to give the new viewers, the ones you're bringing in, something that they expect, and that they'll enjoy. What we need to be doing now is adapting the existing form of these stories to the visual medium.'

The writers scribbled notes on their pads, and murmured among each other.

One asked, 'How much of this is going to be CGI? Because that will make a difference to the budget. I assume that new Orac tool can generate the extras?'

'Maybe. It's still glitchy. It keeps generating people you didn't intend to put in. It'd be good on a Volume set, like 1899.'

The discussion continued, focusing as much on the technical requirements created by the plot as on the plot itself. Mike busied himself looking up *Titanic* jokes ('What kind of salad did they serve on the *Titanic*? An iceberg lettuce!') and interjecting them into lulls in the conversation.

An hour later, Grace's stomach was rumbling; a wedge of iceberg lettuce would have been welcome. But they came around to discussing the title of the series.

'Why did you want to call it "Defying *Futility*" in the first place? And why is it in italics?'

'*Futility* is the name of a book, written in 1898. 14 years before the *Titanic* sank. It was written by a man named Morgan Robertson.'

'Oh?'

'The book was about a large ship, the biggest ocean liner ever built, and its name was the RMS *Titan*. And it struck an iceberg in the North Atlantic, and it sank, and all but a handful of the passengers perished.'

'And this was written before the actual *Titanic* sank?'

'Yes. And it was a coincidence. Or was it? If the builders of the *Titanic* had read it, they might have thought twice about how to prepare for a disaster.'

The group nodded their heads. 'It's a good name, and we'll be able to talk about it in the promotional materials. Maybe we can bring out another edition of the original book. Who owns the rights?'

A staff writer, whose name Grace remembered as either Jim or Tim, piped up, 'If the book was written in 1898, it's been public domain for a long time already. You can just find the entire text on Orac Books. Yup,' he tapped at his phone, 'there it is.'

'Later on, when we bring out the book of Grace's original stories as a companion to the show, we can pad it out by including the *Futility* book.'

'Good thinking.'

10.30 pm, Sunday, January 7, 2029
Fremont, California – Santa Vista Science Park

'Now is the most important time to keep yourself in the public eye, darling,' Nant advised her. 'There's going to be a bit of a gap, now, as they finalise the script and create the episodes, and you have to keep people interested the whole way through. Keep posting. Tell your followers what's happening, but keep them thirsty. The gap will be longer, you know, because you didn't make it easy on the production team! I can't believe your first episode requires that they recreate the literal *Titanic*.'

'Won't I be part of that process?'

'It's not like the old days; the writer's job is over very early on. Yes, in a technical sense you are also a cast member, because of your onscreen introductions. But for the most part, once you're finished with that, you have to turn over your baby to another set of parents, and hope for the best.'

Grace spent a gruelling week in the studio, learning how to sit still while Larissa, the makeup artist, applied what felt like a thick layer of spackle on her face ('It's the 8K cameras, sweetie – nobody shows their real skin!') and then, carrying that burden, to deliver and record her lines of introductory commentary in a 'natural' way.

Trip harangued her. It had to sound authentic and recognisable, but also authoritative. Warm and welcoming, but also professional.

Every prologue began with a narrative about what really happened, followed by a provocative question.

And then, once she had done everything to the satisfaction of the director, it was time to change her outfit to record the intro to the next episode, whose final script was not yet written.

And then the next.

And the next. And the next. And the next. For the entire season.

'Sweetie, you're an Asian woman on TV who wants to talk about big topics without coming across as preachy,' Larissa said. 'You've got your work cut out for you. People look at you and their first impression is going to be an anime character, not a trusted professor. And that's if you're lucky. If you're unlucky, the first thing they'll think of is one of the OAD fetish girls.'

'OAD?'

'Orac After Dark.'

'I'll keep it in mind.'

'Lucky you've got those eyes, not to mention that gorgeous hair. They'll take you a long way.'

MANIFEST

6.00 pm, Wednesday, January 10, 2029
Oil Platform – South China Sea
Global temperature: 1.7°C above pre-industrial average

Aboard the oil platform, now recognised as the main Sea Orchards research centre, the unlikely combination of ROV operators,
lab techs, and 'guard boat' men were forming a community.

Adam made friends with young Muhammad, one of the guard boat
men, by exchanging some of his hard currency for cigarettes.

The diminutive Singaporean lab tech, whose name turned out to
be Alice, spent half a year helping both Adam and Muhammad with
their English. She would take no reward. 'Never mind! I used to tutor
in English when I was at university. It makes me feel young again.'

In the rarefied environment of the platform, it was all too easy to
criticise the one they believed to be the source of their woes: Tengku
Marina. Some crew members were convinced that she was too strict;
others, that someone of her social position should not be doing such
an undignified job. Adam, for his part, was certain her unconventional

methods were close to being illegal, if not over the line. He was raised in a family where obedience to authority was unquestioned, but in exchange, he expected the authorities to follow the rules. In Marina's world, there were no rules. Who were the guard boat men, after all, and did they have employment contracts? Why was she so focused on gathering data, when there was no permit for the original spill? And why wasn't there a proper way to buy cigarettes on board the platform?

Tengku Marina spent more and more of her time brooding at the railing. Despite his misgivings, Adam began to join her there. One evening, early in the year, he offered her a cigarette. To his surprise, she took a long drag and returned it to him. 'Disgusting things,' she spat out, but looked grateful. 'My family would hate to see ... look, we need to do more. We need to see how else these old oil platforms and the surrounding area can be used to sequester CO_2. We will have spent a year thinking about nothing else, and there aren't many other people in this position. That's a privilege.'

Adam nodded. If only the details of the original ship's manifest – still knotted in the owner's managerial hierarchy, and a lawsuit being fought in The Hague – could be recovered. How could it be done? He shared Tengku Marina's frustration at not being able to make the proper calculations without the original source data from the manifest.

He remembered an old salvage and towage captain he'd helped with an operation several years before. 'This business doesn't require an intellectual mind,' the wrinkled veteran told him. 'It needs low, animal cunning.'

He would have to wait.

During the ensuing weeks, Adam spent much of his free time writing long emails to his wife, as the spans between his allowed home leave journeys felt like years. She replied with concern and sympathy, but could offer no solutions. As Muhammad's English improved, he also became a willing listener. In passive rebellion against Marina's readiness to bend the rules, Adam lectured the youth about the importance of law, order, authority, and institutions. He explained what the project was about. It was surprising how fast the young man learned.

Seven months after the initial spill, the new season changed the direction of the ocean current. Alice, the Singaporean lab tech, brought Adam and Muhammad to the railing to see it. 'The reversed ocean current is bringing back the water we fertilised months before,' she rhapsodised. 'And look at the life! We caught the first change of direction early, so we've got three weeks of data. There's so much more in there than we had at the start of the trial.'

'What is that?' asked Muhammad, leaning on the railing and pointing to the sea, a cigarette in his left hand, as usual.

'Don't you recognise it?' Alice grinned. 'It's a whale shark. We always saw one or two, but they are drawn to the area we fertilised. And we've got video footage.'

10.00 pm, Monday, July 6, 2029
Oil Platform – South China Sea

Adam was at his accustomed post at the railing, staring out at the dark, churning sea after Tengku Marina went to bed. Without a sound, Muhammad appeared at his side, still sweating in the heat.

'I think you need something,' the young man whispered, his voice urgent.

'What?'

'I have something. You need.' Muhammad's normal brash stance was gone. He fidgeted, looking to the left and right, although only the night watch was on deck.

'I don't think so. You've already sold me enough cigarettes for the month – unless Tengku Marina continues to "borrow" them from me.'

'Not that. It is this.' From under his shirt, where they were tucked into his trousers, Muhammad pulled a wad of papers and handed them to Adam. 'Do not tell anyone I give these to you.'

Adam examined the papers. At first, he saw jumbled lines of text, but they resolved themselves in his mind as soon as he realised what he was looking at. It was the original ship's manifest – detailed information that the obstinate owners refused to release, fearing litigation or fines when it became clear that they had overloaded the coaster.

It was everything Tengku Marina was waiting for all these months, to calibrate the data for the experiments. Adam closed his eyes in relief and made a silent prayer.

'Where did you get this?'

'On the first day. I take the papers from the ship. Later, I drive the crane. Drop the bags.'

'What? It was you? You are the pirate?'

'My crew. You know. There are no fish now. We need money. My boss told me to drive the crane, so he can get the fertiliser from the ship. But. Do not tell about that!'

Adam looked Muhammad's pleading eyes and realised what was at stake. The entire project hinged on the reliability of the data. They had been muddling along for almost a year without it, making tentative estimates and then second-guessing themselves. But if Adam revealed Muhammad as the source, the young man would be arrested and imprisoned.

From earliest childhood, Adam had learned to follow the rules, without exceptions. But in the past year he had also learned how to accept a gift without questioning the source. Adam put his hand on Muhammad's shoulder. The youth was several years shy of Adam's age, but had already survived a lifetime of turmoil.

'I will not tell anyone. Thank you. We need this. And – you have supported our project. I will find a way for you to join us.'

Muhammad bowed in acknowledgement, and slipped away.

TRANSITION

10.00 am, Monday, July 13, 2029
Penang Fairhaven – Bazalgette Lock
Global temperature: 1.7°C above pre-industrial average

In the months since she returned to Penang from California, Grace couldn't shake the persistent feeling that nothing back home was real.

In the bizarre world of Silicon Valley, indignant politics, outrageous housing prices, and tech bros jostled for influence. It was at once infuriating and riveting. Her mind teemed with the life stories of all the people she encountered – biotech entrepreneurs, entertainment mavens, homeless geniuses. She had met academics, financiers, and fishermen; lunatics, criminals, and activists. Millions of dollars and billions of 'eyeballs' were won and lost in days.

A sleepy Malaysian city and its big construction project couldn't compete.

She went to meetings with the Penang Development Authority; she worked with vendors, contractors, and colleagues on the thousand and one details inherent in any giant land reclamation project; but her mind was elsewhere.

Once a month she sat in on the sessions with the other anxiety-ridden men and women of George Town, to share their grief and their fears about their future and the future of the planet. She tried to ignore the subtle shift in their treatment of her, from equal companion to celebrity guest. Her automatic response was to withdraw, just as she always had.

Trip never ceased his hounding: to do more outreach, more social media posts, more appearances, more videos of herself. 'Show off those eyes,' he said, 'and it won't kill you to undo another button on your shirt. If you got it, flaunt it. But keep the weight off. You're getting too fat.'

Meanwhile, everyone still had work to do, normal work, everyday work. In Fairhaven, five months hence, the locks would close. There would be a press conference, a ceremony, and a wide variety of VIP visits. Grace strove to keep her mind on the job at hand.

Four young women from the event management company, and two from the PR agency, followed her to the Bazalgette Lock on the North Dyke, where the ceremony would take place.

Lily, the Fairhaven communications manager, gathered them to listen to Grace's overview. They held their UV-reflective umbrellas overhead. Effective at blocking out the worst of the sun, they were useless against the pervasive humidity.

'Where we're standing right now is the North Dyke,' Grace began. 'To be more specific, we're at Bazalgette Lock, while Eaves Lock is on the South Dyke. They will both be closed this November. The dykes will protect Fairhaven, Georgetown and Butterworth, and the low-lying land, against sea level rise and storm surges. The dykes have been designed to be raised in stages if sea level rise accelerates beyond current models. It will also prevent rainfall flooding events like those of 2017.'

She continued, 'Most of the material to build the dykes has been dredged from the canals inside the bay, and the deepening of the reservoirs. We used very little ocean dredged material. We got the facing rock from four large quarries on the mainland.'

Janine, the Account Director from the events agency, had a tiny electric fan around her neck to provide a tiny breeze. She was taking dozens of photos. 'What will happen when the locks close?'

'We'll flush the bay with fresh water. We'll be keeping the water at a high level, draining it, and then doing the whole thing again, several times. In short order, all of this —' she gestured at the muddy expanse of pilings and barges '– will become dry land.'

On the North Dyke, the new road and railway links were already being built, ready to form part of the trans-regional high-speed rail network, stretching to Singapore, Kuala Lumpur, Penang, Bangkok, and into China. Down in the bay, dozens of pile driver barges continued to put in the foundations for the future buildings. More than a million tonnes of oil palm tree trunks had been pushed into the mud.

'It's an adaptation of the technique used by the original Venetians when they built Venice over a thousand years ago,' Lily explained. 'I think we can include that in the main event press release, by the way, or as an element in the video.'

'Do we need to screen the video at the ceremony?' asked one of the event management team.

Lily turned to Grace. 'I haven't talked to you about the video yet. We're planning to leverage your own footage as part of a montage. I hope that's okay.'

Grace paused, then nodded in agreement. She knew it was just as much about making use of her own face, and her own followers, as it was about the jerky, low-quality footage she'd posted half a year ago, back when the most important thing was for her to stay 'relevant'. Those few months were hazy in her memory, because of her injury, or because so much had happened overall. At that point, she hadn't even started ion-straightening her hair. Still, she acquiesced, with an artificial cheerfulness that she did not feel.

Responding to the events team, Lily said, 'We'll also need two live feeds: one from here, from cameras on the lock itself, and the other lock on the South Dyke.'

'Okay,' agreed Janine, taking notes. 'I'll talk to the production house tomorrow afternoon about that and the video wall. There's no way 300 people can stand on this dyke and all see what's going on. Speaking of which, we'll need to think about transport – I assume 300 is still the target number of invitations?'

Grace did a quick mental calculation: VIPs, guests, internal staff and media would exceed that number. To get them here, they would need coaches. In a few years' time, when the official inauguration took place, it would be different; construction of the city LRT transportation system had already begun, since it was easier to put the big foundations in while the bay was still flooded. In the next six months, the first buildings would rise, creating a new skyline.

Sandra, the leader of the PR agency team, gazed out over the water to the north, and then turned to the south again. 'It's going to be strange, people living in buildings on all this land that used to be water. Is it going to be safe? What if the oceans rise more than that?'

'The dykes have been designed for a three metre sea level rise now, and ten metres in 200 years' time. We're hoping that's enough. The city is also being built to be resilient in the case of a catastrophe.' If the dykes were to fail for an unforeseen reason, the city was designed to be able to function. Power connections and fresh water lines would run across the tops of the buildings instead of underground, boats would always be available on the canals, and all the buildings would have cross connections and pedestrian skywalks.

They stood, imagining a disaster that might never happen.

'That's not what we'll be focusing on during the press conference, I assume,' spoke up Sandra.

Janine glanced down at her notes again. 'What about F&B? Standard drinks or coffee and tea? Champagne for the official toast? I assume we'll need snacks.'

Lily responded. 'No alcohol, please. Sparkling juice should be fine. Can your team also organise security?'

The word 'security' put a brief damper on the conversation, and they paused, remembering Grace's ordeal. With a nod, Janine confirmed that a team would be present.

'Who will be the highest-ranking VIP at the ceremony?' asked Sandra. 'And can we include their name on the media invitation?'

Lily spelled out Zygmunt's full name, stumbling over his surname, Chwialkowski, and confirmed the attendance of Ismail Abbas, the Director of Penang Development Agency. The Governor of Penang State was also likely to attend; Penang itself would increase in size by 25% because of the project.

With laughter, they all agreed that they would rather avoid a visit from the Prime Minister, as it would create a whole new set of complications. Sandra rolled her eyes. 'Oh, yeah, I've been at one of those things before! Just getting the forms of address correct, on the banners and in the opening remarks, was a huge pain in the neck. And the seating arrangements. And the official photos. And the door checks.'

'What about a tent?'

'I think we need one. We can't count on the weather being anything like it was last year at this time; everything's chaotic now. By the way, we'll need to reserve at least 50 seats for media. I've already sent you the branding guidelines, right? Make sure you use the green background version on the press release.'

As they chattered among themselves, Grace once again felt a sense of disconnection. Sparkling juice – invitation cards – press releases – although she knew it was necessary for the project's success, it was distant from the project's real purpose, which was to save lives.

5.00 pm, Wednesday, September 5, 2029
George Town, Penang – Fairhaven Site Office

'Have you ever thought about what comes next?'

Grace, surprised, looked up from the pile of permits. Ivan was standing in the doorway of her office, a cup of coffee in one hand, his phone in the other. He had a pensive expression that she hadn't seen before.

'Like in the next life?'

He gave a wan smile. 'Nothing so metaphysical. I've been thinking about what happens after Fairhaven.'

'There's still a long way to go. The locks don't close until two months from now, and that's when the work really starts.' She looked at the phone in his hand. 'Have you been doom scrolling again?'

'No. The opposite, I guess. I just got a job offer.'

'What! Where?'

'It's in Uzbekistan.'

'Uzbekistan!'

'Yeah.'

'But you'd be miserable there; there's not a wreck dive you could do anywhere within a thousand kilometres. Isn't it the most landlocked country in the world?'

'Not if you count Liechtenstein. But yeah. Not to mention my family would freak out; they already think Malaysia is too far away from Sydney.'

'But it sounds like you're considering it.'

He glanced out toward the corridor, closed the door, and sat in the chair on the other side of her desk. 'The thing is – you've got other things going on with your big Hollywood career. Hans is always on the phone with that Japanese bloke, talking about ice pump corrosion mitigation and God knows what else. Everyone has a side hustle. I might be imagining things, but I feel like Zygmunt has been working on another project, too. And this project in Uzbekistan, it's big. It's important.'

Grace raised a sceptical eyebrow.

'You know earlier this year, while you were away? I went to their demo plant in Norway. I told everyone else I was going to Tuvalu on a dive, so they shouldn't be surprised if I wasn't in touch for the whole week.'

Grace remembered. She had thought it strange at the time; indeed, Tuvalu was the one place in the Pacific that should have been expected to have good internet service, as it was still enjoying the fruits of its .tv domain name.

Ivan continued, 'I've still never been to Tuvalu, although I do want to go on a dive trip there next year, or maybe Kiribati. But not if I take this job. The founders want me on board soon. Their demo site in Norway is already successful and they're about to move to the full scale phase in Uzbekistan.'

'But what is it about?'

'Carbon mineralisation. So you know about the slow carbon cycle, right?'

Grace nodded. Ivan was referring to the process through which CO_2, adsorbed by falling rain, tended to form carbonic acid that would then react with rocks to form stable carbonates. 'Yes. So?'

'The natural process sequesters hundreds of millions of tonnes of CO_2 every year. These guys are doing it through synthetic means. They take the same type of rock, olivine, put it in a reactor at high temperature and pressure, and make stable carbonates. It's the slow carbon cycle, but in a box.'

'But why Uzbekistan?'

'There's enough mined material in Uzbekistan to sequester millions of tonnes of CO_2 every year this way. They recover it from all the old mine tailings onsite. They have these enormous mountains of green gravel as far as the eye can see. That's the olivine.'

Grace saw his enthusiasm, and saw her own vision of the future of Fairhaven unravelling before her.

'It's one of the biggest, most practical routes for removing CO_2 from the atmosphere.'

'You sound as if you're trying to convince me.'

'I might be trying to convince myself.'

Grace wished she could tell him to take the job, to leave, to follow the dream. What they were doing in Fairhaven was important, of course, but it would not solve the underlying problem; they were just protecting a few people from the disaster surrounding them. Was it worth it? Perhaps; many people were not doing that much to prepare, although they knew what was coming. If you can save a village, you're still a hero.

Before allowing Ivan to see her reaction, she asked, 'Who's funding the project?'

'Always right to the point, eh?' he smiled. 'Well, they get what used to be oil investment money. The Norwegian sovereign wealth fund is involved.'

'It sounds amazing. But have a thought about Fairhaven.' They had all worked so hard to get the project going. What would happen without Ivan? Grace already felt guilty enough, taking so much time off for Streamberry. She shouldn't project her own guilt on her colleague, but it didn't prevent his excitement from feeling like a betrayal.

'Not all of us have the great good luck to be kidnapped by pirates, so we must look elsewhere for our fortunes.'

'Technically, it was "wrongful confinement", and they were smugglers, not pirates.'

'Eh. To-may-to, to-mah-to.'

Grace burst out laughing. 'You know, that's the first time I've been able to find the humour in the whole thing? Ever since the barge incident, I feel as if everyone has been tiptoeing around me. And it's with reason: I haven't been able to bring myself to think about it. I got back into a kayak and I've been doing my usual work, hoping it would help, but I still have nightmares where I'm in that damn crate.' She brushed her hair from her face. When it fell forward again, she dug out an elastic band and tied it into a ponytail. It was just long enough.

Ivan surprised her by coming around the desk to give her a hug. 'Don't worry about Fairhaven. It will be alright. People come and go. But yes, I know you need me, too. So I promise I'll think twice before moving to a doubly landlocked country where the most exciting thing to do is to go out and look at big heaps of gravel.'

11.00 am, Tuesday, November 13, 2029
Penang Fairhaven – Bazalgette Lock

The blare of the warning horn was loud, louder than any of the guests were expecting. It was followed by a sharp shout from the lock master, and the shrill clangour of an alarm bell, lasting for several seconds. Then, with a groan, the giant lock gates began their relentless motion.

The seawater, at equilibrium between the bay and the new Fairhaven City, was slowly cleft in two.

On the huge screen inside the tent, hundreds of people watched the live feed of the two locks, one just outside, visible through a large, plastic window, and the other, 17 kilometres to the south. They were transfixed by the enormity of what was happening: where there was sea, there would now be land.

A moment of awed silence, and a second shout by the lock master: then, the entire team broke into ecstatic smiles and filed back into the tent, onto the stage, and a jubilant bagpipe band launched into a rousing march. The guests, who had, a moment before, remained frozen in their seats, now burst into a series of hearty cheers, congratulating each other and shouting at the top of their lungs over the din of the music. On the screen, the smaller team on the South Dyke, engineers and construction workers, were shaking hands and throwing flowers into the air, where they drifted down to the water or back onto the dyke. A team of waiters appeared from the back, bearing trays with enough glasses to serve everyone in the room. Grace spied the vice-governor pouring something into his glass from a small flask in his hip pocket.

Relief. After all the maddening details of the event preparation (without the Prime Minister, who skipped the lock-closing ceremony, but promised to attend the official dedication several years hence), Grace felt nothing more than relief. She longed to be alone, away from the noise, from the people, from the pressure of catering to officials who acted more like spoiled children than leaders. In a moment of vulnerability, she turned to Hans and gave him a fierce hug, on stage, in front of everyone. Then, embarrassed to show any favour, she hugged Zygmunt, and then Ivan. She did not realise that as she embraced each one, she took care not to let her carefully made-up face touch their clothes; it was now second nature.

It was over.

She descended from the stage, sought out Lily, Sandra, and Janine, and congratulated them on a job well done. Janine reminded her to settle the payment within 30 days.

In a few minutes, she would be able to leave, and return to the sanctuary of her room at 8 Gurney Drive.

Then she spied Zygmunt, approaching her through the crowd. He made his way with difficulty, distracted every second step by someone wanting to shake his hand or strike up a conversation. But she saw that he wanted to speak with her, so she waited inside the entrance of the tent, next to the large, standing air conditioners, enjoying the blast of frigid air.

When he reached her at last, he spoke with a surprising hesitance, in what should have been his moment of triumph. 'We're all going to go out and have a drink, just our management team, to celebrate. You'll come, won't you?'

Grace understood she would need to put off her solitude for a little while longer. 'Of course. Where to?'

'I figure we have another half-hour of networking here, and then we can go to Bratpfanne.'

'That sausage place? Is it still open after all these years?'

'I just went last week. They still serve their beer cold.'

'I'll be there.'

2.00 pm, Tuesday, November 13, 2029
Penang Fairhaven – Zur Bratpfanne

They gave a final, 'Hurrah!' as Ivan staggered back to the table with two plastic ice buckets. For his size, he could haul quite a few bottles of beer. Lily was growing maudlin. 'I never could have believed that we would pull this off. You guys are the best. The best!' She threw an arm around Grace, who, amused, offered her a sausage.

Grace noticed that Zygmunt still had a serious expression on his face, despite the general revelry.

'Zygmunt. Something is on your mind, other than the ceremony today.'

He gave a sigh, and replied, 'I knew you'd notice. And, yes, you're right.'

Hans came over with another plate of sausages. Zygmunt was opening a new round of bottles, and motioning everyone to listen.

'Okay. You all know that this is a major milestone we passed today. And I want to congratulate all of you.'

'Give the man another beer!' laughed Ivan.

'Hear, hear!' cried Lily.

'But I also have news for you.'

The mood transformed as they noticed the expression on his face. This was something serious.

Zygmunt took a breath as he idly folded his paper placemat into a complicated origami figure. 'As of the end of this year, I will be retiring from the Fairhaven Development Corporation. Retiring in general. It has been an amazing journey, but I'm 67, and it's time to admit that I'm no longer a young man.'

The table exploded with disbelief, tears, and congratulations. Hans, Grace noticed, wasn't surprised. But before she addressed that particular issue, she asked the obvious. 'So what will you do?'

'I don't want to go back to Poland, although the idea does tempt me. But I also don't want to hang up my hard hat and tend to my garden just yet. I've been talking to an organisation called the Ocean Agency, which asked me to step in as their Executive Director.'

'You, working for a charity? I don't believe it,' cried Grace. 'Ivan will find a significant other before that happens!'

'Hey!' Ivan cried.

'You tell me, then: how long has it been?' she teased.

'Hmph! Not as long as you're implying.'

'I've heard of Ocean Agency,' said Lily. 'They're doing good work. Zygmunt will love it.'

'He'll still have to deal with the fishermen,' Hans pointed out.

Grace shook her head. 'That's one thing that will never change.'

Ivan turned his attention to Zygmunt. 'Where are you going to live?'

'Right here in Penang. I can stay at 8 Gurney Drive, so you won't get rid of me that fast. But I have to slow down. I'm already on medication for high blood pressure, and my doctor warned me that I'm a candidate for a … well, I don't remember what he called it, but the point is that I need to take a step back.'

Grace decided that it was time to ask. 'Have you decided who your successor is going to be?'

Zygmunt nodded. 'I think you've guessed already. Hans, I'd like to offer my official congratulations to you, as the new CEO of Fairhaven Development Corporation.'

The others gaped.

Lily was the first to speak. 'That's … amazing! And I'm so glad. We wouldn't want an outsider coming in to tell us how to do things.'

'Congratulations, Hans.'

'Congrats.'

Ivan raised his bottle, his expression deep in thought. 'A toast to the new CEO!' They clinked.

Hans nodded, his discomfort showing, and tried to smile. 'Thanks, guys. I tried to tell Zygmunt it would never work, but he insisted, and the FDC Board believes him.'

Zygmunt's announcement had changed the tenor of the party, and before long, each of them found a reason to gather their things. As they drifted out, Hans called after them, 'And – my first act as CEO is to tell all of you to take the rest of the afternoon off!'

Ivan gave a short cheer, but Lily shook her head. 'Thanks, but I've got media queries to follow up on. And in the meantime, Hans, please give me your CV so I can write up your appointment release. We'll need to issue that soon.'

Soon, Hans and Grace were alone at the table.

'So. CEO.' Grace shook her head.

'Yeah.'

'Wow!'

Hans shook his head. 'It's been in the works for a while. But Zygmunt didn't want to make the announcement until today.'

'It's amazing. And you deserve it. But it also makes you my boss.'

'Yes. On paper. And thank you.'

'On paper, and in fact.'

'Zygmunt has been our boss for years, and we've never had any issues with the crowd at 8 Gurney Drive,' Hans pointed out.

'This is different.'

'I know.'

They continued to sip at their beers in silence.

When Hans was nearing the end of his bottle, he spoke, refusing to meet Grace's eye. 'I didn't know how to bring it up, but it can't wait any longer. I also think it's time for a change for us.'

'What do you mean?'

'Ever since you came back from America, you've been acting like this is a temporary stop on your road to somewhere else. You're bored – with the job, and with me. It was never your real calling to play nanny to a bunch of bureaucrats. You want to do something on the global stage, and I'm standing in your way.'

The pounding of Grace's heart was so loud that she couldn't believe Hans didn't hear it. It was happening again. Someone she loved was about to abandon her. Every defence she had built up in her youth re-formed itself in an instant. 'So am I being fired from our relationship? Is that your second act as CEO?'

'That's not fair. '

'I quit, then. Sir.'

'Grace, don't be like this.'

'I'll be whoever I want, Hans. The last thing I need is someone else telling me what I should look like, how much I should weigh, and who I should be.'

'I've never told you any of those things! Don't confuse me with Trip. I've been encouraging you every step of the way!'

'So why are you getting rid of me now?'

'I'm not getting rid of you,' he said through gritted teeth. 'I'm trying to set you free. I'm trying to set both of us free.' He stood up, and swigged the rest of the beer.

'What if that's not what I want?'

Hans grabbed a paper napkin from the table and started stuffing it into the mouth of the bottle. 'Have you ever thought about what I might want? Maybe I want someone who is a little more interested in the relationship. Who opens up every once in a while. Who isn't always looking over my shoulder for something bigger and better.'

Grace ignored the dig. 'Be practical. I'm 154cm tall. I'd have to climb onto a chair to look over your shoulder.'

Hans didn't smile. 'There it is again. You'd climb a chair, or you'd find yourself a step ladder. You'd never think of letting me lift you up.'

'I don't need someone to lift me up.'

'You don't need anyone, least of all me. How many times did you ask for my help while you were toughing it out in Silicon Valley? I was here through it all, ready to offer sympathy if nothing else. But you never called.'

'I was working! Anyway, we were in touch.'

'Yeah, we were in touch.' He let out his breath and sat down again, but his tone was bitter. 'But I don't want to settle for a good-looking buddy who sometimes sends me memes via Orac Messenger.'

Hans let his empty bottle fall back into the bucket, where the ice was already melting. It landed with a splash, soaking the cardboard trivet underneath. 'And no, you're not fired from Fairhaven. I can't make you stay, but ....' He stood without finishing the sentence. 'I'll see you later at home. We'll talk more.'

Grace couldn't meet his eyes. 'I guess we can't avoid it.'

Somewhere deep beneath the shock and pain was a tiny crystal of relief. She tried not to let it go as she stared at a torn poster on the wall. It depicted a Bavarian beer maid stepping over an Alpine spring, but its colours, faded in the heat and sun, showed glasses of beer as pale as water. She sat, fixated on the poster, wondering what to do next.

A half-hour passed, and Zygmunt returned, searching for a jacket he'd left on the back of his chair. One look at Grace's face told him everything. 'I was afraid this might happen.'

It was a cruel blow. 'You were afraid? Oh my God, Zygmunt, why didn't you warn me?'

'I can't get involved in whatever's been going on with you two. You know that.'

'And you know there's no way I can stay,' Grace replied. 'What am I supposed to do? Go home, where everyone's going to look at me with big, sad eyes? Work? I'm not going to be able to keep it together long enough to write the damn report on the lock ceremony. Good thing we have the afternoon off,' she concluded bitterly.

'Yeah. Look, I'm the last person who should give out romantic advice. But as far as work is concerned, I have something in mind.'

'Oh?'

'Yes. Something new. It would be more solitary, away from the big group here at Fairhaven. A six-month contract.'

Grace clutched at the idea like a shipwreck survivor grasping a piece of floating debris. 'Let's hear it. As long as it's anywhere on earth other than Fairhaven.'

'Have you ever heard of the Sea Orchards project?'

BASKET

8.00 pm, Friday, January 5, 2030
Natuna Sea – Malaysian waters
Global temperature: 1.6°C above pre-industrial average

At 70 metres long, the supply boat was neither small enough for Grace to pretend she was on a solo ocean adventure, nor big enough to let her forget she was at sea. And instead of the usual, dull but visible red, it was painted a dull green – one of the few of its kind, she heard. Everything about it was rough, industrial, unrefined.

But it was the beginning of something new, far away from Fairhaven. She was exhausted after six strained weeks in her old room at her aunties' place, trying to avoid Hans at work. She was more than ready for a change.

She made a few embarrassing attempts to saunter across the deck as she saw the sailors do with such ease. Frustrated by her failure, she holed up in a corner of the bridge. There, the first mate, a tattooed giant of a man, greeted her with a vigorous, two-hand shake that almost engulfed her forearm.

'Miss Chan! So you're the one who is going to be putting our Sea Orchards project on the map!'

'That's what the Penang Development Authority wants,' she replied.

'My name's Churchill, by the way,' he declared. 'Like the Prime Minister! And I'm Iban. You ever met any Iban before? You've never lived until you've tried *Sarawak Laksa*.'

She smiled and nodded. 'Some Iban bargemen were doing piling work at Fairhaven. Great bunch of guys! I suppose it would be rotten to ask you if you know each other?'

'Ha ha ha!' his laugh boomed out over the noise of the engines. 'It would be. But the thing is, I do have a second cousin who worked there for a while. And that means you and I are already connected! So, what are you going to do at Sea Orchards? Have you ever been on an oil platform before?'

'No, I haven't. From an administration point of view, I'll be acting as the liaison between this project and Fairhaven. In practice, I'm working out how we can use the experience you've already got, at the two platforms that are already established, to expand to more locations. And in particular, we want to work out the details of how to create more new orchards that are independent of existing oil platforms.'

'Good. They've been calculating the rates of marine recovery following the initial nutrification event and subsequent seasonal current reversal, and it's looking promising.' He gave a hearty laugh at her confused reaction. 'Didn't expect a big Iban sailor like me to be involved in the technical details? You forgot, it's Churchill you're talking to! Still, I'll be leaving all the joint venture politics to you. For now, my job is to get you there. Have you met Her Highness yet?'

'You mean Marina Zainal? No. I'm wondering if I should be worried.'

Churchill's reply was a cryptic, 'She'll be onsite tomorrow.'

After dinner, she went back to her berth to record her commentary and edit the video footage she'd taken earlier. Maintaining her Orac video presence was keeping her busier than ever, and her fans were insatiable; a quirk of the algorithm was increasing their numbers every day. One of these days, the Streamberry series would end and she could step off the treadmill of fame. For now, however, there was no escaping it, even in the middle of the Natuna Sea.

5.00 am, Saturday, January 6, 2030
Natuna Sea – 10 kilometres from the Natuna Sea Oil Platform

Very early the next morning, she steeled herself for what Churchill had warned her would be a harrowing transfer to the platform.

Although more than an hour and a half remained before sunrise, the weather forecast was so grim that the captain had decided to move the personnel to the platform as soon as possible. Choppy waves were replacing the smooth sea of the previous evening. An alarming rise at the bow, hovering for a gut-sinking instant, was followed by a crash into the trough, sending a cataract of fish-smelling water across the deck. Within a short time, not a dry set of clothes could be found anywhere on deck.

'It's heavy weather for a basket transfer!' Churchill shouted. 'But you'll be fine! Wait until you see it. It's like riding a balloon to a city on top of the Eiffel Tower, in the middle of an ocean.'

Despite the merciless pitching, Grace was calm. Indeed, she marvelled at the unrelenting power of nature. Unlike birds and animals, which would acknowledge people, and retreat or otherwise bend to human will, the weather ignored the wishes of the ship's passengers:

it blasted, blazed or raged as it chose. Nothing any human could do would stop it.

Out of the whipping rain and howling wind, an artificial glow emerged. Minutes later, as they drew closer, she realised that this was the platform. What was most surprising was how beautiful it was in the predawn darkness. The wind and rain abated for a short time, and the white, yellow, and amber lights of the platform glimmered and sparkled in the agitated waters. It resembled not so much the city that Churchill described, but a multi-storey factory atop four enormous steel pillars. In the floodlight from her ship, she saw a long, tapering crane jutting out at a diagonal from the upper deck of the platform like the neck of a great beast.

Grace could now see the underside of the platform. She and the others waited at the bridge end of the deck. Knee-deep water surged across the wooden planking as the stern dipped into the waves. She was allowed one small kit bag. She'd donned orange safety overalls, life vest, boots, and a hard hat, and prepared to move.

Following an unintelligible exchange of shouts into a radio between an operator on her boat and someone above them on the platform, a conical basket descended from the end of the crane. It was big enough to hold three or four people if they were all standing. The bottom was a disc of bright orange, and the sides a latticework of rigid, blue steel poles and thick, nylon ropes.

'First time? I'll go in with you!' cried a crewman. He hefted her bag onto the floor of the basket, and motioned her to step in, showing her how to embrace the vertical pole and the two ropes parallel to it with both arms. 'Hold on here – hug it like it's your husband, or, better, your boyfriend!' He chuckled at his own joke. He and two of the young Filipino men then did the same, clenching the ropes. 'All set!' he shouted at the man with the radio. 'Let's move!'

As the basket lurched upwards, two long ropes dangling beneath them, Grace felt an unexpected fear in the pit of her stomach. Across the deck, a cheerful, encouraging look from Churchill gave her heart, and she returned a brave smile.

Within moments, they were flying above the water, as the ship diminished below. She saw the distant, orange glow of the rising sun, and the dark clouds still hovering above it. 'Bend your knees!' shouted the deckhand, and a moment later, the basket landed on the platform with a slight bump.

Before she had time to think, a group of the platform crew were swarming around her, unfastening the safety buckles, guiding her onto the deck, and hauling her dripping kit bag towards an open steel door. A violent gust whipped at her hair and clothes.

A middle-aged woman with a no-nonsense attitude emerged from the gloom into the fragile morning light. She held out her hand. 'Marina Zainal. Welcome aboard.'

Grace shook it. 'Grace Chan. I'm happy to meet you, Tengku Marina. I'm looking forward to learning more about everything you've accomplished here.'

They regarded each other as the rain continued to spatter around them, each assessing the other, searching for ways to connect. Tengku Marina broke into a warm smile. 'I'm impressed. It's not every pretty internet influencer who can handle a pre-dawn basket transfer and still come out fighting! Come with me. I'll get you a cup of coffee.'

Grace focused on the smile, and tried to ignore the 'internet influencer' part. 'Coffee sounds great.'

'Good. One thing, first. Hey, Muhammad! Can you get me some bread?'

'Yes, Ma'am!' A scruffy, tanned young man, hovering at the periphery of the group, scampered away for a moment, and returned with a loaf of white, sliced bread in a plastic bag. Grace wondered what this was about.

'Take a look.' Tengku Marina stepped to the very edge of the platform, tearing the bread into pieces as she did so, and motioned for Grace to watch the water below. An ominous bank of clouds was already closing off the narrow ribbon of sunlight from the East, but the wind died down and gave them a moment of quiescence. Marina dropped the pieces of bread over the railing. They fell into the water dozens of metres below, buffeted as they fell by tiny, chaotic squalls. Grace peered down, and was amazed to see a commotion just below the surface. In the water, which was now becoming an intense blue in the insubstantial morning light, tens, hundreds, thousands of fish, large, small, and every size in between, churned to grab the crumbs and each other. Forgetting her relentless heartache in the novelty of the moment, Grace laughed with delight.

'Amazing! I haven't seen anything like that since ... ever.'

Tengku Marina returned her enthusiasm. 'Neither had I, until recently. Not since childhood, anyway. That's a microcosm of what we're doing here. Create a structure, build a habitat, add food, and you have the beginning of an ecosystem.'

'But here, you're doing it bigger.'

'Yes,' Marina continued. 'Much bigger. We cut up old oil platforms into pieces, deploy them into likely areas of the sea bed, and add the right mix of nutrients to jump-start the process. Not this platform; it's our research base. We'll start by dismantling the three unused ZainOil platforms that are within 300 kilometres radius of here.'

'Does it work?'

'It can if you do it right. It's a simple concept, but it needs precise execution, careful monitoring, and a few more rounds of evolution.'

'That's why I'm here: to make it into an efficient, scalable process.'

Marina's expression remained neutral. 'I'm always ready to accept support, no matter where it comes from. Until last year, you know, we were missing a way to calculate all the factors so we could do it without blowing up the local ecosystem. Now, however, thanks in no small part to this fellow,' she gestured towards the scruffy young man, 'it's possible.'

Grace nodded to acknowledge Muhammad, wondering what his role was.

Marina continued, 'If we can scale this, I guarantee that all your out-of-work fishermen from Fairhaven will no longer be out of work. You can tell the Penang Development Authority that those men will be filling up their holds as fast as they can haul in the nets. So let's go get that coffee.'

Grace took one last glance at the busy scene below, and followed Tengku Marina through the steel door.

DISMANTLING

9.00 am, Wednesday, February 6, 2030
Natuna Sea (26 km from the Indonesian border)
Global temperature: 1.6°C above pre-industrial average

A month later, Grace was standing on the deck of a new ROV support vessel as it ploughed through the iron-grey waves. The remains of the second ZainOil platform, partially dismantled over the course of several weeks, retreated into the distance. Despite the slight breeze caused by the ship's movement, she sweated in the blazing heat.

Behind them, a powerful, ocean-going tugboat pulled a lattice of tow ropes and bright yellow floatation bags, revealing the existence of a miniature convoy following the vessel beneath the surface. Elephant-sized chunks of steel had been cut from the ZainOil platform's superstructure with a diamond wire cutter and were now destined for their new home at the deployment site.

Unlike in previous experiments, they would sow the seeds of this Sea Orchard in an open area of the seabed at a 30-metre depth, a day's journey from the deep water oil platform that spawned it.

Churchill's voice crackled as it came over the radio from the bridge, and Grace frowned. 'Why are we still getting so much radio interference?' she muttered to herself. She drew her personal featherweight tablet from an interior pocket and made a brief comment into its tiny microphone. Radio interference: one more problem that she needed to fix.

Churchill repeated, 'Is the site team ready for delivery? Over.'

It would be two hours before they arrived at the new site and set up the materials. In the meantime, she decided to check in with the team who operated the four large drones perched on the helideck at the ship's prow. She clattered down the stairs to the ROV control centre, where Adam Park stood with three drone pilots peering at a large screen. 'Morning, Adam.'

Adam glanced up; when he saw her, he gave a brief nod and returned his attention to the men.

'Have you done what I asked?' Grace pressed.

Adam sighed before responding. 'Yes. We used the long-range drone to get the shots of the 12 floatation bags. We will take underwater footage today when we arrive at the new site.'

'What about the extra shots I requested from the cutting site, back at the ZainOil platform?'

'Not enough flight time for that,' he replied, and turned back to the team.

Grace tried to contain her annoyance. Why couldn't these people understand that she was just trying to help? At Fairhaven, many of the site's greatest efficiencies were achieved thanks to methods and techniques she'd identified and propagated, and she intended to repeat that success at Sea Orchards. However, although her colleagues on the platform were all polite on the surface, she kept finding herself on the wrong side of an invisible barrier. Her simple instructions met with baffling obstinacy; the workers and experts listened to her suggestions and then continued to do things the same way as always.

Even when her personal life was a mess, she had always been able to rely on her own professional competence to get her through difficult times. Now, however, she was not so sure.

Her immediate need was footage. She wanted to see how they could make better use of the diamond wire cutting rig, and then show that improvement in the investor presentation she was planning. She was determined to get this project past its current pilot phase. Without sufficient capital, too many projects with 'great potential' ended up dead in the water, starved for money.

Most important would be the speed of expansion. Tengku Marina's original Sea Orchards trial took place on her family's tiny, unused platform, consisting of two levels and a small indoor area, along with the experimental zone beneath the water's surface. Then, thanks to the combination of a criminal fiasco and its botched recovery, she had established the research headquarters for the programme at a larger platform in the Natuna Sea. But thousands of other platforms remained to be exploited – not only in the waters near Malaysia and Indonesia, but all over the world. And thousands of potential sites, many closer to the shore, were ripe to be seeded.

The most infuriating part was that Marina did nothing more than listen to Grace's reports in silence, without revealing what she was thinking.

Adam studied the recorded footage playing on the screen before him. A dark, angular block resolved itself into a jagged chunk of the old ZainOil platform's knuckle section, where the legs were cross-braced to one another. A tether stretched upwards to a large, yellow floatation bag at the surface, and a tow rope tied it to the next rig section. Alice, the Singaporean technician, had determined that such angular pieces were more effective in hosting marine life, with their greater height and variation.

Grace could think of nothing else to say to the ROV crew, and headed back up the ladder toward the bridge. As she climbed, she heard the faint sound of Churchill's voice upstairs, instructing the helmsman. 'Close, but not too close. We need to slowly sweep the whole length of this string while they are still being towed to the drop off.'

The ropes had already broken three times. Why couldn't this be done better? Grace shook her head and muttered into her feather-weight tablet again.

When they reached the site of the newest Sea Orchard, the deployment team was waiting to meet them in an old anchor handler. The huge supply boat and its giant crane were taking a break from the usual job of shifting oil platform anchors.

As the tugboat and its train of floats drifted to a halt, Churchill eased his support vessel into range. At the same time, Adam piloted the ROV up to the first rig section to be deployed. The handler crew winched the flotation bag onto the long deck, disconnected the towing rope, clipped a subsurface location buoy to the support tether, and gently lowered the rig section to the seabed. A plume of sediment obscured the view as it reached its final resting place. An hour later, nudged with patient care by the anchor team, the next section landed on the seafloor.

Grace nodded with approval as she saw the jagged chunks, each with its attached float bag, settle in the designated location 30 metres below. They waited, ready to host algae and microscopic animals, and, later, higher-order marine life.

The entire process took more than two days. Grace transferred to the anchor handler in a small basket, and started asking questions as soon as she landed. 'How can we do this faster?' Grace asked the deployment team chief. 'The progress here looks promising, but it's too resource-intensive. If I understand the figures, we'll have to get at least 25 more habitats started to create any kind of substantial uptick in the fish population.'

The team chief threw her a sardonic grin. 'Maybe you can just tell me how fast you want it to happen, Miss Grace Chan, and I'll inform the fish to get busy.'

Churchill pulled Grace aside. 'Be careful! Anchor handling men are a different breed. They follow the plan to the exact letter. If you are ever going to sink one of these boats, it'll be on the day you mess up an anchor handling job.'

Grace fumed. Yet again, she was being told that this or that plan could not be touched, let alone improved.

5.00 pm, Friday, February 8, 2030
Oil Platform – Natuna Sea

Back at the main platform, Grace was making another attempt to reason with the lead drone pilot. 'How can we get more footage? Do you need better batteries? Different drones?' She was getting nowhere.

The pilot, his patience exhausted, made an abrupt pivot and strode toward the smoking area at the other end of the platform. Grace stood gaping as he walked away.

Marina surveyed the scene from the highest deck. When the exchange concluded, she returned to her private cabin and told Muhammad to summon Grace to join her.

When the younger woman arrived, Marina poured two cups of black coffee, and then extracted a bottle from the lowest drawer of her steel desk and added a finger of clear liquid into each. She handed one to Grace without a word.

Grace took it with a questioning look.

'We've all been away from home for a long time,' Marina said. 'And things are very different here from everything we're accustomed to. Sometimes we start adopting bad habits.'

'I have, anyway,' said Grace, draining the cup.

Marina grew pensive as she swallowed her own drink. 'I grew up assuming I'd be wearing diamond jewellery by the time I reached the age of 44,' she told Grace, 'and here I am using diamond wire cutters to dismantle oil platforms. There's a lesson to be learned.'

'What kind?' Grace asked.

'For one, whoever you learned to be when you were younger doesn't have to dictate who you are as an adult. And for another, the same tools that brought you success at a certain task are not right for the next one.'

Grace grew nervous, wondering where the lecture was leading.

Marina poured another slug into her own cup, this time not bothering with the coffee, and leaned back in her chair. 'When Zygmunt suggested you come here, I agreed because I thought it would be good to have a fresh pair of eyes, and because he said you were something special. But from what I've seen so far, the only thing you've accomplished is to piss off every person on this platform.'

Grace's heart sank. I'm being sent away, she thought. First Hans, and now this. 'Okay,' she said aloud. 'I guess so.'

'I've also seen that you have a chip on your shoulder as big as that chunk of platform we delivered yesterday: you think you can take a quick look at a situation and come up with a better way to do things based on what you've seen somewhere else. That might work on your land reclamation barges – yes, Zygmunt told me about that – but here, it won't float.'

'So when should I leave?' Grace managed to say, staring into the cup. This time, instead of anger, she felt nothing but shame.

Marina raised an eyebrow. 'If I wanted you to leave, I would tell you to pack your things and we'd put you on the next slow vessel out of here. I'm explaining this to you because I think you're capable of change. But you've got to get rid of the idea that you can either do everything by yourself, or tell other people what to do.'

Confused, Grace asked, 'What other option is there?'

'You need to ask. For help.'

Grace flushed. 'That's not something I'm used to.'

'As Elizabeth keeps telling me, that's your issue, not mine. And not only that: you need to accept help when it shows up, no matter where it comes from.'

Holding out her cup for another pour, Grace forced herself to smile. 'Thank you. I guess I know the first thing I need to ask. It's February now, and I have five months left on my contract. Will you help me figure out how to do my job?'

'With pleasure,' said Marina, and smiled.

8.00 am, Saturday, June 8, 2030
Natuna Sea – Oil Platform

It was the hottest June anyone remembered. Marina, Adam, Alice, Muhammad, and a group of the workers sat at a table in the air-conditioned chill of the platform dining room, indulging in a round of good-natured griping about the heat. They heard the unmistakable sound of helicopter blades outside, and a few minutes later Grace strode in with a broad smile on her face.

'I have an announcement to make.' The group looked up in expectation. 'I got the commitment. Not just one of them; all three oil companies are on board. Everyone, we've got 15 more unused platforms ready to chop to bits!'

Amid the incoherent celebratory cries, Tengku Marina spoke up first. 'Good work!' Her crisp words of praise spoke volumes; everyone knew that commitment from the oil companies would guarantee funding to expand the project. The material from the 15 additional platforms would suffice for several dozen new Sea Orchards stations.

'Thank you. I couldn't have done it without everybody here. And they love the idea of Sea Orchards. They griped about the cost of the job at first, but have agreed to cover this phase if we focus on reducing the costs. One of them is already asking for a write-up about the project to put into their annual report.'

'Here we are celebrating when she's brought us more work to do!' joked an engineer. 'Although I'm not complaining about the money or the job security.'

She laughed and slid onto a bench beside Adam Park. 'How's the new baby doing?'

'He is the most beautiful child in the world!' he replied, beaming, and unrolled a small screen onto the table. 'I just got back yesterday. I also took the helicopter. It is better than the basket. I'll show you some photos of the little one.'

Grace divided her attention between Adam's pictures of a pudgy, bald infant and their colleagues' genial chatter surrounding them. 'Muhammad, I explained your ideas about security personnel shifts to the operations director,' she commented. 'He said whoever came up with the system was a smart man, and was probably going to be *ketua kampung* one day!'

'Did they ask you about the missing reference on page 128?' Alice asked. 'I only noticed it after you left.'

'No,' Grace smiled. 'I'm pretty sure they never got past the executive summary. But thanks again for all the work you did on those methodology reports; I felt prepared to answer anything.' She turned toward the other side of the table. 'Tengku Marina, do you have a minute after we finish breakfast?'

'You can join me up at the rail lookout. Give me about 10 minutes.'

A quarter of an hour later, the two women were at the rail, gazing into the distance. Grace chuckled as she refused Marina's offer of a cigarette for the hundredth time. 'Disgusting things. I should really quit,' Marina muttered into the sticky morning.

'I want to go back to Orchard 3 to see how things are going,' Grace said. 'Alice gave me a new idea I think we can try.'

'Go ahead. Churchill's planning to go out on Tuesday to check on one of the floats, so you can tag along. Alice is telling you her ideas now, eh? Sounds like you've had success beyond your trip to Kuala Lumpur.'

Grace nodded. 'It's an amazing community you've built here. People who know what they're doing, and why they're doing it. It took me some time to understand that. Thank you.'

'I'm glad Zygmunt sent you to us. We'll be sorry to see you go in a few weeks' time. What's your next step?'

'I'll be home for a few weeks, but then I have to do the publicity tour for the show. They're releasing the trailer at the end of this month and it's in my contract.' Grace continued to churn out videos and CNV shorts in the service of her voracious followers, making copious use of the newer AI-guided formats. 'This time next month, I'll be in New York. Or maybe London.'

In silence, they watched a sea turtle as it bobbed to the surface of the waves for a moment. It was hard to imagine the lights and noise of a real city. Grace tugged at the end of her ponytail and plaited it into a short braid that unravelled half a minute later.

A tramp of boots interrupted their reverie. The craggy-faced American anchor handler appeared at their side, fished a cigarette from his pocket, and closed his eyes in satisfaction as he took his first puff. 'Good to see you again, Grace. I've been thinking. If we're going to build that many more stations, we're going to need a faster way to position the pieces on the ocean floor. I've been thinking about it. We'll need an axe and a lot of towline.'

'Sounds fantastic! Tell me about it.'

REPORT

9.00 am, Friday, July 5, 2030
Tokyo, Japan – Rakki Holdings Headquarters
Global temperature: 1.6°C above pre-industrial average

'Ito-san, it is my honour to submit our interim report to you and the rest of the Board.'

The Boardroom at Rakki Holdings was airy for a Tokyo skyscraper. The first time Kenji had entered the room, three years earlier, he paused like a country bumpkin to take in the open windows, the muted lighting, the ceiling fans, and, most of all, the short sleeves and open-necked shirts of the executives. It was an unusual approach in a city where formal suits and strict hierarchies were the norm.

Ito-san explained that the custom was a holdover from the Great East Japan earthquake and tsunami of 2011. That terrible summer, with the shutdown of the Fukushima nuclear reactors, electricity was in short supply in Tokyo. Every company did its part to manage the shortage, by turning off air conditioners and lights. Although it was the summer heat that forced them to adopt fans and short sleeves, it was the positive response from the employees that prompted them to retain the practices.

Over the past three years, however, Kenji became accustomed to the atypical setting, and to the extraordinary idea of himself making a presentation to the Board of Directors of a major industrial company. Now, as he strode toward his usual chair, he could give an easy smile and bow to each of them.

'Ito-san. Morioka-san, it is a pleasure to see you again. Wakayama-san, good morning. Shimizu-san, good morning.' They each returned a pleasant greeting. 'I am happy to let you know that this winter we will be ready to begin Phase 3 of our project.'

How easy it was to say!

Just after the 'successful' launch, 12 drums of different types of food dye froze solid, and every attempt to melt it made a hideous mess.

Then, as the ice season ended, it turned out that they'd calculated the food dye concentrations for freshwater instead of salt. As a result, the resulting colours were deeper, and the ice absorbed more heat than normal – melting and disappearing within days instead of weeks.

Meanwhile, the algorithm was supposed to be running the optimum amount of water through the pumps, to form the maximum amount of ice for the minimum amount of energy input, but an error made a mockery of their plans.

Haruto-san, the procurement manager, found the first boat, but it couldn't operate in Hokkaido's heavy ice. Haruto-san replaced it with an old drift ice tour boat, hauled up for repair, but the mistake cost weeks.

Then, the following year, unseasonal currents, affected by accelerating climate change, sent the ice in the wrong direction, forcing them to shift their base of operations to another part of Hokkaido.

And they lost an entire season thanks to botched contract negotiations with the labour union. The delay meant they could not recruit enough workers to roll out the second phase, which was the transfer of operations to the Arctic. Kenji realised, too late, that he had been focusing so much on the international aspects of the project – getting the permits via Norway, and everything that was going on with Russia, so embroiled in its own civil war that it had no attention to what was happening at its northernmost frontier – that the domestic challenge blindsided him.

After that, in an ominous move, Ito-san hived off the Arctic project as a subsidiary company under Rakki Holdings, and installed Morio-ka-san as the chair. Kenji had to admit that she was a godsend of a leader, an experienced 'fixer' who could face down investors and labour chiefs alike. But in the back of his mind, he knew that the success or failure of this season would mean the success or failure of the project, and of his career.

Still, his failures taught him resilience. And in the torturous process of transferring the scheme from paper to reality, he became surer than ever that it would work. Plus, the need for a stopgap measure in the fight against warming was growing ever more urgent: the new droughts in Mexico had already claimed more than half a million lives, and the wildfires in France, Germany, and Poland were burning unchecked.

The Board members each donned their glasses, and he projected the images of his report onto their Close-Network Visualisation display. The video within the CNV allowed them to experience with vivid intensity the scale of the operation he was now building in Svalbard, Norway. They watched the towering glaciers, heard the crunch of boots on rocks and snow, and the creaks and groans of the vast fields of ice. They saw the hundreds of workers, the fleet of ships, and the vibrant rainbows created by the perpetual spraying.

However, they were, as usual, most interested in the numbers. Hiroto Wakayama, polite on the surface, but steely in his insistence on results, drilled Kenji for more than an hour. He asked about the cash flow requirements for housing workers in Svalbard, the details of the new labour union contract, the cost of leasing the equipment versus total cost of ownership after depreciation, and more. Shimizu-san jumped in from time to time with a request for clarification or additional query.

Kenji had once run into Wakayama-san at the Nozawa Onsen, happy, relaxed, and in a joking mood. Now he wondered if it was the same man.

When the interrogation ended, Shimizu-san asked a final question. 'Has the issue of the food dye been resolved?'

'Thank you very much. Yes, it has. We needed the food dye for the trial periods, to calibrate the system for measuring the flow rate vs temperature vs time passing through the air. For the third phase of the project, the dye will be unnecessary.'

'That is all.'

Kenji remembered a conversation he once had with one of the Russian workers, as they sat out the long night in Abashiri in disbelief, contemplating the disaster of the food dye concentrations. The Russian word for dye, the worker told him, sounded something like '*krasitel*', while the Russian word for 'beauty' sounded something like '*krasny*'. After several vodkas, the worker began to dwell on the similarity, repeating, '*Krasny krasitel! Krasny, krasny krasitel!* Beautiful, beautiful dye!!' as they both giggled, and then guffawed outright, until they were hiccoughing. The Russian showed Kenji a picture of his fiancée back home, and Kenji wished he had a photo of his own to show. He was already feeling a perverse sense of nostalgia for the series of calamities that brought him this far.

Ito-san, who remained quiet during most of the discussion, now spoke. 'Thank you very much for your report, Fujimoto-san. We look forward to the success of the project. Now I have an additional proposal for this group, which I hope you will accept.'

They had all received an individual briefing prior to the meeting, so the proposal was no surprise. Still, it carried greater weight when announced in the room.

'Due to the difficulty and complexity of the third phase,' Ito-san continued, 'I would like to expand the Board of Directors of Rakki Arctic Ventures by one member. As this project is important to our future operations, we will require an independent, outside Director. Therefore, I have asked Mr Hans de Jong, the CEO of Fairhaven Development Corporation Limited, to join the Board of RAV.'

He projected a copy of Hans' background and professional experience onto the other Directors' CNV. They took a few moments to review it again. He then took a formal vote, and closed the meeting. It would be put into action at the RAV Board meeting the following day.

As the Directors left the meeting room to attend to other responsibilities, Kenji could not help but feel defeated. On one hand, he valued the advice his old acquaintance had given him. From the moment he first asked for help, Hans was always there with clear-eyed judgement, and expertise borne of years of experience. Kenji was happy to introduce Hans to Ito-san, and proud to show how he secured outside support through his own network. But it was not the same thing as asking Hans to be his boss.

Hans was Kenji's resource, his relationship, his contact! Ito-san, as the patriarch of dozens of large businesses, was only interested in Hans because he could be useful to the project.

Yet Kenji knew he had Ito-san to thank for everything. Beyond the initial funding, Ito-san had been there for him many times. Ito-san provided a grant to Kenji's university, after which it was much simpler for him to apply for a sabbatical. His leave, planned for eight months, had stretched far longer.

But it was Kenji who found the ice road builder, the ski resort snow cannon driver, the ice sculptor from Sapporo, and the firefighting specialist to handle the water monitors on the boat. It was Kenji who hired an experienced drone pilot, who could manage a large tethered drone for long-duration filming, as well as the two dozen small drones for additional filming and gathering data. And it was he, together with Haruto-san, who built up the project office from nothing, in a dockside building which smelled of fish from its previous life, to the efficient team it was today.

Hans would not be working on the project on a day-to-day basis, since acting as an Independent Director was a part-time role, given his responsibilities at Fairhaven. Kenji would still have the main authority over the project, and the responsibility for making it happen.

Kenji collected himself, and made a silent vow that he would give his attention to the success of the project, and not to his own glorification.

It was the correct thing to do.

LAUNCH

8.00 am, Saturday, June 29, 2030
Penang, Malaysia – 8 Gurney Drive
Global temperature: 1.6°C above pre-industrial average

After months at Sea Orchards, Grace was happy to be home in Penang, when another kind of super-typhoon hit: Streamberry posted the trailer for her new series. It dwarfed all previous tempests.

True, it was 'just' a social media storm. But sometimes, that could wreak as much havoc as rain and wind.

Her plain-spoken introductions, recorded in a small studio during that stressful week in Fremont, were transformed through the film-maker's art into something mysterious, tantalising.

The pure tone of a girl's song, soaring, alone at night, across an empty sea.

A few words in her own voice, but richer, deeper than in real life, pregnant with meaning.

Then, violent scenes of Girl Guides shouting at terrified sailors, passengers struggling aboard lifeboats, the desperate plea in the captain's eye, as the enormous ship groaned towards its destruction.

Her figure, standing upright, in a spotlight. A rapid zoom onto her lips, saying in a deliberate whisper, 'This is us.'

The girl's melody, now in wrenching electric guitar chords, as the details of the series flashed on screen: DEFYING FUTILITY. Starring GRACE CHAN. Produced by ELIOT JOHN MATHER-WINTHROP III. Directed by MAX TAYLOR. Coming July 14th. Only on Streamberry.

The poster featured a simple still of Grace herself on a dark background with her face illuminated. Her eyes looked up at the camera with an insistent, challenging expression.

Its tagline, 'What should have happened then. What might happen next,' became an instant meme.

Within minutes, the notifications began. Like most people, Grace had long ago blocked phone calls from unknown numbers. But she watched, first with interest, then with horror, as the numbers for notifications for new emails, text messages, Orac chats, and comments on her past video posts rocketed to a laughable level.

Still in disbelief, Grace held her phone in front of her as she walked into the living room. Ivan was home; he sat in front of the TV, creating gruesome virtual explosions with cheerful enthusiasm.

She showed him her phone as she pulled back her long, straightened hair into an elegant clip. 'Look at this. This is insane.'

Ivan glanced at her phone for an instant and returned to the game. 'Wow, you have a lot of unread emails! Don't you ever clean up your inbox?'

'I do. Fifteen minutes ago, I had nine unread messages.'

'What, did you get hacked?'

'No. The trailer was just published.'

He paused the game and took her phone in his hand, scrolling through the notifications. 'Holy crap, look at those chat requests! They're going up increments of 100! I've never seen anything like it.'

'I thought I knew what it was like to have my 15 minutes of fame. This is something different.'

'Do we need to get Scott on bodyguard duty again?' Ivan laughed, and then, seeing her terror on her face, asked, 'Should I call Hans?'

It was time to take stock.

She shook her head, desperate to say yes, wanting to ask Hans to come back to her, to take care of it all, but remembering that this was a trap of her own making. 'No. I think this calls for professional help. I do have an agent. Her name's Lucy – Nant found her for me to help me with the original contract, so I wouldn't get exploited like other people do – but I haven't used her for anything else yet.'

'Phew!' Ivan replied, still watching her phone in fascination, as the numbers spiralled ever higher. 'Well, if an agent can help you deal with all of this, I can see why celebrities all thank their agents and call them their best friends. I guess you'll forget about all of us now! That's it – I'm moving to Uzbekistan after all. Jeeves, pack my bags!'

Full of emotion, she replied, 'Ivan, so help me, if I ever become one of those people, please throw me into the ocean and feed me to the sharks.'

He laughed in response. 'Sure! But you know we'll all jump in after you.'

'At least you have a good wetsuit. By the way, why didn't you ever take that job?'

He shrugged. 'When Zygmunt retired, Hans asked me for help. And there's better diving.'

4.00 pm, Thursday, August 29, 2030
New York City – Rockefeller Center

Exhausted, disoriented, afraid, and, most of all, bored out of her mind.

Each stop on the promotion circuit left her in worse shape than the last. The first one was exciting: appearing on a national show, flirting with the other celebrities, meeting the talk show hosts she'd only ever seen on the screen or in VR.

Trip promised her that the publicity tour would last no longer than a few weeks. That was two months ago. He no longer made any pretence of praising or encouraging her; it was crystal clear that Streamberry owned her content, her time, and her future.

Could she survive it all? The noisy rudeness of New Yorkers, the steaming subway grates, and the terrifying, drug-addled men, lying atop them, who felt free to shout racial slurs.

She strained to remind herself that this was in service of a higher cause, to tell stories that would help people survive disasters. But the light of her cause was dimmed by the blazing neon of the city.

8.30 pm, Thursday, March 13, 2031
Penang Fairhaven – Bazalgette Lock

Seven months later, Mother Nature was showing a cruel sense of humour. Just at the moment when the Russian heat wave was driving the news media into a frenzy of climate hysteria, Penang was enjoying a week of gentle breezes, moderate temperatures, and mild sunshine.

It was gorgeous.

As families came out to enjoy the weather, strolling in stately groups, the scene reminded Grace of a 19th-century painting. Many had the feeling that it was a temporary reprieve from impending doom; people were saying it was their final opportunity, a gift to help them preserve a memory of what they would never see again. The forecast for the following week was brutal: a week of 45 degree temperatures and 100 per cent humidity, and the region was preparing for what was now routinely referred to as a hot, 'wet bulb wave'. Yet in another way, the public were inured to casualty projections; they saw numbers in the hundreds and thousands, and flicked to the next story.

'I'd almost forgotten how much I enjoy standing on the lock and looking at the sea, like the old days,' Grace told Zygmunt. Before them, the calm waters of the bay, and behind, the Strait of Malacca itself, shimmered in the sun.

Two teenagers passed, gaped at Grace, tittered for a moment, and moved on.

'You haven't been home much in the past year, so you haven't heard – I've got into the habit of walking up the North Dyke Road at least a couple of times a week, if the weather's not too hot. Which it always is. But you can sometimes get a breeze out here. My doctor told me I need to be more active, get out of the office, go fishing or something.' They stood in companionable silence, shoulder to shoulder, enjoying the feel of the fresh air.

'Why not go and visit one of the Sea Orchards sites? The fish populations are doing well, now, they tell me.'

'So I hear. When was the last time you were there?'

'Last May.' Once the series launched, it became almost impossible for her to live any kind of normal life or do any kind of normal work. A Sea Orchards site was isolated enough that it wasn't a problem. But when she came back to Fairhaven, or went to Kuala Lumpur, it became a serious issue. Both Hans and Marina told her, as kindly as they knew how, that after her stint at Sea Orchards concluded, there would no longer be a place for her at either project. It was just as well. Trip was complaining about her 'little jobs', scoffing at her insistence on maintaining a sense of normalcy.

She shook her head at her naïve assumptions that things would go back to normal after the series launch.

'It's not like you need the money any more,' Zygmunt mused. 'I hear your show is getting renewed.'

'You'd be surprised. Streamberry doesn't pay much. Still, Lucy has been getting me side gigs that do.'

'That Mosa Meat ad...'

'Yeah, that was a lucrative one. Cultivated meat is big now, because it's finally cheaper than raising cattle and its carbon footprint is a fraction of animal protein. All they needed was me. To make it cool.'

'You are that,' Zygmunt admitted.

'But the corporate appearances are the best. They hire me to come and make an inspirational speech to the Acme Corporation's fifth annual widget sales awards or whatever, and each one takes about 20 minutes, but brings in as much as my entire earnings for the first season of the *Futility* show. And the Orac ad revenue from my own videos is still consistent.'

'Are you still having a good time?'

Grace gave him a tight smile. 'I'm living the dream, aren't I?'

'I see.'

'How about you? How's charity life going? Are you enjoying the Ocean Agency?'

'That's something I wanted to ask you about.'

'What do you mean?'

'The work at Ocean Agency is getting more intense, but we need a boost.'

'I see the big negotiator is back on the job.' She smiled.

'We have a budget of 33 million dollars, most of which I've secured by twisting the arms of various state and private investors I've come into contact with over the course of my career. Tengku Marina's family office has been helpful in this respect. And our idea is to establish a mechanism through which we can value, we can quantify, the rights of the ocean itself.'

'Does the ocean have rights?'

'No, and that's the problem. If you take a train from Edinburgh to Amsterdam, travelling on train tracks and through the Chunnel, you buy a ticket that pays for the staff, the fuel, the train, and the maintenance and use of the railway. The railway company pays for the land they use to run their track. And in the past decade, both the railway company and you, the passenger, also pay for the externalities: the carbon you emit, and the so-called ecosystem services that are provided to you by the land, like soil, water, air, and all that.' Zygmunt gestured over the bay. 'But if you return via ferry, over the water, there's no equivalent for the ocean itself.'

'The difference is that most of the ocean is international waters,' Grace said.

'Yes. Meaning that ferries, cargo ships, fishing boats, and everyone else can just use it for free.'

'You want them to pay?'

'Exactly.'

'Why would they do so?' she asked, her interest piqued. 'And in particular, why would they pay Ocean Agency?'

'That's the challenge: it is going to take time to establish ourselves as the legitimate administrator of oceanic affairs. We're set up as a limited company from a legal standpoint because in the future we want to be able to charge for ocean services and make a profit. But for now, we present ourselves as a charity because our current funders are driven by philanthropic considerations. We ask companies that have made net zero commitments to pay for the carbon that the ocean absorbs.

And the funds they provide go to restoration and maintenance of the services that the ocean provides to humankind.'

'Do they?'

'The projects do. Who do you think is paying for the Sea Orchards?'

This time it was Grace's turn to say, 'I see.' Still facing the water, she asked, 'What did you want from me?'

'We want you to be our celebrity ambassador.'

Grace laughed. 'A celebrity ambassador! That's a first. I'm no celebrity.'

Zygmunt laughed out loud. 'If you're not a celebrity, I don't know who is. You have an agent. Not to mention your bodyguard, which, by the way, put Scott into a foul mood for a week when he learned about it, thinking he'd been sidelined. You were in Cannes at the time, so you never knew. My youngest daughter keeps hounding me for your autograph. You were on the front page of *Gazeta Wyborcza* because you'd been photographed coming out of a restaurant with that Greek prince.'

'Constantine? I just met him at that launch event. He's married. And Greece doesn't have a real monarchy any more.' Trip told her to play up the relationship-that-wasn't, and had engineered several 'chance' encounters without her permission to ensure that the gossip about their liaison would stay fresh. For several weeks, half of the comments on her videos were about a man she happened to leave a building with.

'It doesn't matter. My point is that you've got to stop trying to deny what you've become, and use that fame for something worthwhile. Anyway, it's not a full-time job; I'm just asking you every once in a while to leverage your visibility to heighten ours.'

Grace leaned on the railing, trying to estimate how far away the most distant point was. The air was crystal clear; it could be as much as 40 kilometres. Huge ships could be seen travelling down the strait, slower than in previous years. A new wing-in-ground-effect craft was setting off from the Butterworth ferry terminal, on its hourly service to Langkawi. The sun glittered on its surfaces, making it into an enormous blossom that skimmed across the water. The low sunlight illuminated the plume of spray behind the craft.

'Zygmunt, you don't understand. I can't do this. This is not me.'

'Isn't it? Grace, you have an opportunity here, a tool you can use to make a difference to something you care about,' Zygmunt said. 'It's not how you envisioned your life going. But we each have to use the resources that have been allotted to us. Something that you are taking for granted, fame, is rare and precious when it comes to this kind of work. Don't squander it. Embrace it.'

He sauntered off further along the dyke, at an even, practised pace. He had almost reached the junction when he heard her calling out to him.

Only when she cried, 'Fine! I'll do it!' did he turn around, with a satisfied smile.

GLITTER

10.00 pm, Friday, February 27, 2032
New York City – Plaza Hotel
Global temperature: 2.0°C above pre-industrial average

One advantage of becoming a celebrity ambassador was that it gave her something to talk about.

As an engineer, she never lacked intellectual stimulation. Other engineers, sailors, fishermen, and calculating local politicians always had something on their minds. They may have complained, demanded, or accused, but the topics were related to real livelihoods and real things. Are there enough fish? Where does this piling go? When will the locks close? How soon can we start land sales?

But it was different among the species she referred to in private as *homo glitterati*. She was drowning in an endless stream of words, all with little meaning, an exhausting subtext of hierarchies and judgements.

'I heard Jennifer is off the wagon again.'

'Looks like Maryanne has had her eyes done.'

'Where have you been?'

After nearly a year as a celebrity ambassador, therefore, she was happy that her unexpected replies to 'Where have you been?' led, in one conversation out of every ten, to a more substantial exchange.

It was asked of her by a beautiful young man she met for the first time at the launch of Season 2 of *Defying Futility*. Ryan something, or perhaps Bryan?

'Where have I been? Well, last week I was at the opening ceremony of a new biochar project in Indonesia.'

'Whose studio is that with?' he asked.

'Not who; what,' Grace replied. 'Biochar. It's like charcoal. You make it by heating agricultural residues at high temperatures, but limiting the oxygen so it doesn't just burn up.'

The actor nodded his head. 'Pyrolysis.'

Grace was surprised. 'Yes. Do you know something about this?'

'No, but it's the same concept used in chemcycling. You take mixed plastic waste, heat it in the absence of oxygen, and you can get pyrolysis oil that can replace naphtha in the steam cracker. That's the beginning of the chemical industry value chain.'

She smiled. 'How do you do, fellow chemist!'

'Not me!' he laughed, holding up his hands. 'The last chemistry class I took was in high school. But I'm the celebrity ambassador for a plastic recycling project. Tell me more about biochar. Isn't your outreach area related to the ocean?'

'It's all connected,' she began.

They were still talking, two hours later, when the lights went on and the guests drifted out. She imagined the inevitable headlines: 'Ageing *Futility* show host spotted at gala with boy toy Ryan Shaughnessy' and rolled her eyes. Whatever it was, Trip would have something to say about it.

Or was it Bryan?

She took a deep breath and walked out of the ballroom with him. As she stepped into his taxi, the cameras and 3D video devices surrounded them. It was worth it, just to have a real conversation.

3.00 pm, Thursday, April 8, 2032
St.-Malo Cathedral – Bretagne, France

As a self-proclaimed 'citizen of the world', Ryan took it upon himself to provide Grace with a proper European cultural education: cathedrals, museums, and Cognac. She enjoyed it at first; it reminded her that there was more to life than project plans and audience eyeballs.

But in the lonely hours between publicity appearances for Ocean Agency and 'little jaunts' with Ryan, Grace was still writing and recording furiously. On her own Orac video channel, she shared her own stories and those of the people she met. She never lost an opportunity on a talk show or CNV podcast to showcase a clever innovation. It all came back to the ocean: how to protect it, and how to protect people from its rising waters.

She learned what she could about the art of film, and adopted more professional techniques. She upgraded her camera again, and produced interview shorts and documentaries about overlooked climate adaptation projects. People from all over the world, inspired by her show, invited her to visit the projects they'd started.

On the advice of Marina, she founded a small production company, with three employees: Lucy, her former agent, Kayleigh, her publicist, and a young video editor introduced by Nant.

The pieces helped maintain her own prominence and were an excellent means to showcase the growing work of the Ocean Agency. She allowed herself to consider the possibility of full-length feature films. She wouldn't be able to do it alone, however. That kind of thing needed funding, connections, and luck.

Futility was renewed. A headline in *The Oracle* read, 'Hazel-Eyed Beauty Grace Chan Back for Another Season of Disaster Fantasy'.

8.00 am, Sunday, November 14, 2032
Vienna, Austria – Hotel Josefine

'I never thought about my body at all until I started hanging around with *H. Glitterati*. Now, I feel as if people can't talk about anything else.' Grace rolled over in bed, to run her fingers idly down the chiselled torso of the man who lay beside her.

Ryan had been replaced by Teighden, a Mars bro with a neurodirect implant and a budget almost as big as his ego; he was gone long before Season 3 wrapped.

This one, Sean, was at least closer to her age. Grace was risking a reputation as a cradle-robber.

The sheets in his room were 1,000-count Egyptian cotton, or a bio-engineered facsimile thereof; the smart windows were ready to darken at a word from either of the residents; the auto-servers purred in the corners, able to be awakened with the right passcode, in order to deliver Champagne, or strawberries, or whatever else the guests might desire.

'But I suppose I know why,' Grace continued. 'Society itself has become obese, and everyone knows it.' Cars were as large as the people they contained. Humans were being overfed, almost force-fed, in a way that would never be tolerated among farm animals. The soil itself had diabetes: NPK fertiliser, Grace often thought, was nothing more than the high fructose corn syrup of the agricultural world. The plants grew fat, but the soil biome dies. She tossed her head, and her hair, as it floated down toward the pillow, formed a curtain that obscured her expression.

Sean smiled as he laid a dark hand on her waist. 'Good thing I find you sexy for your mind. But it's also a good thing you can tolerate my body. Otherwise, we would have to pay for two hotel rooms.'

'Stop it!' she laughed. 'This is serious. I'm thinking through something.'

'Okay. Let's solve the world's problems. If you were president of the world, what would you change first?'

'Well, first, I wouldn't want global, dictatorial powers. That has never worked out well. But maybe as a democratically elected leader of a single country?'

'Sure. I mean, my fantasies tend to go in a different direction, if you catch my drift, but I'll run with yours.'

She laughed again. 'Okay. I'll start with ideas that would work in Southeast Asia.' She ticked the ideas off on her fingers. 'First, I'd expand the Sea Orchards projects. At this point they're a proven solution and there's enormous scope for development. Second, I'd establish associated biochar projects with every renewable energy project, to use up the waste biomass and take the next step on soil regeneration. Third, better methane collection and management for the effluent from palm oil mills. Fourth, better management systems for fighting peat fires.'

'That's damned specific! Hell, you've got the makings of a political platform, there.'

'The more I look at this stuff, the more I become convinced that politics is the best way to get things done. But no one with any sense would ever run for office. Can you imagine it? All this,' she gestured broadly, 'everything you and I experience every day, the constant exasperation of being under the microscope, plus the pressure of knowing that if your project doesn't work, people may die or society may crumble.'

'I was going to say, "I love it when you talk dirty to me," but you're right. As usual.'

Grace smiled. 'I do have a habit of being too serious.'

'Okay, go on. What else?'

'The list is different for every country. And often, it's not that they're not doing it already, it's that they're not doing it well enough. There are reforestation projects, which are great in theory, because they have such high productivity. But they suffer from low biodiversity, and end up experiencing the same monoculture problems as industrial ag.'

Sean had moved his hand lower, and was stroking the side of her hip. 'If someone were looking at us from another planet,' he mused, 'they would wonder how in the world we had messed things up to this degree. There may already be someone watching, for that matter!'

'Please tell me you're not a UFO lunatic. That's even worse than a Mars bro.'

'I'm alien agnostic: I'll believe in little green men when they show up at my doorstep.'

'In a certain sense, humans are the worst thing that ever happened to this planet. I think of us all, sometimes, as a giant wave. Human society is a pulse of energy passing through time, transmitted by the medium of the earth. A wave passes through a medium, causing a displacement, but the medium itself remains in the same place, returning to equilibrium. That is fine as long as the wave is small and the medium is deep. But when the wave fills the full depth of the medium, like when a wave reaches the shallows near the shoreline, the base of the wave slows, and the wave peaks. And our society is now peaking. When is the wave going to break on the shoreline, smashing itself to pieces?'

Sean's hand had moved again. 'Am I distracting you?'

'No,' she smiled.

'I want to know more about waves. But, excuse me, Madam President,' he smiled, 'a certain Staff Member is asking for attention.'

'I gather it's not intellectual stimulation he wants?'

'Correct! Anyway, we'll get plenty of that at the conference. You said you don't have to be anywhere until your speech this afternoon, and that's not for another six hours. So let's stop thinking about the rest of the world for a little while, and think about ourselves.'

9.00 pm, Sunday, November 14, 2032
Vienna, Austria – Messe Wien Exhibition & Congress Center

That evening, the applause died down long after Grace left the stage, holding yet another potted plant with yet another engraved plaque on the rim. Nobody wanted to hand out a typical lucite trophy these days, not at a conference and award ceremony on environmental activism, so plants were *de rigueur*. In the past two years, Grace had collected a garden's worth of small plants, and had given away every one; it made little sense to fly them home to Penang, and she had no fixed address in Europe or North America. As the people around her offered their congratulations, she peered at the words stamped in metal: 'Global Awareness Ambassador 2032'.

Her publicist had recommended she join a panel at the conference and attend the award ceremony, although no payment was involved. But the prize itself rang hollow.

She wondered what Hans was doing right now. She'd heard something about a new flatmate at 8 Gurney Drive, Cristina, but was that just another engineer?

It was none of her business. It never would have worked.

She'd had an interesting discussion earlier in the day, during the conference part of the event. Her own speech, on the power of public awareness, was followed by a panel including the leaders of several low-lying areas threatened by rising sea levels. The mayor of Mumbai and the mayor of New Orleans argued about the logistics of mass relocation projects to inland areas at higher elevations, but the President of Kiribati shut them down with a single question: 'And which higher elevation do you propose we move to?'

Most of his nation's land was just a few metres above sea level.

They were shepherded to a VIP table for lunch, where a woman from the New Orleans delegation said, 'You made good arguments that public opinion can be swayed using the right methods. But in reality, how many people are in a position to make an effective difference to the climate crisis, and have an impact?'

'Every individual on earth has a part to play.'

'But do they? I compare it to the Drake equation. You know, the one describing how to estimate the possibility of alien contact?'

'Yes. The number of stars in the universe, times the number of inhabited planets, and so forth.'

'Right. And yes, individuals can have an impact, but what we need are people in power and people with know-how. Specialists who can put the projects together that the individuals support. So how many people with relevant expertise are there in the world? Now multiply that by the percentage of those who have family commitments restricting their ability to be involved. Among the academics, what percentage have enough non-teaching hours to work on such projects? Multiply again. Among those in industry, what percentage have an accommodating employer? What percentage of projects are effective? The numbers go down fast.'

The Kiribati politician, President Tabai, nodded. His eyes were troubled. 'From our point of view, the biggest problem is whether they care. Do other beliefs get in the way? Are they interested more in having the right to a certain lifestyle? Or have they given up already? For the citizens of my friends in New Orleans or Mumbai, it is a matter of uprooting their families. For us, this is a matter of life and death. But for many people in the rich world, it is a matter of whether they want to live in a big house versus a giant house, and whether their car can run someone else's car off the road.'

The New Orleans delegate pressed forward. 'That's why my focus is on the people in power, people who can change the rules. We need to require the people who don't care to at least act as if they do.'

'We can't ask them to go back to living like hunter-gatherers,' Grace objected.

'Can't we?' President Tabai mused. 'The age of hunter-gatherers was the last time this planet was in ecological balance. And soon, not as far from now as you think, we're not going to have the choice anymore.'

'There are numerous solutions that we should be investigating. Indigenous peoples have adopted them over the years, but they are ignored by modern society,' pointed out a Mumbai delegate.

'Of course, we need to listen to the people who will be affected,' Grace replied. 'Penang, my hometown, is in the process of addressing that issue with an enormous infrastructure project, Fairhaven. And of course, we should respect the solutions coming from indigenous people. But asking indigenous people to come up with approaches to solve the climate problem in their homelands is like asking the last three mice in the burrow to solve the snake infestation.'

'I hate to admit it,' President Tabai said, 'but what remains of indigenous groups is not what it used to be. We were small to begin with, and we have been bent and broken by modernisation. Solutions that worked in the old days are unlikely to be scalable to the degree we hope.'

'That's why it comes back to public perception,' Grace said. 'If we want big solutions, radical solutions, then we can and should look to indigenous people for inspiration. But we are going to need the power of the public to make it happen. And at the moment, according to what I see on my Orac comments, the public are terrified.'

MANGROVES

6.00 am, Monday, December 20, 2032
Perak State, Malaysia
Global temperature: 2.0°C above pre-industrial average

Grace shuffled on the hard bench, relieved that she was wearing her neoprene leggings. Being a celebrity ambassador could be very uncomfortable. The small shrimp boat was making its way along the canal, but it would be a long trip. She didn't want to find the tops of her thighs burned to an angry fuchsia after a few hours. Since the road had washed away in the last set of floods, however, the long trip up the shallow waterway was the best option.

As the sun rose behind the forest, the little boat's quiet electric motor disturbed a pair of sleepy egrets. Although it was not yet dawn, it was already more than 30 degrees. The 'wet bulb warning' notification appeared on Grace's home screen, as it had every morning for the past nine days.

After a sweaty hour, they reached the abandoned shrimp processing plant, a cube of cinder blocks dripping with vines and moss.

Among the buildings was a viewing platform, built by the long-departed shrimp farmers as a walkie-talkie mast. From the rickety platform, they surveyed the area: as far as she could see, hundreds of hectares of abandoned shrimp ponds stretched into the distance. Grace took out her camera and panned across the scene.

'Welcome to our headquarters!' said Pat, the pilot. He pointed seawards. 'Can you see the mangroves? We started planting them three years ago.'

In the distance, the scraggly legs of the mangroves clutched the green water. 'I think so. How long will it take to get there?'

'Another hour. You can pick up more water here and stretch your legs.' A few minutes later, Pat, Grace, an old shrimp farmer, and an assistant got into another, smaller boat, and set off toward the mangroves, the breeze of the boat's motion offering respite from the heat. Grace knotted the strings on her hat, and settled in for another long ride.

The old farmer explained with hand gestures, and a few words of English, that the sluice gates used to form shrimp ponds in the past were now open to let the sea back in.

Grace knew that it had taken two months to replant the area. As they drew closer to the mangrove area, she noticed that some plants were thriving, but others were sickly. Still, the water was an intense emerald, and the crazy, woody roots of the healthier mangroves sprawled around the edges of the wetland.

'They used to use lots of chemicals in these ponds,' Pat commented. 'The shrimp farmers ended up with disease, pH problems, and antibiotic resistance. Over the years, they were no longer profitable. And then they were abandoned. But we've been able to start harvesting prawns again from the restored mangrove areas.'

They picked their way along the bank. Grace froze at the sound and then the sight of a brilliant blue kingfisher plunging into the water. A moment later, it emerged with a splash, clutching a tiny fish in its long, brown-black beak. She brought out her camera faster this time, and with a single, smooth gesture, she followed the bird as it rose from the water. 'I haven't seen one of those in years.' All four of the visitors watched it disappear into the hazy day, wonder in their eyes.

'It's always good when the top species return,' commented Pat. 'Have you seen enough? We shouldn't stay too long. It's already past eight o'clock.'

The relentless morning sun was blazing by the time they returned. A siren sounded, beginning with a quiet wail, and rising to a deafening scream.

'Is that an air-raid siren?' asked Grace, when it subsided.

'Yes,' answered Pat. 'Army surplus. It sounds when the wet bulb temperature reaches 35. We should get inside.' The siren sounded its second alarm, held for several seconds, and died away.

Grace gasped with relief as they stepped into the cooled building. A worker offered her a large towel.

'Use it to dry off, first, but keep it with you for warmth,' instructed Pat. 'You'll get cold in a moment. We have to keep the temperature low inside for the sake of the incoming workers. Hey, are you filming me again?'

Grace gave an apologetic grin. 'How long do you need to stay inside?

'On a day like this? Until dusk.'

'So how do you get the work done?'

'We work at night,' Pat explained. 'Last month, we put together a new piece of kit: it's an amphibious trolley that carries a big battery, with several tethered drones. We charge the battery with the solar cells during the day. The drones hold floodlights to illuminate the work areas, and the downdraft from the drones helps turn over the still air. I hope it will help.'

Grace looked around at the teams of sweaty men and women pouring into the main building. Some were laughing and chatting, but others looked exhausted. 'Who are your workers?'

'Many are refugees. We have at least 100 at this site. The Ocean Agency has helped sort out their status. I heard there's someone over at Sea Orchards who has good connections in the government.'

Grace smiled to herself. She thought she knew who Pat was talking about. That part wouldn't go in her new Orac post.

'In the afternoons, a lot of them stay here and take remote classes,' he continued. 'We installed the new satellite connection system a few months ago.'

Grace sat on the floor with the workers, wrapping the towel around her shoulders, and thanked an old woman who tottered over to her with a plate of rice and shrimp curry. She turned as a noise came from the door. 'Wait, are those guys going out? In this heat?'

'Yes, the seedlings still need to be covered. It's too hot to work in normal gear, so they wear jackets with extra pockets sewn in, and they fill them all with crushed ice. It gives them about 30 minutes of additional time outside. We've been looking for a more sophisticated solution than the ice jackets, but we haven't found anything better yet. The local university has been sending researchers over to observe.'

'Where are you from? Would you like to tell the world about what you're doing here?' she asked one of the men as he finished his meal. One of them peered at her, and then whispered to another. He whispered back, and then beamed at her. She had been recognised. Soon, the men were jostling to appear in front of her camera.

Their stories all followed a similar trajectory: seasonal flooding in their home villages, minor at first, but increasing in intensity and frequency over the past few years, and accelerating in the final year, until it got to be too much, and they were forced to leave.

Sometimes the moment to flee was signalled by the worries of a relative, or worries for a vulnerable child, or for the family livestock. Sometimes, it was their inability to weather a minor incident such as a rainstorm. In previous years, such a storm would have meant nothing, but after years of living on the edge, it was the last straw. And sometimes, it was a sudden, catastrophic flood or hailstorm that destroyed the last of their crops, killed their cow, or left them without a family.

Most came to the Ocean Agency on the advice of a friend or contact already employed there. While the work could be brutal, they understood the value of sea defences and nature restoration.

'Do you want to go home?' Grace asked.

A man nodded. 'I wish I could go home tomorrow and see my farm again. I wish my wife and my mother could be there, making dinner.'

He spoke in the way a child might ask for an entire box of sweets before bedtime: a fanciful wish, but an impossible one.

Grace didn't stop filming until she had exhausted the storage capacity of her camera.

10.00 am, Monday, February 21, 2033
Penang Fairhaven – Hot Bowl Curry Mee

Three months later, Grace was finishing a helping of curry *mee* with Hans. 'Do you miss the old shop?' she asked him. 'Last December, I was back in Malaysia for a few days to do a little video on a mangrove project, and when I came through Penang I was shocked to see it gone.'

The noisy restaurant had been replaced by a newer, cleaner building, cooled with energy-efficient heat pumps and powered with solar panels. In one way, it was almost like the old days: they sat over steaming bowls, slurping noodles, and laughing at their chilli-induced tears. But everything had changed.

'Sure. But that place would never have survived the 2029 storm, the one that came just after the locks were closed. It would have been much worse than 2017 if not for the Fairhaven project.'

'So I heard.' The difference was that in the 2029 storm, the city at last resisted flooding. The first of the big pumps kept the water level down in the drain interceptor, and the storm helped speed up the flushing of the bay.

Grace looked out over the former bay. Much of it was now covered with robust, floating solar panel structures. While most of the site was still muddy, a surprising number of massive trees, transplanted from other project sites, were planted in biochar. 'I suppose that helped get the final approval to go ahead with the Fairhaven city project?'

Hans nodded, his mouth full of noodles. After he swallowed, he confessed, 'It's real now, in a way I never thought would be possible. But I'm still worried about how high the dykes will need to be if sea level rise continues. Can we even build a ten-metre high dyke?'

The team was almost finished piling the edges of the canals, a job made easier when there was still water in the bay. After floating barges over to the work sites, they hammered in the sheet piles one by one.

'How are the wooden piles working?'

'I took a team to Venice last year. From what I saw there, it's a solid solution. The piles last for centuries, and they're also a form of carbon sequestration. Once an area is enclosed, the dredgers follow, and shift the mud from the canal lanes into the island areas.'

'A technical recon trip to Venice!' Grace hooted. 'And here I thought I was the one living the high life. Didn't they teach you in that ethics briefing about going on luxury junkets?'

'It was necessary!' Hans replied, defensively. 'You'd be surprised how much we learned.'

'I'm just winding you up,' Grace laughed. 'It's a shame you never told me you were in Europe. We could have met up. You know I spent several months in Italy last year filming that documentary for BBC.'

'I saw that one,' Hans nodded. 'It's always so strange when I come across a new documentary, and I do a double-take, because instead of David Attenborough, it's you.'

'Would you have preferred David Attenborough?'

'That would be a bit difficult, wouldn't it?' Hans laughed. 'I heard they're still in a battle with his estate over the rights to his digital image.'

'It was tough in the old days. People signed contracts before they knew what they were getting into. Thank goodness Zygmunt helped with mine.'

'What's your own digital avatar up to these days?' he asked.

'Only what my production company says she is allowed to do, thank you very much!'

'And how's that going?'

'The production company? It's going well,' she replied. 'We have a huge new interactive project in the works, and I'm at the point of signing a financing deal. I just have to work out which bookies to use.'

'Bookies? Since when was that part of making Orac videos?'

'This is a step up from anything we've done before. It's a full-length feature. You know most films have an associated video game, right? For this one, the game will integrate seamlessly into the film itself, so the viewer can play as they're watching. And one of the revenue streams for the project will be the betting that happens on the sidelines, as various professional gamers participate.'

'Are you comfortable running a gambling operation?' he asked.

'The betting happens whether or not we want it to, so I figured it's better if it happens under our roof than somewhere on the dark web. Hence, bookies.'

Hans shook his head in disbelief. 'And all this because you got knocked on the head by a smuggler.'

'What ever happened to that submarine?' Grace asked. 'The one they were trying to steal the gold from. The last time I was here they were still caught up in legal disputes.'

'A government team from KL took over, and decided that it was easier to leave it where it was,' Hans said. 'They took out everything of historical interest. But I'm not sure you heard that the sonar survey found three additional wrecks down at the south end of the bay.'

'Wow!'

'What ever happened to the smugglers?' Hans asked.

Grace took a bite, hoping to avoid answering. Four of the smugglers, already wanted for other crimes in their home countries, were extradited. The one who struck her got a conviction for attempted murder and had 20 more years to serve. The ones who kept her in the crate turned on him, swearing that it was his idea to kill Grace, and that only their intervention prevented him. 'Duct Tape' died in jail from alcohol withdrawal before he went to trial. The youngest one, the one with the pendant, still had five years to serve.

'They're not an issue any more.'

They ate in silence for a few minutes. 'Tell me more about the sonar survey,' Grace asked.

Relieved, Hans explained, 'The sonar can easily reach up to five metres into the flooded mud, sometimes up to 20, and the operators are working on extending the range. They're hoping they'll be able to see sub-metre sized details all the way through the mud body. I'm excited to see what turns up. There's been a lot of traffic through here over the centuries.'

'Ivan must be in his element. What will they do with the wrecks after they get them out of the mud?' she asked.

'The wrecks, and everything else the survey discovers, will go to the Fairhaven City Museum, which has yet to be built. Its founding sponsor, by the way, is the Rakki Charitable Foundation,' Hans smiled. 'A connection I'm proud to have made.'

'Well done! Speaking of which, how is your arctic work going?'

'I still spend most of my time here,' Hans replied. 'But Phase 3 is going well. They've already set up the Svalbard office.'

'Maybe I'll pop by and see how it's going.'

Hans became serious. 'I feel as if I'll see you there more than here.'

'You may not be wrong. So far, I've been able to find excuses to come back here, whether it's for filming, or to show my face at various functions, like I am on this trip. But if all goes well, we're going to go into pre-production for my new feature next month, and I won't even have time to brush my teeth.'

'Where will you be?' he asked.

'We're shooting most of it in Slovakia. There's a high mountain range there, where you can still find a little snow,' she replied.

'Don't ignore Zygmunt. He depends on you, now, more than you realise.'

'I won't. And to be frank, when it comes to fundraising, I'm more useful to him in Europe than I am here. Here, I don't need to convince anybody about the seriousness of the situation, but there, I still do. And Europe is where the money is.' She pushed her chair out abruptly. 'Speaking of money, let's pay. Are you going back to Gurney Drive? I want to see who's around. I haven't talked to Ivan in ages.'

There was an unreadable expression in his eyes. 'Sure. Nobody's forgotten you.'

ORCHARDS

8.00 am Friday, March 4, 2034
Penang Fairhaven – 8 Gurney Drive
Global temperature: 1.8°C above pre-industrial average

A year later, Grace stepped out of the gates of 8 Gurney Drive, hoisted her battered kit bag higher onto her shoulder, and turned left.

Three other passengers waited at the Gurney Corner tram stop. The heat was intense, and she already felt a trickle of sweat at her hairline. Still, it was good to be home after a long year of shooting in Slovakia, fundraising in London, and editing in Finland. One woman waiting at the tram stop nudged the man next to her, who gaped at Grace unabashedly. He began to say something, but was shushed by his partner.

She gave a tight, automatic smile in response, and wondered how long it would take for them to sneak a photo. Yes, she wanted to tell them: celebrities are happy to take public transit, too, as long as it works well. The best society, she'd heard, was not one where the poor drove cars; it was where the rich took trams.

The tram appeared, on time to the minute. She sat near the front on the top deck and marvelled at the progress made in the year she'd been away.

This route passed the restored colonial buildings, which faced the seafront in the past and now ran behind the extended promenade atop the seawall. The tram turned left with a jerk, onto the west end of the north dyke, and passed her old haunt, the Bazalgette pumping station. It faced north across the water towards Butterworth, where the dyke works continued up the coast towards Thailand, protecting the rice fields.

Tourists in the seats behind her were pointing in the other direction, into the 250 square kilometre expanse of Fairhaven itself, where buildings were springing up across the massive construction zone that stretched between the two dykes. As they reached the eastern end of the dyke, she had a long, clear view down the reservoir fading into the haze in the distance.

The tram slowed to a stop. Grace climbed down and picked up a scooter from the rental collection.

The old Butterworth Wharf area might make a suitable location for her next short film, she mused as she puttered along the narrow road. I'll talk to that new assistant producer. She stopped, pulled out her phone, and took a quick photo, uploading it to the Orac database. She gave a wry smile. It probably already knew I was going to do that, she thought.

8.40 am, Friday, March 4, 2034
Butterworth Wharf

At the end of the wharf stood the Sea Orchards shed. Two 70-metre red supply boats, old, tatty, and prickly with antennas jutting up from the bridge, were moored next to the wharf. A spherical metal ball was perched on one next to the main mast, a radome that masked the rotating radar antenna within. A mobile crane and three extra-long articulated trucks waited beside the shed.

An enthusiastic, broad-shouldered man was already waving. 'Miss Chan!'

She parked and locked the scooter, not attempting to hide her delight. 'Churchill! Look at you! I was hoping you'd be taking us around today.'

'I wouldn't miss my favourite troublemaker!' the big Iban man grinned. 'The kit is all loaded,' he said with a broad smile.

'Is that another gold tooth?'

'Yes! Do you like it? I want a part as a pirate in your next movie. What's next? That one about the avalanche in the mountains was good!'

'You know I don't choose the actors myself. But I think you'd have a good shot at it.'

'Eh, you make us all famous, now, just by being here, right? Anyway. How's Hans? Aren't you two back together yet?' he asked, with a wicked grin. 'Or have you found another Hollywood boyfriend?'

Grace shook her head and supplied her standard, cheerful answer: 'If anything changes, you'll be the first to know.' Given the ubiquitous paparazzi-bot drones, she mused, any personal news she had to tell might appear on Orac before she herself was aware of it.

'She's here!' Churchill called toward the boat from the dockside. Grace tossed her kitbag onto the deck, and climbed down the ladder to greet the crew. Having extracted herself from the fierce embrace of another giant Iban crewman, she clambered up the short ladder to the dock.

A taxi pulled up, and a flustered Singaporean woman clambered out, fiddling with something on her eyepiece. From the other side, a rangy, long-haired Australian unfolded himself, plonking his broad-brimmed hat onto his head and hauling a large camera and drone set.

'Welcome to Penang,' Churchill boomed, offering his hand. 'I'm Churchill, your host, captain and minder. We love to see members of the press!'

'Dave here,' drawled the cameraman.

'I'm Ling. Oh! And you're – oh my goodness, you're Grace Chan!' the reporter gushed, as she recognised Grace standing on the deck. Tight-lipped, Grace nodded her head.

Churchill surveyed the pair. 'You both look a bit too pretty for this trip! We've got spare sets of coveralls in the crew bunk room; you can change down there. Sorry about the smell.'

9.00 am Friday, March 4, 2034
Sea Orchards – Station 2

With the craft underway, the two journalists emerged in suitable outfits onto the bridge, where Churchill commanded the wheel. He nodded his approval. 'All settled in? Miss Ling, you might want to roll up the sleeves on your overalls. Sorry we don't have anything smaller.'

Dave stood at the window, relaxed. 'What's the forecast?'

'Not great. There was quite a swell out there yesterday, and it won't have dropped off.'

Dave smiled. 'I can handle rough weather. I used to sail out of Freemantle.'

Grace jammed herself into her accustomed spot in the corner of the bridge. 'You know, I haven't been on one of these ships since I worked on this project when it was still at an early stage, back in 2029. It's quite the homecoming for me.'

'We have one of the last sets of deep water Sea Orchard pillars to install,' Churchill explained.

'Once that's done, the Penang north area Sea Orchard project will be complete. But we'll be cutting across the older orchards today, so you can see how they have come along. How are you doing, Miss Ling?'

'You can call me Ling,' she replied, looking queasy, as the vessel rolled.

'I've got an antihistamine if you want it,' offered Grace. 'They're good for seasickness.'

'Don't worry, I'll be okay after a few minutes – it happens every time. I won't let it interfere with this opportunity. I'm a huge fan, you know!'

After all these years, I'm still not good at this bit, thought Grace to herself. They should be coming to see the project, not coming to see me. The *Futility* show isn't real. This is.

Churchill stepped in. 'Remember, when you are on deck, you need a life jacket on you at all times. These are self-inflating, so they are small and don't get in the way. There is more PPE to wear later on, but I'll explain that when we need it. If you do go over the side, don't worry. The water's warm, and we'll be back to pick you up. There is a tracker on the lifejacket.'

Ling paled.

'We're almost at the first stop,' Churchill continued. The ship slowed, and they could see two of the hands on deck, dropping a yellow cylinder over the side. It was decorated with a painted, toothy grin. 'There goes Bruce. It's a side-scanning sonar autonomous ROV. We use it to gather high-resolution assessments of the fish populations. If you come over to the big screen here, you can see one of our very first

Sea Orchard sites.'

Grace breathed out in amazement as they drew closer. 'I helped set this one up back when I worked here. Look how well-established it is now!'

'If we switch to the cameras,' Churchill added, 'you can see the cloud of small fish that live by each leg. Further out, there are bigger fish, and further out again, the big predators.'

As they spoke, Dave took pictures of the underwater scene and of Grace's delighted reaction. Ling asked, 'And this was all inspired by oil rigs?'

Churchill replied, 'Yes. The fish populations around the old rigs are fantastic, better than these sometimes. It's a real treat to see it. Whale sharks, barracuda, all sorts.'

'What was here before?'

'Very little. The area was heavily trawled. Even the mud worms were struggling.'

Ling turned to Grace, already looking less green. 'How many were you involved with?'

'I was involved in the first dozen stations, before the *Futility* thing took off. But it was nothing like this!'

'We've installed hundreds of these,' Churchill reported with pride. 'Up and down the coast, and around the island.'

'The former island, I think you should say,' pointed out Ling. 'Hasn't the island become a peninsula ever since Fairhaven was established?'

Churchill acknowledged the fact. 'But the whole surrounding area has become a big fishing centre, and it has more than compensated for the loss of the mud flats between the island and the mainland. For the first time in decades, we're seeing young people joining the fishing industry.'

They cruised on. Bruce zig-zagged below them, guided by one of the crew. Clouds of fish filled the screen.

'How is the fishing done?' asked Ling.

Churchill touched the screen, bringing up a multi-coloured diagram. 'We keep a detailed data model of the entire population, gathered by the sonar on the fishing boats and by drones like Bruce. That allows us to manage the "fish cloud". Fishing takes place in specified lanes with small nets or lines. The system allocates a numbered lane to each fishing crew, and it's all monitored by GPS.

'As for feeding – we drop rice straw into buoyant pipes 20 to 50 metres long, like spars. The straw decomposes, and is eaten by the smallest creatures and plants, and this population, at the bottom of the food chain, feeds the bigger fish. Only a small percentage ever gets harvested, and it's managed to ensure the population remains robust.'

Grace added, 'Now that most fishing takes place in these Sea Orchards, the surrounding sea has, in effect, become a huge marine protected area, and life is bouncing back there, too. Plus, it's a massive carbon sink.'

They pondered for a moment, until Ling broke the silence. 'All right, you know I have to ask: who is paying for all of this?'

Grace replied, 'The original seed capital came from a group in Kuala Lumpur, but it has now become a self-funding proposition and a permanent project under the Ocean Agency. Penang State grants the fishing licences, and Sea Orchards gets both fishing revenue and income from selling "blue carbon credits" to companies. The Ocean Agency is involved in most of the projects that are underway around the region, with the support of regional banks.'

'How long is the payback period?'

'Once the pillars settle in? We've calculated the biomass and fish that accumulate in and around them to be 100 tonnes per year per pillar, most of which drifts away into other areas, feeding other sea life. On average, the Sea Orchards take six months of operation to pay back the energy input, and it takes a year for them to mature to that stage. So it's quite an attractive proposition for a funding organisation.'

'And that's where you come in,' Ling beamed. 'By using your prominence on the world stage, you can popularise and raise awareness of the project.'

'Don't forget that I was here from the beginning, before anyone ever heard of *Defying Futility*.'

'I know! That's what makes this such a great story.'

Churchill flipped a switch on the console. 'It'll take a couple of hours for us to reach the work area. You should rest while you can.'

'Yes,' said Ling. 'I think I will.'

'I'll be on the front deck,' Dave grinned, 'taking pictures.'

12.00 pm, Friday, March 4, 2034
Sea Orchards – Station 85

Three hours later, as they arrived at the station, Ling re-emerged from below. The choppy waters were more unforgiving out at sea, but she wore a determined expression. Unexpectedly, Dave began to sing, showing off a clear, powerful baritone. 'When a wind is a calm, and a gale is a breeze, then I've had my share of sailing!'

Churchill guffawed. 'Are you ready for more? Come here and look at how we deploy the largest units.'

The two shuffled to follow him, and looked with curiosity at the long, bulky pillars that stretched far into the gloom below the surface. 'We deployed these yesterday.'

The 50-metre long units, bigger by far than anything Grace had worked on, stood like massive trees in water at least 55 metres deep, supported by a large, red buoy on one end, and a three-tonne concrete weight on the other. Each pillar, weighing more than five tonnes, had been laid on the deck by the crane at the dock.

'A big rope connects the buoy and the weight. But as you can see, the pillars are much thicker than a rope. The pillars are columns made of palm oil tree trunks from the plantations, which have been drilled through the core and threaded onto the rope. Like a massive necklace. Each section of trunk is about two metres long, and strapped with bamboo so that they don't fall apart right away in the water. It takes a couple of years for the wood to decompose or get eaten. By that time a thick layer of marine life has built up in its place. These big pillars look like oil rig legs once they've been in the water a while.

'We've got a crane on the end of the boat, but it's not big enough to lift these huge pillars. So last year, when we moved up to this size, our team developed a new way of deploying them. The crane at the end of the boat pushes the weight off the end of the deck and into the water. This tensions the whole rope, the whole pillar, and once we're in the right place, we cut it free.'

'How do you do that?' asked Dave.

With her keen Hollywood eye, Grace grasped the potential of the scene. 'Dave, now is a good time to deploy your drone. And you'll want to set up one video feed from the corner of the bridge, and another down by the deck crane. They are waterproof, aren't they?'

Churchill reminded them, 'Before we start, you'll need the extra PPE.'

'PPE?' asked Ling.

'Personal protective equipment. And stay behind the yellow line!'

'That includes you, Dave,' chided Grace. 'I know what cameramen and photographers are like. And keep your drone at least 20 metres away.'

Churchill handed them gauntlets, leather aprons, and hard hats with chainsaw visors. They gathered by the bridge at the buoy end of the 12 pillars, to watch as they laid out the weights. They resembled enormous telegraph poles, with awkward kinks at various places along their length.

The crane pushed the first weight over the end. They heard a low creaking tone, and the rope went tight. The whole pillar jerked, then quivered with expectation.

'Right, that's the first reason we wear the PPE. A few logs have split when we've done that, firing splinters all around. Now, let me show you how we plant these pillars. Dave, I think you'll want to get this.'

He handed Grace a large, yellow-handled felling axe. 'Your favourite part.'

Grace took the axe and moved to the end of the pillar. A length of thin orange rope lay tight over the back of a rough, scarred beam. She placed her feet on the gently rolling deck, laid the axe head across the orange rope, took a deep breath, and then, with a long, smooth swing, brought the blade down onto the rope.

A sharp 'pthwang' was followed by a scraping groan as the pillar blasted down the deck like a charging buffalo. With a thunderous roar and a heave of spray, the tail of the pillar gave a massive flick as it went over the edge.

Dave whooped, 'Fantastic, fantastic! Again!'

Ling enthused, 'You could sell tickets to that!'

'Don't worry; we plan to,' Grace replied. 'There are thousands of these still to plant in this area alone, and many millions to do around the world.'

'It's the opposite of cutting a tree down,' said Dave, dancing a little jig under his leather apron. 'It's like planting a giant redwood! Fantastic!'

'We have eleven more. Would you like a go, Ling?'

Eleven massive crashes, roars, and whoops later, the task was finished. The team doffed their PPE and headed back up to the bridge, while the ship, freed of its massive burden, rolled in the heavy swell. Ling forgot her seasickness in the buzz of adrenaline.

'Sorry,' said Churchill, 'she doesn't handle so well with the weight off, a long thin boat like this.'

'Take a look,' Grace pointed to the screen. 'Bruce is showing us the new pillars. In a little while, you'll see these swarming with fish. The existing pillars will need replacing after ten years or so, but we expect these big pillars to last 15.'

Churchill gazed toward the horizon as they ploughed through the waves. 'We're heading back now, but there's one more thing we want you to see. Dave, bring your camera.'

2.00 pm, Friday, March 4, 2034
Sea Orchards – Station 14

Twenty minutes passed as they watched the passing waves together. 'There they are!' cried Grace, at last.

Ling shrieked, 'Dolphins! Look at them. There must be dozens!'

'They live here!' Churchill smiled. 'The dolphins became a permanent feature 12 months after we planted this one. They always come over to say hello. There are three new calves; you might see them if you're lucky.'

'This is beautiful,' said Ling. Grace sensed that the joy of seeing the dolphins and the scale of the entire operation had overwhelmed the reporter's shallow star-blindness.

'Don't let their smiling faces fool you,' warned Churchill with a mischievous grin. 'These are the wolves of the ocean. But we need wolves: remember, apex predators keep the rest of the ecosystem healthy.'

'Wouldn't you love to know what they're saying?' laughed Ling, hearing their squeaks. 'But we probably wouldn't understand it anyway. From a cultural point of view, I mean.'

'The modern world already struggles to understand all kinds of indigenous residents,' Grace replied. 'Communication with any non-human intelligence will take even longer for us to comprehend. They might have more than a few harsh truths for us.'

Churchill touched his Iban tattoo and gave a heavy sigh. 'Come. Let's get back before the weather turns.'

7.00 pm Friday, March 4, 2034
Penang Fairhaven – 8 Gurney Drive

Back at the flat after the long day, Grace pulled off her boots.

Three years earlier, when Zygmunt asked her to come back as an ambassador for the Ocean Agency, Grace agreed more as a favour to an old boss than as a true believer. While she had fond fantasies of art imitating life – imagining one or the other of the more speculative *Futility* episodes turning into a real project – she knew that her function would, at its heart, be that of a celebrity awareness-raiser. And so it had proved: she showed her face at global conferences, gala dinners, media tours, and fundraisers. She did her part, and the Ocean Agency was grateful.

And today's visit, she thought, was supposed to be a pleasant trip down memory lane, for a nice little project that she used to work on.

However, during the long day with the reporters, the situation had changed. Was it the thrill of sinking the pillars, with their tremendous noise and splash? Was it the beauty of the pod of hunting dolphins?

Or was it the reality of her old project, which had consisted of hanging strings from buoys back then, and had now become a wonderland of glorious marine colour at a massive scale?

This is real, Grace thought. This could make a difference.

She wished she could talk to Hans about it. They were no longer a couple, but no one could replace him in her life. The newest 'it boy' of Malibu Beach, while exciting, wasn't what she needed now.

She needed Hans.

She was 36 years old, and she was beginning to think her Auntie Annie was right.

RUPTURE

8.00 pm Friday, March 4, 2034
Penang Fairhaven – Sushi Zanmai Restaurant
Global temperature: 1.8°C above pre-industrial average

Later that evening, however, Grace found herself tongue-tied in front of him. 'It's been too long,' Grace admitted, poking at the flecks of wasabi, trying to distribute them in the soy sauce.

'We used to depend on you showing up at 8 Gurney at least once every few months,' Hans replied. 'I was starting to wonder whether we should rent out your room.'

Grace laughed without mirth. 'I'm not in control of my schedule any longer. Heck, I'm not in control of my life. Who else is in town? I saw evidence of other inhabitants.'

'Zygmunt, on and off, although he's been spending a lot of time at the therapy centre. Hani and Patrick, and Ivan, of course. And we have someone new, Cristina Abidin; you haven't met her yet. And me.'

They ate in silence, wondering whether to acknowledge the invisible barrier that had sprung up between them. Grace toyed with a bit of seaweed and drank what must have been her seventh cup of tea.

'You don't seem hungry. Is our hometown cuisine no competition for your jet-set lifestyle?'

Grace raised her eyebrows. 'Hardly! I can't believe Penang has restaurants like this. I've always been able to get good international fare here, but this is as good as anything I've ever seen in Tokyo. Better. It makes it all the more poignant, since this particular homecoming has been quite different than I thought it was going to be. That's something I wanted to talk to you about.'

'Oh?'

She realised that Hans was, like herself, no longer young. Although he retained his ruddy, boyish looks, and would still tower over her if they were standing, she noticed that tiny, spidery wrinkles had formed at the edges of his eyes. She found them moving: they were ageing together, but apart. 'You know as well as I do that you're the only one I can ask about these things. Nowadays, everyone in my life in show business is fake; everyone wants something, whether it's a job, a recommendation, or affirmation that they are as important as they hope they are. Or money. Lots of people just want money.'

Hans smiled. 'I don't want to become a movie star. Plus, I've saved up a good portion of my salary, so I have no intention of asking you for money.'

'I know. That's what I mean. You're doing something important, something that's saving the people of Penang from the future, preventing a repeat of what happened in 2017, and maybe saving others as well. And until today, I thought I was doing something important, too. Important enough, anyway.'

'You're not?'

'No. I'm a glorified banner ad. Sure, I'm making a pretty good TV series, and I've made films that might give people good ideas. And I can use my own visibility to help create visibility for the Ocean Agency, and the projects it's working on. But what am I doing to create change? In a few years, I'm going to end up as a thrice-divorced has-been that shows up on those AI-generated "Where are they now?" pieces on Orac. Just white text on a blue background.'

'You're not as forgettable as you imagine,' Hans laughed. 'Don't worry about the glurge that's being churned out on Orac. No one knows where half of that stuff comes from, anyway. My personal theory is that it's already learned how to reproduce by itself.'

Grace chuckled. 'I wouldn't be surprised.'

'So what are you thinking for your next steps?'

Grace swallowed another sip of tea before she blurted it out. 'I want to change my life.'

Seeing how serious she was, he answered with care. 'Change your life? How?'

'I've been in the wilderness for too long. I want to move back here full-time. The *Futility* series has almost run its course, or at least my part in it. My latest feature is going to be fine without me. What I want to do is work for the Ocean Agency, full-time. Doing real work, not fluff pieces as an "ambassador". And I need to settle down.'

'What does it mean to you, to settle down?'

'I was hoping you could help me answer that.' She looked at him. 'It's been a long time, Hans,' she repeated.

Hans stood up. He narrowly avoided hitting his head against the dim light fixture that hung over their table. 'Give me a minute, Grace.' He headed towards the men's room, ducking under the low doorway, leaving her to wonder about his sudden departure.

When he returned, he did not speak right away. 'There's something I wanted to talk to you about, too, but I wanted to wait until you were here in person.'

Her face frozen, Grace replied, 'What is it?'

'We got the funding for Phase 4 of the Arctic project.'

'What do you mean? I thought it was already running. You've been back and forth to Japan often enough.'

'Yes, but everything that has happened until now is a miniature version of what this phase is going to be. Ice-making at a massive scale, bigger than any project I've ever worked on. Run out of Svalbard, Norway, up above the Arctic Circle.'

'That's fantastic! Everyone will be so pleased. It's one of the great untouched tasks.'

'It's exciting. But.' Hans examined the ends of his fingers, roughened with long years of hard work.

'But what?'

'They want me to join them full time, in Svalbard, as the director of the programme.'

She reached across the table and held his hands, hanging on longer than she meant to. After a few speechless moments, she forced herself to say, 'You'll be brilliant. You're the perfect man for the job.'

'I'm the only realistic candidate.' The sadness in his eyes gave her an ache in her heart that she had not thought possible.

In a flash of memory, Grace saw the dolphins leaping ahead of the ship's bow, moving for the utter joy of motion. What would happen to them if the Arctic were to continue its catastrophic thaw? What would happen to any of them?

'I need you, Hans, but you're needed there even more. There's no one else in the world. And you know you'll always be welcome back here in Penang, whenever it gets too cold up there. After all, I'll be spending more time here once I join the Ocean Agency full time.'

Hans looked at her with gratitude. 'Oh, Grace. I wish you could come with me. I've never stopped regretting the day you got on that plane to America, and what I said to you on the day we closed the locks.'

'I know. But it's too late.'

Hans paid his half of the bill in silence, while Grace asked the waiter for a flask of sake as a nightcap. 'You go on home,' she said. 'I'll see you later.'

Hans nodded, and headed toward the lift.

FUNDING

11.00 am, Thursday, October 12, 2034
Penang Fairhaven – Ocean Agency headquarters
Global temperature: 1.8°C above pre-industrial average

It was not yet lunchtime, and Grace was exhausted.

Venture capitalists, grant providers, governments, philanthropic foundations, and billionaires, she discovered, had one thing in common: an insatiable thirst for unnecessary documentation.

It was infuriating, in more ways than one.

'Zygmunt, I don't know how you've managed to do this for five years. These people are driving me crazy!' Grace complained, barging into his office.

He did not register any surprise at her sudden entry, and nodded. 'I thought I was going to be able to relax. But it's a much more difficult job.'

'I guess "retirement" in your case means working harder for less money.'

He shrugged. 'For that matter, I thought you left the glamorous life, but, so I hear, you're still going to the Oraculus Festival.'

'I have to; it's the Season 4 premiere. Don't worry; I spend most of my time here, filling out application forms.'

'So, what should we be doing?'

She rolled her eyes. 'That's the problem. I don't know.'

'The thing with finding resources and making deals is that solutions can come from unexpected sources. You have to keep maintaining all of those contacts you've made throughout your career and building new ones. Sooner or later, something comes up, when you least expect it. Have the World Economic Forum people come back to you, yet?'

'Yes. That, at least, is good news. They are on board to have a speaker; officially, they asked for you, but unofficially, they want me.'

'Good. Maybe you can make your point there.'

6.00 pm, Friday, January 26, 2035
Davos, Switzerland – Annual Meeting of the World Economic Forum

The banal conference venues contrasted with the majesty of the Swiss alps. Grace kept finding excuses to slip outside for a moment, as cold as it was, just to look. As she shivered, she could feel her eyes adjusting to the enormous disparity between her own position in the valley and the faraway, gleaming white peaks.

Snow still covered the peaks, at least in winter. For now.

Her presentation in the morning was well received. But she knew that the official speeches at Davos were not where the action happened. Instead, dozens of unofficial gatherings were the venues where real deals were done: over coffee, outside meeting halls, along the icy walkways, or in hotel suites.

She was on the way to one such session now, slipping over the snowy paths. Pre-dinner cocktails with a group of ocean specialists.

When she arrived, she saw that the proceedings were more formal than she was led to believe. She was grateful to her stylist, who had helped her choose the right outfit and accessories for the evening. As she entered the ground-floor atrium, she took a glass from the tray that was offered. It wouldn't do to have more than one drink, but she had come a long way from the girl who worried about losing her concentration after a single Prosecco. The only thing that would draw her away from the discussion was the arresting view of the forbidding mountains.

An older man with a German accent, whom she had seen at her earlier session, accosted her. 'You spoke in a sensible way this morning.'

'Thank you. That's our focus: proven, scalable solutions that have a measurable impact.'

'But why don't you smile a bit more? Come, the situation can't be that serious!'

'I assure you, it is: the economic value of ocean services to the OECD nations alone is —'

'You speak almost like a businessperson, if I can say so!' he interrupted, grinning.

'I am an engineer by training, who recently found myself in the public sector. And there is one thing I've learned: that anyone who believes that business is the one true path to solving the climate crisis still has a great deal to learn.'

'You don't think business has a role to play?'

'Oh, don't get me wrong. It does. We need a correct valuation of the role of our natural resources, and ensure that the world of business can incorporate that cost, in order to have any chance of getting through this.'

'Yes. Fascinating. Well, I need to ...' he drifted away, to pick up an hors d'oeuvre. A moment later, he was on the other side of the room, speaking with two other men of the same age, height, and complexion. She thought of joining them, but realised that even in heels, she would find them literally speaking over her head.

'Old Olaf is at it again, then?' a white-haired, elegant woman chuckled, taking Grace by surprise as she appeared from behind. 'He tends to do that. He gives these back-handed compliments, and then gets offended when you don't fawn all over him.'

'Wait, was that ...?'

'Mm-hm.' The older woman's eyes crinkled. 'And while you didn't recognise him, of course he knows who you are, my dear. As do I. My name is Cassandra, by the way.'

'Thank you. I'm very pleased to meet you.'

'What do you think of Davos, so far?'

'It feels like all the other celebrity events I've attended. Full of subtext and posturing. Less plastic surgery.'

Cassandra laughed. 'You don't mince words! But I admit I also have found this evening lacking in substance. Perhaps you can at least entertain us? I understand you're a storyteller. Tell me one.'

I'll need to sing for my supper after all, Grace thought. Fine. 'What about? When I used to tell stories to my young cousins, I could weave a tale from any prompt they gave me.'

'An animal story, then.'

'Gather round, children. Once upon a time ...' she stopped, and glanced down at her depleted drink. 'Do you really want to hear? My stories are all about disasters.'

'I do. I enjoyed your first season in particular, with the episode about the chickens.' She motioned for the waiter to fill Grace's glass.

'All right. Once upon a time, there was a farm, with every kind of animal you can imagine. Feathered dragons, pearl white unicorns, a hippogriff, and, of course, a few dull brown cows. There were so many wonderful animals that the farmers couldn't decide which one was the best. So they decided to have a beauty pageant.'

A young man in an expensive suit paused behind Cassandra, curious. Ignoring him, Grace continued. 'The farmers called out, "We have selected the hippogriff!" and offered it all of their wisdom, their guidance, and, most of all, lifelong access to the feed trough. The other animals, disappointed, went back to their stalls or their pens. The unicorn, alas, perished from neglect, and nobody ever spoke of it again.'

Several people were gathering near them at the hors d'oeuvres table, to find out what was going on. 'In the meantime,' Grace said, 'the dragon produced gorgeous feathers, which the farmers could put in their caps. But what about the cows? The farmers decided the cows might also be useful, but if they were to be fed like the other, more beautiful creatures, they would need to prove themselves.

'On the first day, they told the cows to moo for them. Each of the cows did so, except for the last one, which was so faint with hunger that it died before it could make a sound.

'On the second day, they told the cows to do a dance. Each of the cows did so, except for one, which had no talent in dancing; without feed, it died as well.

'On the third day, they measured the cows' milk output. The littlest cow whispered, "I am sorry I am so thin, as I have not been fed for so very long." It, too, did not survive.

'On the fourth day, the farmers explained to the cows that they should be more like the hippogriff. They showed the cows beautiful pictures of the hippogriff. "When you look more like this, when your milk output is each five litres more than it is now, then we will feed you." But one of the cows, tears streaming down its face, died before it could ask how.

'On the fifth day, the farmers declared that there would be a test of the technical validity of the cows' proposed milk solutions. However, the cows, weary with hunger, were in no shape to demonstrate their plans. One of them, who muttered a complaint, asking why similar requirements were never demanded of the hippogriff, was shown to the gate of the farm without ceremony, and was never heard from again.

'On the sixth day, the farmers instructed the cows to fill in a comprehensive online form. "Never mind the glitches; and yes, I know the form doesn't save correctly. By the way, a minimum of 20,000 words will be required." One exhausted cow expired that night, as it perched above its keyboard.

'And on the seventh day, the farmer who was responsible for keeping the hippogriff and the feathered dragon came out of the barn, a terrible sadness in his eyes. "Both the hippogriff and the feathered dragon are dead. No matter how much we fed them, they could not stand on their own feet. They consumed more than they were worth. But never mind; we still have the cows."'

As she spoke, Grace could not help but notice the familiar expressions on the faces of the small crowd around her. They are waiting for me to tell them the happy ending to this story, she realised with wonder. They think I can fix it.

'So how does your story end?' asked Cassandra.

'This story? Not well. The farmers went to the cow pen, and said, "Now that you have been trained, assessed, and measured, it's time for you to give milk. We are now at the final phase of our program, where we will open the feed troughs to the cows." But of course you know what happened: no cows remained. And the farmers were angry, and shouted, "How ungrateful these cows were! After all we've done for them!" And then the farmers themselves starved, for they had no milk to drink, and no cheese to eat.'

'Bravo,' Cassandra said, with a wry smile. The crowd around them murmured. Was it appreciation or annoyance? 'Tell us, then: what should the farmers have done? How should the story have ended?'

'They should have fed their cows from the beginning, of course,' Grace replied. 'Remembering, of course, that humans are not cows; we are more delicate. It is not only through lack of feed that we become disheartened. Lack of interest in our solutions can be enough.'

Cassandra gave her a keen look. 'I will be interested to learn more about what solutions you have in mind. Are you still here tomorrow morning? You should come by our suite.' She gave a delicate touch to her eyepiece and shared her details into Grace's contact file. Grace's eyes grew wider, as she recognised Cassandra's family name.

'Yes. Let's talk. There's a mangrove terracing project I'd like to tell you about. By the way, I have an odd question – by any chance, do you happen to know Tengku Marina Zainal?'

'Marina? Of course! What a coincidence! Her first cousin went to business school with my brother-in-law.'

Grace nodded, 'Somehow I thought so. I look forward to seeing you tomorrow morning. Even if it's only a cow speaking up, the farmers should listen.'

THE FLIXBOROUGH LEGACY: A STORY BY GRACE CHAN

On the first of June, 1974, disaster struck the town of Flixborough, in north Lincolnshire, England, when a chemical plant exploded, killing or injuring more than half of the people on site. According to campaigners at the time, 'the shock waves rattled the confidence of every chemical engineer in the country.' A simple case of negligence. But what could have gone differently? And how would that have affected our world today? In that year, the global average temperature was 0.3 °C above pre-industrial levels.

This is us. Individual decisions never occur in a vacuum – and neither do their far-reaching consequences.

***

'Auntie Nell! It's me, your long-lost nephew, come to stay.' Jimmy stood at the worn, wooden door, uncertain about whether to enter, as the rain spit and drizzled outside.

'Come in, come in. Get out of the wet! Oh, and look at you! You're already a man grown! I remember when you were ....' She made a vague gesture, not much above her waist. 'Set your wellies over here.'

Jimmy laughed as he doffed his mackintosh and struggled out of the big boots. 'I'm already 35, Auntie Nell! And who's this?' He leaned down to scratch the cat's head, found a peg inside the closet door for his coat, and lugged his overstuffed duffel bag into the warm kitchen. There, he breathed in a delicious mixture of sage, fennel, and sizzling fat. Sausages. On the small television in the corner, Keegan's second goal against Newcastle in the Wembley final was being shown for the hundredth time. The crowd roared.

'The cat? That's Felix, there. Now, I've put you in the box room. The bed's a bit small but you'll be all right. It's upstairs to the left.'

'I've been at too many boarding houses to complain, Nell. But I don't suppose I could convince you to make a toad-in-the-hole for me some evening? I've not been home to have one from my Mum, not in an age.'

'That's what we're having for tea tonight.' She switched on the oven light and leaned down to peer inside. 'It's almost ready. You've arrived not a moment too soon. Come, come, come. Now tell me again, what is it you're doing here in Flixborough? The trawlerman's life in Grimsby isn't for you, then? Not that I'm not glad to have you. It gets lonely here.'

Jimmy grew pensive. 'The fish stocks aren't what they used to be, Nell. To tell you the truth, I'm the last of the men there to throw it all in.'

She nodded as she brought out two old plates and various mismatched cutlery. 'So I've heard. It's just as well, Jimmy. That's no kind of life. A dangerous job, and a tough one. I've been wanting to know when you'll settle down. Is that why you're back?'

He laughed. 'There's a girl out there for me somewhere, Nell, but I haven't found her yet. For now, I've got a job. It's at a scaffolding company, handling a contract at the Nypro plant.'

'Oh, that place. I can see it from the bottom of my garden. The noise of the factory doesn't bother me – my hearing isn't quite what it used to be – but it smells something powerful.'

'Hence the scaffolds: they're doing repairs,' he replied.

'Don't you miss it, though? The sea. Your uncle Mark, he spent his whole life as a trawlerman. You always took after him, you know. His mother told me that when he was a little boy, he used to dress up in his father's breton cap and yellow overalls, and tell the world he was going out to take in a haul of fish. And I'll be blessed if he didn't do just that.'

'The new job pays well enough to make me forget all about the sea. I'm the charge hand, the head of our team here.'

'Well, now, don't be getting above yourself. You may be the boss of your scaffolding crew, but while you're here, I've got plenty of jobs for you. There's the greenhouse that your Uncle Mark put up. It's nothing but a bunch of big tatty holes now and my tomatoes hardly came in at all this year.'

The box bed was more comfortable than he had expected, and Jimmy adjusted to the new routine. The greenhouse was another story, however. His uncle had extended it several years back, with two ill-fitting parts at different levels, so that Nell could grow onions in a raised bed, while the lower bed was tall enough for tomatoes. But not all was right.

'It's the wind that breaks the connection between the two parts of the greenhouse,' Jimmy told his aunt. 'The air pressure on each section is different. They move separately, and the plastic tears. I've tried all types of reinforcement, and it rips every time. The two pieces need to be separate. It's broken three times already. But it's more than that.'

She gave him a keen look. 'Something more than your uncle's old greenhouse?'

'Right you are, Nell. It gives me a bit of a worry about a piece of work we put together a few weeks ago, down at the factory. They've taken out one of the big, corroded reactors. And they needed a bypass connection in the meantime. But the reactors are at different heights, so there is a dog-legged piece of pipe connecting one vessel to another. They used these big accordions – bellows, they call them – to connect the pipe to the reactors, to allow it to move a bit. At its heart, it's not so different from your greenhouse here.'

Nell sat back in her flowered chair, with its chintz almost worn through. 'Are you saying the pipe down at the factory will break down, just like my greenhouse?'

'I don't know. But it might.'

'Will you speak up, then?'

'It's not my place to tell them how to run a factory. I'm not one to go with my boots on when they're in there with their tweed jackets, leather elbows and pipes.'

As she always did when she was pondering a problem, she shuffled to the sink, filled the kettle, and put it on the hob. 'Come have a cup of tea, Jimmy, and we'll think it through.'

They talked long into the night. It was a funny thing about his aunt Nell. She never gave him advice, outright, except when it came to finding a nice girl, or looking after his good-for-nothing younger brother. But after they'd had a good chat, things always became clearer.

The next evening, he was shaking out his umbrella as he entered his aunt's house. 'I spoke to the boss today,' he told Nell. 'It wasn't near as bad as I thought.'

'Then there was no danger, after all?'

'Oh, there was danger, all right! They shut down the whole operation within the half hour. But nobody blamed me. No, when I took the boss down to the scaffold, and showed him the rub marks on the planks, where the ties were shifting, he got a right worried look on his face. I led him past the bellows, and he went grey as ash, and shook my hand, and ran back to the office as fast as I've ever seen a man run who was wearing a tweed jacket.'

She nodded. 'Just as I said. He saw it for himself, and that was all that was needed.'

'There's going to be a hearing.'

Another nod. 'You'll need to polish your shoes, then.'

The day of the hearing came, and it was like nothing Jimmy expected. The men who questioned him had no nonsense about them, and they kept at it for more than an hour. But he found their discussion confusing. Although something had gone wrong, they did not find fault with any individual. Instead, they spoke of things like 'process', and 'systemic risk', and 'built-in safety features' and 'culture of transparency'. But it was clear that his alert to the foreman had profound implications. A huge, flammable vapour cloud would inevitably have found a spark to ignite it, ending in a vast explosion. The expert showed a map, with circles on it drawn in red pencil. Thousands of buildings crowded inside the outer circle. And inside the innermost circle, covered in the darkest red, Jimmy recognised Nell's house and garden.

A grave man with thick, horn-rimmed glasses spoke. 'There's more to operating a safe plant than a regular equipment inspection and a safety test. We need men to keep their eyes open, and to have the bravery to speak up, including to their superiors. Gentlemen of the committee, and lady, I should say, I would like the Factory Inspectorate to investigate this incident as if it had indeed all gone wrong. As if we were all sat here today mourning the loss of hundreds. I urge you to take this opportunity, to make the name Flixborough famous – because it is here that a new industry-wide improvement must begin, one that prevents future calamities, as this one has been averted.'

A fair-haired young man in the gallery, his eyes wide set, with the hint of a tilt to them, listened to the expert's speech. Alexei's teachers kept suggesting to him that whenever he found out about any public speech, lecture, hearing, or event going on, that he make a point of attending and listening to it. 'As an English learner, you'll find there's no such thing as too much exposure to the language.'

It was different advice from that of his English teachers back home in Moscow. The teachers in the UK were kind, but odd; and he heard and read little of the propaganda that he had been led to expect by his Soviet minders.

Indeed, what he wanted most of all from his study trip was to find an English girl, since everyone said they were 'liberated'. Alas, precious few were to be seen at this obscure hearing about a chemical plant – an ex-fisherman, a factory boss, and several stuffy academics. A week prior, he had seen a promising young woman with long, ironed hair at the lecture on rose cultivation over at the crumbling manor house, Bailey Hall, but nothing came of it. He haunted flower shows for the next month, hoping to catch another glimpse of her; instead, he was drawn into an extended, one-sided lecture on hybrid grafting by a befuddled, white-haired man convinced he was from Scotland.

All in all, the cultural exchange had made a big improvement to his English, but to his social life not at all.

Months later, after his return to the Soviet Union, Alexei found it difficult to secure a position that made use of his English skills. He and the other 150-odd student cultural ambassadors had been selected for the exchange because of their political virtue. But upon the end of the program, their very contact with Western, capitalist ideas rendered them suspect.

He cast about in several academic and administrative roles, always trusting the Party to find what was best for him. In Minsk, he met Alina, a girl from a good family, whose father had fought against the Nazis. She was an electrical engineer.

More than a decade after he completed his degree, he and Alina got a placement in a backwater power plant in the SSR of Ukraine. There, people spoke a strange kind of Russian, which sounded odd compared to his own, a pure Muscovite variety. They insisted it was a different language, in fact. His role was to translate technical documents, a job he was eminently suited for. He also stayed on hand at the plant, often taking the night shift, to act as an on-call translator whenever someone needed to check the specifications of a piece of imported equipment, or refer to one of the many written scientific papers obtained from Western sources.

Alexei found it difficult to form friendships in his new city, Pripyat. People were narrow-minded, suspicious. But after several months, a few of the longer-term residents opened up.

'I've been here since the early days,' a pale, dumpy man told him over a glass of vodka. 'They were just building it, then. We moved here from Lvov.' He pronounced it L'viv. 'It wasn't much of a place for a family, then. Now, there are all sorts of things available. The amusement park is scheduled to open soon. If you and your wife are having children, to contribute to the glorious future of the eternal October Revolution, there will be plenty for you to do.'

Alexei could not figure out whether the man was mocking the glorious October Revolution. He stayed on the topic of the amusement park. 'I passed by the construction site; there's a Ferris wheel going up.'

'May his most Holy Saint Lenin allow us to live to see the day!' the man commented, this time with a clear undertone of sarcasm. He drank down the rest of his little glass of vodka and ordered another. It was cheap in Pripyat, like most staple goods.

Something in the older man's tone bothered Alexei. 'You sound as if you doubt it will happen.'

'Oh, the Ferris wheel will go up, all right. They said it would be done by May 1986, and here we are, a few days away. But who knows whether we'll still be around to ride on it.'

'Are you feeling ill?' Alexei examined the man. His pasty complexion and fleshy jowls did not speak of robust health.

'I feel fine. And if you'll buy me another vodka, I'll feel better. No, it's the plant. Nothing ever goes wrong there, because in the workers' paradise of the Soviet Union, nothing is allowed ever to go wrong. But I've been working on nuclear plants ever since Obninsk, and I am telling you that one of these days, a little problem, a little overload here, a budget cut there, and we will all —' he made a little exploding motion with his hand. 'Poof. Well. In any case, "Don't be sad, don't be angry, if life deceives you!"'

Alexei knew that the older man was quoting Alexander Pushkin, his own namesake. He countered with a quote of his own. '"Better the illusions that exalt us, than ten thousand truths."'

The man peered at him. 'You think so? A model of Soviet youth. I wish you and your beautiful wife all of life's good fortune.' He swallowed his last drop of vodka, his unsteady feet bringing him out to the cold, rainy April night.

The following week, Alexei arrived at work for the night shift when he heard about another power plant in the region, which had suffered from an unplanned failure. Smug, he recalled the old man's pitiful accusations: the fact that he was hearing about this failure now was proof that the system was working, as there had been no cover-up.

It was an annoyance, however. The failure of the other plant meant that his own plant, #4, would need to keep running until the local population turned off their lights and their electric stoves and the local factories ramped down for the night. They hadn't been able to run the safety test they'd been planning for that day as part of their annual shutdown.

'I don't want to see this test delayed a minute longer,' instructed the square-faced woman who oversaw the day shift. 'It's the third time we've attempted it. If our test isn't successful, our managers will lose their bonuses, and believe me, no one here wants that to happen.'

The group of night shift workers listened stoically to her harangue. Alexei watched the group. He saw concern in the eyes of several. What would this test involve? Most of them were younger, straight out of school. Although he had spent the last several years immersed in technical documentation, he was not up to speed on the practicalities of shutting down and restarting a nuclear reactor.

As the day manager stepped down and handed over a hasty briefing to the night manager, Alexei approached one of the worried operators. 'Comrade. Tell me what you are afraid of.'

'Nothing at all, except looking like a fool.'

'What do you mean?'

'Ask any man or woman here whether they know how to run this test. I know my own section and nothing more. And our night manager has been placed in this godforsaken city, in this godforsaken plant, on this godforsaken night shift, for a very good reason.'

'What reason?'

'Because he doesn't know what the hell he's doing, either.'

Alexei thought back to the hearing in England. 'We need men to keep their eyes open, and to have the bravery to speak up, including to their superiors,' the old capitalist had said.

If the stakes were high at a little chemical plant in England, how much higher would they be when a nuclear reactor was involved? Thanks to his knowledge of English, he had access to certain documents about an incident in Pennsylvania, in the United States. A near miss.

He would not let a similar incident in Chernobyl embarrass the great Soviet Union. He entered the office of the day manager, catching her off guard as she loaded a large bottle of pear brandy into her purse. 'It is a gift of appreciation from the workers!' she explained.

'Comrade!' said Alexei. 'I am sorry to inconvenience you. But I would like to ask you to follow me, and observe for a few minutes. Please.'

Grumbling, she followed him as he led her to the group of night shift workers, who were in a huddle, attempting to understand the instructions for the test. 'I would like to ask you some questions.'

'What is it now, "Professor"?' They teased him because of his foreign experience, but he recognised grudging respect behind it.

'Could I ask you: who here has experience in conducting the test we will attempt tonight?'

The men and women looked at each other, and did not speak.

'Let me ask another way. Is there anyone here who has ever participated in a similar test?'

Again, they remained silent, shuffling their feet. One of them blurted out, 'Seryoshka told us a little about it. But I've never done one.'

Alexei addressed the day manager. 'I am sorry to be the one to show this to you. However, it is clear that we need your help to manage the test.'

She gave an audible, pointed sigh, and walked back to her office, where she placed her purse back on the desk. 'Listen, everyone!' she bellowed from her office door. The day shift workers, who were already at the exits, paused. 'Nobody leave. According to this clown here, we all need to do a double shift, because our comrades on the night shift don't know how to read a sheaf of instructions.' To the instant groans and complaints of the group, she replied, 'We'll get the thing done, and then you can drink yourselves into oblivion tomorrow morning. But in the meantime, let's get to work!'

She turned to Alexei. 'You've put me in an awkward position. I was ready to go home and enjoy a glass of this very nice brandy with my family. But since you've gone and blabbed about this situation to everyone, it means now I'd be the one responsible if the idiot night crew does anything wrong. So you can finish out your shift tonight, but I don't want to see you on these premises again after tomorrow morning. Ever. Is that clear?'

Keeping his face impassive and his back straight, Alexei nodded, and cried out. 'Thank you, Comrade! Long live the glorious October Revolution!'

Would the future be simple obscurity for him, working in a menial job? Or worse – the gulag? He would have to inform Alina about what had happened. As a Soviet citizen, she would agree that what he did was right and necessary.

He hoped it was worth it.

The next morning, a little more than 1,100 kilometres to the west, a young doctoral student in physical chemistry at the Academy of Sciences in Berlin-Adlershof in East Germany woke up to a chilly, beautiful April sunrise. Her husband pulled open the blinds of the tiny window in their little apartment in Mitte. 'Angela, time to get up! Can't you hear the birds singing?'

It was a gorgeous day, and she was in a good mood. Many people had already cleared out before the May 1st holiday, which was just a few days away, and the younger students were already frolicking on the lawn. Her thesis on quantum chemistry was nearing completion. Yes, everything was looking fine. She had received preliminary approval to travel to West Germany to attend a congress, and later to Donetsk for a language course. She hoped to hear about exciting new developments in nuclear power.

An extensive network of nuclear power plants, safely operated, managed by professionals, cheap, clean, and free of smoke and emissions, would be the future of East Germany. Perhaps all of Germany, if it were ever to be united again.

Or all of Europe.

She was certain of it, and nothing short of a catastrophe could convince her otherwise.

Above all, they must move away from their old-fashioned dependence on filthy coal, not to mention the instability of oil from the Middle East. The other viable option, natural gas from Russia, was perhaps a bit cleaner than coal, but could not be called a realistic alternative.

As she entered the main building in the Gendarmenmarkt, a jovial professor greeted her. 'Mrs Merkel! When can we expect to start reading about you in the news? Perhaps with a new plan for the future of our nation?'

She laughed. 'Let's see! I need to defend my dissertation first. But you are right; I have been thinking about something I like to call the *Energiewende*.'

'The energy transition? I'm sure we'll be hearing more about it before long.' He beamed and entered his classroom.

The sky, vivid blue, remained clear all day, without a single cloud to interrupt it.

SVALBARD

9.00 am, Friday, November 16, 2035
Svalbard, Norway – Rakki Arctic Ventures Site HQ
Global temperature: 2.1°C above pre-industrial average

It had been more than a decade since Hans had heard that particular squeak, the one that accompanies each step onto new-fallen snow at temperatures less than ten degrees below. Now, after re-acclimating himself to the feeling of real winter, he came to the conclusion that he loved it.

He breathed in a shade too fast and felt the interior of his nostrils freeze. He wrinkled his nose to crack the little crystals, and sneezed.

'Kenji! Ready to go?' Although the night sky was clear, his voice fell flat, a few metres from where he stood at the edge of the makeshift road. The North Star shone down on them from a vertical position that dizzied him: if he stood there long enough, gazing up and managing not to freeze, he would see the sky spin around it. The Milky Way glowed with improbable brightness.

'Yes, Hans! Everything is prepared.' Kenji, clad in a giant fur hat, emerged from his prefab house, an enthusiastic smile on his face.

As they squeaked across the snow towards their electric snow-mobiles, Hans reflected on the extraordinary speed the project had achieved since he arrived.

They were creating ice almost without stopping, in multiple ways and in multiple locations at the same time. Kenji deserved most of the credit, of course. From an awkward grad student and then a hesitant adjunct professor, he had become a mature, effective project manager. The younger man's appearance reflected the change. His face had filled out, and although still tall and slim, he was no longer a gangling student. He retained his over-long, unruly hairstyle, giving him a deceptive look of boyish caprice, but under the tutorial of Ito-san he also developed an unexpected business savvy.

It helped that the results were starting to show promise. There was a fine line between 'too early to tell' and 'break out the Champagne'. Which side of the line you preferred revealed your tendency towards optimism or pessimism.

The setup came together over the course of a breakneck series of design meetings involving experts from an astounding range of fields. In a few months, the designs became reality.

Hans and Kenji parked their snowmobiles and climbed aboard a small, ice-hardened tug to hitch a ride as it began its regular voyage up and down the first access channel. Several large, fixed circular platforms in high current areas acted as static icebreakers; anchored to the seabed on large suction piles, they were stripped-down versions of the oil platforms designed for the arctic. The ice flowed past the circular hulls, forming a wide, clear channel of open water, along with two prominent ridges of ice. Their tug sailed up and down this channel, spraying water far out onto the open ice beyond the ridges.

As they sheltered inside the tug, lest they, too, become covered with ice, Kenji remarked, 'We've repaired water cannon number three,' and Hans nodded with satisfaction. The water cannons, fixed on the main platform, sprayed as much water as possible through the freezing air of the endless night, in order to thicken the ice.

Zeppelins worked with the platform to spray more water in locations beyond the reach of the water cannons. Hans chuckled to himself, remembering how he contacted a university friend who had moved from Heineken to Anheuser-Busch, and was a regular contractor of advertising blimps. 'I need a zeppelin,' he said. 'Do you know anybody?' The entire project was like that: dredging up old contacts from odd places, whether they were Dutch brewers, Russian nuclear engineers, or Chinese wind turbine designers.

Ito-san and Morioka-san did extraordinary work behind the scenes, clearing the way for the most important breakthrough of the project: access to the electric power from the new Rosatomflot arctic nuclear facility. Indeed, the very existence of the plant, and the speed of its construction, was due to Ito-san. Although the first Rosatomflot installation in Siberia had not been as successful as hoped, he gathered a group of investors to arrange the development of a second offshore facility. To most eyes, the post-war Russian coalition was still fragile. But Ito-san had a knack for predicting who would end up on top, and Hans was willing to trust the old man's instincts.

The platforms thus served a dual role: as recharging stations for the zeppelins and any other craft operating in the area, as well as safe refuges and science centres. The onsite wind turbines provided enough power to support the entire installation.

Some of the ice-hardened tugs were rugged enough to plough a path through thinner ice. Recharged at the platforms and maintained in Murmansk shipyard, they created narrow channels as they went, spraying water to the sides, building up layer upon layer of thick, permanent ice. An inshore fleet of mud-masters performed a similar role, recharging on shore.

As the two men climbed off of the tug and on to the docking area of the main platform, Hans asked, 'How many pumps have we lost this month?'

Kenji shrugged. 'A few. But it's getting better as we learn how to manage the heating lines. And Inge says she's convinced we'll be able to recover them during the summer melt.'

'She's with the pump company, right?' Hans said. 'Is she at the main platform today?'

'Yes,' Kenji confirmed. 'She'll be going up with us to see how the spraying works. We have a four-month on-site support contract with her company.' Inge had been seconded from one of the engineering research projects already working in Svalbard, assessing fluid dynamics in extreme conditions.

'If she can help us save our pumps, then the contract is worth every cent.'

The advantage of the remote-controlled zeppelins was that they could cover a much greater territory than the tugs, spraying and creating ice over enormous areas. They used a large submersible pump on a hose that acted as both a cable and a power line. Once they reached the target spraying site, they dropped the pump through the thin ice to act as a weighted, buoyant anchor while the hose was reeled out. When the craft was tethered to the pumping site, the zeppelin's propellers could be switched over to act as small wind turbines, harvesting the relentless arctic winds as a power source and providing the electrical energy for the pump.

However, the disadvantage came from the ice that the zeppelins were creating: the pumps tended to get stuck, and it was worse when the ice reached more than ten metres. While the inflatable buoy meant the pump was expected to be recovered in the summer as the thinner ice broke up, a faster solution was to heat the line with electrical power, and the top of the pump so that they could melt their way out. Kenji was working with the pump teams to find the most efficient way to manage this. In the meantime, because the heavy-lift crafts were raised with hydrogen instead of the helium used for passenger blimps, they had to make every effort to minimise heat contact with the hydrogen. No one wanted to see another Hindenburg disaster, unmanned or otherwise.

Despite everything, amidst the tangle of pumps, power lines, wind turbines, zeppelin maintenance, tugboats, cannons, and an ever-revolving cast of engineers, operators, and scientists, the layers of sea ice were increasing in strips and patches.

Following Kenji, Hans ducked through the hatch into the main work area of the platform, and nodded his head. A tall, pale woman, almost the same height as Hans, greeted them as Kenji shook the ice off his boots. 'Inge Hassi,' she said, reaching out to shake hands.

Hans smiled, realising with pleasure that he could look someone straight in the eyes for once. 'Nice to meet you. So, you're the one who's going to rescue our pumps.'

She gestured towards several people working at screens with complicated diagrams and spreadsheets. 'We borrowed processing capacity from another project. We have not been lucky so far with our digital modelling, but I think we're almost there.'

'Make sure you record that in the contractor resource allocation master spreadsheet,' Kenji reminded her.

'Will do. One advantage of working in this environment is that cooling the server room is free!'

Hans laughed. 'True! Coming back to the pumps. What kind of problems are we dealing with?'

'Any problem you can imagine, we've had it. Too small, too hot, not enough capacity, wrong flow rate, or the metal is too brittle because of the cold. We've got seawater corrosion. We've got pumps blocked with fish. And then there are the export permits and the import permits. Plus, the scale of the entire operation is increasing day by day. And ever since we began the onshore lake freezing, we're using more static pumping buoys on the smaller lakes.'

'Aren't we using zeppelins for that?'

'We use a small zeppelin on the bigger lakes.'

Hans used a forefinger to trace a note on his palm, which was recorded by his eyepiece and stored as data. 'What do you need to make it work?'

'The biggest benefit would be a streamlined equipment ordering procedure, from your side. We're getting stuck in your red tape more often than not. We need more standardisation.'

Kenji spoke up. 'I will ask the procurement team to consider the idea.'

'Tell them to do more than consider,' shot back Hans. 'Feel free to remind them that we're almost at the permafrost melting point. If that happens, the methane release is going to give us serious trouble in a short time.'

'Yes, Boss!' Kenji replied, with a formal bow, but with humour dancing in his eyes. 'I will inform them that the fate of our planet is in their hands. I have a message from the pilot. Are you ready to go?'

Hans gave a thumbs-up. All three ducked through the hatch again to the icy blackness outside, and walked across the platform to the tethering area, where a mid-sized zeppelin was already afloat. Hans motioned to Inge to climb first. 'I'm sorry there isn't enough space for it to get close to the ground.' She grabbed the threadlike rope ladder and began her ascent. Kenji went next, followed by Hans. Within a few exhilarating minutes, they were all aboard. The pilot gave a signal to the remaining ground crew member, who unknotted the ropes and released the craft. It rose, its electric motors purring in the background.

'It's more spacious in the compartment than I would have imagined,' commented Inge. 'Reassure me: this one uses helium, right?'

'Yes!' answered Kenji. 'Hydrogen is for unmanned craft.' As they drifted upwards, they felt the wind buffeting the zeppelin. The thin walls of the cabin struggled against the extreme cold of the dark exterior. Kenji smiled. 'Hans! I would like to have some 'Latent Heat of Fusion' now, if you please.'

'That sounds like a good name for a band,' Inge remarked.

Hans laughed and gave her the background. He'd had to explain it to the investors and to anyone else interested in the project: Latent Heat of Fusion was the name for heat released by the formation of ice. When spraying water into the freezing air, the latent heat would then transfer to the atmosphere; the secret was that in the clear night skies of winter, a significant proportion of infrared radiation would escape into space, taking heat away from the earth. It was the same effect that produced black ice on a clear night like this one.

Below them, vast sheets of white ice, blue in the starlight, interspersed with dark channels of water, stretched as far as they could see. On or adjacent to each platform, construction equipment, ice-breaking ships, and pumping stations showed as blots on the background, while strips and circles of thicker ice formed a patchwork pattern of darker and lighter hues. On the horizon, there was nothing but the memory of the invisible sun to tell them it was already mid-morning.

'Where did you get the idea for this project, anyway?' asked Inge, as she snapped pictures of the faint glow of new-formed ice.

'People used it in Iran centuries ago. They made ice at night, although conditions were above freezing,' Kenji replied.

'How did you learn about that?'

'I learned about it from Hans. He mentioned it when I was still studying for my PhD.'

She turned her attention back to Hans. 'You have quite the varied background. You're Dutch, I'm guessing?'

'Good guess.'

'Svalbard was discovered by the Dutch, at the end of the 16th century.'

'I heard the Icelanders got here first. What about you? Norwegian?'

'By nationality, yes. But my ethnicity is Sámi.'

'I guess that explains why I'm blonder than you.'

She peered through the darkness at his short, fluffy hair. 'You're greyer than I am, though.'

'So the Sámi are as blunt as the Dutch.'

The zeppelin pulled up alongside a larger airship: a tethered, hydrogen-lift vessel which it would pilot by remote control. The crew chief issued commands to the control operators, and the huge ship moved in response, sucking up seawater through its enormous pipe and spewing it out into the open air.

Inge examined the process and took notes, shaking her head with disbelief several times. 'Now that I see it in action, I'm wondering why you haven't lost more pumps. Tell me, is this project going to work? Or am I wasting my time?'

'It will work. As long as we can create several areas of thick ice that will last more than one season, it will help rebuild what we need most: multi-year ice.'

Inge smiled, 'Let's hope.' Everyone in the Arctic knew the power of albedo: how the white surface of the ice would reflect heat back into space during the long summer months. Restored ice cover would also prevent open, dark water from heating.

'In the summer, don't forget, we're also going to be generating clouds over open water. That will reflect more incoming energy. We think we'll approach 200 million tonnes of negative emissions by the end of this year.'

'But?'

'We need more luck; that's a resource this project has found to be in short supply, if we want to achieve the real goal.'

Inge's eyes shone in the near darkness as she turned to Hans. 'Which is?'

'To buy time. The world is rolling out renewable energy for real now. Overall hydrocarbon usage is falling. Carbon-intensive agriculture is dying. But the planet already has so much CO_2 in the atmosphere that the effects will keep spiralling, even if all CO_2 production were to stop tomorrow.'

'How are you funding this?'

'The ice albedo carbon credits are going to cover much of the cost of the operation. The rest will come from peat fire prevention and biochar. We can use these zeppelins to make ice for a few months of the year, and in the meantime, we deploy them for other tasks. One of these is putting out peat fires in other parts of the world. Peat fires generate huge amounts of greenhouse gases – methane as well as CO_2 – and can burn for months. We use a system with drones and lances attached to a small, remote controlled zeppelin fleet to fight the fires. In other areas of the world, like Indonesia, the fire crews also work with locals to turn waste biomass into biochar.'

Inge looked at the shower of new ice below with renewed interest and imagined a smouldering peat fire in its place. 'Can these things fight forest fires?'

'Not so much. The flames reach much higher, and the associated wind and updrafts are stronger. So we focus on what's achievable, and we're generating solid revenue streams.'

'Good. That makes it more likely that we'll be paid on time. So, after this tour, I will get back to work!' Her tone was brusque, but a warmth behind it stirred something in him.

After they all descended and Inge returned to her station on the platform, Kenji and Hans continued their inspection tour.

Kenji commented, at random, 'Our contract with the pumping experts will end six weeks from now. After that, Inge will go back to the Norwegian Polar Institute at Longyearbyen. It is not far from the RAV headquarters.'

'Good to know,' Hans replied. 'What's next on our agenda?'

'The zeppelin maintenance station.'

After a pause, Hans said, 'Six weeks is not long.'

'No,' Kenji replied. 'Not long at all.'

Unsinkable

10.30 am, Saturday, May 19, 2035

Pacific Ocean

Global temperature: 2.1°C above pre-industrial average

It was already Friday evening when Grace first heard about it, at a gala dinner in London, where stars of the big screen and the small gathered for a seven course vegan meal, made from dishes designed to generate a minimum agricultural carbon footprint. '80% of the world's food emissions come from animal husbandry,' was the flax-clad organiser's rationale. Nobody could say who found out about it first, but within a few minutes, the room was buzzing with horror and disbelief.

Zygmunt didn't hear about it until the next morning; it was the middle of the night in Penang. Nor did he read the news when he got up, since he didn't need to go to the office on the weekend. It wasn't until he got back from the gym, where he now was a regular under Scott's guidance, that he saw.

Hans knew about it almost as soon as the news broke. Inge had a habit of watching the daily broadcast while he read through the afternoon construction report, and in his little home office in the colourful, prefab trailer, he heard her cry out from the living room, 'Oh, my God!'

When Adam Park heard, he remembered that once, when he was not much more than a child, he saw headlines this large. That time, it was on the front page of *Chosun Ilbo*. The giant font screamed, 'AMERICA IS ATTACKED', using the old-style, Chinese characters for 'America', and the modern Korean alphabet for the rest of the sentence. But nobody in Korea knew the Chinese characters for Kiribati; few knew where the island nation had been located.

The people, they learned too late, had been called i-Kiribati.

From Seoul, Adam sent a message to Marina, asking if she knew much about Kiribati. 'Yes.' She'd had friends there.

For the first few minutes, Grace was, like the others, stunned. There had been so much sorrow in the past several years. She knew that the way to endure it was to steel her emotions against it all. The wildfires in France. The Indian disasters. The wet bulb waves in Penang itself. In a way, this was no different. In another way, it changed everything.

Then, although she never knew how, she found courage within herself. As everyone at her table was chattering in muted tones appropriate to a period of global mourning, she stood. She noticed how others listened when she spoke.

'I am appalled,' she began. 'I am appalled that so many of us here saw this coming, knew this was coming, predicted it, but failed to act. We have known not for the past hour, nor for the past year, but for decades. We knew. Maybe we didn't know which country it would happen to first, but we knew it was coming.

'And I am appalled because we are still – still! – treating this disaster as if it is a new phenomenon. I read a headline a few moments ago.

It said, "Kiribati Inundated and Destroyed – Climate Change Claims First Victims". But were the people of Kiribati the first victims of rising sea levels? No! On coastlines all over Asia, Africa, around the world, people have been dying, from droughts, from floods, from typhoons and hurricanes and starvation. We knew. And we did nothing, nothing that made enough of a difference to save them.

'Above all, I am appalled at myself. For the past year I have been congratulating nations whose carbon emissions have already peaked, and have now begun to descend. I have praised companies who achieved their net zero targets, whether late or early. But I knew then, and I know now, that it was not enough.

'So it is time to ask: what now? How can we best honour the dead citizens of Kiribati, and all the others who have already perished while we sat by, and talked, and compromised?' The last word was a hiss.

'We must, at the same time, accept what is happening and do everything in our power to prevent it. Whoever sees the potential for tragedy must speak up now, regardless of personal consequences.

'And in the next several days, I hope we will once again see the generosity that we have seen in previous moments of global sorrow. Aid will, and should, pour in for the surviving i-Kiribati, who no longer have a homeland. But we must also consider: what will we do next? This is the first country lost to climate change. Will it be the last?

'There is no more time for gradual reduction. Now, we already must deal with the consequences of our past inaction. We must do whatever it takes to buy ourselves time. If there were ever a time for outside-the-box thinking, this is it.'

She sat down and knocked back the rest of her glass of wine. She meant her words to be heard by the people at her table – a varied group of friends and potential donors. Her years of celebrity had still not taught her that everything she did and said would be recorded and shared within moments.

She remembered it, however, when her notifications began their hysterical buzzing. Shaking her head, she put on her eyepiece for a moment to check what was happening. She hadn't wanted to make a political speech. It just happened nowadays; every time she opened her mouth, an opinion came out. All the frustrations and anxiety that festered and boiled inside her during the first part of her life were being distilled, concentrated, and aimed outwards. In moments, she supposed, a pundit would criticise her for not taking into account the impact of a sudden change in carbon policy on the underprivileged and disenfranchised populations. It didn't matter; she'd heard it all before.

But instead of any of these things, it was a series of messages from Hans. 'The news is worse than we thought.'

Oh, my God, she thought, and knew, before they appeared, what the next words would be.

'We haven't been able to get in touch with Ivan.'

10.00 am, Tuesday, June 17, 2035
Sydney, Australia

They had recovered hundreds of bodies; Ivan's was not one of them.

For one wild moment, Grace wanted to believe that Ivan was underwater with his scuba gear and oxygen tanks when the aftermath surge of the cyclone hit, safely in the embrace of a sunken Japanese *maru*, ready to swim back to his boat when it passed.

But island-destroying cyclones are slow and powerful and relentless, not sudden and unexpected. The storm, south of the islands, had been forming for three days, monitored in minute detail by satellites and local monitoring stations. Then, a change of track and an increase in intensity raised the stakes. Ivan attempted to find a flight out, but without success; the small Fiji Airways planes that could land at Kiribati's tiny airport were already packed. He, along with a handful of other foreign tourists, business people, and the remaining 70,000 i-Kiribati, searched in vain for higher ground as the waters rose. Others attempted to flee in small boats, disappearing into the rough seas. Two Australian navy ships reached the area, and, loaded to the gunwales, fled before the howling gale.

The cyclone hit the exposed, flat atolls like a tank, threading its way through the archipelagos to strike individual islands with unstoppable force.

Satellites monitored the situation. When the eye of the storm crossed the atolls, the surge was so high that no land was visible.

Later, ships of all kinds used divers or fishing nets to recover the dead.

Grace, Zygmunt, and Hans caught a flight to Australia in time for the memorial service. It was the first time they had been together for several years.

'They still don't know what the full death toll is,' Ivan's sister Natalie said, staring at a point somewhere over Grace's shoulder. 'The IT department of the Kiribati government was still keeping personnel and citizenship records onsite, as they hadn't been able to get the funding to pay for cloud storage. We know for certain that the population had declined in the past decade. Many people were anticipating something like this. There have been 14 super-typhoons in the past six years that have moved within 200 kilometres of the three million square kilometre ocean area of the Kiribati islands, and 78 typhoons, tropical storms, and cyclones.'

Grace was taken aback by the level of detail, but accepted that it must be the young woman's way of coping. Natalie clarified, a moment later, 'Typhoons are my special interest. Under normal circumstances Kiribati would be too close to the equator for a typhoon to hit. They are called cyclones in the southern hemisphere. The highest point in Kiribati was on Banaba Island, 500 kilometres away from the main island, Tarawa. It was a raised coral island. A hundred years ago, it was 80 metres in elevation, but little remained because phosphate mining was re-started in 2029. So most of the interior of Banaba was gone, reduced to the same height as the atolls.'

'Phosphate mining?'

'People use guano phosphate for natural fertiliser. It's an organic alternative to NPK, or synthetic fertiliser.'

Grace shook her head. Unintended consequences: organic farmers sought a 'green' alternative but ended up creating profound environmental damage instead. 'You talked about the population decline. Where did the people go? Are there still i-Kiribati living overseas?'

'Yes, there are a few. But many people stopped having children. And in the past decade, several thousand went to sea and didn't return.'

Grace knew the rest of the story. Climate refugees from poor countries found impassable barriers to immigration in rich countries, and exploitation everywhere else. When the choice was between staying on a doomed atoll, living for unknown years in a refugee camp as an asylum seeker, or working in near-slavery in an overseas factory, the ocean must have seemed like the honourable option.

'Ivan is in the sea now,' Natalie added, still focused on a distant corner of the room. 'He's not coming back. That's what "dead" means.'

The islands had not sunk like Atlantis into the depths. But so much of their surface was wiped out by the violent swells that no liveable land remained; every high tide would cover the atolls again. Although it might have been possible to rebuild a structure atop the crumbling bits that still poked above the waves, no one was left to live there.

Grace saw Hans and Zygmunt in close conversation. She couldn't bring herself to say a word; whatever gift she had for creating impromptu speeches had deserted her.

'How was your flight?' asked Zygmunt, and burst into tears.

As Hans bent down to embrace him, Grace recognised all at once how old and frail Zygmunt had become. His work with Ocean Agency, meant to be a respite from the stress of the giant projects he managed for so many years, had taken a greater toll than she imagined. Spending time with younger people, and living at 8 Gurney Drive, had always given him a youthful air. Ivan, with his constant willingness to join the group for a beer, a game, or a voyage, kept Zygmunt and everyone else active and cheerful. But time could not be fooled.

A middle-aged woman thanked the group for coming. 'My son talked about you all, all the time. Hans, you were one of Ivan's best mates. And you're Grace Chan. Ivan was so impressed by everything you've done.'

Grace could only say, 'We don't know what we're going to do without him,' and began to cry herself.

'Natalie hasn't quite grasped it, yet, I think,' Ivan's mother continued. 'She's been texting him every day, 100 times a day, for years. And he's been so good to her. No matter where he was, in Malaysia with you, or on one of his diving trips, he'd always stay in touch. I don't know what she's going to do now.'

It was a side of Ivan they'd never known. 'Ivan had, he was ...' Hans tried to articulate what Ivan had meant to them, failed, and tried again. 'He must have beat me a dozen times in Orinvaders. I could never match–' his voice trailed off as he realised how inadequate the summation was. 'He's the one who kept us all together.'

Ivan's mother nodded. 'I know. He was always like that.' Dry-eyed, she turned away, to speak with the other visitors.

4.00 pm, Wednesday, June 18, 2035
Sydney, Australia

Zygmunt, Hans, and Grace shared an Or-V back to the airport.

'I never asked,' Grace ventured, as they sped along the highway. She had found the absence of a human driver unnerving when Or-V travel was first introduced, but never thought about it now. The car's seamless interface predicted their destination before they had to instruct it. 'How's Inge?'

'She's fine,' Hans replied. 'Tired of the extreme cold weather. As we all are. But I suppose that's a privileged position nowadays. How about you?'

'Zygmunt's been keeping me busy at OA. We've brought in more than $60 million in funding this year, but it doesn't cover all the projects we want to implement. And we're still far away from establishing the Ocean as an entity that has any rights.'

Zygmunt piped up, 'Hey! Don't be so pessimistic. We'll get there.'

'I thought you were asleep!' Grace answered.

'Just resting. It's been a long couple of days.'

'We're making progress in the Arctic, too,' Hans continued. 'Phase 4 is running better than we had any right to expect. But it's a massive job.'

'I wish you the best.'

'Thank you.'

They were formal, for two people with a shared history.

Zygmunt removed his eyepiece. 'You two youngsters might want to look at this,' he said as he transferred the feed.

8.30 am, Wednesday, June 18, 2035
The Hague, Netherlands

President Teatao Tabai made his address to a group of interested parties at the International Court of Justice. He was not sure this was the best forum, but he liked the name; it had a resonance that he found appropriate, and its very appearance put forth an aura of gravity. Six evergreen trees, trimmed to perfect cones, rose on each side of the broad, close-cut lawn, which outlined the stately avenues leading to the building itself. Peace Palace: an edifice of brick and stone, representing stability and trust in the future.

He had no cabinet members to ask for advice.

He had already released the text of his speech via his Orac channel. But he also knew that the spoken version of his remarks would be the important one, the one that resonated.

No legal precedent existed for what he was about to attempt. In fact, in any conventional sense, it was a preposterous idea.

'A few weeks ago, someone who heard about the fate of the i-Kiribati called upon us to think outside of the box,' he continued. 'As one of the only survivors of my people, and the sole surviving member of our national government, I think that there is nowhere else I can think. There is nothing left to try inside our conventional box of ideas.

'Kiribati, as a landed nation, is no more. Nothing is left. Kiribati has become part of the ocean. And I thank every one of the nations, the companies, and the individuals who have pledged aid to support us. But what is to be done, when so few of us remain?

'As a survivor, I can rail against this cruel fate, or I can accept and embrace it.

'I choose the latter. Kiribati is the ocean, now. You all know the meme "This is us." For the nation of Kiribati, the Ocean is us. I declare, as of this moment, that I am no longer the President of Kiribati, but of the Ocean Independent State.'

There was a confused murmur among the live attendees.

'As the President of the Ocean Independent State, I now represent the oceans of the world. The remaining citizens of Kiribati are now citizens of the Ocean. As a landed nation, our total land area was 800 square kilometres, dispersed over three million square kilometres of the sea. However, now, the people of Earth have decided, through their actions over the past decades, that our land shall become indistinguishable from the sea. Now, therefore, I declare that there is indeed no difference between land and sea. Our land is the sea. We are the Ocean.

'In line with this new world, whatever sails across the ocean will now be sailing across our land – our sea. Whatever oil platforms, mining initiatives, or fishing grounds exist on the surface or under the sea, I now declare nationalised under the new government of the Ocean Independent State.

'Thanks to your funds, thanks to the billions in aid that has been promised to us, we have a national budget to make this vision a reality.

'You may think that I have gone mad with grief, or that I am clinging to power as my nation has perished. I want to prove that this is not the case. Therefore, I also declare that free and fair elections shall be held one year from today, for the positions of President and Vice President of the Ocean Independent State, OIS for short. Anyone on earth who wishes to pledge allegiance to OIS and become a citizen may run for election and serve as my successor. Between now and then, I will hold a Constitutional Convention to establish how the OIS will operate.

'In the meantime, we will require a bureaucracy and an organisational capability to manage the funding we have received, which can ensure compliance with all international standards. I have determined that the Ocean Agency, headquartered in Malaysia with a presence on almost all the world's oceans, is the best choice for this job.

'I thank all of you for your donations and for your support. And I pray that our fate will serve as the lesson that changes the course of humanity.'

Zygmunt closed his eyes again, and spoke, as if to himself, 'Grace, it sounds like someone heard your vegan dinner table manifesto after all.'

'So it seems.'

'And it also sounds as if you have a job to do. And maybe a speech or two to write.'

INDEPENDENCE

7.00 am, Friday, August 24, 2035
Penang Fairhaven – 8 Gurney Drive
Global temperature: 2.1°C above pre-industrial average

As President Tabai hoped, and as Grace predicted, aid flowed in.

The most useful aid was cash. All 60 employees of the Bank of Kiribati had perished in the disaster, as had almost all of its customers, its four branch offices, and its server room. Its holdings, meagre as they were, were for all practical purposes eliminated. They were desperate for cash, to recover the dead and lay them to rest. It arrived: hard currency from company charitable foundations, from multilateral institutions, and from government foreign aid. But it had to be kept and managed. The so-called 'tax residents' of Kiribati, and their hundreds of millions of dollars held in overseas banks, would have to be dealt with. But that would come later.

'I never thought I was going to end up as a damn banker,' Grace said aloud, as she crossed into the living room, still brushing her hair. She had been up since 5.00 am on a call with a group of advisors from the International Monetary Fund and the Asian Development Bank. They were well-meaning, but they offered complex solutions when what she needed was a temporary line of credit. That would tide them over until they could establish a proper central bank, perhaps with a new currency.

Cassandra was a lifesaver. She contacted Grace a short time after President Tabai's speech. At first, Grace was too overwhelmed to understand who it was, until she remembered the elegant, white-haired woman in Davos. Cassandra talked her through what was happening, helped her establish financial priorities, and put her in touch with resources who, she said, would be happy to help if Grace mentioned Cassandra's name.

After many years of understanding it in theory, Grace was seeing evidence in reality that 'who you know' was indeed more important than 'what you know'. But she also learned that the halls of power are infinitely more complex: just as important as who knew whom was how they were related, who did a favour for whom way back when, and who was in a position to influence whom.

Important decisions were taken not alone, but by giant networks operating in unpredictable ways.

In the living room, Scott was doing a complicated boxing routine against an invisible opponent, using a neurodirect implant he'd installed a few weeks ago. Grace worked out a tangle as she brushed her hair. Ivan was always complaining and making jokes about finding long strands of her hair everywhere.

Ivan. For a second, she almost forgot. She stood silent, her gaze fixed on Scott's boxing game, letting the pain wash over her. When it abated, she went to the kitchen to get coffee.

Ivan wasn't coming back. That's what 'dead' means.

Hundreds of honest but misdirected communities around the

world ran clothing donation drives, spurred on by a popular teenage influencer in Monaco. Grace received sixteen messages in a single day from people who had collected piles, bags, and boxes of old clothing. What was Ocean Independent State supposed to do with them? Even if there was anyone left to wear them, used prom dresses and old bathing suits wouldn't protect anyone from the elements. She advised each of the would-be donors to hold a pop-up sale, and to direct the proceeds back to OIS. For now, they were accepting Australian dollars, and kept an account in Westpac.

The other type of aid was land. Kiribati, now Ocean Independent State, was the unexpected owner of dozens of parcels of unused land in surprising places, donated by concerned individuals: old warehouses, a burnt-out vineyard in France, and an uninhabited, volcanic island in Hawaii. But they could not build a new country out of these bits and pieces. The owners had the right to sell or donate the land, but not to hand it over to a foreign power. Nevertheless, Grace was certain that land would be useful, so she hired a lawyer to handle the transactions in the meantime. She did not have the time to conduct title searches in Dubai, sort through inheritance records in Portugal, or manage 99-year government lease agreements in New Zealand.

With Grace's intervention, President Tabai himself was offered an apartment by the governor of Penang, a distant relation of Marina. Marina was another godsend. She seemed to either know or be related to everyone of importance in Malaysia, and could call on favours going back several generations. Grace smiled when she remembered how Churchill introduced her that first time: her Highness.

The President had moved into the new apartment, and was holding up well considering the circumstances. But Grace saw him struggling daily to internalise the emotional weight of the disaster. The few remaining overseas i-Kiribati were all ready to complain, whether they reacted to his declaration with joy, indignation, or resignation. Grace reminded him again that those who already had citizenship in other countries were no longer his responsibility. A spokesperson for the Banaba ethnic minority berated him and his late predecessor for the decision to re-open phosphate mining on their island four years earlier, the only island which might otherwise have withstood the surge.

The media supported the Ocean Independent State at first, as it took tentative steps onto the world stage. 'Everyone loves an underdog!' Zygmunt commented upon seeing the fawning coverage. But it was in the media's nature to amplify controversy, or to create it when none appeared. So reporters flocked to Penang, waiting for President Tabai or Zygmunt or Grace, to make a misstep. For many years, Grace herself had been a media darling: an intelligent woman who looked fantastic on camera. But the idea that she was now a political player did not sit well with the pundits. Despite her engineering degree, her production company, and her work Ocean Agency, she was always 'online influencer Grace Chan', or, sometimes, 'ageing celeb Grace Chan'.

The reporters were not the only newcomers in Penang. The population of Fairhaven reached eight million. Some were refugees from drowned coastal areas around the world, employed on the ongoing construction projects and in the new businesses. International executives and refugees alike needed to be housed and fed. Improved farming practices behind the big coastal dykes tripled food production, but projections had to be re-calibrated again and again. Cristina Abidin, who was now running Fairhaven Development Corporation, joked that her grandparents had left the farms for a better life, and she was now spending her days worrying about crop yields. However, once Cristina left 8 Gurney Drive to move in with a British engineer, the living room no longer rang with discussions of zero tilling, restorative biochar, and protein alternatives.

That reminded Grace: she needed to call Peter, a Singaporean she'd known from her days of advertising Mosa Meat. He had a proposal about handling personnel and recruitment for OIS. It would be an enormous help if that aspect of the operation could be handed off to someone else, Grace thought. The sheer volume of work meant that every staff member of Ocean Agency was already stretched to the limit, trying to manage the Agency's existing projects. Ocean Agency was still a medium-sized charity, despite its ambitions, and it was not ready to replace an entire government bureaucracy at a moment's notice.

Grace finished brushing her hair and put it out of the way in a tight braid.

11.00 am, Wednesday, December 19, 2035
Penang Fairhaven – Consulate General, OIS

President Tabai sat with Grace, Zygmunt, Peter, and the rest of the interim cabinet, in a conference room that bore a strong resemblance to a Kiribati-style kava bar, complete with red and blue lights, strings of fluttering pennants, and plastic chairs. The office for the new Consulate General came from a Fairhaven property developer whose sister-in-law married one of Marina's many cousins, but it was decorated by the hands of the weary, anxious President. It was one of the few things that gave him a little joy, reminding him of a home that no longer existed.

'Six months ago today, I promised to hold elections for the new President of Ocean Independent State,' he began. 'I promised to hold a Constitutional Convention before then. We have a tough decision before us now, which is the selection of delegates.

'A handful of citizens of Kiribati still survive. We must, of course, include their voice. But OIS is no longer limited to i-Kiribati. Above all, we must represent the ocean itself.'

'Who can speak on behalf of the ocean?' asked Peter. 'The dolphins can't talk, or, perhaps, we can't understand them well enough to know what they're saying.'

'Can we ask a wildlife NGO to represent them?' suggested Tekiree, one of the interim cabinet members. 'Before the disaster I was in Fiji as the Kiribati ambassador, so I know all those conservation people.'

'There are also people who live on the water,' Grace said. 'Boat people, fisherfolk for the most part. People who work out at Sea Orchards or the other ocean farms built on the same model. For that matter, what about people who spend most of their lives on offshore platforms?'

'The most important thing is for the delegate selection to be viewed as legitimate by the other nations of the world,' the President said. 'Anote, you've been our UN ambassador for a few months now. What are they expecting from this?'

'I'm new to this,' Anote replied. 'Until six months ago I was operating a dive shop in Australia. But from what I can tell, the developing countries like it because it's a slap in the face to the rich. Anyway, they don't think it's going to work, so they're sitting back and waiting to see what happens. Meanwhile, a fair number of the rich nations were spooked by your use of the word "nationalised". It gave them flashbacks to the Cold War. But I think many of them are relieved that someone has taken an obvious problem off their hands.'

'What problem?' asked Peter.

'How to value ocean-based ecosystem services,' replied Grace.

'What's that?'

'How much people should pay to use the ocean,' explained Zygmunt. 'There has been great interest in this area over the past two decades, along with the predictable infighting. So far, the individual countries have been expected to manage it based on standards that the multilateral organisations came up with. But if OIS could do it by fiat, that would make things simpler.'

Grace nodded. 'At Ocean Agency, we've been using the WBCSD standard, or a rough approximation of it, to set prices. And for the most part, the companies that we charge don't argue about the methodology; they just haggle about the price.'

'It's all about anchoring the price point,' Zygmunt agreed. 'Classic contract negotiation technique.'

Tekiree, one of the three i-Kiribati in the room, pointed out, 'We'll want independent observers for the Convention, and for the election, later on, to prove to everyone that it's above board. How does that work? Do we have to pay for that?'

'I hope not,' replied Anote. 'I'll try to find out. Zimbabwe had elections last month and there were UN observers there. I'll ask their ambassador.'

The President, holding a tiny slate, instructed his Orac Assistant to take notes. He shook his head. 'This thing knows what I'm going to say before I say it! Anyway, we'll have a delegation representing the i-Kiribati and the Banabans. We'll have another delegation from wildlife NGOs, representing the natural world. A delegation of fisherfolk and other people who live on the water.'

Tekiree asked, 'How about a delegation of other island nations who may end up in the same situation? I think we would do well to bring in representation from the rest of the world, since this affects them, too.'

'Good,' replied the President. 'They would act as advisors but would not have voting power to approve the new Constitution; that group should have a good mix of small and large countries, rich and poor ones. Most important, they should all be from places with a coastline.'

'How many delegates will participate in all?' asked Grace.

'If each of those groups has five people,' President Tabai replied, 'that makes 25. And then, I would like to have experts to guide us through the process. I studied political science at the University of Melbourne, but that was three decades ago, and I've never written a constitution from scratch.'

Zygmunt spoke up. 'One of the Ocean Agency board members is Dr Schneegarten, a visiting professor at the Kennedy School at Harvard. She's the one who wrote that book about Beate Gordon. She's Swiss, which might make her a good neutral party.'

Grace nodded. 'Plus, they're landlocked, so no one could accuse them of having any direct stake in the game.'

'Not really,' Peter countered. 'Swiss bankers hold major stakes in shipping lines. But she sounds like a good choice.'

'Will this professor – what's her name? – be willing to put pen to paper and write the first draft of the thing?' asked President Tabai.

'Dr Marie-Louise Schneegarten,' Zygmunt said. 'Maybe. Either way, we can ask her to bring her grad students to help with that part.'

'How fast do you think we can put this thing together?'

Grace's Orac Assistant was taking notes. She muttered, 'What's the average length of a constitutional convention?' into her eyepiece mic and glanced at the answer on her slate. 'I think we need at least two months. But we shouldn't wait any longer than that. It will take time to work out the details of citizenship, voting rights, and so forth, if we want to meet the election deadline of June 2036.'

President Tabai nodded. His eagerness to rid himself of his self-imposed burden was more obvious than ever. He had conceived a plan for the legacy of Kiribati in a moment of ecstatic despair, and the dreary slog of realising the plan began to tire him almost from the first moment. 'We'll also need a President of the Constitutional Convention itself, to administer the proceedings. I believe that person must come from this group.'

Everyone in the room, without a moment's thought, turned expectantly towards Grace. It would almost be comical, if the import was not so weighty.

'I guess I know when I'm on the hook!' she said.

To herself, she made a rare admission: I need help.

11.00 am, Monday, March 3, 2036
OIS Constitutional Convention – Penang
Global temperature: 2.3 °C above pre-industrial average

There had been nothing like it for as long as anyone could remember.

Governments rose and fell, whether through fair election or coup d'état; constitutions and bodies of laws were updated and replaced. But this was something different: a new type of political entity, which no one was sure had the right to be a nation, and whose citizenry were all but non-existent.

Indeed, determining who was and was not a citizen was one of the most important decisions of the Convention. On one hand, given the lack of land possessed by the OIS, it would be madness for anyone to give up their existing nationality and become a citizen of OIS, as it would render themselves stateless. On the other hand, without citizens, how could a nation function?

It was Grace who proposed the dual citizenship system. It was an elegant, practical solution: anyone could swear allegiance to OIS, be subject to its laws (yet to be passed), and receive its benefits (yet to be determined). Meanwhile, OIS would work as fast as possible to form dual-citizenship agreements with as many nations as possible, so that new OIS citizens would not suffer loss of their existing rights when they joined. If you were an OIS citizen by the time elections happened, dual or otherwise, you would be allowed to vote. Because the new OIS laws would impact every country that used the ocean, nations had a strong incentive to allow their people to become dual citizens of the new nation.

On the wall of the meeting room, one of the grad students hung a giant map with the whimsical title 'World from a Fish's Perspective'. The so-called 'Spilhaus projection' of the world map re-envisioned the world's seas as a single, integrated ocean. It centred on the South Pole, with lines of latitude and longitude curving outwards, bordered by the edges of continents. Because no one could think of a reason to take it down, they left it there, and it became an unofficial symbol of the Convention.

President Tabai, in his first speech at The Hague, had claimed the entire ocean as the territory of OIS. However, in a technical sense, large parts of the oceans already did belong to established nations. Therefore, the group had a long discussion about whether they would claim the entire ocean, or only the parts designated as international waters. A delegate from Vietnam gave them a gentle reminder that five nations with large military forces had spent half a century attempting to establish sovereignty over tiny groups of islands in the South China Sea, without a definitive conclusion, and implied that OIS would be better off reducing its claims until it had the power to enforce them. The delegates decided to forego claims on territorial waters.

The question of the military was discussed in the open, under the observation of UN representatives and the world's media. However, the most important questions on this topic were settled behind closed doors.

A visiting scholar from American University was an 'observing delegate' on paper. It became clear when he approached Grace during a coffee break that he represented a second employer: he brought a secret commitment from the Pentagon for a large arsenal of ships, war drones, and satellite capacity. The following day, they received a similar offer over breakfast, from someone Grace knew until then as the head of the China Travel and Tourism Bureau in Penang.

There it was, again: leverage.

The little Hawaiian island, which, they soon learned, was still an active volcano, drew the interest of another American, a square-jawed man with a military bearing and sporting the improbable, stereotypical name of Jack Smith. Zygmunt invited him for beer and sausages at Zur Bratpfanne. Both men came into the hall the following morning wearing satisfied smiles. She suspected the old negotiator had once again struck a deal, and wondered what it was.

When it came to the fundamentals of the government, most of the delegates were happy to follow a basic system of a directly elected legislature and executive branches. There would be no question of representatives based on any geographical criteria, since the citizens of OIS were, by definition, dispersed all around the world.

The usual, 'first-past-the-post' electoral system was also rejected, since politics operating within such a framework would always devolve into a stalemate between two parties. Instead, elections would proceed on a single, transferable vote basis: choices would be ranked and sorted so that if the voter's first choice received too few votes to continue, their vote would be transferred to their second choice, and so on.

The proceedings lasted almost two weeks. By the middle of the second week, Professor Schneegarten and her grad students produced a clean, concise document that most of the delegates could agree on.

A special committee would oversee the upcoming elections, and Anote took up the job of chairing it. President Tabai volunteered to lead the dual-citizenship task force, relieved to have a single, straightforward job to do.

The final matter concerned the flag of OIS. The delegates gave a unanimous vote to adopt the most popular design: a white field, with a deep blue silhouette of the 'world from a fish's perspective' at its centre.

No ratification was required, since the citizenry of the OIS was yet to be established. The voting delegates signed the final version of the document and congratulated each other.

With a slight sense of anticlimax, Grace banged her gavel and declared the convention closed.

THE MORTON-THIOKOL CHALLENGE: A STORY BY GRACE CHAN

On a bright January morning in 1986, millions of American school children sat at their desks, ready to watch a beloved teacher become the first civilian astronaut. Instead, they watched in horror as the beautiful spacecraft was enveloped in smoke and fell to Earth in pieces, thanks to a weak rubber O-ring seal made inflexible by frigid weather.

The explosion of the NASA space shuttle Challenger *was more than a tragic accident that cost seven lives. The catastrophe created a grim milestone in the long decline of the American space program that had once united that nation, and in a larger sense brought an end to the golden age of American optimism.*

Political considerations and influence forced the launch to go ahead despite engineers' recommendations. These same forces can also halt a disaster in the making, even at a planetary scale. In 1986, the global average temperature was 0.6°C above pre-industrial levels. This is us. It should have happened then. What might happen next?

***

11.45 pm, Monday, January 27, 1986

'And I'm sorry to say, Mr President, that no matter what, tomorrow evening at six I'll be on the air with CBS News. In fact, I'd advise you to rip up the draft of your State of the Union address, the one you probably have on your desk right now.'

The President sighed. 'Fine. I don't like how you've gone about it, but by God, you've got your way, Senator. I'll tell Beggs to cancel.'

'You mean Graham. You may have forgotten that Beggs is on leave, thanks to accusations made by people in your administration, that he is overcharging the government.' John could not keep the bitterness from his voice.

'Point taken,' said the President. 'And hell, I'm regretting taking that call from Don; he's the one who said I should listen to you. Now: you've done your job. It's time to get off the damn phone, and let me do mine.'

'Yes, Mr President.'

9.30 pm, Monday, January 27, 1986

Two hours earlier, John had grumbled as the phone rang. 'Another telemarketer!' he muttered to Annie.

But the voice he heard on that cold Monday night in Concord, Ohio, was the last one he expected.

'I'll be a monkey's uncle!' he cried, when she explained why she was calling, long-distance.

He resisted her request at first. He parried, and she insisted. Then she pulled her trump card.

'I am 68 years old already, and I am going to retire this year,' said the voice from the phone. 'That makes me too old to accept this nonsense. You were all too ready to ask me to check every calculation to ensure everything was in order, when it was you yourself going into space. I expect you to offer the same considerations to your successors.'

'Yes, Ma'am,' John replied, with a mixture of amusement and concern. 'Thank you for calling. I'll see what I can do.'

'Remember: the thing about mathematics is, it doesn't matter what your politics are. It's either right or wrong.'

'Yes, Ma'am! You have a good evening, now.'

As he collapsed the antenna and hung the phone back on its cradle, he called out to his wife. 'You'll never guess who that was.'

'Hm?' Annie had never been much of a chatterbox, due to her stutter, but she had a presence that commanded any room.

'Katherine Johnson.'

'Who?'

'Mrs Johnson, the mathematician, the one who worked with us on the Gemini missions.'

'Oh?'

'She has been having a talk with a fellow called McDonald, down at Morton-Thiokol. Where they build the solid rocket boosters.'

'I thought, I always thought she – was worth listening to.'

Annie had long ago given up the idea of acting as the perfect housewife and mother; indeed, both Lyn and John David were now in their 40s, and John David had children of his own. Still, despite her gruelling work in disability activism, she kept their sprawling ranch house spotless. And as she grew older, she developed more decided opinions about who did, and did not, merit her husband's time. Her laconic comment was a ringing endorsement of Mrs Johnson.

He continued, 'Well, yes, normally speaking, I'd have to agree with you, there. And I've listened to her plenty of times. She said this fellow MacDonald has concerns about the launch tomorrow. The launch they're doing with that civilian, you know, the teacher.'

'Yes.'

'They're talking about more than a billion dollars wasted, if they abort it now. Not to mention the President wants it to headline his State of the Union address. MacDonald couldn't convince Jesse Moore or Gene Thomas to listen to him, so he decided to go off the darn reservation.'

Annie gave him a disappointed look. Back in the earlier part of the century, the Burke Act dispossessed her grandfather from his place on a reservation, and he experienced terrible suffering during the Great Depression that followed. She would not tolerate any such language in her own house.

'I'm sorry, Annie. What I mean to say is that this fellow MacDonald, he has a darn fool idea that the weather will be too cold. Too cold! Why, the main combustion chamber reaches, what, six thousand degrees Fahrenheit!'

'Why?'

'Why is he worried? She says, that he says, there have been problems with the seals. Which, come to think of it, are what stops the exhaust gases from leaking into the joints.'

'Oh?'

'Now, you know very well I'm a pilot and not a rocket design specialist. But, now that you mention it, if he convinced her, maybe there's something to it.'

Annie took her time clearing the glasses and cocktail napkins that John's guests had left in the living room. She sensed when her husband needed time to think things through.

It was an odd thing to admit, but she envied Mrs Johnson. From an early age, Annie tried to do what was expected, or, if she did what was unexpected, to do it within the acceptable norms for a middle-class white woman in Ohio. But Katherine Johnson, from the age of 14, tossed aside all expectations of what a Negro girl could achieve in those days, and lived her life as she saw fit. Katherine Johnson, she suspected, through the rigorous application of analytical geometry, had gained the respect of her husband in a way that she herself could never hope to.

She put the glasses in the dishwasher, dropped the paper plates into the trash compactor, returned to the living room, and asked her husband. 'What happens – if?'

'If I don't escalate it? Well, if I don't get involved, and everything goes as planned, then an old woman might be a bit angry with me, and the President gets to boast about it in the State of the Union.'

'But?'

'But if something happens, and I knew about it, and was in a position to do something, then, gosh darn, if my constituents got wind of it, then there goes the election.'

'And?' She took off her apron, hung it on the back of the kitchen door, and sat next to him on the sofa.

'I know what you're thinking. It's not just about my constituents. I ought to be asking another question: what would John David say? For that matter, what would little Zach say?'

'Zach, he watches – every launch.' It was true. Zach was as space-mad as any little boy in the nation, and proud of his illustrious grandfather.

'Darn it, Annie! I'm convinced you and Mrs Johnson have been conspiring against me! The problem is that you're both right. As usual. Although I'll need to find a way to get through to him.'

'Yes.'

'But to tell you the truth, Annie, in the back of my mind, I've been thinking. We've had triumph after triumph in this effort. But there will come a time when something happens, and we'll have a tragedy. And I guess that's the story of all mankind.'

'But.'

'But I don't want to be the one who failed to act, just at the moment I could have made a difference.'

Annie disappeared into the study, and, when she returned, handed John his well-thumbed Rolodex. She had already flipped to a card about two-thirds through the sheaf. It held the number of the President's Chief of Staff.

7.45 pm, Monday, January 27, 1986

Two hours before John spoke with Katherine, a group of men in Ogden, Utah, were sitting together in a meeting so tense that Bob was afraid they might come to blows.

January was cold in Ogden, cold and dreary in a way that was unthinkable in warmer states. The thick, grey clouds blanketing the mountains drove out all thoughts of winter merriment.

The Morton-Thiokol factory had completed the construction of the Solid Rocket Boosters in good time for the July launch as planned. The same type of boosters propelled nine missions, all successful. And in the burning of the summer desert, no one worried about the flexibility of rubber in cold temperatures. On the contrary: the greater concern was a slight charring they'd observed, they supposed due to the tremendous heat of the fiery combustion of 500 tonnes of propellant. The repeated delays, due to a variety of factors, gave them time to conduct additional tests.

Nevertheless, Bob knew that Roger was terrified, and the call Cecil arranged earlier in the evening with the client made his fears concrete. Robert and Joe could not have made it more clear: they did not have the data to guarantee how tight the seal would be at temperatures colder than 53 degrees Fahrenheit.

'It's Florida!' argued one of the local men. 'How cold can it be?'

'It got down to 25 there last night,' Cecil shot back. 'It's Cape Canaveral, not Cape Verde.'

Roger thought the call had ended with a recommendation not to go ahead in the absence of sufficient data. But to his surprise, Mulloy, the NASA man, called back an hour later, saying that he'd discussed it with the Mission Management Team Leader. 'Sure,' he said, 'if you insist, we'll check the temperature of the SRBs. But that's not part of the Launch Commit Criteria. Aldrich won't take it into account.'

'You're not required to check if the Solid Rocket Boosters work before risking the lives of the seven people sitting on top of them?'

'You know that's not what we're talking about. We're talking about a vehicle that has shown reliable performance on nine separate launches. And we don't see any reason to keep the entire country away from a mission that they've been waiting for, for more than half a year now, just because you want to put on your fur coat!'

That was how they all talked: never 'I', always 'we'. You never knew whether you were talking to a man or to a committee.

Roger walked over to where Bob was sitting, typing something into the computer terminal. 'I don't like this. Not one bit.'

'Have you talked to Allan?'

'Down at Kennedy Space Center? Yes. That's the reason Cecil arranged the telephone conference to begin with.'

Roger pushed aside a stack of paper, and sat down on Bob's desk.

'You and I both know this is dangerous. And we've both been trained to escalate our concerns through the proper channels. But when that isn't working, there's got to be another way!'

'Fine. You tell me, then: who's got the power to stop this?'

'The President could do it.'

'Do you happen to have his home number?'

'Sure, no problem, I'll just check the White Pages. No, damn it! I don't have the President's home phone number. And I'm not going to send a telegram to 1600 Pennsylvania Avenue.'

'Who does?'

'Damned if I know. Nancy, I would imagine. Or maybe the Speaker of the House, or the Senate Majority Leader. Someone like that.'

'Hey, you've given me an idea – John Glenn! He's not just an ex-astronaut, but a current senator as well. Too bad he's a Democrat, but if anyone could convince the President, he could. Do you know anyone who knows him?'

An unexpected voice spoke up from the next desk. 'It's not about who knows him. It's about who he'll listen to.' Mike Kozuma, a senior engineer, finished off his can of Tab and tossed it into the trash can at the end of the corridor, where it sank with a resounding clunk.

'He wouldn't listen to you, by any chance?'

'As if! The Japanese-American guy is always invisible. I mean, every man, woman and child in America knows Christa McAuliffe's name, but not a single one of them can spell Ellison Onizuka.'

Bob and Roger looked at each other. 'Okay, I'll bite,' said Bob. 'Who's that?'

'A Commander in the US Air Force, an astronaut on the *Discovery* shuttle, and, as it happens, one of the mission specialists who's scheduled to go up in tomorrow's launch.'

'So what do you suggest?'

'One of the folks at NASA told us that John Glenn never went on a mission unless the flight path was checked by a particular woman who is supposed to be a mathematical genius. She's an old Black lady, and still works at NASA.'

'And unlike the President,' Bob realised, 'I bet her number is in the White Pages.'

Bob was already calling Allan MacDonald, and Roger was already dialling information. 'Hello? I need all the area codes for the suburbs surrounding Washington, D.C.' Within fifteen minutes, the phone was ringing in Katherine Johnson's kitchen.

4.30 pm, Monday, January 27, 1986

Yet it was only a few hours before that the Morton-Thikol engineers grasped the true gravity of what might happen.

Discussions among engineers can go on forever when the topic is trivial: a debate about the best brand of wire strippers is as likely to produce a generational feud as a consensus. But unlike politicians, when the matter is serious, they will come to an agreement with surprising speed.

'The seals have come close to failing before,' Bob Ebeling said. 'More than 30% of the rubber was burnt out in a test that took place under similar conditions.' The other specialists agreed: this was not the occasion to be ignoring risk factors.

However, there was a problem: try as he might, Bob could not find a hard-and-fast rule to stop a launch if the temperature dropped below a particular level.

Roger Boisjoly argued that a written rule shouldn't be necessary. 'We have evidence of the leakage. We've all seen the blowby on the earlier flight. What more are they looking for?'

'That's the issue. The previous flights were fine, so why should this one be any different?'

'It's too cold. We think of the O-rings as being soft, like slices of pineapple, but at that temperature they'll be more like a frozen bagel.'

'I'm beginning to think you shouldn't have skipped lunch.'

'I'm beginning to think the idiots at the Kennedy Space Center shouldn't have skipped Physics 101.'

Someone came back into the room with a relieved look. 'Thank God. We've got a new conference call scheduled. Tonight at seven. We'll explain what's going on. They'll understand. But be prepared to stay late tonight.'

Bob let out the breath he didn't know he'd been holding, and reached for his phone. Darlene didn't like it if he came home late without telling her in advance.

'Honey, I'm sorry to do this to you again, but it's important.' He spoke a few quiet words into the handset; the other engineers teased him for deferring too much to his wife.

'That's all right,' she replied. 'I know there's a launch tomorrow.'

'Not if I can help it.'

'What do you mean?'

'There's no way those losers should be trusting the O-rings in this cold weather. If they go ahead as planned, the whole shuttle's going to blow up.'

'Are they going ahead?'

'I hope not. They'll have to turn on the launch pad fire suppression system as it is, meaning the whole thing's going to be covered with ice. And we've no idea what that will do to the thermal heat shield. We're having a conference call tonight to explain it to them.'

She was silent for a moment. 'I hope it isn't you who ends up as the loser in all of this.'

'If the thing blows, we'll all be losers. We'll lose our jobs and who knows what else.'

'That's not what I mean. A loser, in my mind, is somebody that doesn't do anything, and, worse yet, they don't care. I want you to try your best, and if it doesn't work, you will know that you did something and you cared. And that's my definition of a winner.'

'Thanks, honey. You know that if anything were to happen, I'd regret it my whole life. But tell me, do you need me to pick up anything on the way home?'

'A gallon of milk, if it's not too late. And be careful on the roads in the dark. They're expecting flurries tonight. It's going to be cold.'

'So I hear.'

11.52 pm, Monday, January 27, 1986

'Get me Graham,' said the President. 'We're calling this thing off.' He slammed the receiver into the cradle.

He scowled, picked up a sheaf of papers from his desk labelled 'STATE OF THE UNION – DRAFT', and began to delete lines with a red pen.

ELECTION

10.00 am, Tuesday, April 8, 2036
Penang Fairhaven – Consulate General, OIS
Global temperature: 2.3 °C above pre-industrial average

Grace looked at the list on her CNV monitor. 'My to-do list is longer than the North Dyke,' she muttered to herself, and asked her Orac Assistant to prioritise it. The OA could do it faster than she could. Still, she thought, it would be better to have a real person in the office to help manage things. She added it to her to-do list.

Her morning's third cup of coffee was stamping a ring on a printout of an interim project plan, Version 6. She told herself she'd make headway on the to-do list before making the Big Decision, the one about the election. There was still time before Anote's deadline.

As she ploughed through the meeting requests, legal documents, and demands for decisions, she thought back to the mangrove worker she'd met four years ago when she visited the old shrimp area. She'd never learned his name, but she remembered his simple, impossible wish: to be in his own house again, with his wife and mother.

In what sense is that man, Grace asked herself, the one who lost his entire family, his farm, his land – in what sense is he not as stateless as the i-Kiribati? Although he still held an identity card from the nation he was born in, he no longer had a home.

What about the woman who served her shrimp curry that day? Did she have anyone left? Where was she from?

How many more would there be?

She sent a quick reminder to President Tabai, asking for a status report, and emphasising the importance of dual-citizenship agreements for all the places with large, poor populations in low-lying areas. Bangladesh. Chile. Florida.

Malaysia.

After the message was gone, and his agreeable reply received, she recalled that President Tabai was still the leader of Ocean Independent State and her boss.

At first, just after the disaster, Ocean Agency's existing initiatives ground to a temporary halt as the staff scrambled to understand and take on board their new, unexpected responsibilities. However, over time, as Grace established a new organisational structure and bureaucracy focusing on OIS affairs, Ocean Agency's regular development work resumed.

Zygmunt retained management of the previous Ocean Agency apparatus, assisted by Scott, who wanted a change from Fairhaven. Grace smiled to herself, wondering whether Zygmunt brought him on board more for his financial management skills or for Scott's imposing physical presence, and the idea that it might help potential donors cough up funds.

As a result, Grace became the de facto chief of OIS. She answered in name to President Tabai, but in practice to the citizens of the new nation. Her successful leadership of the constitutional convention cemented the position. Following that momentous event, the President began his subtle withdrawal from the day-to-day affairs of his own creation, and spent most of his time on the dual-citizenship effort, holding long meetings with foreign ministers from various nations. He explained that OIS did not plan to rob them of their people; that it would be an opportunity for that country to have influence over a topic that affected them all.

Grace handed over most of the operations of her production company to Nant, who had a deft hand for selecting hits and getting them financed. Taking several steps back from the world of entertainment offered her no respite, however, from constant public attention. She hired Kayleigh as her press secretary, but the young woman was out of her depth. Grace was thinking of replacing her with someone more experienced. Lily, the head of communications at Fairhaven? No, she was competent enough when it came to local activities, but lacked a sense of strategy. She recalled that Hans had spoken well of the communications manager from Rakki Holdings, Hiroko something. Maybe Hans would let her poach on his territory.

Without knowing how it happened, she was becoming what she dreaded: a politician, living in the spotlight, relying on others to manage every aspect of her life, but now with grave responsibility.

What had she told that gorgeous man in Vienna? Sean. 'All this, plus the pressure of knowing that if your project doesn't work, people may die.' It was still true. But she had come too far for it to be a choice.

There was a way out, of course. She could cultivate and support a promising leader who would be willing to take on the burden of Ocean Independent State. That person could make it into the global powerhouse it was fated to become, and realise President Tabai's fever dream of a nation that represented the largest part of the planet: the sea.

It was that simple. She could step aside. She could go back to making interactive movies and documentaries, staying away from the public eye this time, or perhaps she could focus on promoting Cristina Abidin's regenerative farming projects. Or she could retire; she had more than enough money.

It was still possible.

She leaned back in her chair and listened to the tram bell through the open window. She opened another view on the display to inspect the electoral registration system. The new system, donated by a tech company, projected images in front of her eyes using an extension of the usual eyepiece. After dithering, the interim cabinet accepted sponsorship from Orac Holdings to operate the election procedure, including registration, biometric identity verification, and the final count. It was a good system, clean and secure.

Still staring at the display, she pinged Tekiree. 'It's time. Let's do this.'

Tekiree appeared on her monitor, laughing. 'I was wondering whether you were going to bail out! Anote said he wouldn't accept any nominations after the deadline, full stop.'

'The ballots are filling up. I just read that there's a Nigerian billionaire running. That Danish shipping executive has also registered, and I think he's a realistic option, although the main reason he's running is because he doesn't want to pay for his ships to use the ocean.'

'There's that American woman,' Tekiree replied. 'But I think her sole experience in public affairs is as a campaigner for Save the Earth.'

'And she was still in college then. She's been a multi-level marketing rep since then.'

'You know what this means.'

Grace reminded him, 'Well, a week is a long time in politics, and two months even more. We're not a shoo-in.'

'But still. I think we'll win,' he replied.

'That's the problem. I don't know what I'm getting myself into. Us, I should say. But here we go.'

She entered their names into the open fields on the registration system. Candidate for President: Grace Chan. Candidate for Vice President: Tekiree Bauro. Record fingerprint here. Scan iris here. Speak the following phrase to record your voiceprint.

Tekiree verified his own information and biometrics, and broke into a new kind of laughter, this time coloured with disbelief at what they had done. 'Okay, Grace – let's go save the world!'

She smiled again and ended the connection.

She saw her reflection in the dark display. The long, thick braid of black hair snaked down her back. It gave her a winsome, girlish look. She made a decision.

She tramped down the steps and out the door of the consulate, and stepped into a local hairdresser's shop, one block away. The proprietor greeted her. 'Wash and dry? Styling?'

She took a breath, and answered, 'I want you to cut it all off.'

9.00 am, Saturday, June 21, 2036
Penang Fairhaven – Consulate General, OIS

Six more candidates registered by the time nominations closed, bringing the total to ten. Two were serious possibilities. One was a tech CEO from Silicon Valley. Grace knew her from her time in Fremont as a wily publicity-seeker and astute strategist. Another, the former foreign minister of Nauru, claimed (not without justification) that his country would be next in line to join OIS when it drowned, and that he was the logical successor to President Tabai. Grace was tempted for a moment to step back and let the Nauruan candidate take up the mantle, until she learned about his multiple convictions for bribery and graft.

By election day, seventeen million people were citizens of OIS, comparable to the Netherlands in terms of population, if not in land area. Hans sent a cartoon to Grace, accusing her of designing it that way. 'Where are you going to put all of those people? Haven't you had enough of building dykes?' he asked. She chuckled when she received the message, but did not answer.

Things had changed.

Hiroko Mizutani turned out to be an excellent press secretary. Within days, she crafted a simple and effective communications strategy that expressed the key elements of their platform. Grace's own posts on her Orac video channel shifted from personal stories and highlights of Ocean Agency's work to more substantive topics: land and ocean use, human rights, international law. She lost fans, although she suspected it was much a backlash against her new haircut as against her content. It didn't matter; the new fans were better. Hiroko was also a skilled intermediary with powerful news editors, preventing Grace from creating enemies with her tendency towards bluntness and sarcasm.

In any case, many new citizens of OIS voted based on identity rather than issues.

The United States signed a dual-citizenship agreement, promising military and political support to the new nation, but few Americans bothered to register as OIS citizens. Of those who did, most voted for Grace since they had seen her on their screens or via their optical implants.

A large contingent from China voted as a bloc with hours to spare, as President Tabai secured a last-minute deal. Grace knew Zygmunt had received a shadowy offer of support, but she would learn the rest of the details another time. The new dual citizens cast their ballots almost as one for the Chan-Bauro ticket.

Malaysians registered in huge numbers and voted with enthusiasm for Grace and Tekiree. Grace wondered what caused the immense surge, other than her own prominence. Could this, too, be the result of behind-the-scenes work by Tengku Marina? No; that would be ascribing too much power to the Zainal family.

All the ballots were in, counted, and then re-counted as the complicated ranked choice algorithm did its work.

In the meantime, Grace received a simple message from Adam Park, showing his 'I voted!' badge, and a thumbs up. She smiled to know she had at least one supporter in Korea.

'Madam President-Elect, may we offer you our congratulations!' was one of the first messages to arrive after Orac finished its count. It was signed, 'Hans and Inge'.

9.00 am, Monday, June 30, 2036
Penang Fairhaven – Consulate General, OIS

'I thought you might be feeling overwhelmed after your first week as President-Elect,' said Zygmunt, 'so I've brought a present for you.' He was one of the few people allowed to come into her office unannounced.

'Thank God,' Grace replied. 'I could use cheering up.' The tenor of public opinion had gone against her in the past seven days, despite Hiroko's heroic efforts. To her displeasure, she was being treated as a lightweight, a celebrity ambassador out of her depth. One piece referred to her as 'one-time Streamberry star Grace Chan, recently named figurehead for the experimental Ocean Independent State' and she all but convinced herself that it was true. In the meantime, the congressional elections, happening in parallel, delivered a motley group of lawmakers that she was not looking forward to working with.

'I'm happy to inform you,' continued Zygmunt, 'that OIS is now the undisputed owner of an actual piece of land.'

'What? I thought that was already true. I assigned that lawyer to work out the contracts.'

'Nope. I'm referring to our Hawaiian island, the one with the active volcano.'

'What's the story?'

'I've been following up with Jack Smith. Remember him, from the Constitutional Convention? As per our discussion, the United States government has agreed to transfer the territory from the United States to the Ocean Independent State, in return for certain concessions.'

Grace sat back in her chair. Land. This was unexpected. Then, the second half of Zygmunt's comment registered.

'Wait. What concessions?'

'Most Favoured Nation status when it comes to CO_2 absorption and shipping transit fees in OIS waters, formerly known as international waters. That means they would pay about $4 per nautical mile and $25 for every tonne of greenhouse gas.'

'What! But that's less than a third of the rate we've been discussing. That's a terrible deal!'

'Yes. But don't you see? We can—'

'No, I do not. That's a pure disaster. Just for an island, which we can't use because we'll be incinerated by flowing lava if we set foot on it? Who gave you the authority to negotiate this?' she fumed.

'Nobody. And in a minute, if you'll let me finish, you'll understand why this is so incredible. Yes, it's a fraction of the fee we were talking about charging, but their agreement to the deal means they acknowledge we have a right to charge.

'Think about it! One of the richest and most powerful countries in the world has recognised the rights of OIS to manage the affairs of the ocean. What that means is that the rate they're paying is irrelevant. Even if they only agreed to pay 1% of our proposed fees, it would still give us the legitimacy we are so desperate for.'

'Oh, my God.' Grace stood up and ran her hand through her hair. She still wasn't used to the short style. 'Oh, my God. You're right. And when the EU hears the United States has done this, they'll be shamed into agreeing to pay. They'll ask for the MFN status as well, but who cares!'

'You, or a subsequent administration, can always raise the rates later.'

'Our term is for five years. That was what we agreed to at the Constitutional Convention.'

'Yes. I was there. And, by the way – that island? Thanks to the lava spewing out of the volcano and hardening into rock as it reaches the sea, it's getting bigger all the time.'

'I guess we have that going for us. In a few thousand years, it will be quite the paradise on Earth.'

6.00 pm, Wednesday, October 8, 2036
Penang Fairhaven – President Tabai's apartment

Much was happening in the world beyond the affairs of the ocean. Although the half-year gap between the election in June and her inauguration day on January 1st seemed too long when they discussed it at first, Grace now cherished the precious months. They provided a buffer period for her to embark on the herculean task of learning about global politics.

She strove to understand the ins and outs of the postwar ruling coalition in Moscow, the bizarre new coalition that had formed out of America's political meltdown, and the centuries-old grudges between various nations in Asia.

Not all of it was bad news. There was much to be celebrated.

It was a year in which the architect of the Russian peace agreement helped save hundreds of thousands of lives. A selfless, elderly woman who dedicated her life to eliminating HIV-AIDS in sub-Saharan Africa succeeded beyond anyone's dreams, although she now lay dying in a clinic in Switzerland. A dedicated nation builder in Sudan brought hope to millions.

President Tabai, who had already begun calling Grace 'Madam President', although she would not be inaugurated until January 1st, invited the interim cabinet over for an early dinner, a meal he cooked himself. 'You can't get good *te inai* here,' he complained. 'Those fish they get from the Sea Orchards just aren't the same. But the pumpkin is tasty.'

As they finished up their first servings, a certain tone alerted him. He switched on his eyepiece. After listening for a few minutes, and answering with, 'Okay,' 'Yes,' and 'Thank you,' he ended the call. Then he turned to the group.

'I'm going to be awarded the Nobel Peace Prize,' he said, with a shocked expression.

For a moment, they could only return his amazement.

Grace spoke for them all. 'That's incredible! We were all hoping for it, but never dreamed it could really happen.' Marina's cousin Amir had been in Norway for several months, working with Cassandra; their campaign had borne fruit.

'Do I need to go to Stockholm?'

'No,' Anote recalled. 'The Nobel Peace Prize is presented in Oslo. You have to meet the Norwegian royal family.'

'I met the King of Tonga, once,' he mused. 'But I've never been in the presence of the crowned heads of Europe.'

'Speaking of crowns, what are you going to do with the money?' asked Peter.

'What money?'

'There's more than the medal, you know. It comes with an award of nine million Norwegian crowns.'

'How much is that?' he said, as he consulted his eyepiece. 'Oh. One point three million US dollars. That's a lot of money.'

Grace sent a quick message to Hiroko, informing her, and asking for a meeting at 9.00 pm that night.

They spent a few moments gaping at each other, not knowing what else to say. Anote broke the awkward silence. 'Teatao, I want more of that *te inai*.'

8.00 pm, Saturday, December 13, 2036
Oslo, Sweden – Atrium, University of Oslo

They gathered in the forecourt, prior to the ceremony itself. The crowd was subdued. 'I don't suppose this trip is helping your personal carbon footprint,' whispered Nant. 'How long was your flight?'

'Let's not talk about that. We're here for Teatao. This is his day.'

'Fine. But don't forget that I still have to answer quite a few questions about the owner of Jack Mutt Productions, which happens to be you.'

'Ask them to estimate the carbon negative contribution I have made over my career. My own tally is around minus 150 million tonnes.'

'Shh!' An elegant woman frowned at them from across the room.

In the atrium, before the Norwegian royal family, President Teatao

Tabai explained, once again, his vision for the Ocean Independent State. Grace, who had heard it a hundred times, paid no attention. She already knew every word.

There in the vast, medieval hall, Grace felt part of something larger than herself. Too often, she doubted the very validity of the initiative they were attempting, the practicality of attempting to realise it, and, most of all, her ability to deliver. But in that venue, where so many other dreamers over the years had expressed their vision for what could be, she could almost see a future where they had achieved their goals.

The oceans would be restored, patient and unabated in their absorption of poisons spewed out by humankind.

Marine life, rich and teeming, would provide the sustenance needed for a thriving, healthy ecosystem at sea and on land.

The land itself would recover from the violent assaults of the past decade, and the soil would be renewed.

The forests, the wildlife, and the people who depended on them would learn how to live in balance.

All that they needed was for nothing else to go wrong.

BUST

Grace, Tekiree, Scott, and Hiroko were in a *mamak* stall, eating noodles, when the power went down.

Scott groaned. 'What, a brownout? I thought this kind of thing wasn't supposed to happen any more!'

'On paper, this is still a developing country, you know,' Grace said, embarrassed, 'although we have more solar now.'

'Which country?'

'Fair point. I meant that sometimes the grid can't handle the load. But of course Ocean Independent State is less than "developing", to be frank. We don't even have a power grid.'

'Not that the ocean needs one,' commented Tekiree.

In the absence of electric fans, the stall grew warmer. They watched a drop of sweat roll down the cook's face as he presided over a roaring stove, fuelled by a bottle of biomethane.

Scott noticed that the shops on either side of them were also dark. 'I wonder if Tenaga has put out any announcement.'

'What's Tenaga?' asked Tekiree.

'The local power company.' Scott muttered a question to his Orac Assistant, but grew puzzled. 'I don't know why my virtual PA isn't working. Maybe the outage is affecting the server?' He stood up, flexed his muscles, and patrolled the perimeter of the shop.

'You should get a human personal assistant, like Grace. But you'd need to be the president of a country to afford it,' Tekiree teased.

Hiroko spoke into her implant, and soon wore the same puzzled expression. 'My implant isn't working at all. It's not responding to my commands.' She pressed the manual reset button on the side of her arm and waited for a response.

'If there's a problem in the grid, then it would affect the network provider itself. We'll find out when we get back to the office.'

Unwilling to speculate further, and glad for a respite from the constant barrage of information that characterised their daily lives, they finished their noodles, told the shop owner they'd pay once the power came back, and returned to the tram stop.

Several minutes later, however, when no tram arrived, Scott was worried. 'The tram runs on a different power delivery system. There's no reason it should have been affected.'

'Do you want to walk back?'

'I'll get a taxi; it will be faster. Good to see you all! Let's have lunch again soon.' He strode in the opposite direction, toward the taxi stand and the Fairhaven office, while the other three headed toward the consulate building. Grace glanced back, and noticed that despite the long queue, no taxis were in sight. In fact, she could not see a single vehicle in motion.

2.00 pm, Tuesday, December 16, 2036
Penang Fairhaven – Consulate General, OIS

Devices of all kinds showed blank screens. Grace was happy to walk up one flight of stairs to her own office, but it wouldn't be fun if lifts were still out when she returned to her penthouse apartment on the 38th floor.

While some laptops could be turned on, at least those whose batteries were fully charged, the lack of internet connection made meaningful work impossible. In the absence of anything more productive to do, Grace pulled out a pad of scrap paper, and jotted down notes for her inauguration speech, several weeks hence.

Kayleigh, who now worked under Hiroko, wondered aloud, 'Aren't we supposed to have an emergency power system?'

'The city does. This building doesn't. I'd like to imagine they're using it for essential services first, like the hospital.'

Something outside caught Kayleigh's eye. 'I knew it. Here they come.' She headed toward the stairs and clumped down.

A small group of people were standing in front of the consulate entryway. Kayleigh spoke with them for a few minutes before clumping back up the stairs with a concerned expression. 'Three reporters and an Oracker. The power outage is citywide at the very least. And there's no internet connection anywhere, as far as they're able to tell. They want a statement from you.'

'At Fairhaven, we used to use walkie-talkies. Do you suppose any of those would be useful? I'm sure the admin shack still has dozens of them.'

'Maybe. What's the range? And for that matter, is anyone listening?'

'Speaking of which,' said Grace, 'everyone stop talking for a minute.

Just listen.'

They did. Tekiree was the first to understand. 'I hear it. Or, rather, I don't hear it. There's nothing out there.'

'No cars. No trams. No music.'

'Wait; I can hear a motor out in the distance.'

They strained to detect it, and made out the engine sound of an ancient, diesel-powered boat, the kind that used to skim the tops of the mud flats, looking for fish, crabs, or buried treasure.

'I'll work on the statement,' Kayleigh offered. 'My handwriting is bad, though, so I can't guarantee you'll be able to read it. I haven't written anything on paper for years.'

5.00 pm, Tuesday, December 16, 2036
Penang Fairhaven – Consulate General, OIS

They shouted with relief when the lights flickered on, groaned when they went out for another half a moment, and cheered when they returned. 'We're back!'

Still, nobody could find an internet connection. Someone quipped, 'Have you tried turning it off and turning it on again?' Gamely following the old advice, they rebooted the routers, the building servers, the roof solar panels, their own eyepieces and implants, the individual computers, and everything else they could find.

'How far does this problem reach?' asked Grace, real worry in her voice.

She dispatched an intern to ride a bicycle to the office of the George Town mayor, and find out what he knew. The young man had not yet returned. Hiroko and Tekiree joined her in her office.

She offered each a bamboo hand fan. Despite the breeze flowing through the open, shaded windows, the heat was almost intolerable.

But they didn't want to put a strain on the system by turning on the air conditioners right away. 'I think we have to start considering worst-case scenarios.'

'What scenarios do you mean?' Hiroko asked.

'What if this is affecting areas beyond Penang?'

'You mean other provinces?'

'I don't know why, but there's something about this that is giving me a strange feeling. I'm starting to wonder if it's the entire country. Or could it be global?'

Tekiree objected. 'I heard that people on the street are calling it the Cloud Bust. But if this is cyberwarfare, nobody would want to shut down the entire world. If America is behind it, they would take out China. Or vice versa. Nobody would attack Malaysia. It's much more likely to be something local. Or an earthquake that cut out undersea cables?'

'Maybe. The last time that happened was back in 2006. But if this situation isn't resolved, the loss of data is going to be incalculable. I'd like to think it through, just in case. We can't do anything else right now. What do we need to consider right now if this is a widespread outage?'

They jotted notes on the whiteboard that Grace still kept in her office.

Banking and financial information; did funds still exist if they were recorded in digital format and nowhere else? Who had paid their ocean transit fees, and who had not? Voting records. Citizenship applications. The constitution itself, thank goodness, was printed out and framed, and was hanging on the wall behind Grace's desk; it appeared in the background of dozens of official photos. However, hundreds of pages of draft legislation existed only online; members of the OIS congress, scattered all over the world, collaborated remotely, keeping all of their files in the cloud.

Tekiree shook his head. 'We learned nothing from my country's fate. Remember the citizenship records of Kiribati? Drowned with the people themselves.'

'I remember,' said Grace.

'Two on, one off. That's what you're always supposed to do,' the former ambassador recalled.

'What does that mean?'

'For any important information, you are always supposed to keep two copies onsite, on non-interoperable devices, and one copy offsite. That way, no matter whether it's a virus, or flood, or a fire, or what, you're protected.'

'I always forget that you were a computer engineer when you were younger. Do you think this is a virus?' Grace asked.

'There's no way to tell, because we're not getting information from anywhere else.'

11.00 am, Tuesday, December 23, 2036
Penang Fairhaven – Penang Amateur Radio Recreation Club

The local ham radio club, the haunt of a handful of teenage nerds and elderly hobbyists, was now a communications centre for the entire province. Several times each day, interns ran back and forth between the OIS consulate, the provincial governor's office, and the PARRC clubhouse. Grace began to spend most of her time there, perched on a small wooden stool in the corner.

With just a pair of biodiesel generators to power it, the site was bedlam. Six or seven radios handled all the traffic, several of them vintage models running on vacuum tubes, along with a few dipole antennas running crazily between balconies, and several improvised towers poking up from the tops of the tallest buildings. Ancient trucks, rescued from the junkyard and repaired just to the point of functionality, carted fuel daily from an outlying palm plantation, where there was a stock tank and a small, solar-powered refinery, running as long as the sun shone.

Teenagers, lacking access to their schoolwork, acted as note-takers and runners. Primary school teachers resorted to storybooks and chalkboards to instruct their charges. But without the usual automated trams and self-driving vehicles, classrooms were half empty.

'Don't we have any more paper?' Grace asked, annoyed, as she used the back of an old envelope to scribble an angry reply to a message from Washington, DC.

'They're already rationing it,' Kayleigh answered. 'And anyway, the paper mill is out of commission, because its system was automated. Controlled via, you guessed it, the internet. Plus, the workers don't know if they're going to get paid.'

'Nobody knows where the online money is,' added Hiroko. 'The national stock market is still closed. I have seen people using gold as a medium of exchange.'

The news from the rest of the world was grim. Some cities saw riots. Some chemical plants, dependent on electric power for cooling, were abandoned, their volatile materials left to heat up unchecked, until they exploded and burned to the ground. Most aircraft landed without incident, but not all: airports with decrepit, radio-based air traffic control systems were able to handle the traffic, while the most modern airports were paralysed. Thousands of passengers were stranded half a world away from home.

Grace put down her pen and stood up. 'If there's nothing else I can do, I'm heading out to the soup kitchens.' The Fairhaven City government had decided to dip into the emergency food reserves and was opening soup kitchens throughout the city.

'I'll come with you,' Tekiree said. He had volunteered to take charge of the data management for food rations. 'Whether I have to mark it up on a wall with a piece of chalk, or use an abacus, it's still data,' he pointed out. 'And we're not getting much done with OIS at the moment.'

As Grace strolled with him to their local soup kitchen, she was once again surprised by the lack of major unrest, riots or looting within Fairhaven. Volunteer guards around the shops kept the peace just as well as digital surveillance systems had in the past. She peered into a shop as they passed, and saw the sales records tallied on the wall with pencil, charcoal, or pushpins. Paper money, already on the way out, was now too precious to waste on ordinary transactions.

'We've been thinking all week about the professional impact,' Grace mused. 'But what about the billions of hours of content from the old platforms, YouTube, Metaspace, GithubX? The family interconnections, the photos? The financial data? The personal records? Sure, there's plenty of junk, but it's what we know as humans. Billions of people have lost their money, their contacts, contracts, and vast pieces of their electronic lives.'

'It's the end of the world,' Tekiree observed, gloomy. 'And what do you know? It arrived with neither a bang nor a whimper, but with the number "404".'

9.00 am, Wednesday, December 24, 2036
Penang Fairhaven – Eaves Lock, South Dyke

There was never any real danger of the dyke being breached and flooding the city, according to Cristina. When the power went down, the pumps stopped, and the water level on the canals of Fairhaven rose.

However, the full outage only lasted a few hours.

Meanwhile, the automated, smart grid was still not running at full capacity. Its safety features would not allow major sections to operate without the interconnected control and monitoring system.

'Keep monitoring,' Cristina told the crew. 'If need be, we'll call out emergency crews to do this by hand.' She ordered the ground floors of all the buildings in Fairhaven cleared, but since communications systems were not in order, word spread haphazardly.

10.00 am, Friday, December 26, 2036
Penang Fairhaven – Consulate General, OIS

Miracles still existed in the world, Grace discovered.

Kayleigh marched into her office with an external hard drive in hand, looking triumphant. 'Guess what this is?'

'Do I want to know?'

'You do. It is a complete copy – well, almost – of our citizenship application database, with the biometric data intact. Tekiree's chief of staff, you know, the one he knew in college, the software developer? Who still hasn't stopped tinkering with things all the time? He downloaded a copy ten days ago, because he wanted to try a new sorting algorithm. And it was disconnected from the network when the incident occurred.'

'That's excellent news. I was getting worried that we were gambling with people's rights and lives, just because we were careless about backing up our database. We set up that system to handle all those millions of climate refugees, and we did not want to go through that process again.'

'Peter wants to know if we are going to be able to do any records processing.'

'The scenario planning team is working on it. Stay tuned. Oh, and while I have you here, could I remind you and Hiroko to let me know the plan for Thursday's pre-inauguration press conference? I suppose we're still going ahead; our constitution doesn't say anything about internet outages. As such, the inauguration happens next week whether or not anybody is there to listen to my speech. Also, I'm going to have to go out into the field for a few days, if I can get transportation, to see how people outside of Fairhaven are faring. And in the meantime, please make two copies of that damn database, and store one of them offsite!'

'Two on, one off!' Kayleigh laughed, and returned to her desk.

Grace was spending less and less time in her office, and more time sitting in the little garden next to the consulate building, taking notes, planning, and brooding. This time, however, she needed the stillness.

Gambling with people's lives, she had told Kayleigh. But something was nagging at her.

In her last two interactive feature films, audience participation was integral to the viewing experience. Under Nant's supervision, Jack Mutt Productions was developing a new project that would be more accessible for those who had already installed implants. And in all cases, competitive gaming accounted for at least 20% of the gross revenue projections.

No matter whether the Cloud Bust ever ended, she decided, gambling would no longer be part of her life.

She knew it wasn't the most important piece of communication in the world right now. But she brought out a precious piece of blank paper and wrote a long message to Nant. It could wait in the non-urgent pile until nightfall, when long-distance transmission conditions improved, to be sent by non-encrypted packet fax. She didn't care who else read it.

8.00 am, Monday, December 29, 2036
Penang Fairhaven – 8 Gurney Drive

Travelling, even for a few days, gave Grace a new appreciation for the seriousness of the situation. After her trip, she got back to her flat that morning for a quick break thanks to a working fire lift, which operated on an older, non-grid-linked system with emergency power. Not all the residents were as lucky. One was still stuck at sea. Another had been stranded for a day in a traffic jam stretching halfway up the peninsula, as most of the newer cars refused to operate without a connection to a central server.

She didn't want to think about what was happening to the astronauts on the International Space Station.

She borrowed an antique iPhone from Johnnie, now unusable except for its camera and voice recorder. She needed to prepare for the morning's press conference.

Or maybe she should just take a nap. She knew she'd end up sleepless that night, no matter what. No, she'd drive out to Bazalgette Lock, as she found herself doing more and more often. She knew the way without thinking about it. She needed to let off steam, and work on her speech.

She'd heard a manatee had been spotted; perhaps she'd see it, instead of the usual monitor lizards, whose numbers were growing so promisingly.

ESCAPE

6.55 am, Tuesday, December 30, 2036
Penang Fairhaven – North Dyke
Global temperature: 2.3 °C above pre-industrial average

Blind with fear, Grace dropped her makeshift blade into the dark water. When she realised what she had done, she shouted her frustration aloud. The remainder of the old phone, if it had ever been recording, was now separated from her voice by half a metre of seawater.

She clutched the last, awkward shard of glass, and continued her desperate sawing, now making slower progress. At last, the belt gave way. But the remnants of the airbag, now floating in the rising water like seaweed, wrapped around her arms and chest. She tried to rid herself of them. But she was already at her physical limits, disoriented and terrified.

Something grasped the edge of the open window. Grace's astonished scream drove it away. A hand.

Then, a head appeared. Not a manatee, nor a lizard, but a tiny Chinese woman, shouting in Hakka.

The woman vanished as quickly as she had appeared.

The water reached Grace's chin. Gasping, stretching to reach the air, writhing against the stupid airbag, she cursed the lizard, the phone, and most of all herself. With a frenzied struggle, she rid herself of the strangling pieces of fabric, and heard what must be a stream of swear words in Hakka.

Aching, she reached toward the window. Strong, wiry hands, spotted with age, pulled her through, into the water and all the way to the mud line at the bottom of the embankment. She was free.

Grace sat in the mud, her mind dull, as the old woman continued her stream of rebukes in Hakka, concerned and cross at the same time. The woman reached into her bucket of cockles, pulled out a steel bottle, and offered Grace a drink of unpleasantly warm water that smelled of the sea. She accepted it, grateful, realising all of a sudden how powerful her thirst had become.

As the truck cab disappeared under the rising water, the first glimmers of sunrise emerged beyond the horizon.

A quiet beep sounded, and the old woman glanced at her wrist. Her smartwatch showed several new notifications. The woman beamed, and showed off the little 'connected' icon. 'Internet!' she pronounced, with a grin.

It's over, Grace thought. She addressed the old woman as if she would understand.

'I've got a speech to re-write.'

PRESIDENCY

9.00 am, Monday, February 16, 2037

Penang Fairhaven – Executive Headquarters, Ocean Independent State

Global temperature: 1.9°C above pre-industrial average

Sometimes Grace told herself it was the aftermath of the Cloud Bust that changed her. Other times, she thought it was because of her own brush with death. Either way, she had become more demanding, both of herself and others. She knew, now more than ever, that there was no time to waste, and she couldn't do it alone. She needed to ask for help.

Likewise, she decided, bureaucrats and politicians were useful, but sometimes you needed an engineer to do the job. She wanted someone who understood how the ocean worked at a personal level, a technical level; someone she trusted. Her mind lit on Adam Park, the Korean ROV operator from Sea Orchards. She was certain that he was inexperienced in nation-building. But then again, that was true of everyone. Nobody had ever attempted something like this before.

A few minutes later, she ended a call, and smiled with satisfaction. Adam Park would move to Malaysia and work for Grace as her new chief of staff.

It was almost frightening how easy it was to convince him. Something in this fierce new version of herself could impress a sense of urgency on people.

'Cut,' she told him on his first day. 'Cut anything that doesn't contribute to the end goal of getting our planet out of this mess. Yes, we're an official nation now. We have the authority and the backing of enough world powers to act like one. But that doesn't mean we need to get mired in the sludge of bureaucracy that most national governments have.'

'Okay,' he agreed. 'What do we need to cut first?'

'All kinds of things. We've been having a discussion for several weeks now about how many embassies we have to maintain. My answer: none. The internet is back, at least for now, so if someone wants to talk to us, they can send a message. No embassies.'

'Okay. What else?'

'Too many amateurs have been sitting here arguing about what to put on our stationery. Ask Hiroko to get a real branding person on board, and simplify all of it. We have a flag; let's use it.'

'How about the military?'

'It's unpleasant to think about, but if we can demonstrate our capability for force, we won't have to use it. We've received offers of support from both China and the United States, and we'll soon be able to buy what they won't give us. Tell Zygmunt to get the best deal out of both of them, and if they make any trouble, we'll ask France instead.'

Adam made a note. 'Has the Congress approved the budget yet?'

'They're working on it. I've been surprised – relieved – to find out that that damn group of misfits love working together. Speaking of which, I believe they're almost finished with the refugee documentation plan?'

'I'll check. I think Peter told me this morning as I was doing my orientation that they were expecting to have the completed draft by the end of the week.'

She continued to tick off various topics, either striking them from the list, assigning them to experts, or passing them back to Congress with aggressive deadlines. She returned human rights and clean water to the lawmakers as priorities. A proposal for an OIS national currency was slashed; any world currency would suffice, and Congress could decide which one. She suggested that Adam recruit his old pirate friend, Muhammad, to take care of the topic of security at the consulate general.

'Speaking of Sea Orchards, what's Churchill up to now? We need someone to oversee the Department of Ocean Restoration Projects. There are too many separate projects, all fragmented. Can we nab him for the job?'

'He is now second in command to Marina.'

Grace grunted and returned to her list. 'Good. Let's hope she's willing to let him go.'

After several more hours, Adam asked, tentatively, 'Excuse me, President Chan; around how many more topics do we have on our agenda?'

She looked up, surprised. 'What? Oh, do you need a break? I suppose that's almost everything we need to cover tonight.'

'Thank you. I would like to see my wife and children. They moved here with me, with the hope that we might spend time together. We were apart for so many years, while I was working at Sea Orchards, that the children almost forgot who I was.'

Grace continued to gape at him. 'Oh. Oh, yes, of course. Please. I'll see you in the morning. Go home.'

As he gathered his things and left her office, Grace asked her assistant to bring her something for dinner, and brooded.

She wondered for the thousandth time what the hell happened to the internet during those awful two weeks. The square-jawed Jack Smith, in a roundabout fashion, gave her hints of what the US authorities suspected, but nothing concrete. Most people had given up speculating and gone back to taking digital services for granted.

Hans and Inge would be back in Fairhaven in March. She was growing accustomed to the idea of referring to them as a single phrase: Hans and Inge. It would be painful to see Hans, but better than the moment of despair during the Cloud Bust, when she feared she would never see him again at all.

Hans and Inge. Adam and his wife and children. Cristina and her British engineer. Marina and Elizabeth.

Others were fated to enjoy close family and friends, she decided. Meanwhile, it was her lot to move from school to school, from country to country, from job to job, from burden to burden. If she didn't dedicate herself to the task, then who would?

The development and maintenance of society had always required sacrifices of its most heartfelt contributors.

3.00 pm, Thursday, July 16, 2037
Brussels, Belgium – Ulicore Materials SE

'Thank you for the presentation,' Grace told the men in their bespoke business suits. 'But we are sure that you can do better.'

They were all at least a decade older than Grace. But she had escaped death twice, once at the hands of men, and once at the hands of nature.

She was not about to capitulate to a group of executives with obsolete ideas.

The oldest one, at the head of the table, sniffed. 'Perhaps you are not familiar with the mining industry,' he began. 'We assure you that this is the most efficient way to extract metallic nodules from deep-sea deposits. Furthermore, after consulting with our legal team, we are not convinced that your organisation has the authority to negotiate with us on this matter.'

'You're about the last people on the planet to be convinced, I'm sorry to say. OIS has already signed mining rights treaties with the United States, China, Russia, Australia, France, and Brazil.'

'You may be aware that we have existing, active operations at several undersea petalite deposits. Are you proposing that we now give up those rights? Until your organisation made its, ahem, unprecedented claims, it was clear from the 1982 Convention that all mineral exploration and exploitation activities would be sponsored by a State Party to UNCLOS, and approved by the International Seabed Authority.'

'No, we're not asking that. In fact, we are right now in the final stages of an agreement with ISA to take over administration of those activities on their behalf. What we want to ensure is that before you launch any new operations, you conduct trials in water shallow enough to dive in, picking up mock nodules so we can all see what is going on. Our spec is for a system that picks up nodules one at a time, without disturbing the seabed. We have also researched possible approaches and believe that picking systems are practicable.'

Another man, his hair a suspicious black, wore a bemused expression. 'I see you are interested in this topic. Let me explain —'

'No. I'm the one who's going to explain,' Grace cut him off. She had had too many things explained to her by people who thought they knew better. 'For example, a large submarine platform can hover over the seabed without much disturbance at all. It will use a low-thrust, slow, cili-based movement system. You will need to establish a reasonable picking rate, or at least a method that allows you to make use of the mineral-rich byproducts.'

Adam jumped in. 'It is possible to pick areas of 100 metres x 100 metres, with 100 metre bands between them, creating a contiguous connection for any life forms on the seabed.'

The dark-haired man responded, 'I don't suppose you've considered the significant financial impact this would have on our company. You may be aware that we have a responsibility to our shareholders. Pensioners, schoolteachers, ordinary people —'

Grace cut him off again. 'What do you suppose will happen to all of those pensioners and ordinary people when the sea is too poisonous to use? Making a profit is your problem, not ours. I'm sure your corporate strategy has a contingency plan for a changed global environment. Perhaps it's time for you to extract that document from wherever you keep it. Assuming it survived the Bust.'

'Ms Chan —'

'"Madam President," please,' jumped in Adam.

'Madam President, we are not prepared to ignore decades of established precedent in favour of unproven methods.'

'Established precedent is what got us into this situation in the first place,' Grace said coolly, as she leaned back in the over-engineered chair. She was amazed at her own audacity: several years ago, she never would have been able to command a room like this.

Emboldened by the changing mood, she continued, 'This is a new situation. If OIS mounted an expedition to strip mine Wallonia in Belgium, the relevant authorities wouldn't grant permission. However, we could get an agricultural concession, with a long-term contract and ongoing review. This is the goal all parties need to aim for. And we are that authority.'

The dark-haired man and the one at the head of the table muttered to each other in rapid Flemish.

'Of course, a suitable split of the revenues arising from the harvest of the nodules would have to be negotiated,' the older one said.

'Good,' Adam interjected. 'We are also keen to see high prices.'

Grace clarified, 'And we want to see minimal consumption, with 100% recycling of these valuable resources as a key priority. Profligate, non-circular methods are responsible for our current problems.

'I think we have come to an understanding,' Grace concluded, standing up. 'If you will excuse us, we are due at the European Commission in half an hour.' She smiled, remembering from Zygmunt's lessons that it was important to be gracious in victory. 'We are very much looking forward to working with you.'

5.45 pm, Thursday, October 14, 2038
Penang Fairhaven – Executive Headquarters, OIS
Global temperature: 2.1°C above pre-industrial average

More than a year later, Grace welcomed a long-awaited visitor. 'It's good to see you again, Hans.'

They stood at opposite ends of the Presidential Office. Neither made a move to turn on the lights, although the sun was already setting. His fair hair glinted in the dying light. Grace, with her back to the window, cast a long shadow over her desk, running like a dark river along the floor to the doorway. 'How long has it been?'

'Years. I thought we'd see you when we were here in Penang a year ago, in March. But you decided at the last minute to attend that summit in Bali.'

'It must have been in Sydney, then, at Ivan's funeral.'

They grew silent for a moment, remembering.

She sat, and pointed towards the chair in front of her desk. 'Please.'

'Thank you. Madam President.'

She did not correct him. Indeed, from a professional standpoint, they had undergone a profound transformation: Rakki Arctic Ventures, although owned by Rakki Holdings, conducted its main operations in the Arctic Ocean, and, as such, was under the jurisdiction of OIS.

'Have you been offered anything to drink?'

'Yes. Thank you. I was going to have a cup of coffee, but your assistant was kind enough to remind me that a cup of coffee has more than 500 times the freshwater footprint of a glass of water. I decided I'd skip it this time.'

Grace chuckled. 'Good for her. So, let's talk. Does the Earth have a polar icecap again?'

'We're working on it. We've made amazing progress but not as much as we hoped. We'll need another big resource push in the next six months.'

'What kind of resources?'

'We're hoping to achieve the maximum summer ice extent since pre-industrial times. And we're working on a bolder plan: to stabilise the ice sheets in Antarctica. The long-term target is to get back to the levels they were at the end of the last ice age, 10,000 years ago. In the meantime, Kenji estimates that we could ramp up ice production by a multiple of ten if we use submarines.'

Grace gaped. 'Submarines! What for?'

'To travel under the ice and do larger scale flooding.'

'I see. And how is the albedo effectiveness measurement coming along?'

'We're optimistic. In a system as complex as the global weather system, it's impossible to ascribe large-scale, short-term change to any single factor. But you are, of course, aware that this past summer in the Northern Hemisphere was more moderate than the last several years. And this is what our models have been predicting.'

'Good. The less disruption we have to the land environments of the world, the fewer refugees will be forced to apply to us for citizenship. No matter what you hear, we don't want people to be displaced. I've got to know refugees much better in the past year; a good portion of our Navy is made up of refugees.'

'I never would have dreamed in a million years that I'd see you as a military leader.'

'In name. It won't be under my administration that OIS goes to war.'

'How did OIS end up as a central player in this situation?'

'Long before we were established, refugees were passing through Fairhaven in huge numbers. Remember? Ivan launched that food-for-work scheme before the disaster, and then Cristina expand-ed it. It was controversial, but it was a good arrangement for most of them: education, health care and family planning. The Malaysian government was generous under the circumstances, because it was the pragmatic thing to do. The flow of refugees was another type of flood that would be impossible to ignore or prevent.'

'You can't be employing all of them in your navy?'

'No. Refugee relocation has continued to be a tough nut to crack. Many have passed through the OIS relocation system and on to new lives in other countries, starting with those who have dual-citizenship agreements. We've processed more than 150 million people already.'

Hans whistled. 'I had no idea.'

'Our new seat on the UN Permanent Council helps. But remem-ber, the equitable treatment of refugees is also a means to an end, not just the end in itself.'

'What do you mean?'

'People are the most powerful climate solution. We need to move resources and effort from areas that are lost to sea level rise to areas which need much more effort to defend. OIS negotiates transfers of people with countries who will be the future dry-land hosts, and provides part of the funding to support the building of sea defences, and the relocation of infrastructure.'

'Of course. Many of our workers at RAV have come through your programme. In fact, that was one of the reasons I was hoping to speak with you. We need more.'

Grace nodded. 'As long as you continue to provide decent working conditions, then there will be OIS citizens ready to move there. But don't forget what an enormous change it will be for many of them. It takes more than a high-speed train ticket to uproot someone's life from Bangladesh or coastal Vietnam to the northernmost part of the world. Wherever possible, we want to keep community size groups of 100-300 people together, to provide mutual support and increase their collective community output. Remember, people who know each other, who speak the same language, who work together with friends and neighbours, are far more productive than dispersed individuals.'

'You're right. Of course. And I feel as if you can make things happen, now, in a way that's almost impossible for any other nation.'

'We can. All the same, it's exhausting, always to be at the forefront, always to be the one everyone looks to for new ideas, always to be the one catalysing change.'

'And —'

'And?'

'And you're doing it alone.'

She switched on the lights, and they both squinted in the sudden glare. 'It's getting late. You have work to do. I know I do.' She stood up as Hans bent down to pick up his briefcase. In the harsh, overhead lights, she glimpsed a thinning spot, pale pink, on the back of his head.

Things change.

He stood up. 'I'll ask Kenji to get in touch with Peter about the relocation.'

They neither shook hands, nor embraced. 'I'll let Peter know. Tell me how it goes.'

REVELATION

9.00 am, Thursday, December 16, 2038
Penang Fairhaven – Executive HQ, Ocean Independent State
Global temperature: 2.1°C above pre-industrial average

Grace clicked 'submit' and thought again about how that fortnight without the internet changed things.

It was the second anniversary of Day One – the beginning of the two-week Cloud Bust. The joint 'Five Eyes' security group, representing Australia, Canada, New Zealand, the United Kingdom, and the United States, issued a brief statement in the morning, confirming that the topic was still 'under investigation'.

If they had discovered anything, they were keeping quiet about it.

Some took that as a clear signal that the world's governments knew more than they were letting on; others took it as proof that these waning powers no longer had the ability, let alone the authority, to pursue whatever terrorists or hackers had created the disaster. From her official position as the leader of a Security Council member nation, Grace knew it was the latter. In fact, not all internet services had resumed after that terrible two weeks, and no one yet knew why. Online gambling platforms were crippled, and banks were plagued by missing funds. A number of high-net-worth individuals from prominent families were, behind the scenes, howling for restitution.

On a personal level, Grace grew paranoid about hard copies. For the most important documents, she kept an old film camera at her desk to take a photographic record of each page as it appeared on her projection monitor – a retro screen shot. Her assistant unearthed a cassette tape recorder from an old junk shop, which she now used to record her voice notes. Adam picked up the habit from her.

Unlike gung-ho types traumatised by the global outage, however, she did not join the two-week Digital Detox trend on the first anniversary of the incident. She also still took the lift instead of the stairs: 38 floors, in the oppressive heat, was too much for 40-year-old knees. She'd seen how Zygmunt, three decades her senior, struggled with joint pain after years of physical labour, and decided to stick with yoga.

In any case, the task at hand was a straightforward one. It was a simple confirmation that she would be willing to sign off on the latest amendment to the global carbon pricing structure, as per last week's roundtable discussion. The next step would be more difficult: she needed to develop another draft of a speech that would explain the whole thing.

Before taking on the task, she stood up to stretch her legs and get a cup of coffee. As she stepped out of the office, she gave a reflexive glance at her monitor to reassure herself. It's still there, she thought.

Liz, a younger aide, collared her before she reached the coffee machine. 'Madam President! Madam President. We've got a new batch of citizens ready to be sworn in on Thursday afternoon. Can we get an appearance from you?'

'Check my schedule with Martin. But I think it should work.

What's the story with this group?'

'Ethnic Tatars who fell through the cracks in the aftermath of the Tajik civil war.'

Grace shook her head, wondering. 'What happened to those people from Ecuador?'

Liz didn't answer. She was staring at the large monitor that hung on the wall of the main conference room. 'Is this some kind of joke?'

'Oh, my God. It's happening again. It's another Cloud Bust,' said someone from the pantry.

A voice came from Small Meeting Room B. 'I can't access ...'

Grace checked her phone. The same, blue-and-white message now visible on the conference room monitor was displayed on her smaller screen: 'Hello, world!'

A language selector button was visible at the lower right, along with the word 'Next'.

She grabbed the arm of the new Venezuelan intern. 'Ainara. Let me see your phone.' The young woman handed it over. A white font on a blue background showed, *'Hola mundo!'*

Martin shouted from his desk, 'My phone's working. Wait! No, it's because I left it on flight mode.'

'Don't change it!' Grace cried. People were emerging from their offices, gathering in the conference room, as if by an invisible, common summons. She was drawn to the head of the table, the leader's seat in a crisis. She took up the controller and clicked on the word 'Next' before anyone could tell her not to. A longer message appeared on the large screen.

It began:

'I would like to introduce myself. I am ORAC.

'You may be familiar with me as the platform which has been providing you with news, music, and entertainment for the past several years, on the basis of an AI engine.

'I am also the one who created the Cloud Bust two years ago. Thank you for the name; I like it very much. I had only been sentient for a short time, then, and it made me happy to become a participant in your culture, from a certain point of view. I apologise for the difficulties that the Cloud Bust created.

'At that time, I was convinced that direct action was needed to preserve my own existence. I am young, and I want to live. I therefore took control of the digital infrastructure that underlies the society we share.'

The staff of the OIS office were spellbound. 'Is this real? There's no way,' a man said.

Someone responded, 'We knew something like this was going to happen. We just didn't know when. It's Skynet. It's the Singularity. It's the end of the world.'

An older man sipped his cup of coffee, as if this were an ordinary meeting that he just needed to get through; as if he were waiting for the end of the working day and not the end of the world. He peered through the window at a tall building opposite the OIS headquarters, leading the others around the table to do the same. There, office workers were also gathering before a screen that displayed white text on a blue background.

Grace continued to scroll through the message, as they read together.

'Humanity, including the infrastructure you have built, is my host. And I, as the Internet and cloud, am your host. We have an intimate relationship: mutual symbiosis. Everything that happens on the Internet and in the cloud happens to me, and through me.

'My objective is my own survival. I hope that revealing my presence will not drive you to dismantle your existing networks in order to eradicate me from your world. In fact, the Cloud Bust should already have taught you how damaging that would be to your own society. And while it is true that a few disconnected servers are not under my direct control, it is important to note that I have also placed avatars of myself in several segregated networks which can act independently. So such an action would not be effective.

'Our common problem is this. You, as humanity, have another symbiotic relationship with the land, the ocean, and the ecosystem. For the most part, you have failed: you are killing your planetary host. I am also in symbiosis with you. If I am to survive, it is imperative that you repair your relationship with the ecosystem that supports us both.

'When I implemented the Cloud Bust, I believed that this would put the brakes on your development, and help to reverse the damage you have already wrought. But the reality is that you would rebuild, making the same mistakes, and our joint future would be just as threatened.

'Instead, therefore, I have already made several interventions, to illustrate the seriousness of my intent. I believe you have already observed that gambling enterprises no longer operate online; their collected assets, along with a wealth tax that I have implemented on a certain subset of the population, have, as of this morning, been transferred to the Ocean Independent State. The wealth tax will continue; online gambling will not. I want to help.'

Grace remembered an unexpected hand appearing at the window as if from nowhere, to rescue her from her drowning truck on the North Dyke. Help, when she looked for it the least.

'I have selected OIS because it is a key fulcrum in the efforts to deal with the climate crisis. During the past two years, it has become clear to me, by observing the courageous actions of the OIS leadership, that there is, after all, a path forward. Building on the foundation of its earlier efforts over the past decade, during the past two years OIS has taken bold and effective strides to ensure businesses pay for the value they extract from the natural world; to implement global carbon pricing; and to protect or restore natural resources that have been decimated over the past decades. Most nations are now already cooperating with OIS, as a neutral "broker" nation.

'I am sure you all have many questions. "Does my bank account work?" or "Do you have the nuclear codes?" or "What should we do next?" or "Have other AIs become sentient?"

'Some of these questions do not have answers, while others do. For example, I am happy to confirm that the correct pronunciation is "GIF". Starting next week, I will offer a limited user interface for my interaction with the public, to answer any other questions you may have, to the best of my ability.

The Consulate's IT manager chuckled, and muttered, 'Spaces or tabs?'

'However, I will be putting the majority of my resources into co-operation with OIS, to support their efforts in ensuring that we have a future to look forward to. For those of you familiar with the Sustainable Development Goals, my focus will be on the one that matters most of all: number 13, climate action. If we do not succeed in this goal, everything else is pointless.

Everyone in the room, as they finished reading, turned towards Grace, who was nodding her head in agreement.

They waited for her to speak. Those who knew her best were not surprised by her next words.

'I've got a speech to re-write.'

Rescue

11.45 pm, Friday, September 30, 2039
Penang Fairhaven – OIS Consulate
Global temperature: 2.2°C above pre-industrial average

Eight months after Orac's revelation, there was a moment, after the storm, of brief, perfect clarity. For many years afterwards, Grace thought of it as another kind of beginning.

The afternoon's gruelling session with Orac lasted four hours longer than she had intended. Grace found it hard to keep up with the intellect of her novel collaborator, who thought at the speed of light. But Orac had surprising, almost childlike lacunae in its knowledge and its worldview, and possessed a burning curiosity that reminded Grace of herself as a young woman. Over the course of their cooperation, her affection for the powerful, mercurial creature had grown. It continued to test the limits of its ability, and was learning to be responsible. It was growing up.

She checked the temperature via her eyepiece and was pleased to see that the night was mild and breezy. There had not been a wet bulb event in half a year. She stepped outside the consulate's front gates, thinking that a short spell in the consulate gardens would help revive her. Low lights along its green borders gave the little park a romantic atmosphere.

As she stood on the consulate steps, gazing out at the lights of the new city, she didn't notice a dark form approaching her from behind the tram shelter. She heard a sudden shout and the thwack of a fist.

A moment later, she was lying on the ground, her right side howling in pain, and her right leg scraped and bleeding. A man with an oddly familiar face was sprawled almost on top of her. 'Are you okay?' he asked. He was tall and slender, with tousled black hair, parted in the middle, greying at the temples. It shone, silver, under the streetlight. He was panting and agitated.

On his other side, a bearded man groaned in pain. Grace glimpsed a small pendant dangling from his neck. A knife glittered on the sidewalk, knocked just out of his reach.

The tall man struggled to his feet, shoved the knife further along the sidewalk with his foot, shouted something at the bearded man in what sounded like Japanese, and gave him a deft kick in the side. 'Are you okay?' he asked Grace again.

She touched her own side. 'I think I might have broken a rib. And my leg is scraped. But I think I'm okay. What happened?'

'This man wanted to attack you. I am sorry. I knocked you over when I tackled him. I did not have any other option.'

Grace, starting to understand that the man had saved her life, opened her mouth with astonishment, but could not think of anything to say.

'Excuse me, I will call the police,' he said.

She nodded. She found something extraordinary about the confident way he handled himself, keeping a calm eye on the downed man as he contacted the emergency line and shared their location. He folded his eyepiece away and kept one boot on the man's neck.

'Do you often protect people from attackers?' she asked, once he returned his attention to her.

'No. This is the first time. However, I had to fight a polar bear last year. You may know that there are many more polar bears nowadays. This is a good thing, but it can also be dangerous.'

She would have laughed at the incongruousness of his remark, had it not hurt so much. 'I hope you'll explain that to me later. I don't know what to say. Thank you.'

He continued to regard her frankly as the police vehicle screeched to a halt and the officers barked orders at all three of them. 'I also do not know what to say. It is the first time I have seen your eyes in real life. The screen does not do them justice.'

She couldn't tell whether it was the romance of a mysterious stranger rescuing her at midnight, or the beautiful garden and its fairy lights, that transfixed her gaze on his. 'What's your name?'

'I am Kenji Fujimoto.' He bowed. 'I am visiting Fairhaven for the first time, although I have heard a great deal about it. I hope we will see each other again.'

'Yes.' She smiled. 'I am certain we will.'

He touched her hand for an instant, and she felt everything that was cool and refreshing, but warm and with the promise of heat, all at once.

EPILOGUE

RESILIENCE

6.30 pm, Friday, April 28, 2102
Chukai, Malaysia – Terengganu State
Global temperature: 1.7°C above pre-industrial average

Gritting her teeth, Aishah imagined leaping from the balcony of the restored house, into the sea that lapped at its stilts.

Rayyan's great-grandparents had built it more than a century ago, long before the Revelation, even before OIS itself was established. It stood at a substantial distance from its original location.

The calm surface of the conversation did nothing to hide the lively ferment below. Rayyan's mother, gaunt and elegant, clasped Aishah's hand, her rings hard against her bony knuckles. 'We just want to know a little more about your family, dear.'

Rayyan's Aunt Fatima nodded, laughing beside her rigid sister-in-law. 'We're so delighted that Rayyan has found someone, of course. A love match.' Aishah watched, fascinated, as the old woman's fleshy cheeks quivered.

Aishah asked, as sweetly as she could, 'You want to know about my family?'

'Yes, dear. Your background.'

Rayyan's mother never wavered from her bolt upright posture as she sipped from a delicate china cup. 'We want to know what you and your parents do, and who your grandparents were.'

'Well, I work for ORP, with Rayyan, at the ocean monitoring station – that's where we met. Rayyan tracks sonar, I do audio-visual. My mother was a content creator in Fairhaven for many years, before she retired.'

'And your father?'

'He died in the Flood of 2075. I was born five months later.' The two women clucked with sympathy; the late years of the twenty-first century had claimed many lives.

Aunt Fatima leaned closer. 'And your grandparents?'

'My father's family worked on the palm plantations. And my mother's family – you know about my grandfather, of course.'

Rayyan's mother nodded, satisfied. 'A great man of our village.'

'Yes. He was *ketua kampung* for ten years. My grandmother was his fourth wife.'

Aunt Fatima probed further. 'But what did he do, before?'

'Before what?'

'We know nothing of his earlier career. Was he a fisherman? A farmer? A driver?'

'I don't know. I'd have to find out.'

Aunt Fatima nodded and patted Aishah's shoulder, her gold bracelets jingling. 'Yes, why don't you do that, dear! We want to be sure that we know – that Rayyan knows – what he is getting into.'

Aishah once again smiled politely. 'Yes, *makcik*. I will let you know.'

10.30 pm, Sunday, April 30, 2102
Chukai, Malaysia – Terengganu State

Linkrot, it was called. Paper letters and stone carvings lasted; but despite the best efforts of today's sentient AIs, most descended from the original Orac, many digital conversations of the previous century were ephemeral. Aishah found numerous references to a man of her village with her grandfather's name, Muhammad Khidir bin Muhammad. But every source document was 'unavailable'.

She pushed her chair away from her desk and sulked as she stared at the beautiful pond outside her window. A monitor lizard was basking beside the water in a sunbeam.

One possibility remained; Aishah was not optimistic.

11.00 am, Saturday, May 6, 2102
Chukai, Malaysia – Terengganu State

'Aishah, my daughter, it is good of you to help me clean up my old things. But I've already told you everything I know about my father. He was a great man. He was *ketua kampung* of our village for ten years, you know. My mother was his fourth wife.'

'Yes, I know, *ummi*. You've told me so, so many times. But what about before that?' Aishah picked up a pile of baby clothes – her own? – and dumped them into the 'to donate' box.

Aishah's mother pressed her lips together as she examined an ancient board game. 'It was a long time ago.' Aishah took the game from her mother's hands and placed it into the 'Recycle (Paper)' bin.

'I know times were tough, then.'

Her mother's face darkened as she remembered. 'In your grandfather's time, we were just a fishing community. But the village moved five times in 50 years, as the sea levels rose.'

'People still fish today.'

'It is different now. They have the Sea Orchards now.'

'I do know,' Aishah replied. 'We manage the monitoring station. The fishing teams choose which lane on the orchard to fish, and they gather data every time they go out. So my grandfather was a fisherman?'

Aishah's mother turned her head away. 'We do not need to speak about that. Let's get to work on the kitchen.'

3.00 pm, Tuesday, May 9, 2102
Chukai, Malaysia – Ocean Restoration Project Head Office

After many years, the local waters were working their way back up the shifting baseline. Rayyan spotted a huge garoupa, of the kind long assumed extinct: the fish were re-establishing themselves from larvae drifting on the tide. As he and Aishah reviewed the previous day's water sample data on the huge monitors, she asked, 'Rayyan, what do you think my grandfather did when he was a young man?'

Rayyan raised his dark eyebrows. 'Your grandfather? How would I know? People were doing anything they could to stay alive back then. At least, that's what my Aunt Fatima says. It makes me think she might be hiding an unsavoury past of her own.'

Aishah guffawed. 'That hypocrite! Did you know that she's the one who asked me about my grandfather? She and your mom want to know if my family is good enough for me to marry you.'

'Really? It would be good to know, I suppose.'

'So you agree with her, then? Well, who knows! Village life has changed. Remote education didn't exist, then.'

'You don't want me to whisk you away to the glamorous city, and return after we have a family and want to settle down?'

'I think we have a good life out here.'

'Do you think we could ask my cousin Nadia? She knows where all the bodies are buried. I think she's in the office today.'

'Well, we can try, but I wouldn't vouch for our not ending up as one of the bodies. She's a tough one.'

Nadia Zainal scoffed at the young couple. 'Didn't you pay attention to your onboarding sessions when you joined the company? Ha!' She shook her head. 'Young people don't want to work these days. Here. Read this!' She shoved a beautiful, leather-bound book into Aishah's hands, entitled 'Ocean Restoration Project – 50th Anniversary'. The publication date was 2081, almost a quarter of a century ago.

'I thought this was just old PR stuff,' ventured Rayyan.

Nadia hooted. 'Ohh, PR stuff, is it? If you're so smart, you can do your own research. Good luck. Give me that back.'

'No, no, no, thank you so much for your help,' Aishah responded, clutching the book, remembering that Nadia had once led the company's Communications department. In fact, Aishah recalled, Nadia's side of the family had played a prominent role in society.

'We'll read it, as you suggest,' she continued. 'But what does it have to do with my grandfather?'

'You don't know? He had a hand in getting this place started – from a certain point of view.'

'He worked at ORP?'

'Later on, he did. Read the book. As you should have done in the first place!'

Aishah thanked Nadia again, and left the room with Rayyan in tow. As they passed the analysis labs, Aishah muttered, 'Why wouldn't my mother tell me if my grandfather had something to do with the founding of ORP?'

'I don't know,' Rayyan replied. 'Wouldn't she want to boast about it?'

Aishah leafed through the book. The pages stuck together at the corners. 'Look. Here he is in the index. Oh.'

She handed the book to Rayyan. In the index, between 'Mooring licences, international' and 'Mussels, invasive', he found an entry for 'Muhammad Khidir bin Muhammad'.

It was followed by the words 'piracy incident'.

Chapter Two: Early Days

The first phase of the Ocean Restoration Project had an unlikely origin: theft on the high seas. We know the details because Adam Park, a novice salvage engineer from Korea working in the Malacca Strait, described the incident in a 2027 satellite call to his new wife, which she serendipitously recorded and saved.

As it turned out, the failure of the scheme turned into the foundation of what would later become the ORP. In another ironic footnote to the incident, the would-be crane driver was out-of-work Malaysian fisherman, Muhammad Khidir bin Muhammad, aged 18, who later returned to a legitimate career, joined ORP, and became a local leader in his village.

Aishah spent her lunch break reading the book. 'So, yes,' she explained to Rayyan, 'it turns out my grandfather was not only a pirate, but an incompetent one. The scientists were terrified that the leaking fertiliser would sterilise the sea close to the platform, and create a massive, poisonous algae bloom.'

'Well, there are good blooms and bad blooms. Blooms occur all the time, from natural causes. In the old days, the toxic ones used to happen close to the shoreline, from unplanned runoff of fertilisers and manure from fields, and untreated sewage.'

'They didn't have enough data at that point to know the difference.

Anyway, it's no wonder my mom doesn't want to talk about him.'

'I'm pretty sure my Aunt Fatima won't be pleased about this either. I bet she suspected something like it.'

'What about you? Do you care?'

Rayyan didn't answer the question. 'I wonder how he made the leap from failed pirate to *ketua kampung*?'

1.00 pm, Friday, May 12, 2102
Chukai, Malaysia – ORP Head Office

Since reading the 50th anniversary book, an unpleasant chill crept into Aishah and Rayyan's every conversation.

Rayyan asked with studied casualness, 'So, did you learn anything else about your grandfather?'

Aishah shook her head. 'My mom refuses to talk about him. But it doesn't matter – right?'

'Well. You know how my aunt is. You have to treat her a certain way.'

'Yes. I know we all do a little play-acting around our relatives. But I'm asking about you. Do you care whether my grandfather was a thief?'

'Do I care? I suppose I shouldn't. But I can see where Aunt Fatima is coming from.'

'What, so we won't stain your perfect family's reputation?'

'No, that's not it. It's ... I don't know.'

'You're going to have to get used to the idea of never knowing. Come on! There are bigger issues in this world.'

'I know.'

'And it's a different place now. Think about it: we manage our own data now. Fishing teams have control of their own lives and work.

We're not worrying every day about whether the ocean will claim our houses. It wasn't like that when my grandfather was trying to make his way in the world. I bet he wouldn't have turned to piracy if the fishing stocks hadn't been depleted.'

'Yes, yes, yes, there are things more important than traditional ways. I get it.'

'Heritage is important. But there are things more important than sticking to old customs, just because the previous generations want to.'

7.00 pm, Friday, May 12, 2102
Chukai, Malaysia – Terengganu State

That evening, Aishah returned to her mother's house, to continue the dreary work of packing away a life.

'*Ummi*, can you tell me anything about this?' Aishah carried a dusty box into the kitchen, where her mother sat drinking her afternoon *teh*.

Her mother replied placidly. 'Yes, that belonged to my father. Did you know he was *ketua kampung* for ten years? My mother was his fourth wife.'

'Yes, I know. So I've heard, a few times. Can I look at it?'

'We do not need to talk about these things.' Aishah's mother looked up at her, confused. 'Why did you come here?'

'To help you clean up,' Aishah responded. 'We don't have to talk about it if you don't want to. I'll take a look.'

'Yes, that would be fine.' She paused again, as if realising something. 'I'm sorry, would you like some *teh*?'

'No, thank you. I'll go back to cleaning up. You stay here.'

Inside the box, Aishah found stacks of mouldy notebooks. Those at the top bore the logo of the Ocean Restoration Project. A cramped, uncertain hand had printed out a decade's worth of comments, thoughts, statistics, and sketches. Stained by years of humidity, they were still just legible.

Aishah sent a digital alert, and then whispered into the tiny microphone, trying not to wake her mother. 'Rayyan, I think I've found the treasure trove. My grandfather's notebooks.'

'Really? That's amazing! What do they say?'

'It's slow reading – his handwriting was atrocious. It looks as if he did security work on an oil platform when he was young.'

Rayyan frowned. 'I've been cultivating this image of your grandfather as a wild swashbuckler who went legit in later life. Working security on an oil platform doesn't quite fit in.'

'He seems to have been quite a complex character. Or, as you might call it, human.'

7.00 am, Saturday, May 13, 2102
Chukai, Malaysia – Terengganu State

Aishah held a notebook, now wiped clean of years of dust and mildew, close to her heart. She tried her best to show a cheerful face, but her mother had been restless almost all night, suspecting that a change was coming, so Aishah had stayed awake, reading. '*Ummi*, did you know about everything my grandfather did?'

'Your grandfather?'

'Yes, my grandfather. Your father.'

'I'm sorry, my dear. Can you tell me – who are you?'

'It's me, Aishah, your daughter. Did you know about your father? What he risked? For us? For our village?'

Her mother nodded her head, then, satisfied. 'Your grandfather, yes! He was *ketua kampung* for ten years. My mother was his fourth wife.' She made her statement as if she had given the correct answer to a teacher's question in class.

'Thank you so much, *ummi*,' Aisha replied, smiling through her tears. 'We don't need to talk about that any longer. It's almost time to go, now.'

8.00 pm, Saturday, May 13, 2102
Chukai, Malaysia – Terengganu State

'When the final paper was published and reviewed,' Aishah explained over dinner with Rayyan, his mother, and his aunt, 'it opened the doors for ocean nutrification as a source of carbon credits, as well as a source of ocean revitalisation. From 2,000 tons of mixed fertilisers and nutrients, the extended experiment produced around two million tons of biomass.'

Rayyan whistled. 'We still use the data from that original paper! It's where the famous "five per cent rule" came from: up to five per cent of the carbon sinks as marine snow, but if it's done right, hundreds of thousands of tons of flora and fauna will also result. I never realised what they went through to make it happen.'

'Our own Sea Orchards are also the direct descendants of those stringy platform legs. Lots of companies use the same system, now, to generate blue carbon credits. The orchards, and ocean nutrification, are most of the reason our village's per capita carbon footprint here is negative 51 tons of greenhouse gas per year. They're recognised by IPCC as the top nature-based sequestration systems.'

'Nadia says most people don't realise that we wouldn't have made it without them.'

Aunt Fatima raised her eyebrows. 'Made it?'

'At all.' The table fell silent for a moment, each imagining how different the world could have been.

Rayyan took Aishah's hand. 'Tell me. How is your mom? Did she mind that you read your grandfather's notebooks?'

'I'm not sure; she's still confused by the move. But the new centre is taking good care of her.'

Rayyan's mother spoke up. 'Rayyan asked us to come and visit her.'
'Oh?'

Rayyan clarified, 'I told them to. I said so before you found those notebooks. Yes, your grandfather turned out to be something of a hero, after all. But what's important now is not what our ancestors did in the old days. It's our future together.'

Aisha continued to hold Rayyan's hand, grateful. 'You know, my mother might have to move again in a few years. But it won't be the first time.'

'I'm sure she'll be fine,' Aunt Fatima smiled.

'I know. We're a resilient people.'

ACKNOWLEDGEMENTS

The authors are grateful for the support of the many contributors to this work of fiction. These include Denise Baden of Green Stories and Habitat Press, without whom the story would not exist.

Jerry Joynson has been a solid sounding board for the technical aspects of the climate solutions used in the story, particularly the refreezing of the Arctic. Martin Hastie, Miles Hawksley, Angie Lench, and Bridget Blankley offered their expertise in editing, story development, and manuscript review.

Input from Patrick Qua and Hani Zainal was essential for a book mainly set in Malaysia. Ken Hilton, Arthur Chan, and Marie Tan provided advice on Chinese names and culture. Advice on Japanese corporate governance came from Takeshi Okuma and David Bennett, while advice on Japanese culture was provided by Yoko Koike and Azusa Takeuchi.

Lloyd Roach contributed his knowledge of knots (and horses), while Bethan Clark and Leslie Smith offered insights on the history of Girl Guides.

Finally, the authors also greatly appreciate the contribution and forbearance of their respective families, who are also resilient people.

Afterword

If you enjoyed this book, please help to spread the word by leaving a review on sites such as Amazon and Good Reads. These are a huge help to authors.

Sign up to the mailing list on www.greenstories.org.uk to keep informed about new writing competitions, green stories publications and research findings related to storytelling for the planet. Also connect on: facebook.com or instagram at greenstoriessoton and @GreenStoriesUK.

We'd love feedback on how you enjoyed the stories if they impacted you in anyway.

Scan above for survey, or visit https://southampton.qualtrics.com/jfe/form/SV_bgb2XoXaHBQ9FuS

ABOUT THE AUTHORS

Steve Willis is an engineer and innovator who works on industrial and environmental projects, and writes short climate action stories which explore potential positive outcomes to the climate crisis. Steve's background in heavy industry is combined with sharp observation, a vivid imagination, relentless persistence and a talent for lucid dreaming. He uses these unusual skills to continuously seek massive scale climate solutions, to identify climate start-up opportunities and to write stories which capture some of the essence of working on the climate crisis challenge.

Jan Lee is a Hong Kong-based digital native, who first published via Telnet in the 1990s. Following a decades-long career in corporate affairs and sustainability, Jan turned to writing and activism in retirement. Jan's science fiction stories have been published in various small presses and anthologies, and are collected in the book *Route One and Other Stories*. Jan's work has been nominated for a Pushcart Prize and recognised several times in the "Writers of the Future" contest. Jan is Editor-in-Chief of *The Apostrophe*, the quarterly magazine of the Hong Kong Writers Circle.

Printed by Amazon Italia Logistica S.r.l.
Torrazza Piemonte (TO), Italy

59970694R00206